WIND RIVER COWBOY

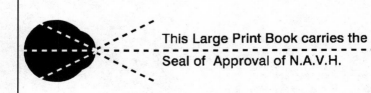

This Large Print Book carries the
Seal of Approval of N.A.V.H.

WIND RIVER VALLEY

WIND RIVER COWBOY

LINDSAY MCKENNA

THORNDIKE PRESS
A part of Gale, a Cengage Company

Farmington Hills, Mich • San Francisco • New York • Waterville, Maine
Meriden, Conn • Mason, Ohio • Chicago

Copyright © 2017 by Nauman Living Trust.
Wind River Valley.
Thorndike Press, a part of Gale, a Cengage Company.

ALL RIGHTS RESERVED
Thorndike Press® Large Print Romance.
The text of this Large Print edition is unabridged.
Other aspects of the book may vary from the original edition.
Set in 16 pt. Plantin.

LIBRARY OF CONGRESS CIP DATA ON FILE.
CATALOGUING IN PUBLICATION FOR THIS BOOK
IS AVAILABLE FROM THE LIBRARY OF CONGRESS

ISBN-13: 978-1-4328-5963-3 (hardcover)

Published in 2018 by arrangement with Zebra Books, an imprint of Kensington Publishing Corp.

Printed in Mexico
1 2 3 4 5 6 7 22 21 20 19 18

*To all the men and women in the military
and those who are retired veterans.
Thank YOU for your sacrifices
for all of us.
Freedom is never free.*

CHAPTER ONE

"Ambush!"

Sergeant Kira Duval's earpiece rang with the warning from Army Captain Aaron Michelson, the Special Forces A team leader. The night was black and an RPG exploded right in between the two Humvees they were riding in. The twelve-person team halted and all hell broke loose.

Kira exited the vehicle, hearing the hollow *thunk* of another RPG being fired in their direction. She heard more orders in her earpiece as she threw herself on the muddy Afghan ground, hands over her head, mouth open.

The night erupted into red, yellow and orange flames as the second RPG hit the first Humvee, which Aaron was in. She wanted to scream, but the blast lifted her off the ground, hurling her several feet, and she started rolling to minimize the impact. Keeping her mouth open to equalize the pressure between her lungs and the outside air so they wouldn't melt into jelly, Kira had the M4 strapped in a harness across her chest. She fell hard on her side, the weapon jamming into her rib cage, making her cry out.

Another explosion erupted. Her eardrums were pounded. The pain in them caused her to grunt. The shouts, screams and orders roared into her head. She saw dark shadows exiting her Humvee, the other four men trying to escape and run for cover.

Someone jerked her up by the shoulder of her uniform harness, dragging her along, heading for a group of shadowy rocks. Gasping, Kira struggled and then lunged to her feet with the help of Sergeant Garret Fleming, who was at her side. He was screaming into his mic for the four operators, ordering them to get to the safety of the rock fortress just ahead of them.

Another RPG was fired. AK-47 fire was like a fusillade slamming into the escaping Special Forces survivors. Kira didn't have time to cry. The first Humvee was twisted metal, flames roaring into the dark sky, sending long, dancing shadows across the muddy soil. She slipped, but Garret kept a tight gloved hand on her uniform, keeping her on her feet as they raced three hundred yards to safety. They had to get cover or they were all dead.

Her mind spun. There had been six men in that first Humvee. Had any of them made it out? She heard Garret yelling into the mic for Captain Michelson, but there was no answer from their leader. Oh, God! She'd lived with this team for three years. Each of these men were like beloved brothers to her. They couldn't be dead. They just couldn't!

Sobbing, tears burning in her eyes, Garret suddenly went down. She heard him curse. He released her shoulder, sending her spinning and falling to the left of him. Bullets were digging up mud all around them, geyser spouts flung into the air. They were not only ambushed but surrounded on half of the area where they were scrambling to find cover. Landing hard on her knees, she twisted around, the mud making everything slippery. Kira saw the shadows of two other A team members running in their direction. Bullets mowed them down. Screaming, Kira lunged for Garret, who was grabbing his left leg, blood spurting from his calf.

Just as she reached Garret on her hands and knees, a second bullet struck him in the head. He suddenly collapsed, lifeless, on the ground.

No! I love him! You can't kill him! You can't!

Kira grabbed Garret's shoulder. The man was six foot two inches tall, two hundred and twenty pounds without counting the seventy pounds of gear he wore on his body. Jerking at him, she managed to get to her feet. Adrenaline gave her the strength of two men and she hauled Garret behind the rocks that stood five to ten feet tall in a semicircle around them. She called for their 18 Delta medics. No answer from either of them. There were two on each team. Were they *both* dead?

No!

Gasping for breath, Kira knelt down by Garret, seeing the blood pouring from his calf. With shaking hands, she pulled off the tourniquet he kept on the epaulet of his left shoulder, quickly fashioning it around the upper part of his right calf. Yanking it hard, she stopped the bleeding on his leg and tied it off. Hauling the M4 off her shoulder, she took a position at the end of the rock pile.

Her earpiece came to life as she heard Warrant Officer Ethan Torrence radio for Apaches to come help them. She heard him calling off the coordinates, asking any black ops in the immediate area to race to their aid. Kira wasn't aware of any other friendlies who were around their sector. She sighted her M4 against the rock, firing at the muzzles of the AK-47s spewing out death into their compromised position. Her breath was coming in huge, ripping gulps and sobs. The tears stopped and she huddled in a kneeling position, continuing to slow fire and take out Taliban who were in the rocks across the road from where the Humvees had been attacked.

She saw another of her brothers go down, slammed forward by several bullets. He was so far away that she couldn't get to him. The superior Taliban force would kill her if she exposed her location again. Throwing a glance behind her where Garret lay unconscious, Kira didn't know if he was alive or dead. She saw black liquid alongside his head where he'd been struck by an AK-47 bullet.

Another RPG exploded between the rock fortress and the last Humvee. Kira knew the Taliban was trying to destroy it as well. She didn't know where the other four men were. Three were lying between that Humvee and her position. None of them moved. Her heart ripped in half. These were men who were married, had children, loved their wives. *Oh, God, no!*

Kira jerked awake, screaming, bathed in sour-smelling fear and sweat. It took her precious seconds to realize she was in a

11

motel near the Pentagon in Washington, D.C. Sweat burned in her eyes. Little whimpers tore between her compressed lips as she fought not to cry. She had to get a shower. Water always soothed her. Dazed, her white cotton nightgown clinging to her damp body, she stumbled into the small bathroom. The water was tepid coming out of the nozzle. How she wanted nearly scalding hot water. A hot shower always helped tamp down her anxiety from her PTSD. But not this morning. She scrubbed her hair and body, wanting to get rid of the nightmare that haunted her weekly. Sometimes more often, depending upon the stress she was under.

Today, she was a civilian, no longer in the US Army thanks to her wounds and PTSD. But her old commanding officer, General Barbara Ward, US Army, had ordered a meeting between them — in person. That had been two weeks ago.

Kira felt broken as she climbed into a black wool pantsuit with a white blouse. She liked General Ward, who had asked her to take part in a secret operation. Kira had become one of the twenty women volunteers from the Army to be trained by the Army Special Forces. She'd already passed the Special Forces schooling when she had been invited into the inner, top-secret operation. For three years she'd been assigned with her twelve-person A team in Afghanistan.

She'd loved those years, never regretted them. But nearly a year ago she'd lost ten of her brothers in that horrific nighttime ambush. Only one other man had survived: Sergeant Garret Fleming. And as much as Kira had tried to find him after she'd been transferred from Landstuhl Medical Center to the Walter Reed National Military Medical Center in Bethesda, Maryland, to recover, she never had. Garret had literally slipped off the map. She had no way to find out where he was, how he was, or anything else. Hurting, Kira's mouth thinned as she pulled on a dark green parka. It was cold and rainy on this late October morning. She had no umbrella, but the hood would protect her. Her heart was heavy. Why was General Ward insisting upon seeing her in person? The Army had jettisoned her shortly after discharging her from the hospital. They had handed her her walking papers, separating her permanently from the military. Her PTSD was bad. She had nightmares. Anxiety. Insomnia. She refused to take medication because she hated how she felt during and after taking it. The adverse side effects were worse than suffering with the symptoms without taking them.

Was that what this meeting was all about? Kira left the motel room with her purse and headed to the parking lot. Her father had given her an old Ford pickup when she'd come home and it was her wheels now. The Pentagon was two miles away in the pall of gray, cold rain.

Barbara cared deeply about the women under her command. She'd helped create the concept and training to prove women were equals in combat alongside men. That they could do the job just as well. And Barbara had proven that, hands down. Kira felt warmth for the Army general. Barbara had never rejected her even after the military had. She called her every month to see how she was doing.

On her part, Kira had gotten so she dreaded the monthly check-in phone calls because they would be time to tell the general she'd been fired from another job. Why? Because her PTSD symptoms hiked up her anxiety due to the stressful demands of the job, and she'd either quit or get fired. Usually, she was summarily dismissed. Kira felt like the bottom had fallen out of her life, and now she was in free fall. No helping hand was going to shoot out of the darkness, grab her and stop her plummeting into nothingness. Depression haunted her like a good friend.

She parked near the Pentagon and climbed the shiny white stone steps leading up to the front entrance to the octagon-shaped building. Inside, Kira had to go through several layers of security before being allowed to find General Ward's office in the "E" Ring.

Kira was used to the questions, the tests and working with the general's staff who rated and watched each woman in the top secret test. But this was different, and it left Kira feeling wary and worried. Nothing else in her life had worked out. She'd fallen in love with Garret Fleming, never told him, but had spent three years with a man who made her so happy. And he had disappeared from her life.

She'd lost eleven other brothers, the men of her A team. It hurt so much to visualize each one of them, to remember them, their wives, their children and parents. Kira had loved those three years with her team. They'd been the best of her life until the Taliban ambush had killed everyone she'd ever loved, with the exception of her father, who was still alive.

Rubbing her forehead as she walked down the highly polished hall, Kira tried to ignore her depression. Her mother had been born with severe depression. She'd committed suicide when Kira was nineteen, unable to stand it any longer. And she had mild depression — a genetic predisposition for it, Kira supposed — brought to roaring life thanks to her PTSD.

Entering the office, Kira gave her name to a red-haired office assistant, a civilian woman named Trina Smith, in her forties. Sitting down, Kira waited outside the closed door that would lead to the general's office. What did she want? It couldn't be good, Kira surmised. The rest of her life was a certifiable disaster, an unending mess of bad news and being constantly fired from jobs. She was on welfare. All she had left was food assistance.

Trina stood and came around her desk. She smiled at Kira. "The general will see you now." She opened the door that led to a hallway. Kira was familiar with Rooms A and B. The assistant pointed to Room A.

"Just go in there, Ms. Duval. May I get you some coffee? The general has already ordered some Danishes for the two of you."

Why not? Kira nodded. "Yes, thank you, Trina. That's very nice of you."

The assistant stepped aside, gave her a warm smile. "Not at all. It's the least we can do for you ladies. I'll be back with your coffee shortly."

Kira removed her parka and left it on the chair, pulling her leather purse across her left shoulder and walking past the assistant. The door was half glass, pebbled so no one could see through it, with gold stenciling announcing: GENERAL BARBARA WARD, US ARMY, across it. Taking a deep breath, Kira tried to gird herself for more bad news. It was the only kind she ever got these days. Knocking on the door, she heard an "Enter . . ."

General Ward was a powerful military woman, and one of the youngest women generals in the US Army at fifty-six. She was in her Class A dark green winter uniform. Kira entered and the general came around her huge maple desk, a welcoming smile on her face. Kira tried to return that warm, genuine smile. She was surprised as Barbara threw her arms around her and hugged her hello. When she released her, Kira felt her hopes rise as she looked into the tall woman's intelligent, narrowed green eyes.

"Thanks for coming, Kira," she said, gesturing for her to follow her to a long, polished table in the next room. "Come on, join me for breakfast?"

Following her, Kira felt deflated. At one time, before the ambush had occurred, she'd had that quiet, powerful confidence that radiated from the officer. Now, she felt anything but confident. Kira hated feeling hopeless. Looking toward the long table where she had sat before, she saw a plate of Danish rolls, two gold-rimmed porcelain plates, white linen napkins and flatware. Barbara pulled out the chair to the left.

"Sit down, Kira. Are you hungry?"

Kira sat down and placed her purse in her lap. "Not really, ma'am."

"Well, eat one anyway."

"Yes, ma'am."

Trina brought in a container of coffee, cups and saucers, along with cream and sugar. She poured them both steaming cups and Kira thanked her, pulling over the coffee. It warmed her cold fingers. She hadn't brought gloves from home and didn't have money to buy a new pair.

The assistant left, and reluctantly, Kira used the aluminum tongs alongside the plate of Danishes and chose the smallest one possible. Her stomach was tied in knots and she had no desire to eat anything.

Barbara sat down, giving her a sharp look. In front of her was Kira's personnel file, opened to her quarterly assessment. She had monthly check-ins and, every three months, a physical. "You've lost more weight."

Grimacing, Kira sipped the black coffee, both hands around the cup. "I don't have much of an appetite anymore, ma'am."

"I see." Barbara studied her in the growing silence. "You've had it rough. This last report indicates you've run out of money."

Shrugging, Kira said, "I've still got a little left, ma'am. I make ends meet by translating Arabic on an Internet website. My father sent me some when I told him I got fired from my last job." That hurt to say it, too. Her father, Les, had wanted her to stay home to recover, but her nightmares, the screaming, was keeping him up half the night several times a week. Kira felt so ashamed of herself, and the fact that she couldn't stop or control them, that she left. Her father was a hardworking man running a lumber business and he needed his sleep. If it wasn't for his generosity, she would have starved by now.

"Is the stress and anxiety stopping you from holding a job, Kira?"

Nodding, it hurt to admit it. Shame, deep and invasive, flowed through Kira. Her stomach tightened until it felt like a boulder was sitting in it. Barbara had requisitioned the money for her truck trip, reserved her a motel room and given her a food stipend to get her here because Kira couldn't afford to do it on her own.

"Eat."

Kira forced herself to bite into the sweet apricot Danish.

"My placement team has a lead on a job for you," Barbara said briskly, choosing a lemon Danish. "One of the things my team is tasked with is to get returning black ops women who have PTSD long-term employment."

Kira knew that. The team had found five jobs for her in the past. She'd been fired from all of them. "Yes," she whispered, unable to meet the general's eyes. She'd failed her, too.

Reaching out, Barbara gripped her lower left arm and squeezed it. "I'm not disappointed in you, Kira. You have PTSD. You were one of two survivors in your team. You saved your fellow sergeant's life. And for your valor, you were awarded a Silver Star, not to mention a Purple Heart. You should be proud, not ashamed. You've done nothing wrong. You've served your country with courage and honor."

Hollow words. They only deepened Kira's sense of hopelessness. At one time, she had been the cream of the crop as far as women in combat went. She was good at what she did. And she'd never failed Barbara or anyone else in those three years. Her teammates admired and respected her. General Ward was pleased.

Until the ambush . . . and since then, her life had been in free fall, all her control over herself taken away. The only place Kira knew she was headed was down a rabbit hole she couldn't see any end to. "With all due respect, ma'am, it doesn't mean a thing to most people in America. Military people comprise one percent of the US population. We're a niche minority at best."

Grimly, Barbara nodded. She pulled a piece of paper from the file and nudged it in Kira's direction. "My team has found a place for you to apply for a job."

Kira stared at it. She wanted to cry. To run. To hide from life. She tucked in her lower lip between her teeth, afraid she'd burst into tears of humiliation.

Barbara kept her hand on the paper. "This one is different, Kira. I talked to the owner of the Bar C in Wind River, Wyoming, yesterday. Her name is Shaylene Lockhart. She's a military veteran who was in the Marine Corps. She served in Afghanistan until she was given an honorable medical discharge."

"Does she have PTSD?" Kira asked, unable to meet the general's gaze.

"Yes. She came home on a hardship discharge because her father, who ran the ranch, had a stroke that partially paralyzed him. By the tenets of her mother's will, the ranch legally went to her when her father was incapacitated, and she now owns it. The place was in pretty bad shape because he's an alcoholic." Barbara's husky voice lowered with feeling. "She decided to hire only military vets as wranglers. Vets like herself, who struggled daily with PTSD. They're slowly bringing this ranch back to life, as well as healing."

Kira's heart leaped with hope and she lifted her chin, gazing into the officer's patient, warm eyes. She was like a fierce mother at times, and now Kira was on the receiving end of her ability to nurture others. "But — I'm not a wrangler."

"I sent Mrs. Lockhart your résumé by fax. She e-mailed me and said you'd be a good fit for the ranch. I think the fact that you worked in your father's timber business, know mechanics and can fix equipment, was helpful in making her decision, Kira. And in the Special Forces team, you were their mechanic. You can fix anything."

"I guess," she whispered, wrapping her arms around her middle. She couldn't even fix herself.

"Look," Barbara said, "this isn't like working for a company. You'll be assigned to a real house with all the amenities. You'll work five days a week and have weekends off. Fifteen percent of what you make as a translator goes into the ranch account. Everything else, you keep. There's a weekly vet session where you sit down every Friday night with everyone else. A woman psychologist holds the session and her specialty is PTSD. Every person there, Kira, has PTSD as bad or worse than you do. And the four male vets who are there are all improving, thanks to Mrs. Lockhart's vision. I think you will, too."

"If I could save some of my translation money, that would help a lot," Kira admitted quietly. "And I wouldn't mind a weekly get-together and therapy session with other vets."

"Especially ones who have PTSD like you. Mrs. Lockhart has a good program in place and I'm very impressed with it. I've placed her on our list of employers for any future women in black ops who may end up with PTSD. I think getting back to nature, working around horses, cattle and being outdoors, is helpful to vets like yourself."

Kira gave the general a kind look. In her heart, she knew Barbara Ward was a fierce mother-protector of all her women. She knew all of them on a personal basis. Barbara had flown to Bethesda shortly after Kira'd come in from Landstuhl Medical Center in Germany, and spent time with her. The general cared for the women under her command, no question. And now she was feeling hopeful once more. "I love horses. I used to have one growing up . . ."

"I think your lumber company experience is going to be a good fit with a ranch life, Kira. We've seen time and again if a PTSD vet can work around animals, be it dogs, cattle or horses, get out of the city and into a rural country environment, it helps his or her symptoms. The other jobs you were given were in the city. Looking back on it, we should have been a little more circumspect and placed you in a rural community. I think you'll do very well at the Bar C."

Rubbing her face, Kira muttered, "I'm so tired of being fired, ma'am. I know I do it to myself —"

"Did you ever quit in the middle of a firefight?" Barbara demanded, her eyes narrowing on her.

"Of course not."

"Then see this time in your life like a fire-fight, Kira. It's survival reflex time, and I know you have that in spades." Barbara patted her hand and pushed the paper toward her. "Give this a try. My assistant will contact Mrs. Lockhart and let her know you'll be driving out there. Make the most of this. You'll be around people who understand your situation and symptoms. And all of them are fighting to get better, to get their lives focused and back on track. The ranch will serve as an incubator of sorts to help you make this work."

Her emotional words buoyed Kira. She forced a little smile and took the paper. There was a photo of the ranch. It looked peaceful and beautiful. "This is a different kind of job offer," she agreed.

"It's right up your alley, Kira. These people care deeply for one another."

"Kind of like a new A team?" she ventured.

Barbara smiled a little. "Yes, a new A team. Where everyone becomes extended family to each other in the best of ways."

Kira was afraid to hope. The job sounded so good. She studied the paper with the information. The ranch looked like a dream to her. A way out. A way up, not down.

"You've talked to Mrs. Lockhart?" she

asked, looking at Barbara.

"Yes."

"Was she . . . nice?"

"She was kind and warm. She just got married to one of the vets who was working on her ranch, Reese Lockhart. I liked her spirit, Kira. She has a passion to help vets like herself to find a place in the world where they can lead productive and happy lives, despite their PTSD."

"I see on this list of things I'm expected to do is some caretaking of Mrs. Lockhart's father, who's partially paralyzed?"

"Yes. Ray Crawford is fighting back and getting better. As you can see, you're wanted for housekeeping, providing him three meals a day, plus driving him to doctor or other appointments in town. You okay with that?"

Nodding, Kira said, "I miss my father . . ." Maybe Ray Crawford would be good for her, but then she remembered he was an alcoholic. She had no experience with anyone with that problem.

"In time," Barbara said gently, "maybe you'll heal enough so you can actually go back home, where your father would like you to be."

"I tried that, ma'am. We both wanted it to work, but it didn't."

"I know. A lot of vets go home and then

have to leave. Have you ever read any of Joseph Campbell's books?"

"My mother loved them. I confess, I don't have much interest in myths and how they parallel our lives."

Shrugging, Barbara said, "Do yourself a favor. Read his book on the Hero's Journey. I think you'll recognize yourself in that myth."

Intrigued, Kira sat up, more hope drizzling through her. It was far better than feeling hopeless. "What? That I'm a hero?"

"Campbell uses the word *hero* in a different way," Barbara assured her. "It's about the journey many people take in a lifetime, the ups and downs, but eventually, the rewards for their courage under fire are given to them."

"Well," Kira said dryly, "mine was literal."

Sitting back, Barbara nodded, studying her intently. "It was in one respect, Kira. In another, like the hero of Campbell's book, you got knocked down. And you're struggling to get back up."

"Oh," Kira said, "I'm down the rabbit hole, ma'am, no question."

"Read the book. I'm not going to order you to do it, but I want you to sit down with it and really absorb it. It's really your story, Kira."

"What? That I'm the princess? And I kiss a frog and he turns into my prince?" she scoffed mildly, seeing Barbara grin a little.

"A hero's journey is comprised of many things known and unknown," she said enigmatically. "There are challenges, falls from grace, learning to get up and move forward whether you feel like it or not. I can't promise you a prince or a frog at the end of it."

"Sound's like Campbell's hero had PTSD like me." And the last thing Kira wanted was a relationship with a man. She was a mess. She was mature enough to know that in her present emotional and mental shape, no relationship she entered into would have a happy ending.

Chuckling, Barbara's grin broadened. "PTSD isn't mentioned in his book. But who knows? Maybe the hero did have it before a time when it was diagnosed and given a medical name. And maybe it was part of his — or — her challenge to work through and struggle to move to a higher level of being alive, despite it."

"Just as long as there's no frog in there I have to kiss. I'll make sure to pick up a copy of it, ma'am."

"One of the greatest lessons to come out of this story is the people the hero — or heroine — meet on the journey." Barbara waved a finger at her. "Keep your eyes open, Kira. I've always said our best teachers are the people we draw to ourselves. I believe working at the Bar C may symbolize getting out of your ordeal and it will instead become a place where you can regain yourself."

CHAPTER TWO

"Do you have any questions about what I just covered with you, Kira?"

Kira felt bathed in the warmth and care of Shay Lockhart as they sat in the kitchen of the Bar C's main ranch house. She'd arrived shortly after lunch, met two of the military vets, Noah and Harper. Shay had fixed her a late lunch, introducing her to her husband, Reese Lockhart, who went down the hall to his office afterward. That left Kira with Shay to go over the employment opportunity. "No questions. You've covered everything pretty well."

Shay smiled and said, "Are you interested in taking the job?"

"Absolutely." Kira's hope had climbed in the last two hours as Shay had outlined the responsibilities of the position. Earlier, they had bundled up in their coats on the cold but clear day, and Shay had taken her around the main buildings on the Bar C.

Kira was impressed with what the vets had done to repair the broken-down ranch. They were slowly fixing, building and bringing it back to life.

Shay's father, Ray Crawford, had met Kira and shaken her hand. He was nothing like her father but felt she could certainly do weekly housecleaning plus make his meals. Shay was more than fair about financial compensation and that made Kira want to work for someone like her.

"Okay, then the only other thing left to do is assign you to a house," Shay said with a smile. She took a pen and wrote "House A" on the file.

Kira knew there'd been four new homes built on the ranch property not far from the main house. Shay assigned each vet to a home. The fourth house was for Ray Crawford. There were two bedrooms in each home. And Shay had designed the homes to hold two vets each. All told, Shay had informed her, she wanted to eventually hire six wrangler vets. Kira would be wrangler number four, and the first woman vet.

"Okay," Kira said.

Shay frowned and looked across the trestle table at her. "Are you sure you're okay living with a strange guy underfoot?"

Kira smiled a little. "He's a military vet. I

31

don't think I'll have an issue with him, Shay."

"Well, not everyone gets along with each other," she said. "I'm assigning you to Garret's house because he's been here the longest. In fact, he was the first vet I hired. I feel he can show you the ropes, be kind of a mentor in some ways to you, introduce you to the ranch rhythm and the duties around here. He's a good go-to guy and is very helpful. But if you feel it's a problem, Kira? Just tell me and I'll move you to another house."

"Thanks, that's good to know. He's got PTSD, right?"

"Oh, yes. It's pretty bad." Shay shrugged. "But then, what PTSD isn't bad? He has nightmares, insomnia and anxiety just like the rest of us."

"I'll fit right in." She found herself more than a little curious. "You said his name is Garret?"

"Yes. Why?"

The front door to the ranch house opened and closed. Both women stopped and looked toward the entrance.

"Oh," Shay said, "that's Garret coming back. He was up in Jackson Hole for the last two weeks. He's a heavy equipment operator and he had jobs on two ranches down there. Jackson Hole is fifty miles north of here, so he stayed at a bunkhouse on those ranches, not returning nightly to the Bar C. It snows a lot and he didn't want to risk driving on icy roads for several hours both ways."

Nodding, Kira heard the vet stomping snow off his boots in the mudroom. "Makes good sense."

Shay smiled. "Well, you'll get to meet him in a few moments. He had to see Reese when he drove back from the work assignment. He'll be coming by the kitchen here any second and I'll introduce you to him."

Kira nodded. "Are you sure he won't mind a woman in his house?" Her mind snapped back to another Garret who she'd known for three years. The man she'd fallen helplessly and completely in love with, who had been part of her A team. Kira wasn't sure Garret had loved her; he'd always treated her like a sister. But she had secretly fallen in love with him. Utterly. Rubbing the red sweater she wore, Kira felt her heart ache without relief. She'd never known what happened to him. Where was he now? How was he doing? That part of her life was a black hole. A blank slate.

"Garret is easygoing," Shay assured her. "All the men know that sooner or later they'll get another military vet living in the same house with them. And they're all okay with it."

Kira heard the echo of heavy boots meeting the oak hardwood floor out in the hall. "What military branch was he in?"

Shay was about to answer when Garret came around the corner, his black Stetson in his hand.

Kira froze. Her eyes widened enormously as Garret Fleming stood in the doorway, staring at them. Her heart crashed in her chest. His hazel gaze snapped to her and stopped. And then he blinked slowly as he absorbed her sitting at the table.

Shay felt a palpable shift of energy in the room, as if a bolt of lightning had suddenly slammed into it. Confused, she looked at Garret and then at Kira.

"Kira?"

Garret's low, deep voice, filled with disbelief, plunged through her heart. Kira's lips parted as she wrestled with the shock bolting through her. "Garret?"

"Yeah," he rumbled, scowling. "What are you doing here?"

Kira gulped. "I — uh —" and she choked, unable to speak, her hands against her heart as she stared up at his tall, powerful form. Garret Fleming was six foot two inches tall, two hundred and twenty pounds of pure, rock-hard male muscle. He no longer wore a beard, which all Special Forces men in the teams did when in Muslim countries. His face was scraped clean and she saw how ruggedly handsome he really was. A beard hid so much of a man's face. Her heart stuttered and she felt swept away on a giddy joy that avalanched her. Garret had a square face, large, wide-spaced intelligent eyes that glittered with green, brown and gold flecks as he stared at her in disbelief. She wanted to get up and hurl herself into his arms. To kiss him. To celebrate he was alive! To Kira, he looked so strong and healthy, his face darkly tanned, exuding the vitality she'd known when she was on the team with him.

"What's going on here?" Shay asked, puzzled.

Garret shook his head and gave Shay a wry look. "Kira was a member in our Special Forces A team for three years."

"Oh," Shay whispered, her hand flying to her lips, her eyes suddenly huge as she stared at Kira.

Kira managed a jerky nod, her gaze never leaving Garret's. "Y-you're okay? I tried to find you, Garret, but I never could . . ." and her voice died into an aching whisper of regret. She saw his eyes grow stormy, that well-shaped mouth of his thinning as he regarded her.

"It's okay," he rumbled. Pointing at his left temple, he said gruffly, "I had amnesia for six months after I was flown to Bethesda. I didn't even know my own name until my memory came back on its own." He gave her an apologetic look. "I tried to find you, but I never could. I'm sorry, too . . ."

His low, emotional explanation filtered through her shock. A lump formed in her throat and she couldn't speak for a moment, overwhelmed with so much that had happened to them during the ambush. "I-I understand," she managed hoarsely, "you were shot in the head. I-I remember . . ." Kira remembered everything. Her weekly nightmares guaranteed that. She saw Garret's face crumple with pain for a moment before he put on his game face.

"Oh my God," Shay said, looking at first one and then the other, "you worked together?"

"Yeah," Garret said, moving his shoulders as if to get rid of tension. "Black ops, Shay. Top secret."

Shay stared at Kira. "I-I didn't know you knew Garret."

Kira managed to look at Shay. "I didn't know he was here." She waved her hand in a helpless gesture. "We were both wounded in a firefight. I was sent to Bethesda after being at Landstuhl and lost track of him." Swallowing hard, Kira held Garret's unfathomable look. She could feel the bombshell reaction inside him, but it didn't transfer to his game face, which remained unreadable. She honestly didn't know if he was glad to see her or not. A year had passed since they'd last been together. A year that felt like a lifetime of pain and anguish to her without his larger-than-life presence in it.

Now he was standing six feet away from her, incredibly handsome, confident, the old Garret she knew from the team. His face had deeper lines around his mouth now, given the terrible circumstances they'd barely survived. It told Kira of the suffering he'd gone through, too.

Reese Lockhart ambled out of his office and down the hall. He stopped in the kitchen doorway, nodding hello to Garret. "What's going on?" he asked his wife.

Shay quickly filled him in.

Reese gave Garret a long look, and then his gaze drifted to Kira. "Looks like you two have a lot of catching up to do, then," he said. "Kira, are you okay still being assigned to Garret's house? Or would you rather not?"

Kira looked at Garret. He seemed as surprised as hell at the question. But then she saw an emotion in his eyes, a flash for a second that she couldn't translate. "Well . . . I-I don't know. It's up to Garret —"

"It's fine," Garret told them in no uncertain terms. "Kira is welcome to stay with me."

Relief avalanched through Kira. For a brief moment she saw a thawing in Garret's hazel eyes. Her heart squeezed with powerful emotion and she felt suffused by joy. She didn't know how Garret felt toward her. They'd always been friends, as she was with all the men of the A team. Nothing more. And she'd held secret her love for this man who was so heroic, a warrior and a good person, who had helped so many in those three years they'd worked together.

Her feelings for him were still her secret. Even now. Probably forever. Some of Kira's joy dissolved. They had never talked about how they felt about each other. Always friends. Never anything more intimate.

Reese touched Garret's broad shoulder. "You got the paperwork from those two jobs?"

"Yeah," he said, rummaging around in the pocket of his sheepskin coat. Garret handed them to Reese.

"Great," Reese said. "Let's get business out of the way and then you can take Kira home with you."

Giving a nod, Garret said, "Sounds good." And then he looked at Kira. "This won't take long. I'll be right back."

Kira didn't know whether to laugh or cry. She so badly wanted to hug the hell out of Garret, to welcome him back into her life. Shay was watching her with some confusion and she offered, "We were on an A team in Afghanistan for three years."

"I know Special Forces teams try to stay together for long periods of time." Shay searched her eyes. "But you're a woman. I didn't know they had women in A teams."

"It was a top-secret operation," Kira hedged. She couldn't speak to anyone about it. Not ever. Garret knew because he, like the other eleven men on the team, had signed legal documents swearing to keep the operation confidential. Shay sat back, digesting the information.

"Okay," she said, "but is this going to be a stress or pressure on either of you? It looks like you lost track of each other."

"Yes, we did. I didn't know he had amnesia. It would explain why he never tried to contact me," Kira said quietly. She clasped her damp, cool fingers in her lap beneath the table, all her emotions in play. For the last year she'd thought Garret had chosen to remain out of her life. Now . . . she knew differently.

"You tried to locate him afterward?"

"Yes," and Kira held on to tears that burned in the back of her eyes. She closed them, taking in a ragged breath. "Our team was so tight, Shay. We were family . . ."

"Garret only told us once, during a therapy session, that of the twelve men in his team, only two survived." Shay gave her an anguished look. "That's so tragic."

It hurt to breathe at that moment because it brought everything back to Kira. Avoiding Shay's compassionate look, she whispered brokenly, "Y-yes, all of the other guys . . . dead. It was — horrible — awful . . ."

"Garret never said the other survivor was a woman."

"He couldn't. Legally, Shay, I was part of a top-secret operation. It couldn't be talked about. Not even here, not even with other military vets."

"God," Shay whispered, her hand against her throat, grief in her expression, "that had to be so terrible on both of you . . . to lose so many friends all at once that you'd known for so long . . ."

Unable to breathe for a moment, Kira wrestled with all her grief, her loss. "I-it lives in me every day, Shay. Three years of my life were with those guys. Every one of them was a stand-up man. They were brave men who did good things for the people of the village we lived in." She compressed her lips, hanging her head and closing her eyes, trying not to cry. Shay was so kind and caring that it made it easy for Kira to talk with her, to allow her feelings to surface. General Ward had been right: Shay Lockhart was a true maternal, loving woman. And it was something she'd missed so much, no longer having her own mother in her life. At the same time, Kira knew her top-secret life in the Army had to remain as such.

"Listen," Shay said softly, "I'm here for you, Kira. I understand what top secret means, but it doesn't stop you from talking to me about your feelings. We all need someone to lean on when trauma happens in our lives. If you ever want to unload, come and see me."

Warmth cascaded through Kira as she lifted her head and met Shay's kind blue gaze. "Y-yes, maybe in time. I need to prove my worth around here first."

"I'm sure you will. I'm here for you, Kira. Just remember that. Okay?"

Kira heard men's voices drifting down the hall, honing in on Garret's deep voice. She heard laughter between the men and then the heavy, thunking sound of Garret's boots striking the oak floor, coming in their direction. Her stomach knotted. Her heart started a slow pound, adrenaline leaking into her bloodstream. What was she going to say to Garret when they were alone? What was he going to say to her? Or do? Her mouth became dry and Kira seesawed between heaven and hell. She felt so tentative, so unsure about Garret. How did he feel about her? She honestly didn't know except that he always had been her friend on the team. But so was every other man.

Garret pulled a hard rein in on his emotions. He'd been Special Forces for a long time and knew that emotion, when uncontrolled, could lead to people getting killed.

As he drove Kira over to the house in the truck, he felt trapped. He had nowhere to run to hide from the past. He'd fallen hopelessly in love with Kira from almost the moment she'd joined their team, and then suppressed it, not allowing it to surface. He felt gut-punched. Kira was a brutal reminder of his past and that firefight he'd buried so damn deep within himself. He'd struggled to make sure it never surfaced again. Now, with her beside him, going to be a part of his life twenty-four hours a day, he felt scared and unsure. She was the only other survivor. She was a reminder of everything he never wanted to feel or remember again.

Garret was shocked by how she looked. Kira used to be strong, vibrant and darkly tanned. Her smile had been constant, her teasing not hurtful but infectious. The children of the village had adored her, called her mother in Pashtun. She was a hard worker, a team person, someone every man could count on.

He'd fallen helplessly in love with this woman from his past. And he'd thought he'd lost her. But she was sitting beside him. The violent need for her, to pull her into his arms, crush her against him, feel her woman's body and heat, savagely tore through Garret. He was wrestling with the fear of the past rising up to overwhelm him right along with his powerful yearning to hold, kiss and love Kira until they melted into each other.

What the hell was he going to do?

His mouth thinned as he drove slowly around the ranch house and down the newly created road that passed in front of all four houses that had been built about fifty feet apart from one another. Snow glittered like diamonds across the covered tops of the dark green, steeply sloped tin roofs. Already, the snow that had fallen last night had slid off the roof, keeping the excessive weight from causing the entire area to stress.

His gloved hands opened and closed around the wheel as he tried to figure out how to handle this situation. What had led him to say it was all right that Kira lived under his roof? What the hell was wrong with him? All she'd do was be a raw, constant reminder of everything he didn't want to remember or feel.

What kind of sick, twisted life had he been living since the firefight? Chaos seemed to be part and parcel of Garret's life ever since he'd awoken in Bethesda not even knowing his name. It had taken six months before everything suddenly downloaded and he'd had his complete memory back. Some of it, he wished fervently, hadn't returned. The deaths of his ten friends haunted him without relief.

Pulling up to the house, the snow on the ground from an October storm had fallen two days earlier, the bright sunlight glancing off the western side of the sprawling ranch house, Garret said gruffly, "Here's your new home, Kira. Let's go in."

He tried not to be affected by her thinness. Or the dark smudges beneath her glorious gray eyes, which used to sparkle like soft diamonds when she laughed. An ache settled deep in his heart as Garret walked to the cleared concrete sidewalk sprinkled with salt pellets and took the four steps to the back porch.

Opening the door, he gestured for her to go in first. The Kira he knew had been vibrant, vulnerable, easily touched and accessible to the rest of the team. Now, as she moved past him like a ghost from his lost past, he saw how closed-up she'd become. PTSD did that to a person. It had done it to him. Noah and Harper were the same.

Mouth compressed, Garret hungrily watched her move onto the mud porch and stomp her boots to get the snow off. Feeling like a starved wolf sexually speaking, he wanted her all over again. There hadn't been a day that went by in Afghanistan that he hadn't hungered to take her, bury himself into her hot depths and share her returning fire and need. He looked at her bare hands. Kira had long, thin fingers that were so graceful it made his lower body throb with need. How many hundreds of times had Garret dreamed of those hands roaming his body? Exploring him, learning what made him feel good? Imagining what it would feel like as she glided her fingertips across his hardened flesh?

Groaning inwardly, he went inside and closed the door. He'd never let Kira know any of his desire for her. It would have destroyed the team in so many bad ways, so he'd stuffed it. Just as he'd stuffed his horror over that firefight. Out of sight, out of mind. Now Kira was here and Garret could no longer forget any of it. Or his feelings toward her.

Kira stood, hands shoved in the pockets of her nylon parka to warm them, studying Garret. He saw sadness and grief in her expression and it kicked him in the gut. Dammit, he'd spent six months violently shoving down all his emotions since remembering that deadly ambush. There was no way he wanted to connect with any of those feelings. He tried not to remember any of his friends. Their laughter. Their personalities. Their wives . . . their children he knew as if they were his own family. His heart felt like it had a deep, unending ache within it, getting more painful by the minute. Scowling, he wanted to blame Kira for bringing up all the shit he had so viciously tried to avoid.

Garret strode past her and opened the

door that led directly into the kitchen. He hated that she gave him that look of vulnerability, as if seeking his protection against something. What? Him? He knew he was growly and irritable. PTSD at work. Kira looked down, her hands jammed deep in her coat pockets, and slipped by him like a wraith. He could smell her feminine scent along with the cold, clean winter air. It was like breathing life into his dead body; he couldn't get enough of her, wanting desperately to grip her shoulders, turn her around and yank her into his arms. That's what she needed, Garret realized. Kira felt stripped and naked thanks to her PTSD; he would bet anything on that. The look in her eyes wasn't something he'd never seen before. Once, she'd been such a strong, confident, outgoing young woman. Full of life. Full of promise. And he'd never stopped loving her.

Garret took off his Stetson and dropped it on a wooden peg next to the kitchen door. He turned, seeing that Kira had stopped near the granite island in the middle of the large, bright kitchen. She was so damned pale. In Afghanistan, she'd been deeply tanned, her black hair short, blue highlights dancing through those thick, silky strands.

Kira had never worn any makeup of any kind in the Army. The odor of cosmetic products would, first of all, alert the enemy that they were nearby if on a mission or patrol. Hell, she didn't need anything anyway, her black lashes long and thick, a frame for her incredible dove-gray eyes that were truly a window into her soul, to her many emotions.

She could never hide anything from him. She cried when an infant, just born, died shortly afterward. She held the mother, who rocked the dead baby in her arms, crying with her. Kira was so easily touched. Now? Garret could feel the wall around her. Trying to lock whatever she was feeling within those walls, keep the rest of the world out. She was afraid anyone she let in would shred her raw and bleed her out. That's how he felt every day with PTSD. It was an endless, tiring and wearing exercise. And he could see how worn down she had become.

His heart twinged. "Come on," he said, softening his gruff tone, gesturing for her to follow him, "I'll show you to your bedroom."

Walking down the oak hall, their boots echoing, Garret pushed open a door on the right, swinging it wide. He stepped aside and said, "This is yours . . ."

Kira hesitated. "Where is your room, Garret?"

Lifting his thumb across his shoulder, he said, "Right across the hall. Why?" Because he saw her wrinkle her nose, her gray eyes darken.

Giving him a shy look, unable to hold his penetrating stare, she whispered, "Sometimes . . . sometimes I wake up screaming at night." She pushed strands of hair off her brow in a nervous gesture. "My own screams wake me. They woke my father every time. That's why I had to leave his house. I kept waking him up." Her lips quirked. "I don't want to wake you . . ."

Garret forced his hands to remain on his hips. He was a tall, broad man, filling up the hallway. Kira was half his size and looked so damned vulnerable. He wanted to slide his hand across her wan cheek, cup it, lean down and kiss her tenderly to reassure her that everything would be all right. Garret knew better. There was nothing right with either of them anymore. They were twisted, wounded, distorted human beings trying to act and behave normally when normal had been destroyed in that ambush a year ago.

He cleared his throat and rasped, "Don't worry about it. I do my fair share of screaming in nightmares, too. Let's look at the positive side of it. We can start a symphony."

49

His teasing eased the tight line of her lips. She studied him, her large, soft eyes widening as she searched his. Heart beating to underscore the ache now centering in his lower body, Garret cursed to himself. He had no damned defense against Kira, he realized sharply. That unstrung him for a second. And then Garret realized the awful truth about Kira: she, too, was facing the demons within her from that ambush. He saw it reflected in her sad eyes, the parting of her lips that tempted him as nothing else ever had. Kira wasn't hiding from what had happened.

That terrified Garret more than anything else. He had successfully hidden from his grief and pain for six months. What was he going to do now?

CHAPTER THREE

Garret muttered, "The bathroom is next to my room," and he made a quick gesture in that direction. "I'll get your bags for you."

Kira nodded, standing uncertainly at the open door to her room. "Thanks," she whispered.

Turning, Garret felt the anxiety that was constantly there amp up like a monster within him. Always, he wrestled the need to run, deep back down inside himself, as he strode through the kitchen. Just getting out in the cold, crisp afternoon air that he dragged deeply into his lungs helped settle his desire to run.

Shaking his head, he walked up the road, around the main ranch house and opened the door to Kira's pickup truck. Inside was a ninety-pound duffel bag. It was familiar and brought back so many unwanted memories. With a curse, he yanked it out of the truck, hefting it over one broad shoulder.

He slammed the door a little harder than he'd intended.

Get a hold of yourself, Fleming. It's not *Kira's fault. Stop blaming her.*

Ice crunched beneath his work boots. Snow fell in the western part of Wyoming from September, onward. The midafternoon sun was melting some of the white stuff but not much. The muddy tracks showed up on the road as he walked with the duffel bag to the house. His gut was a nest of writhing, frightened snakes twisting within him.

Because he'd always loved Kira, he hated himself for thinking this was her fault. It wasn't. He had to stop this immediately. She had been wounded, too, in so many ways, just like him. He could see the suffering in her face even though he also saw her trying to hide it from him. She'd never been able to hide anything from him. But telling her how he felt about her had always been off the table.

Angry and disgusted with himself over his panic and anxiety, his worry about all that crap vomiting up from the tightly held box he kept stuffed within him, Garret knew he had to get a handle on his escaping emotions immediately. People with PTSD often projected their anger and irritation at the closest moving object, usually their spouse.

Kira wasn't his wife, but he was responsible for her now that she was living under his roof. Living alone, he didn't have to shield his anger and irritation when it rose violently up through him. Now he would have to or else. Kira didn't deserve his darkness. She had her own to contend with.

As he opened the back door, hefting the duffel bag into the kitchen, Garret forced himself to settle down and think. Before PTSD, he'd been calm, coolheaded and utterly focused on any task before him. Now things were never like that. Now it was like trying to get all his anxiety, which flowed in many different directions at once, corralled and then tamed into one focus. It took so much energy that by the end of a long work day, he was physically and mentally exhausted.

His boot footfalls echoed down the well-lit hallway. Kira's door was open. His heart rolled in his chest, that damned yearning ache ratcheting up with intensity. How badly he needed her. Garret knew he could find peace in her arms. If he could bury himself in her warm, welcoming depths, he'd find calm, which was something he hadn't felt since the ambush. Kira represented an island of healing for him and Garret didn't even try to deny it. He halted at the door. He saw her at the dresser, some of the drawers open.

"Here you go," he said, taking the duffel over to the queen-size bed. The ladies of the Wind River Valley Quilt Club had gifted it to him. The quilt was a simple quilt made of nine-inch-square patches of summertime flowers in bloom. It was bright and cheery. When she gave him a tentative smile, his heart burst open. For a moment he felt the gnawing in his lower body, reminding him just how much he loved her. Nothing was simple. Absolutely nothing.

"Thanks." She walked over, opening it up. "My whole life is contained in here."

"The Army's still with you."

"It always will be," she answered softly, removing the clothes she'd carefully folded and packed, placing them in neat rows on the bed.

Garret wanted to stay to talk with her. He had hundreds of questions for her. Kira looked exhausted. Her once proud, straight shoulders were slumped. She wore a bright red sweater that showed him the pallor of her skin and emphasized her large, beautiful gray eyes. Her black hair was mussed and he itched to lift his hand to tame a few of those strands away from her high cheekbone but severely resisted the gesture. "Have you eaten recently?"

"Yes. Shay made me a late lunch. That was really kind of her."

He fidgeted inwardly, forcing himself to appear quiet and calm, at least outwardly. Inwardly, there was a battle raging between his hormones, lust and the past rapidly rising up, engulfing his stretched, fragile emotional state. "Are you tired? Do you want to rest? Or would you like to sit with me in the kitchen and have a cup of coffee?" Garret wanted to do something — anything — to relieve the rawness he felt with Kira. It was like she was walking around without her skin to protect her. And Garret knew from long experience, with his knee-jerk reaction to a child or woman who needed shielding, he'd be there in a heartbeat to be that guard. Kira was pushing every button he had in that area right now. And she wasn't doing it on purpose. She might be feeling pretty bad, but she didn't whine, didn't give it voice. She just gutted through it, silently, not asking for help or support.

Like him. *Hell.*

"Coffee sounds really good. Are you sure you don't mind making us a pot, Garret?" and she searched his hard, weathered face.

"No problem. I'm happy to do it."

55

"Maybe we can take a bit of time to catch up with each other. I have so many questions to ask you."

Wincing internally, his gut clenching, Garret nodded. "Yeah, I understand. Come out when you're ready. I'll have coffee waiting for you." He felt unparalleled fear; if Kira started talking about the ambush, about the deaths of their brothers, Garret knew he wouldn't be able to handle it. Digging into her pensive features, feeling her natural warmth and openness, Garret felt like he was lost; the anchor he'd managed to create after the amnesia left had dissolved. To say he was floundering was an understatement.

And yet, looking down at Kira, how thin and small she was in comparison to himself, he saw strength in her eyes, too. *Small but mighty.* He'd always teased her about that. In the team, she was called Trouble. It was a nickname that had a helluva lot of love and respect for Kira behind it. And she did stir up trouble, but not the bad kind. She would see a need, bring it to everyone's attention and something would get done to fix it.

No one on the team ever winced when she brought up a solution for the village people's problems either. She was their secret weapon in getting actionable intel from the women, who clearly loved her, and they were grateful for her generosity to them. But now Garret knew he had another kind of trouble with Kira. And he had to shield her from himself or else. She was suffering just as much, maybe more, than he was. He'd have to find out.

About thirty minutes later, Garret heard Kira's boots scuffing down the hallway, coming his way. He turned from the counter, seeing her enter the kitchen. "Ready for some coffee?" he asked over his shoulder.

"Please." Kira walked slowly to the large, round maple table that had four chairs around it. "Can I help?"

"Nah. Sit down. Make yourself comfortable." He reached for red mugs and poured the coffee, bringing it to the table. Kira had combed her hair, he saw. And she'd changed sweaters. This one, a pale pink, clung to her, and he avoided looking at the soft slope of her breasts pillowed beneath it. She'd also changed from jeans to a pair of black wool slacks. He slid the mug in her direction. "Last time I remember you liked your coffee black."

She managed a slight smile, taking the mug. "At least that hasn't changed in me. This is fine. Thanks."

Garret sat opposite her, pulling the sugar

bowl in his direction from the center of the table. "My coffee taste hasn't changed one iota either." He lifted his mug in a toast. "Welcome to the Bar C."

She smiled tentatively, lifting her mug and gently touching Garret's. "I'm still in shock over seeing you here, Garret." She sipped the coffee, holding his gaze. Setting it down between her hands, she asked huskily, "You said you had amnesia from the head wound?"

"Yeah, for six damn long months." He leaned back in the chair, tipping up the front two legs. "Last thing I remembered was running that night. The next thing the lights went out. I woke up ten days later in Bethesda. The docs had put me into a drug-induced coma, working to stop my brain from swelling where that bullet grazed me here." He pointed to his left temple. "I didn't know who I was. I knew *nothing.*"

"God, that must have been scary."

He gave her a dark look. "At least I didn't know what happened to our team." The words came out low and tight. Garret knew he'd have to cover some of the firefight, but as little as possible. He was going to manipulate Kira as much as he had to in order to stay the hell away from that subject. "The docs told me who I was. They told me I'd been wounded in Afghanistan, but that was all."

"Did they know whether you'd get your memory back?"

"They said it would probably download at some point. My brain was bruised and off-line." He shrugged. "I was bored as hell. I had the wound in my left calf, too One of those bones was broken and it was in bad shape. They had to put screws into it. I spent a lot of time doing physical therapy at the gym facility in the medical center. I've got most of my mobility back, but that's what got me discharged from the Army with an honorable medical discharge."

"Does your leg still bother you?"

"Around here as a wrangler? I can do anything physically asked of me. It's not a hindrance. The Army knew my leg would never stand up to the daily stress and strain of being part of black ops, though." He tried to stop the blossoming love for her spreading through his chest. This was so like the old Kira in the A team. She was a mother hen to the rest of the team. And to the villagers and their children as well. Garret saw that care burning in her eyes for him. It felt good, dammit, to have a woman extend herself like Kira could. Garret had had enough relationships in his life to know Kira was special. She'd always stood out as a woman among their team of males. And it was more than physiology and more than skin deep. It was *her.* She was a compassionate, caring human being. Garret had seen it in a hundred small ways during a day with her at the village.

"God, I'm so sorry all this happened to you. I know how much you loved the Special Forces." She tilted her head, her voice soft with feeling. "And you were so good at what you did, Garret. The villagers loved you. The kids doted on you . . ."

He shifted uncomfortably in the chair, not wanting to go back to that time. "I'm sorry I never got in touch with you," he said, meaning it. He saw Kira's eyes go moist for a split second, and then the tears were gone. "Until my brain dumped everything, my shrink wasn't about to tell me anything about that ambush. I asked the shrink if there was anyone else who'd survived the firefight." Garret's voice went thick. "They told me you were the only other survivor. That you'd been wounded twice. I asked him for a way to get in touch with you." His mouth pursed as he held Kira's softening gaze. "They told me three months after you'd been released from the hospital that you were given an honorable medical discharge. I asked them for your dad's address because I knew you were close to him. They gave it to me, Kira, and I called Les. He said you'd stayed a month and then left for parts unknown. At the time I called, he had no idea where you were." Garret stopped for a moment, wrestling with his emotions as they rampaged through him, mostly grief and sadness. "I didn't know how to find you. God, I wanted to . . . but you were MIA."

Nodding, Kira whispered unsteadily, "I was lost, Garret. I did stay with my dad for a while, but I was having PTSD nightmares nearly every night. I was waking him up. All the time. And he was so upset and worried about me. Neither of us were getting any sleep." She pushed her hands against her face. "I had to leave. The poor guy was becoming sleep-deprived. So was I, but I'm a lot younger than he is and I guess I could handle it better."

With a shrug, she added in a trembling tone, "I'm so glad to know you did try to locate me. When I was at Landstuhl, I tried to find out where they sent you. No one knew. And then they transferred me to Bethesda for recovery. I tried again to find out where you were. No luck." She shrugged. "My duffel bag, or what was left of it, was in a locker in the basement. I knew I had an address book in there. When I could walk and get around, I went to find it. I called your father, Cal."

Wincing, Garret grumbled, "You know he's an alcoholic, Kira. A mean bastard."

"Yes, I remember a number of talks we had about your father," she said. "I figured he'd know where you were." Shrugging, she drew in a ragged breath. "He was drunk when I called. Told me to go to hell."

Garret's hand on the table moved into a fist. He felt rage tunneling up through him, saw the devastation in Kira's eyes. "I-I'm sorry. He shouldn't have done that."

"Hey, you clued me in on him long before that. I knew I was taking a risk, but I needed to find you. I *had* to find you, Garret," and her voice filled with tears. She hastily wiped them away and gave him an apologetic look.

Oh God. Tears. Garret froze, unable to deal with the tears glimmering like soft diamonds in her eyes that were filled with such anguish. He heard so many emotions in her hushed voice, felt it energy-wise, as if a warm blanket briefly, lovingly surrounded him. He still loved Kira. That love he'd held for her those three years hadn't dimmed one damned bit. It stunned Garret. "I'm sorry he treated you that way."

"Don't apologize for him," she said, distress in her tone. "After he told me to go to hell, he calmed down. I asked if he heard anything to call me. I had a cell phone and gave him my number. He said he would. It was the last time I heard from him and I had no idea where you were, how you were doing or anything else."

"I couldn't find you either, Kira." He gently set the legs of the chair down on the shining oak floor. Wrapping his large hands around the coffee cup, he added, "I didn't have a cell phone. After I talked to your father, I told him I'd try to call him from time to time, in hopes you had called him." He dropped her gaze. "When they released me, I had some money in the bank but not much. I thought it would be easy to get a job, but it wasn't." He gave a one-shouldered shrug. "My PTSD."

"Oh . . . that," she muttered, frowning. "I got discharged because of the PTSD, not my wounds."

Garret bit back the question he desperately wanted to ask. No one had told him what happened that night after he'd been knocked out. How had they been saved? He wanted that information, but at the same time that would be opening up a can of worms he didn't ever want to open. There was no one to ask but Kira. But not right now. Probably, never. "PTSD? I thought you were discharged because of your wounds."

Shaking her head, she muttered, "I was an emotional basket case, Garret. I was wounded in the left arm," she pointed to her upper arm, "and my right calf. I had no broken bones, thank God. But my head . . . my emotions . . . I lost it," she admitted, shame in her voice.

Garret sat there, staring hard at her, seeing the moisture in her eyes, the shame for her behavior after the firefight. "Look," he said gruffly, "only two people survived that hell. You and me. I remembered everything up to the moment I was struck in the head. It was hell, Kira. Don't be ashamed of how you feel. Anyone surviving that attack was going to be permanently changed by it. I was. So were you. You don't have to apologize to anyone for what happened to you. Okay?" He felt every protective hackle standing up on his spine and neck. Who the hell wouldn't have PTSD after the firefight they'd survived?

"I guess," she admitted in a low, unsteady voice, her hands gripping her cup, "I never expected post-traumatic stress disorder. Oh, I'd heard of PTSD, but I'd been in the

Army since I was eighteen. And here I was twenty-six and I'd seen plenty of stress and some combat. Like a lot of other people, I thought it was all in your head," and she gave him a wry look. "I know different, now."

"I got a good dose of it, too," Garret admitted thickly. "It runs me if I let it."

"Tell me about it." She touched her stomach. "The anxiety I feel is horrible. General Ward, who I worked under, had an employment team to put us women into jobs after we separated from the Army." She wiped her brow and shook her head. "Five jobs, Garret. And I got fired from all of them." Rolling her eyes, she uttered, "It's the anxiety. If I get stressed, I start losing it. I can't help it. I can't control how I feel. I try, God, I try, but . . ." and her voice trailed off as she avoided his sharpened gaze.

"Did the general find this ranch?"

"Yes. Her employment team came on it and because all my other jobs were in the city, General Ward thought maybe a rural job would decrease my stress levels. I hope it does . . ."

"It will," Garret said firmly. "Shay and Reese are both vets. They have PTSD. There isn't anyone around here who doesn't, more or less. Hell, Noah and Harper have it ten times worse than I do. Noah was a dog handler in the military. He's really good with all animals. He got discharged due to PTSD. Six months ago he wandered into Wind River Valley and Shay saw him in one of the main plazas in town, asking to do any kind of work for money for food. She brought him here and he's been healing ever since. Now he has horses he's training for folks in the valley."

"That's really hopeful," Kira said, sitting up, her voice suddenly stronger. "What about Harper?"

"He came here five months ago. Similar situation. Shay found him sleeping on a bench on one of the plazas; dirty clothes, a beard and no bath for probably a few months. He was a Navy combat corpsman. Saw too much. Got medically discharged with PTSD. Shay got him cleaned up — a shave, haircut, new clothes — and brought him home to the Bar C. He's a handyman and goes around the valley doing odd jobs of all kinds. But he also wants to go to college to become a paramedic, and then either work for the fire department or a hospital. He's saving his money and he's climbing out of his PTSD cellar a little at a time, too. I know he'll make it."

"And what about you?" she wondered.

"How has Shay helped you?"

Garret found it easy to share that with Kira. It wasn't traumatic compared to the ambush. "I came here a year ago. I was looking for work and went to Charlie Becker's hay-and-feed store. He said Shay was looking for a wrangler who had heavy equipment experience. I decided to drive out to see if I could get the job. I liked her immediately. I liked her even more when she told me she was a Marine Corps vet and had PTSD. She told me she wanted to hire only people like herself, who needed a job, respect and a place to heal."

"That's so inspiring," Kira whispered, deeply touched.

"Shay's responsible," he told her. "She's the world's biggest mother hen — with the exception of you." A slight grin lifted one corner of his mouth. "Shay has given us a safe place to heal ourselves, Kira. We get weekly counseling and there's a woman military vet, Dr. Libby Hilbert, who leads our weekly sessions. We can go to her for individual counseling if we want."

"Shay is remarkable. Someone should give her a medal," Kira agreed. She sipped her coffee.

"I'm sure you'll do well here." Garret frowned. "The only potential stress on you will be Ray Crawford."

"Shay warned me."

"He's an alcoholic. Reminds me too much of my father," Garret said flatly. "Shay says he's stopped drinking, but I don't buy it. Alcoholics are the best liars and manipulators in the world."

"Maybe you can be a guide for me, Garret."

"What do you mean?"

Shrugging, Kira said, "My dad, Les, is a wonderful person. I love him so much. We don't have alcoholism in our family like you do. I thought . . . well . . . if I have questions about something Ray does, can I come to you for help? Maybe some advice?" and she looked at him.

"Any time," Garret said. "I worry he'll jump on you like he did Shay. He is, to this day, mentally and emotionally abusive to her. He wants to take back his ranch. Right now, Shay and Reese legally own and run the Bar C. Ray is trying to get well enough from his stroke so he can take the Bar C away from them. Hell, he's the one who ran this ranch into the ground in the first place. He drove off all the wranglers with his cursing, anger and abuse of them." Kira's eyes widened, and Garret realized Shay hadn't told her everything. He was damned if he was going to allow Kira to walk into the line of fire with Ray Crawford. He was a mean son of a bitch and there was no way in hell he was going to let Kira become his target.

"Oh . . ." she managed, swallowing hard. "Shay said he was cantankerous and acknowledged he was an alcoholic. She didn't talk to me about him wanting the Bar C back."

Garret held her gaze; he saw the concern in her eyes. "All alcoholics are manipulative, Kira. They lie to get anything they want. Did Shay tell you to check the cupboards, dresser drawers, the pantry and any other places he might hide bottles?"

Grimly, Kira said, "No."

"You have to do it at least once a week. Also, take a good whiff of his breath. If you smell alcohol, you'll know he's drinking and hiding the bottle."

"Great," she muttered, worried.

"Look, I'll be here to back you up," Garret soothed. "He's not supposed to be drinking, but if my childhood experiences with my old man are anything to go by, I believe Ray is still drinking but not admitting it to anyone. Shay think's he's dry, but I know he isn't."

"Then I need to be careful about checking out hiding places."

"From what I understand, he sits in the living room and watches TV. A van from the local gym picks him up and he goes into town. That's when he could get one of those drivers to buy him another bottle or two of liquor for the coming week."

"I see."

"Do you have to cook for him seven days a week?"

"Yes. That and clean his house once a week." Kira shrugged. "That's easy stuff."

"What kind of translations are you doing right now?"

She smiled a little. "I'm with a big website. I translate business letters and manuals from Arabic into English and vice versa. At the moment I've been asked to translate a five-hundred-page manual from English into Arabic. It's good money. I get five cents a word. That adds up to a nice amount when they hire me. But there can be a week or more when I get no translation requests."

"So you'll put fifteen percent of what you earn into the Bar C?"

"Yes. Shay's interested in me getting a savings account. Part of her overall plan to help me is to get money in the bank for a rainy day. It's not a bad idea. She's really practical about it."

"Everyone loves her," Garret said, his voice thawing a little. "She's doing too much, and when her old man decided to come back here and live on the Bar C again, she bought his lie."

"What was that?"

"That he was coming back because he missed the ranch. The truth is, from what I can see, he intends to take it back from Shay. But she doesn't believe it. I do."

"Have you talked to Reese about this?"

Garret gave her a feral look. "I let him know a heartbeat after I figured it out. I get protective of women, kids and animals. And I don't like to see a wolf in sheep's clothing, which is what Ray Crawford is."

"Wow, there's a lot of intrigue around here," she said, shaking her head.

"You need to know what's going on, Kira. You're right in the middle because you're going to be around Ray more than anyone else on this ranch. You need to be Shay and Reese's eyes and ears. Crawford isn't to be trusted. At all. And don't let him lure you in by being nice to you. If that happens, that means he wants something from you."

"How does he treat you, Noah and Harper?"

"He thinks we're worthless. He disdains us. Calls us cowards and weak because we

71

have PTSD."

Kira made a sad sound in her throat. "But . . . why?"

"Because Ray blames Shay for going into the military. He's never been in and he's antimilitary. Thinks we're on the dole, asking for handouts. He doesn't respect us at all. And he's angry as hell that Shay left the ranch to go into the military. The truth is, she ran away from here because of him. Her mother was already dead. She couldn't handle his abusiveness any longer, so she escaped and went into the Marine Corps."

Kira wrapped her arms around herself, staring down at the table, evaluating what Garret had shared. She lifted her chin. Meeting his gaze, she whispered, "God, it sounds like a war is going on right here. A quiet one. But a war between the daughter and the father anyway."

Garret's eyes gleamed with pride as he looked at her. "You've nailed it, Kira. And you're the party in the middle. You need to watch your six." *And I'll be there to shadow you, protect you.* But he didn't say that out loud to her. He loved Kira. Garret was damned if someone like Ray Crawford was going to hurt her.

CHAPTER FOUR

Kira was nervous and her sweaty palms proved it. Today was her first day of work at the Bar C. She wanted to make a good impression on Ray Crawford. Would he like her cooking? She hoped so.

In the kitchen, making herself breakfast at six a.m., Kira tried to be quiet, knowing that Garret was still sleeping, his bedroom door closed. She reached up into a cupboard that had several dry cereal boxes in it and drew one down. She had slept little the first night, her mind and heart in a free-fall tumble. Right across the hall from her, Garret slept. Lying in bed, her heart squeezed with so much love for him that had no place to go. She'd gone over their first conversation at the kitchen table so many times. Kira was looking for some hint, some sign, that Garret wanted to be more than a friend to her.

There was no hint or sign.

73

She had noticed he was far more hair trigger emotionally, especially when the topic of Ray Crawford arose. In the Special Forces team, she had been treated like one of the men. If they saw her woman's body, no one said anything about it. It was understood that as a top-secret operation, it was designed to see if a woman could not only survive in combat but fight alongside her male compatriots. She was razzed like one of the boys, teased unmercifully at times, rousted out of sleep for her watch just like any other team member would be. Only Garret had been more prickly and protective toward her for as long as she could remember.

Kira lay awake, remembering one night when she'd had terrible cramps from her period. Normally, she didn't have one due to the high physical demands and stresses of the combat environment in which she lived. It was well known that women stopped menstruating for months at a time under this type of duress. She hadn't had a period in four months, but one night, in the mud house she shared with Garret at the south end of the village, she was in horrible pain. The kind of pain that made her double up and cry, and she'd tried to keep from making any sounds. He had his bed, a cot, in another room. He'd awakened.

Kira had told him to go back to bed, that she'd be all right. She was crying, trying not to sob, biting her lower lip to stop any sounds from escaping her. Garret had good night vision and Kira knew he saw the trail of tears down her cheeks. He'd insisted on starting a fire, boiling water in a black iron kettle and then soaking a towel in it. He'd asked if he could gently lay his hand on the area, promising it wouldn't make her cramps worse. The heat from his hand would help. Garret had never, in all three years they'd spent together, touched her like he had that one night.

Kira had hesitantly agreed and closed her eyes, the pain severe. While the water heated, he got up on one knee, leaned over her cot and placed his large hand lightly across the span of her abdomen. The moment Garret's warm, callused palm lay across her flesh, the pain began to ease. He didn't rub her belly. Rather, just the light contact, the heat radiating off his hand, was soothing to Kira. It had sent wild, pleasurable sensations throughout her tense body. Garret didn't speak; he simply knelt there, beside her, getting her to relax, the heat from his hand releasing the tautness. She had never been touched by a man like Garret had touched her that night. Her mind spun wildly afterward, wondering hotly what it would be like to be loved by him. It was then that Kira knew Garret would be an extraordinary and considerate lover. For all his weight, size and bulk, she had experienced Garret's tenderness. For a long time Kira had suspected he would be a wonderful lover, but on that one night, he'd shown her a side of himself she would never forget.

Like a male mama bear, he'd fussed over her and laid the warm, moist towel across her belly to reduce the cramping. In truth, her cramps were nearly gone by the time he placed the compress across her. Within fifteen minutes the cramps had completely dissolved.

Garret had stayed up with her for another half hour, wetting the towel, keeping it across that affected area. For all his size and his shoulders, so wide he'd get stuck in the doorways of many of the small Afghan homes, he was amazingly caring with her that night. Kira loved him so much and she couldn't tell him. Now that she'd experienced his touch, Kira had wanted more. So much more. At some point she'd fallen asleep. When she woke up the next morning, her trousers were back in place around her waist, a blanket drawn over her and

Garret gone.

Those cramps never returned like that again. Even though she'd have a period every three or four months, Kira didn't ask for special consideration or rest. She had duties to perform every day just like everyone else on the team. If one person didn't pull their weight, it placed an unfair demand on everyone else.

Garret had come back to their mud house to see her an hour after she was up, dressed and kneeling at the tripod with a kettle suspended from it. She saw the concern burning in his hazel eyes as he'd ducked down to enter the house. He crouched opposite her and asked how she was feeling. They were nine months into their first year together and she'd never experienced the cosseting side to Garret until then. Kira felt as if she were the center of his world in that moment. The burning care in his gaze had totaled her. She saw something else in them she couldn't translate. Whatever it was, the feeling that washed over her in that moment was like a lover bringing her into his arms and holding her safe. Kira had to shake herself after he'd rose and left, returning to his duties for the day. Had she imagined it?

On nights when Kira felt lonely without him beside her, she would remember that special night when she was on the receiving end of Garret's care. On other nights, when her libido was high and she was gnawingly aware she wanted a man just to have sex with, Kira always visualized Garret in her imagination. She wasn't a woman who hopped from bed to bed. No, she wanted a relationship that had depth and substance to it. But being in Afghanistan, with no way to satisfy any sexual urge, she would remember Garret's hand gentle on her painful abdomen. It was as close as they had ever come to being intimate with each other. They'd never kissed. Never embraced. And now she felt pangs of yearning tremor throughout her lower body, imagining . . . imagining Garret making scaldingly hot love with her.

"Hey . . ."

Kira gasped, turned, a bowl in one hand, a box of cereal in another. Garret's low, sleepy voice echoed from the hall and into the kitchen. He was dressed in a pair of black pajama bottoms, naked from the waist up, wiping his drowsy-looking eyes with his hand. His blatant masculinity slammed into her. Instantly, her lower body clenched. The dark hair sprinkled across his massive chest combined with the breadth of those shoulders, the muscles large and powerful, made her go hot with longing.

"Sorry," Garret mumbled, wiping his face as he halted near her. "Didn't mean to scare the bejesus out of you."

Gulping, Kira tore her gaze from his chest and shoulders. He looked like a sleepy kid, his eyes half open, their hazel depths looking cloudy. "I tried to be quiet in here. I'm sorry I woke you . . ."

Garret stared at her and then shook his head. "What time is it?"

"6:00 in the morning." It was hard not to fall back into military speak with him.

He grunted. "You have to feed Ray at 0700?"

"Yes."

He grimaced at the box of cereal in her hand.

"Put that away. Let me make you a real breakfast." He pointed to the table. "Go. Sit down. I'll be back in a few minutes."

Nonplussed, Kira nodded and put the cereal away. She couldn't shake the masculinity of Garret. Oh, she'd seen him stripped to the waist before, but for whatever reason, it impacted her now a hundredfold. Maybe because they weren't in the Army anymore? She didn't have to hide from her own body and heart and continue to be in denial about her love for Garret. Shakily, Kira shut the cupboard door and poured herself some fresh coffee. Figuring Garret would want some, she filled a mug and left it on the counter for him.

Garret ambled out ten minutes later. His hair was neatly combed, but that three-day growth of beard was still there, giving him a dark, sensual look. Her throat went dry. He had pulled on a tan T-shirt that did nothing but exploit his physique, and her lower body began to gnaw, making her keenly aware that she was long overdue for sex. But if she ever had the chance to go to bed with Garret, it would be so much more than for just sexual relief and an orgasm. Her heart was in the mix and it would make their loving each other so very special. A one-of-a-kind thing. Her gaze dropped to his jeans, which hugged his thick, long legs. He still looked drowsy in a little-boy kind of way that was endearing to Kira.

"You don't have to do this," she protested.

"I want to," Garret growled, quickly gathering a large cast-iron skillet, eggs, cheese, bacon bits and an onion. "You like toast with your omelet?"

"Sure. Can I —"

"No. Stay where you are." He gave her a hard look. "You've got dark rings under your eyes. Didn't you sleep last night?" he demanded.

A slight grin tugged at the corners of her mouth. "My, aren't we cranky before we've had our first cup of coffee?"

Snorting again, Garret set to work making his omelet. "You should wake me up when you get up."

"Why? I can feed myself."

"That's not the point. I want to be here to help you, Kira. Let me. You okay?"

She sat back, digesting his grumpy growls. And that's what they were. "You sound like a snaggle-toothed lone wolf snarling around your lair." She looked at his profile, seeing that beautifully shaped male mouth of his briefly hook upward.

"Not used to living with a woman underfoot."

"Thanks, Batman."

"You can be my sidekick, Robin."

It was her turn to snort. "In your dreams, Fleming." She saw his mouth hitch upward even more. Warmth sheeted through her because this was the Garret she'd lived with when they were with the A team.

"Speaking of dreams," he mumbled, whisking all the ingredients together into a steel bowl, "did you have any nightmares?"

"No. I mostly tossed, turned and couldn't shut off my mind."

"Everything's new here, that's why," he said, giving her a glance across his shoulder. "Adds stress. Brings on the insomnia bigtime because of our PTSD."

"Yeah," she muttered unhappily, gratefully sipping the hot coffee.

"By tonight you'll be so damned tired you'll be ready to keel over after you get done with Crawford's dinner."

"You got that right." Kira watched him move like he knew what he was doing. "You know, you did a lot of the cooking for the team. Are you doing the cooking here?"

"I did over at Shay's house until she married Reese. I made three meals for everyone on the ranch every day using the Wolf stove in her house. We ate at that big trestle table of hers in the kitchen the first year I was here. Now? I cook Sunday dinner for everyone over at their house. It's always a great meal and we enjoy one another's company. A time to catch up and relax a little bit."

"You cooked for everyone for a year?"

"Sure. Why not?" Garret popped the sourdough bread into the toaster and walked to the fridge to find the butter dish.

"I don't know," she said. "Anyone meeting you for the first time wouldn't automatically think *chef*.

"What? More like wrestler? Bouncer?

Mixed martial arts fighter?" and he chuckled, flipping the top over on the omelet in the skillet.

"For sure." Kira felt lighter. Happier. Just being around Garret again was a natural high for her. And if she was any judge, he looked pretty happy, too, although all she could see was his profile from time to time. The breadth of his back and those massive, thick shoulders of his, took her breath away, too, but in a good way. Kira could see each time he moved, the set of muscles contracting and sliding smoothly into the next set beneath the tight-fitting T-shirt he wore. The man was in superb athletic condition.

Garret expertly cut the omelet in half, placing each on a red ceramic plate. The toast popped and he quickly slathered it with butter and placed it over the eggs. He slid a plate toward her. "Now, eat. All of it. I'm gonna start weighing you once a week and keep tabs on your weight."

She smiled a little. "You're really mother-henning me, Fleming. What gives?" She saw that lazy smile come to his face. In the past it had meant Garret was in a teasing mood, something she always loved about him when it happened.

Garret sauntered to the fridge and drew out jars of strawberry and apricot jam. He then brought the coffeepot to the table and refilled their mugs. "I've always been a hen with chicks. You know that."

"Well," she grumped good-naturedly, picking up the apricot jam jar and opening it, "that's true. All the kids in the village, when they first met you, were scared to death of you. I'm sure you looked like the Jolly Green Giant to them."

"Yeah, I scared the hell outta them with my size," he admitted, sitting down at her right elbow. Garret tackled the strawberry jam, taking no prisoners.

"But later," Kira archly reminded him, savoring the delicious omelet, "they found out you were a big, overstuffed teddy bear. All warm and fuzzy."

Garret groaned and closed his eyes for a moment. He opened them, staring at her. "Oh, come on! You're not going to tell everyone here about that, are you?"

Kira gave him a sly look. "I won't if you don't start calling me Trouble again." That was her nickname in the team, and he'd been the one to give it to her and it stuck.

Garret's eyes glistened. His mouth curved ruefully. "I see where this is going."

"Better believe it. I'll keep your secrets if you keep mine." Kira discovered she was starving and rapidly ate everything on her plate. She had half an hour before she had to be over at Ray's house. The thirty minutes was a pure, unexpected gift to her. Just getting to sit with Garret, to see strands of his short, sandy-colored hair dipping over his broad brow, that layer of sleepiness still in his eyes, made her want to reach out and cup his stubbled jaw, lean forward and curve her mouth over his smiling one.

"What? Trouble suited you perfectly at the village. You were always getting into some kind of trouble there."

"Or I was getting out of it," she reminded him, laughing. "You just remember the times when I needed one of you guys to help me."

"Yeah," Garret said drolly, "like the time it had rained for three days straight one winter. And you took our Humvee out and was test driving it and ran into a puddle? Only the puddle was masking a four-foot-deep hole? It swallowed half that Humvee and flooded the floorboards with dirty water."

"Geeze," Kira muttered, shaking her head, "you remember that?"

He snickered and finished off his omelet. "How could I forget it?"

"I hit the brakes, but it was too late, and I was too close to avoid the pothole," she defended herself, relishing their repartee.

"That was the story you told the guys," Garret deadpanned, mopping up the leavings on his plate with the last of his toast. "Everyone bought your explanation except me."

She gave him a dirty look.

"Hey, you got distracted."

"You never said anything about it then," Kira accused, pushing her plate to one side, still grinning.

Shrugging, Garret said, "Well, okay, here's the truth of that little event. Everyone else was on the west side of the village when it happened. I was walking on the east side along the road. I saw a mother goat and her two kids run right in front of you." Garret lowered his voice, holding her gaze. "Instead of hitting them, you swerved and landed in that mud hole."

"You knew?"

"Yep."

"Why didn't you rat me out?"

Shrugging, Garret said quietly, "Because you're a softy at heart, Kira, and if I'd been in your shoes that morning, I'd have done the same thing. Those other guys would have had goat steak for dinner that night and paid the owner for the loss of the animals in US dollars. Everyone would have walked away happy except the goats. You took the high road and did the right thing for the right reason."

"Hmm," Kira said, sipping her coffee, eyeballing him. His voice had gone low and intimate, ruffling the edges of her lower body. Her skin riffled, as if he'd reached out and caressed her. He hadn't, and Kira wished he would. "So, you do keep some secrets." She knew Garret had never mentioned the night she'd had the terrible menstrual cramps to anyone else either. He'd protected her. If the other guys had heard about it, they would have razzed the daylights out of her. But he'd never said a peep to anyone. It had been their secret.

Garret gave her a narrow-eyed look. "I'm just full of secrets."

"Apparently, some about me." Kira watched him give her a teasing grin, his eyes glinting, reminding her of a hunter who had his quarry sighted.

"Oh, more than a few," he assured her lightly, standing and picking up their empty plates. "But your secrets, Trouble, are all safe with me."

Kira burst out laughing, his teasing lifting her spirits higher than they'd been since she'd gotten wounded. Garret had never teased her meanly, not ever. Some of the other guys had, but it was just their way and she didn't take it personally.

She watched him rinse the plates and flatware, placing them in the dishwasher. Absorbing Garret's presence into herself, Kira felt like she was in some kind of dream and was afraid she'd wake up and find it was just that: a dream. The months of suffering and grieving over not being able to find him after she'd been wounded had scored her to her soul. She'd had grief over the loss of ten friends to deal with. Even more for the man she'd fallen in love with and had disappeared off the face of the earth. Kira had thought Garret didn't want to ever see her again, and that was why he'd never contacted her.

How wrong she'd been. Appreciating his maleness as he turned, came back to the table and sat down, she felt a yearning coming from him. It was subtle, but it was there. Hungrily, she basked in his presence, grateful for any small, intimate moments she could share with him. Kira didn't fool herself. She understood this was one-sided. But it was as if she were being given a second chance with Garret, and this time she didn't have to hide how she felt toward him.

What she did have to do was be patient.

She was new to this ranch. It was a job, and one she desperately needed. She had to prove herself worthy of it to the ranch owners. Over time, if something just naturally blossomed between them, she would know. If it didn't, she'd be disappointed, but at least she'd understand where Garret stood with her once and for all.

Garret moved the cup between his hands, his brows dipping. "Listen, you need to go lightly with Ray Crawford. Listen a lot, say little. Okay?"

"Yes," she said, sobering, "I've got it."

"If he doesn't like you, Kira, he'll find some way to get you fired. Shay likes to think she's free of her father's influence, but she's in denial, only fooling herself."

Horrified over that prospect, one she hadn't thought about last night, Kira frowned, holding Garret's troubled gaze. "How do I avoid that?"

"Ray doesn't respect women. You need to be like a subservient Afghan wife."

Kira snorted.

"I'm serious."

"Oh, I know you are. But I hate that role, Garret. I'm not good at playing games. I'm only good at being myself."

"I understand. Ray's a talker. Be a listener. Don't give feedback to the bastard unless he asks for it. Take it all in, but don't give him anything he could possibly use against you. The less he knows about you, the safer you'll be and the fewer feathers will get ruffled as a result."

Her stress level was rising. She could feel it amping up like a hungry monster that had been awakened and was now prowling around inside her. "Okay, I'll do my best."

"You'll do all right, Kira. You were always so good at reading the Afghan people, the guys, even me. You'll figure this out and then go into stealth mode with Crawford. Just pretend it's a black ops situation. You're in an enemy camp gathering intelligence." He grinned a little.

"I can do that," she said, rising. "Thanks for breakfast. You really have spoiled me." She saw a glittering look in Garret's dark green-and-gold eyes. It took her back a pace as she stared down at him. What was that look all about? She was unsure, but it felt like a man wanting his woman. How ridiculous was that? Kira knew she was misreading Garret's energy and expression. He'd never come on to her. Not once. This was her overactive imagination at work as usual.

"I'll make you breakfast every morning unless I'm gone on an assignment somewhere," he promised. "If you need anything,

I'll be in the barn, oiling and greasing the machinery in there. What time are you coming home for lunch?"

Home for lunch. Kira thought it sounded like a husband and wife talking about the day's events. *Home.* Yes, this surely felt like a home with Garret unexpectedly in it. Kira was sure she was still in shock over the situation. "1300, one p.m."

"I like Zulu time."

She smiled and pushed the chair beneath the table. "We're military through and through. We'll probably never take that skin off ourselves." Drowning in the warmth she saw in Garret's eyes as he studied her, Kira felt suddenly nervous. That same feeling, of being wanted by him, embraced her powerfully. This time Kira knew she wasn't imagining things.

Hurrying to the sink, she dumped the last of her coffee and rinsed the cup. "What are you going to make for us?"

"I don't know. What do you like?"

You. Kira gulped, biting down on her lower lip, the word almost leaping out of her mouth. "I — don't know."

"How about if I surprise you?"

She picked up the purse she'd hung on a wooden peg after pulling on her nylon parka. Slinging the leather strap across her left shoulder, she said, "Surprises aren't high on my list, if you know what I mean." Because any surprise — a sudden noise, a sudden movement — spiraled her anxiety and shot it through the roof.

Garret twisted around in the chair. "Okay, how about grilled tuna fish sandwiches with Swiss cheese melted on them?"

Kira opened the door. "That sounds really good. Thank you."

"Oh, don't thank me yet, Trouble."

She grinned and said flippantly, "How many people have you poisoned with your food, Fleming?"

Chuckling, Garret raised his thick, dark brows. "None so far. Want to be the first?"

Her eyes danced with laughter. "I'm done with surprises, being a guinea pig and being first in anything. I'm opting for a very quiet, uneventful life. Aren't you?"

Garret gave her a burning look. "With the right person, life takes on some pretty damned nice aspects."

Kira tilted her head, unsure of what he was referring to, but that burning look was back in his eyes. "I gotta run." She lifted her hand. "See you at 1300, one p.m."

"I'll be here, Trouble."

She laughed softly, shaking her finger in his direction. "Did anyone ever tell you that you're a bad boy trying to act good, Fleming?"

Shrugging noncommittally, Garret murmured, "I've always been a bad boy. I just hid it from you when you knew me before. Now the gloves come off . . ."

"Uh-oh," Kira teased with a lilting laugh, "then I'm the one who's in trouble!" She saw Garret give her a searing look that made her breasts instantly tighten and her whole lower body take off, howling for hot, raw sex with him. The awareness jolted through her, taking her breath away for a moment. The look Garret was giving her was one a woman could very accurately read. He wanted her . . .

CHAPTER FIVE

Kira tried to settle her nerves as she knocked
on and entered the back door that led to
Ray Crawford's kitchen. He was at the
kitchen counter, frowning. When he saw
her, his scowl deepened.

"You're late!" he snapped.

Kira felt the slap of his anger as she shut
the door. "Shay told me to come over at
0700 to make you breakfast," she said, her
gut tightening instantly. The man's small,
close-set brown eyes were filled with rage.
She felt it as if it were the Taliban about
ready to kill her. Her heart began to ham-
mer and she felt adrenaline spike through
her, making her feel as if she were in
combat. At least Ray wasn't pointing a gun
at her. Yet. He looked angry enough to hit
her as he stood stiffly at the counter, his
hands curving into fists.

"I hate that military shit! Speak to me in
English, girl."

"Yes, sir," she said, struggling out of her parka and hanging it up on a wall peg.

"And don't you *sir* me, either. Where the hell is my coffee?" and he jerked his hand across the counter, the parts and pieces of the coffeemaker strewn across it.

Kira walked over, quickly gathering the parts, her hands shaking. She didn't like being this close to Crawford. He might be partially paralyzed, but he was a big, intimidating man. She hated the glare he gave her. "If you'll go sit down at the table, Mr. Crawford, I'll get your coffee made and then your breakfast." Her voice was wobbling, she was so shocked and frightened by his unexpected attack.

Snorting, Crawford grabbed the one crutch leaning against the counter. "I hope like hell you make good coffee."

Relief swam through her as he hobbled awkwardly to the table on the one crutch beneath his left armpit. She winced as he jerked out a chair, the legs scraping loudly against the oak floor. Trying to settle her shot nerves, Kira looked through the cupboards until she located a tin of coffee. Some of the coffee spilled on the counter because she couldn't stop her hands from trembling.

"You're late, you know."

Kira plugged in the coffeemaker and turned. "Your daughter told me to be here at seven a.m., Mr. Crawford. I'm sorry if you're upset that I'm late. Is there a better time for me to be over here to make you breakfast?" Kira felt herself crumpling up inwardly, her stomach tightening. She wanted to run. The urge was so powerful, she had to anchor herself at the counter.

"I told Shay six thirty a.m.! What the hell! Women are so goddamned stupid!"

Anger stirred through Kira and her eyes narrowed on Crawford's angry face. "People make mistakes. I'll be here at that time tomorrow morning," she said in as soothing a tone as possible. Right now she wanted to get the hell away from this man as fast as she could. Her dad was a gentle person who had never raised his voice to her; he'd been her support when she was growing up.

This man, if she could ever possibly look at him as father material, was a raging bull in comparison. Kira suddenly felt very sorry for Shay. Had he been like this when Shay was growing up? She couldn't even begin to understand how she had become as nice as she was. This man was abusive, just as Garret had warned her he would be.

Kira needed this job and she had to get through this bad patch with Ray, who was sitting there breathing hard, his hands in fists on the table, glaring nonstop at her. Garret had said Crawford didn't respect women. *Check that box.*

"I'm hungry, dammit!"

"What would you like for breakfast?" Kira asked, trying to sound pleasant. Her throat was tight with tension. Her body was trembling inwardly, and it was all she could do to stand and look relaxed.

"I thought Shay told you what I liked to eat!"

"She did," and Kira started naming off about ten dishes she'd mentioned. She saw Crawford's tight face ease a little.

"Well, you've got a good memory, I'll give you that. I want pancakes."

It would have been nice if he'd added a *please* with his request, but Kira knew Crawford wasn't interested in being social. He struck her as an embittered, angry person. "Coming up," she said cheerfully, turning to find the items she'd need to make them.

"How soon will my coffee be ready?"

Kira knew he could see the glass pot on the coffeemaker just as well as she could. Bending down, looking in a cupboard for some stainless-steel bowls, she said, "Looks to be halfway done. I'll pour you a cup as soon as it's ready."

Silence settled over the brittle tension in the kitchen. Jumpy, her nerves screaming for relief, Kira's hands were anything but steady. She got this way in severe, stressful circumstances. Wishing she could control it, she tried to focus on making the pancake batter. One of the symptoms of PTSD was the inability to concentrate. Her mind was soaked in adrenaline and cortisol now, the fight-or-flight hormones. Kira struggled by the second to keep her mind on the ingredients.

"Get my coffee!"

Crawford's voice whipped over her. Cringing, Kira looked up to realize the coffee was ready. Distracted, she moved too soon, the spoon flipping out of the bowl, the batter splattering beneath the cupboards and onto the tile backsplash and counter. Panic hit her and she froze, her eyes widening as she saw the batter dripping off the bottom of the cupboards. *Oh, God . . .*

"I want it now. Not tomorrow, girl."

Clenching her teeth, something she did when a panic attack struck, Kira moved jerkily toward the cupboard where the cups were kept. She brought one down. Coffee splashed around the cup, her hand shaking. Taking deep breaths, one after another, she tried to force down the worst of the panic.

"Do you like sugar or milk, Mr. Crawford?"

"Both."

Kira hurried to the fridge and found a quart of milk. It took her a long minute to locate the sugar. And then she had to find a small bowl to pour some of it into, not wanting to hand him the five-pound package. Hurrying, she took the coffee and set it in front of him. Kira knew better than to try to juggle all three items in her hands at once. Not when she was feeling out of sorts like this. Sweat began to trickle down from beneath her armpits. She felt shaky, dying for some fresh, cold air.

After delivering the items, she started back toward the batter on the counter.

"How do you expect me to stir my coffee? What the hell kind of brain do you have in your head? Gimme a spoon!"

Hurrying, she handed him one. Kira went back to cleaning up the mess she'd made at the kitchen counter. As she wrung out the washcloth, everything clean once more, she heard Crawford curse richly.

"Son of a bitch! This coffee tastes like shit!"

Kira turned. Crawford's face was a dull red. Was he going to have another stroke?

She clenched the washcloth in her hands. "What's wrong with it?" Was it cold? Her mind whirled with possibilities.

Ray pushed the cup away from him, the contents spilling across the table. "It's *weak* coffee! Dammit, I like *strong* coffee. Now get your ass over there and make me a pot of strong coffee!"

Kira moved to the table, quickly mopping up the spill and taking the cup away. Crawford's glare cut into her.

His breathing was rapid. "You're gonna give me a stroke, girl. Can't you do *anything* right? I don't know what the hell Shay was thinkin' when she hired another vet. None of you are worth a plugged nickel!"

Compressing her lips, Kira said nothing, remembering Garret's earlier words. *Listen a lot. Say nothing.* Panic ate at her. She was failing at this job. Horribly. Completely.

Groaning inwardly, Kira chastised herself, aiming in the direction of the silver drawer. Think! She had to slow down and think! She was screwing up so badly . . . Worse, she had to come over twice more today to make him lunch and dinner.

Ray Crawford was in no better mood for lunch. Kira double-checked with Shay on the time for lunch and dinner and found it was the same as she'd written down in her notes. The man was sitting at the head of the table, looking at her as if he were a king in his palace and she the lowly servant. It had been snowing out and she shook off her parka on the mud porch before entering the main part of the house. He had a magazine of crossword puzzles between his hands.

"What would you like for lunch, Mr. Crawford?"

"Cheese sandwich, grilled, will be fine."

He seemed less agitated, but she hated that she could feel his gaze following her as she walked to the kitchen counter. It felt like he was drilling two holes in her back, the feeling was so uncomfortable.

"And to drink?" She'd had a few hours to get herself back together again, although she felt gut shot emotionally. Kira knew she had to make this relationship work. Garret's suggestions on how to deal with Crawford had been correct. She hated being subservient to someone like him. In the Army she'd been treated with respect, as an equal. Crawford had demoted her to a second-class citizen because she was a woman.

Kira had failed at five jobs in a row. This was her sixth. She could *not* fail. She *had* to make this work, regardless. Her stomach was in a painful fist. Her hands weren't steady but better than earlier.

"Coffee."

Kira nodded and said nothing, forcing herself to focus as never before. The house was quiet. Painfully quiet. She loved having soft, instrumental music on in the background because it soothed her anxiety and took an edge off her. This house reminded her of a mausoleum.

Repeating Garret's phrases continually in her head as she worked, Kira forced herself not to make small talk with Crawford. Reminding herself that he hadn't spat out curse words about the pancakes she'd made him, Kira considered that minimal progress. So far, she'd made him one meal he liked. At least he hadn't griped about it or thrown it on the floor. Or at her.

Kira had an awful feeling that Shay probably had dishes or God knew what else thrown at her from time to time growing up. It was just a psychic impression, but she knew in her state of heightened awareness she often received them, and they turned out to be right most of the time. What would she do if Crawford threw something at her? Kira was afraid to think, given her PTSD.

In ten minutes the coffee and sandwich

were ready. Kira brought them over to him. He stared at the sandwich.

"You grilled this?"

"Yes." He'd seen her do it. Tensing, Kira waited as he looked at it like an eagle looking at its quarry.

"You used Swiss cheese on it like I told you?"

"Yes, I did." She waited, wondering if he was just going to stare at it or eat it.

"Get me some potato chips and then leave," he snapped.

Kira turned, feeling relief. Grabbing the bag of chips off the top of the fridge, she brought them over.

"What would you like for dinner tonight?"

"Hamburgers. Two of 'em. And I want 'em on buns."

"How about a salad of some kind to go with them?"

He stared at her. "If I want you to talk, I'll let you know. I said I wanted two hamburgers with buns."

"Okay, got it," Kira said. "I'll see you at five p.m., Mr. Crawford."

He said nothing, biting into the sandwich like a mad dog.

More than glad to be leaving the house, Kira looked down at her watch. Relieved she'd only spent twenty minutes with Crawford, she hurried down the recently shoveled sidewalk to the house at the end. The snow was swirling lazily around her, and in the distance she could vaguely make out the outline of the sharpened peaks of the Salt River Range, to the east of the ranch. Looking toward the two huge barns, she saw Garret walking down the slight slope toward the truck parked below.

Her heart lightened with joy. Garret was coming home. Home for lunch. Home to her. So much of her anxiety calmed, just knowing he was going to be with her, that Kira felt the rest of her fear dissolve. Her boots crunched through the melting ice because salt had been laid across the concrete sidewalk.

She had just come into the kitchen when she heard Garret on the mud porch, stomping snow off his boots. In the middle of making them a fresh pot of coffee, Garret emerged into the kitchen, looking left toward her.

"Hey, how's it going with the old man?" He took off his Stetson, hanging it on a wall peg.

"Rough start, but things are slowly improving," she said, flipping the switch on the coffeemaker. Her heart bounded and this time it was with happiness, not dread, as it did when she was at Crawford's place. She saw something in Garret's eyes, a flash of irritation maybe. It didn't feel as if it were aimed at her. Kira knew he was protective of her when it came to Ray. Now she knew why.

Garret came over and pulled down two mugs and set them on the counter. "What does *rough* mean?"

Shrugging, Kira said, "Just misunderstandings is all." It wasn't a lie, but it wasn't the full truth either. She never wanted to lie to Garret. Kira brought plates down for the sandwiches he was going to make. She set them near the stove where he pulled out a griddle. She'd just made Ray the same sandwich.

Garret slid her a glance. "What kind of misunderstandings?"

Her neck prickled with warning. Kira reminded herself that Garret was black ops. He listened intently and missed nothing. Her heart pounded with fear because she didn't want to let Garret know how Ray had treated her. She automatically sensed he'd get protective and go to Shay and Reese, lodging a complaint on her behalf.

That couldn't happen. Kira had a vision of them firing her when they found out the truth. Swallowing, she said, "Just a time issue was all. Shay had told me to be there at 7 in the morning. When I arrived, Mr. Crawford said he'd told his daughter I was to arrive at 6:30 was all. Don't worry; we got it straightened out." She turned away to set the table, praying he wouldn't pursue her explanation beyond that.

"I thought I heard Shay tell you 7:00," Garret said, whipping up the tuna fish in a bowl.

"Makes two of us. It's all right. I'll be there at 6:30 tomorrow."

"That's too damned early. Crawford doesn't have a right to impose that kind of rule on you."

Panic hit her. Kira came over to the counter where he was working. "Just let it go for now, Garret?" She searched his scowling features. "Please? I need this job. If I have to start half an hour earlier, that's no skin off my nose. I'll be happy to do it."

Garret groused, "He's expecting too much. Shay told me once that Crawford treated his wife like a slave, ordering her around, cursing and yelling at her. Shay got so scared she ran to her room and hid. And often, because of the way Ray was always belligerent and angry, shouting at his wife, Shay couldn't eat."

"Her stomach was probably tied in knots,"

Kira agreed softly, wrapping her arms around her waist.

"She said he got that way when he was drinking."

Grimacing, Kira said, "Really?"

"Did you smell his breath?"

Kira hesitated. "Well . . . no . . . I guess I forgot to check." Because Crawford was screaming at her, unnerving her, and she couldn't link two coherent thoughts in a row. And then added, "I'll try to remember later today."

Garret nodded, placing the tuna on the bread. "You look stressed out, Kira."

He'd said it so gently, it caught her off guard. The words, low and deep, were filled with concern, and she got that wonderful sense of being invisibly embraced by him. Right now Kira desperately wanted to walk into Garret's arms and be held. He had always made her feel safe, even in the most dangerous circumstances in Afghanistan. "First days at work are always stressful," she offered quietly.

Garret said nothing else, and in a few minutes their sandwiches were ready. He pulled the chair back for her to sit on and slid the plate in front of her.

Kira felt like she was in two different realities. In one, she was treated like a queen. In the other, like a slave.

"I saw Shay out in the broodmare barn earlier. She said she was going to drop by about 9 tonight and talk with you. See how your day went with her father."

Inwardly, Kira froze. She didn't want to lie. It wasn't who she was. "Okay." She felt Garret's gaze on her. It wasn't upsetting, but she swore she could feel his laser-like attention, as if trying to ferret the rest of the truth out of her. On some level, he knew she wasn't being fully forthcoming.

"It's a pressure cooker for you," Garret said, eating. "You have to try to get the old man to like you. The daughter, on the other hand, who knows what the bastard's like, is worried for you. She's concerned he'll pull the same shit on you that he did on her."

"He's learning to adjust, too," Kira said. "He's probably just as nervous about this as I am."

Garret gave her a dark, slicing look. "I've been here with Shay for a year, Kira. She would confide in me sometimes. She used to go see Crawford three days a week at the nursing home in Jackson Hole. I could tell by how she looked, when she returned, what day she went to see him. She was strained, pale and there was a lot of pain in her eyes. I saw it every time. It never changed." He released a heavy sigh, giving Kira a worried look. "A tiger doesn't change its stripes. I don't care what Shay says; her father is an alcoholic and an abuser. He spent eighteen years bludgeoning Shay and I honestly don't know how she managed to turn out as well as she has."

Kira's stomach knotted because she felt Garret subtly interrogating her, saying things to see what her reaction would be. "Look, I'm not Shay."

"No, but you're a woman, and Crawford disrespects them."

"I had plenty of sexual harassment in the Army, Garret. If Ray throws anything my way, I'll handle it. I have more than enough experience to deal with it."

Nodding, he regarded her through half-closed eyes. "If you start coming home looking like Shay, we're going to sit down and have a serious talk, Kira. I won't let that bastard do anything to hurt you. Understand?"

A heated longing coursed through Kira. He'd said those words softly, with feeling, meaning it. She wanted to shrug off his care, but she couldn't. She didn't want to, but she didn't dare tell Garret what Ray had said to her today. It was verbal abuse, pure and simple. She knew it, hated it, but had bit the bullet and ignored it. And now she was going to have to shade the truth with Shay, too. "Yes," she said quietly, "I understand."

Garret motioned to her food. "You're not eating."

Kira picked up the sandwich and took a bite, not tasting anything. How badly she wanted to tell Garret the whole truth, but she knew if she did, he'd go storming over to Crawford's place. God knew what he might do to the guy. Crawford was only forty-nine, not really an old man as Garret referred to him. He would have been a strapping rancher in his prime if the stroke hadn't slowed him down.

"Are you doing your Arabic-to-English translations this afternoon?"

"Yes. I worked on the manual, plus I have two other clients with several letters to translate."

"Good. I was thinking that maybe in a week or so, after things settle down, we might invite Noah and Harper to dinner. How do you feel about that?"

Perking up, Kira smiled a little. "I'd like that."

"Well, you'll get to meet them in a couple of days when we have our weekly Friday evening talk session. And at our Sunday dinner, too."

"Right. But Noah works with horses and I'd love to know more about what he does."

"He's looking for another horse trainer right now, but it's got to be someone who has experience with trail horse training."

"A person with specialty training?"

"Yes." Garret looked up and said, "He's gonna have to find a military vet, someone who's been a horse handler like himself. I think he'll have problems finding someone."

"Why do you say that?"

"We've got long, damn-cold winters," and he grinned. "Nine months out of every year there's snow on the ground."

She felt her heart open over his partial smile. Garret had never smiled a lot, but when he did, the hard planes of his face softened and changed. He went from looking like a tough operator to someone who was very approachable. Kira had always called it his teddy bear side. The Afghan children certainly figured him out in a few days. Garret might be a giant of a man towering over them, but his hands were gentle and he was outright tender with all the children. In fact, he spoiled them rotten by bringing them candy nearly every day as he strode up and down the streets within the walled village.

Garret had contacted Operation Gratitude in Chatsworth, California, and asked them to donate candy so he could hand it out to the children. The charity, that helped many overseas military men and women with care packages, sent him so much that a quarter of their hut had been piled with boxes of it. Garret never ran out of candy for those children and he had won Kira over once again. He was a warrior, but he was also a kind man who knew when to put his strength and power away and allow his heart to lead him instead.

"We endured a lot of cold, hard winters in Afghanistan," she reminded him. "And we always found ways to pass the time."

"Yeah, you and your journal. You were always writing or sketching in it."

"You and the guys loved Monopoly. You taught it to everyone." She smiled, warmth embracing her with a memory of those times. "Winter was always the quiet time in our cycle. The Taliban left everyone alone because all the passes were closed by snow. We had time on our hands to play games."

Garret finished his sandwich, wiping his fingers on a paper napkin. "I remember them well. The kids would come to our house. They knew you sketched and they wanted you to draw portraits of them."

"I've got a lot of those drawings," Kira said fondly, remembering those times. "But really? They came over to the house because those smart little tykes knew you had boxes of candy stacked to the ceiling and were hoping you'd give them some. I think I was their second objective, don't you?" and Kira chuckled.

Garret's grin grew. "Yeah. Well, the boys were like that. The little girls, though, they just liked to come visit because you held them, sang to them and kissed them." He traded a warm glance with her. "You were their second mother, and every little girl knew that. I think they wanted you to draw them because it gave them just that much more quality time with you. You'd fuss over them, combing their hair, rearranging their thin clothing, and it made them feel important. Loved."

"Well, the Afghan mothers loved their children equally, if not more, Garret."

"Not contesting that." Garret reached out, barely grazing her cheek with his fingers. "I don't think you see yourself, Kira. Those kids did, though. You're full of life; you had so much love to give and they knew it. They orbited around you for those three years. I saw it. I was there."

Her skin tingled in the wake of his unexpected touch. Startled inwardly, Kira didn't move, digesting his gesture. That burning look, one of yearning, lay banked in his green-gold eyes. Her voice was choked. "Yes . . . you were there . . ." Her heart was turning to mush in her chest and she wanted so badly to wrap her arms around Garret's thick, powerful neck and hug him and never let go. "I remember you'd sometimes give me a funny look when I'd hold a little girl, singing to her. I always wanted to ask you what that was all about, Garret." She saw his cheeks go ruddy, something that rarely happened. He was blushing. Little made him blush. She gave him a searching look. "Tell me. What were you thinking at those times?"

Moving uncomfortably, Garret muttered, "I was thinking back to my own childhood. My mother, Jenny, used to pull me up on her lap, cuddle me and sing to me."

"Oh, that's so wonderful," she whispered, suddenly feeling tears burn in the backs of her eyes. "I didn't know . . ."

"Well," Garret said, giving her a wry look, "I didn't exactly go around telling my team about it. They'd have had a field day with that kind of intel."

"No, but I would have understood. My mom used to snuggle me into her arms before I'd go to bed. There was a rocker in my bedroom, and I knew every night after I washed up and got into my pj's, she'd come in and sit in the rocker. I loved jumping into her lap. She'd hold me, kiss me, like I did those Afghan kids. And then she'd read a chapter out of a storybook. I just loved her reading to me . . ."

"We had good mothers," Garret agreed, his voice low and thick.

"Is your mom still alive?"

"No. Died when I was ten." He scowled. "My father is a mean, abusive alcoholic. I remember my mother dying of a heart attack out in the garden. I'd just come home from school that afternoon and she was out there on her hands and knees, pulling weeds. She'd been crying, and I could see the wetness on her cheeks. I'd come up to her to ask her why she was crying, and that's when she had the heart attack."

It felt as if a knife had been plunged through her own heart. Kira gasped and whispered, "Oh, no . . . oh, God, I'm so sorry, Garret. I didn't know." Without thinking, she reached out, gripping his hand. Instantly, his long, callused fingers wrapped around hers. The gesture was intimate and possessive. Kira saw the pain banked deep in his stormy eyes. She squeezed his fingers a little more, realizing he could crush hers if he wanted to. "You grew up without a mom, too."

He gave her a sharpened look. "What do you mean?"

Reluctantly, Kira withdrew her fingers from his hand. Her flesh tingled and she felt that old, gnawing sensation begin deep in her lower body, wanting him. "My mother . . . well, I remember her smiling and being so happy when I was very young. She'd sweep me up into her arms, carry me, hug and kiss me. She loved me so much. And then, when I was around eight, she changed." Saddened, Kira said, "Looking back on it now, my mother, Elizabeth, had gone into a deep depression. And from the looks of it, it's genetic on her side of the family. My grandmother Ivy was depressed all her life."

"What happened to your mom?"

"She committed suicide when I was nineteen." Instantly, she saw Garret's face fall with grief — for her. "I was in the Army, overseas in Afghanistan, when it happened. I got emergency medical leave and came home. My dad was devastated. He loved her so much . . . so much . . ."

"It had to have hit you hard, too."

"Pretty much. She'd been getting worse.

Sometimes," and Kira wiped her eyes, giving him an apologetic look, "I think it was my fault. She begged me not to leave, not to go away to the Army."

"Jesus," Garret growled, giving her a pained look. "She shouldn't have laid that on your doorstep, Kira. You know that, don't you?"

Sniffing, she shrugged. "On a good day I do. On a bad one . . . well . . . because I've had depression since I got PTSD, I really understand some of what she must have felt. That sense of utter helplessness. That dark hole that stares back at you, and you know if you fall into it, you're never climbing out of it. I often wonder if Mom fell down that rabbit hole. That's what I call it. And if she did, not only did she feel helpless, she was lost . . . no rudder . . . no desire to do anything or . . . nothing . . ."

Gripping her hand, Garret rasped, "Listen to me, Kira, you had nothing to do with your mother deciding to take her own life." He stared hard into her moist eyes. "Not. Your. Fault."

She curled her fingers around his, needing him in that moment. His touch fed her, filled her heart and made the hurting stop whenever she thought about her suffering mother. "When I was going to therapy sessions at Bethesda, the psychiatrist wanted to give me meds for my PTSD. I saw what depression medicine did to my mom. She got worse. I refused to take any meds. I told the doc I'd rather suffer and not become like my mother."

Just the warm solidness of his hand around hers buoyed her, took away some of her guilt and anguish. "And then, after I got kicked out of the Army, I went home. My dad was so glad to have me back. And I was glad to be there. I really needed him. The day he met me at the airport and threw his arms around me; I'll never forget it as long as I live. I was hurting so much. Grieving. Unable to sleep. Unable to stop remembering. And he's a big man like you, so when he pulled me into his arms and held me, it was the most incredibly healing moment of my life." She felt Garret's hand hold hers a little tighter. It felt so good, smoothing out her ragged emotional state. Kira didn't want to let go of it.

"How long were you able to stay home?" he asked, frowning, watching her closely.

"Two months? Days ran together for me, Garret. I lost track of time, to tell you the truth. I was screaming in the middle of the night, waking myself up. Waking him up at least four times a week. The poor guy was so shaken by what was happening to me. At first when I had those nightmares he'd find me wrapped in the bedcovers on the floor. I was in a flashback. They're a lot worse than a nightmare." Lifting her head, Kira met his darkened hazel eyes. "You know the difference. I know you do." She saw Garret barely nod.

"So you left because the PTSD had full control over you?"

"Yeah," she admitted, misery in her tone. "I thought moving out, finding a job somewhere else, would help me regain control over my life." Her mouth pursed. "It didn't."

"Seems to be the norm," Garret said, his voice gentle. "I got fired from a lot of jobs until Shay gave me one here. You aren't out of control, Kira. It's the stress that amps up our anxiety, and we can't handle it."

"No, I'm not out of control anymore . . . at least not as often as before. A lot of my symptoms have become less intense." She motioned toward the hall. "If I couldn't write in my journal . . . draw things . . . just jotting down things that are eating me from the inside out, have helped. If I didn't have that journal, Garret, I don't know what I'd have done. I think I'd have gone insane . . ."

He took his other hand, smoothing it down her lower arm in a gentle, quiet motion. "We all get slammed up against that wall," he rumbled. "PTSD does it to you." He slid his other hand beneath hers, holding it, watching her. "You've come a long way on your journey back to who you used to be, Kira." He looked deep into her eyes. "And now you have me. I'll be there for you. All the way. Let me be that support for you."

CHAPTER SIX

Garret felt himself start to unravel as he listened to Kira's admissions. Intuitively, he knew there had been a lot more than what she'd shared with him about Ray Crawford. He could see anxiety in her dark gray eyes, the worry that she was going to be fired from this job. Holding her hand, warming it up between his, sent waves of incredible happiness through him. This was the first time he'd ever been able to do this. It wouldn't have worked when they were together in the A team. It would have torn the team apart.

When he felt her fingers shyly curve against his, it told him so much. *So much.* If there wasn't something unspoken between them, Kira would have pulled her hand out of his immediately. Because holding her hand went beyond that line in the sand of a friendship. His action was intimate. More than anything, Garret hoped desperately that Kira realized he was interested in her as a woman. As someone he wanted to know so much better than when they'd been in the team together.

He forced himself to release her hand and stand up. "I've got to get back to work," he said, apology in his tone. The history of Kira's mother tore heavily at his heart. He saw Kira rally. It was then that Garret began to understand the power and influence he had with her. Some of the dread in his chest lifted because, more than anything, he wanted to give Kira a safe harbor in her 24/7 fight with anxiety that came with PTSD. She seemed calmer. More settled. Maybe even relaxed. Garret wasn't sure about that, but her eyes told him so much. Some of the darkness had lifted from them and he took it as a sign that she was feeling calmer. There was so much he had to relearn about her. She was a shadow of her former self, and he grieved for her, knowing what the ambush and then the PTSD had stolen from her.

"Yes, I need to get to my translation duties," Kira said, rising.

"I'll clear the table. You go to work," he said. "I'll see you at 7:00 tonight? I'm making us baked chicken with rice along with a poultry gravy."

She nodded, then hesitated in the hall leading to her room. "Sounds good. See you then . . ."

Garret cleaned off the table and put the few plates into the dishwasher. His conscience needled him and he looked down the hallway, now empty. What the hell was Crawford doing or saying to her? *Something.* But Kira wasn't telling him. *Dammit.* Maybe he'd find out more after Shay grilled her about her father tonight after dinner. He hoped so, because Kira was acting like a frightened rabbit. Like a big, bad wolf was circling her. Crawford could be up to his usual abusiveness again.

The question was whether or not Shay would turn a blind eye because she was in denial about her father. It was a sticky issue and one that wasn't going away anytime soon. Garret could only do so much. But he was damned if Kira was going to become tied to Crawford's whipping post. He needed her to come clean with him. He had to figure out a way to get her to trust him enough with all the truth, not just half of it.

"Well, how was your first day?" Shay asked Kira. The three of them sat at the table with coffee mugs in hand. Garret had made a white cake, just slathered chocolate frosting on it, and he'd given each of them a slice on a plate. Shay eagerly dug into hers.

"It was a day of learning curves," Kira said, pushing the cake around on her plate with her fork.

"What do you mean?"

"Your father said I was late. I'd gone over at seven a.m., as you'd asked. He was upset and told me I was half an hour late."

Shay grimaced. "I told him seven."

Shrugging, Kira said, "He's had a stroke. Maybe he forgot. I mean, I don't know the extent to which the stroke has affected his memory."

"It's affected him in different ways. He does get forgetful. It comes and goes. He didn't yell at you, did he, Kira?"

Shaking her head, she offered, "I apologized and told him I'd have coffee waiting for him at six thirty tomorrow morning."

"That's too early to ask anyone to start work," Garret grumbled, giving Shay a warning look. "Don't you think?"

"Absolutely," Shay quickly agreed. "I had written down the schedule for my father, Kira."

"Maybe he misplaced it."

"That's always possible. I'm so sorry, Kira. I was hoping this would be a smooth transition for him and you."

Garret gave Shay a searching look. "I think part of the solution is to buy your father a coffeemaker that has a timer on it. Kira could make him coffee the night before, have it turn on at 6:30 a.m. and then I could show up at seven to fix him breakfast. What do you think?" He saw instant relief come across Shay's face because he sensed her worry over the issue.

"That's a great idea," Shay said. "I'll go out and buy one tomorrow." She looked at Kira. "Would you mind going over there at six thirty tomorrow morning just this one time?"

"No, not at all."

Shay gave her a relieved look and reached out and touched Kira's arm. "Thanks. I'm so sorry about this. The stroke has left my father with on-again, off-again memory issues."

"You'd warned me about that," Kira said, giving her a small smile. "It's okay. We've got a fix for this and hopefully, after you talk to your father and assure him I'll always come over at seven to make him breakfast, it will resolve itself."

Garret said, "Shay? Your father needs things written down. Maybe you have to put the paper in every room of his house so he's reminded. I don't want him going after Kira like he went after you." He saw Shay's face drain of color; she knew damn well what he was talking about. He'd found out that Shay hadn't covered the darker aspects of her father with Kira. And he wasn't going to have Kira be a target for him to vent his rage. *Not a chance in hell.* He watched Shay's pale expression and knew the tone of his voice got the message through to her. He hated putting pressure on her, but it couldn't be helped.

"Yes, I'll make that happen tomorrow." She swallowed and gave Kira a searching look. "H-he didn't yell at you, did he?"

Garret saw Kira wince. It wasn't obvious, but he saw it. Operators saw a lot of subtle human expressions and expertly picked up on body language.

"No, he was fine. Really. I'm sure this will get straightened out and everything will go smoothly. He's in a new environment, too. Change often is upsetting until you get used to the new routine."

"Well, he was waited on hand and foot at the nursing home," Shay told her. "Here, he's pretty much on his own."

"As it should be," Garret growled.

"Yes," Shay agreed. "He wants to get better, get stronger, be able to walk without the assistance of crutches, so this forces him into doing most things for himself."

Garret scowled. "Shay? If at some point your father does get to that level of mobility, are you going to make him start feeding himself? Kira shouldn't have this as a forever job, right? She's far more valuable to us as a translator."

"Absolutely," Shay murmured. "Reese and I see this as a temporary assignment for you, Kira. We do want you to continue your translation duties, plus, we sure can use someone like you when it comes to mechanics around here. Harper's great, but sometimes he's away for a week at a time, and then we have no one with his skills. As soon as my father can walk on his own again, he's already been told that we expect him to feed himself and take care of the housekeeping duties at his home."

Garret saw Shay's explanation give Kira some purchase, saw some of the anxiety in her eyes dissolve. Kira needed to have this kind of support if she was going to weather whatever Crawford was doling out to her. It bothered him that Kira wasn't coming clean with him. He understood her terror at being fired again, so she wouldn't divulge the real truth to Shay. But to him? Somehow, he had to get Kira's trust. Deepen it. Widen it. Get her to open up to him. But how?

■ ■ ■ ■

Garret suddenly awoke. He was bathed in sweat. Breathing hard, his heart slamming into his chest. *Dammit! Another nightmare.* He hated them. Pushing his legs over the side of the bed, he thrust the covers aside, pissed. Looked at the clock on the dresser, which read two a.m. He wiped his sweaty face, needing to get up. It wouldn't do any good to lay in bed; his mind would just churn over that fucking ambush like it did at least once a week.

His pajama bottoms clung to his body. Muttering a curse, he turned on the lamp on the bedstand and stood. Pulling the pj's off, he could smell the fear sweat surrounding him. Adrenaline was still making him jumpy and tense. He'd take a hot shower and that would calm him down. Make some tea and go sit at the kitchen table and let himself come down off this cliff. What he hated most was the grief that always stalked him along with the flashback. Violently, Garret shoved it deep down inside himself as he threw the damp pajamas to the foot of the bed. He walked naked to the dresser, yanking open the drawer and found a pair of jeans, a T-shirt and a pair of socks. A pair of boxer shorts could wait until he went to work in the morning.

He'd nearly opened the door when his preoccupied mind remembered Kira was in the house. Normally, he'd stalk naked down the hall to the bathroom.

Muttering to himself, he grabbed his dark blue bathrobe, shrugging it on. He hoped Kira was fast asleep and opened the door quietly so as not to disturb her.

As he stepped into the hall, he saw her door was open. *What the hell?* Twisting a look toward the living room down at the other end, he saw a light on. Was Kira up? Unable to sleep? Scowling, Garret needed that shower. He needed to get the stink off him. He'd find out why she was awake after getting cleaned up.

Twenty minutes later, he emerged in a black T-shirt, jeans, his feet in the black socks as he halted at the lip of the living room. Kira was sitting in the middle of the black leather couch, her legs tucked beneath her, that old, scarred leather journal laid out across her thighs. He saw a set of colored pencils and an ink pen, beside her. She was wearing a flannel, ankle-length, pink granny gown, looking beautiful.

"I didn't wake you, did I?" she asked.

His flesh reacted to the smoky quality of

her voice, that low tone that always made him want her. "No. Had a friggin' flashback wake me up out of the blue."

"Want to sit down?" Kira gestured to the overstuffed chair across from the coffee table and couch. "Would you like some tea?"

His mouth tugged at one corner as he drank her in. Right now Kira looked peaceful. Garret wasn't picking up that tense, frenetic energy that had been around her earlier, when Shay had arrived. "Probably. Would you like some?"

"Sure." She started to set her journal aside.

"Stay put," he growled. "I'll get it for us," and he turned, padding silently through to the kitchen. As he made chamomile tea, he wondered what the hell he was doing. Kira seemed so vulnerable in that baggy, shapeless, pink flannel nightgown. But she looked so damned fetching to him, too. Garret wanted to run his fingers through her hair, tame some of those errant strands back into place. She looked more like a young girl in her teens. Innocent. Fresh. And he wanted her. All of her. His body stirred and he ruthlessly suppressed the desire.

Retrieving a wooden tray, Garret set it down between them on the coffee table. There was something sweet and tender coming to life within him. He saw Kira brighten, lay her open journal aside and sit up. Her feet were bare. Small, delicate feet. Like her. Sometimes, Garret wondered how someone half his size had handled combat and been just as strong and rugged as the men on the team. Kira had been a valuable member of their group. The height and weight of a person didn't tell anyone about the size of a person's heart or their courage. The strength of their soul. He saw her gray eyes were clear, but he noticed dried tear tracks down her cheeks, too. Wincing inwardly, he said, "Here you go."

For a couple of minutes the *clink* of a spoon against the ceramic mug, the stirring sound as she put some honey into the clear brown liquid, the fragrant scent of the tea, filled the air. Garret sat down, his legs open, resting his elbows on his thighs, the cup balanced between his hands. Kira sat back, tucking her feet beneath her.

"Aren't your feet cold?"

"A little."

"You could have worn socks."

She shrugged and sipped the tea. "I love going barefoot. I love my feet feeling the shiny gold oak beneath me, the texture."

Garret nodded, starved for this kind of intimacy with Kira. They had never talked like this before. He knew she loved to push her toes into the red sand, and sometimes he'd seen her do it with the children, who were always barefoot because there was no money to buy shoes. "What are you doing with your journal?" He craned his neck a bit, looking at the opened pages. The book was leather-bound, with creamy, thick paper. He saw an ink drawing and a lot of writing on the opposite page.

Kira set her cup down on the coffee table. She reached for the journal, turning it around in her hands, tipping it so he could clearly see it. "Sometimes," she began softly, "my grief wells up like a tsunami inside me. When that happens, I get up, open my journal and look at the sketches of the guys we lost . . ." Her voice trailed off and she caressed the page where she'd drawn a soldier, his head and shoulders. A lump formed and her voice grew soft. "I'm not much of an artist, but this is Captain Aaron Michelson." She lifted her chin and looked at him. "I need to cry for them . . . for their wives or girlfriends . . . their children . . ."

Mouth hardening, Garret felt gut-punched. The ink drawing he was looking at was as good as a photograph of Aaron. He was turning his head, his eyes narrowed with that keen intelligence he possessed. At thirty-five years old, Garret remembered clearly their captain had been married for ten years and had three children, two boys and a girl. His gut rolled and his throat closed off with sudden grief. Looking down at his cup, he said roughly, "Close the book, Kira. Please?"

Startled, she frowned and closed it, setting it down beside her. "I-I'm sorry."

His head snapped up and he met and held her confused gaze. "No. It's not you. It's me," he said harshly. His hand tightened around the cup. Garret hadn't expected this kind of violent reaction. It was his repressed grief rising strongly within him.

"I drew all the guys. Even you," she began. "I did it while I was recovering in the hospital. I didn't have any photos of the team and I missed everyone so much." Kira pressed her hand against her throat. "For me, Garret, the drawings help. They comfort me when I feel that grief wave rip me apart again. I don't want to ever forget any of them." Her lower lip trembled. "Not ever . . ."

Ah, hell. Garret gritted his teeth, watching tears fall silently down her cheeks as she stared at him. They hit him like a sledge-hammer to his heart. Above all, he loved Kira. She didn't know it. Not yet. *Probably never.* But Garret wasn't going to let her be savaged by Ray Crawford either. And the only way to get her trust was to be there for her. Listen to her. Watch her cry. Jesus, he wanted to hold her so damned badly he could taste it. "We'll never forget," he said quietly, his voice raw. Garret didn't want to do this. He didn't want to talk about the men he'd loved as brothers. He felt that fist of grief he'd buried starting to shove up into his chest, felt the suffering that came with it. What was he going to do? How was he going to be able to keep it stuffed down and still gain Kira's trust?

"When I got out of the hospital, after my discharge," she said softly, leaning back against the couch, her gaze up on the ceiling, "I made a promise to all of them."

His brows drew down. "What promise?" he demanded.

Her gaze turned to his. "That I'd travel around the country and see each wife and their children. I saw Brady's fiancée, Alicia. And the girlfriends of Tony and Mark."

Garret stared at her. "You did that?" he asked, disbelief in his tone.

Nodding, Kira said, "I had to, Garret. I knew the Army wouldn't tell them anything. I knew they all lived in a special hell, never knowing what really happened. I sat down with each one and told them what I could. I know we were black ops, but they deserved to know how their loved ones died." She lapsed into silence, the cup in her hands. "Someone had to tell them and I couldn't find you. I didn't want them to hang in that painful limbo any longer than they had to, so I took it upon myself, for our team, to do it."

He could only stare at her as if she were an alien from another planet who suddenly had landed and walked up to him. His heart was pounding with such urgency as pain flooded into his chest that Garret couldn't speak. He opened his mouth, but nothing came out. The expression on Kira's face was one of peace. Acceptance. The grief was in her eyes, but so was the solace.

How could she have done that? Garret had often thought he should see the surviving families, to give them closure, but he was a coward and knew it. His soldiers deserved his best effort. Team members looked out for one another, looked out for their families as well. They'd been such a tight-knit group. He'd never found the strength to go visit any of them. To do so would mean he'd have to live through all those feelings, over and over again, and Garret knew it would destroy him if he did. Fear ate at him as he held Kira's soft, moist, gray eyes. The kind smile on her mouth, that compassion she'd always possessed, was there for him to see.

"You did something incredibly good for them, Kira." He choked. *Because I couldn't. I still can't do it.* What did that make him? Garret didn't look too closely at himself to answer that one. Kira's strength over-whelmed him. For someone so small, she had the heart of the bravest men he'd ever known. She was a class act. As always, she'd done the right thing for the right reasons. Garret knew Kira had to be hurting badly, grieving herself, and yet she'd pushed beyond her own pain and visited all those families . . . God . . . how had she done it?

"It had to be done," Kira whispered, giving him a shrug. "I was the only one left to do it."

Because she couldn't find him. Because he had amnesia. Anger and frustration thrummed through Garret. He should have been there for Kira. If anything, they should have done it together. It should never have been left on her small, proud shoulders to carry the entire team's grief. But she had. She was so friggin' brave he could barely sit still at that stunning realization. Garret wanted to hold her now even more. She'd suffered alone, without help, without support, trying to find herself after her world was blasted apart. And where was he? Where? In some ways, Garret still felt so damned lost that he couldn't even find words to describe where he was at. The PTSD had fractured his soul, maimed his ego, torn so much of who he thought he was away from him. And he was sure Kira felt the same way. Yet whatever was left of her, she'd had the grit and stamina to do what she could for their team. *My God . . .*

He closed his eyes and hung his head, the cup warm in his hands. Emotions came up whether Garret wanted them to or not. There were feelings of pride for Kira, love for her, and the realization that he didn't deserve someone as beautiful and courageous as she really was. It hurt to feel, and Garret opened his eyes, rubbing his chest over his heart. Kira was sitting there, relaxed against the couch, her eyes half closed, warmth for him reflected in them. Or was he seeing things? Garret knew she couldn't love a coward, which was what he was. Kira deserved someone a helluva lot better than him. His mind was spinning with what to say to her. What could he say that wouldn't sound inane?

"Are you okay, Garret?"

Her low voice broke through his tortured state of emotions. He raised his head, meeting her worried gaze. "Yeah . . . it's . . . just a lot. I didn't know," he rasped, the corners of his mouth pulling inward, "that you'd done that, Kira. It was a good thing. I'm just sorry I wasn't there with you . . . Thank you for doing it . . ."

She gave him a tender look. "You had amnesia, Garret. You didn't know. You look so guilty right now and you shouldn't. Really, don't feel like that way, okay? The women who loved all our guys are in a better place now. Only one of us had to do it. And I was glad it was me." Kira managed a weak smile. "I'm a woman. It's easy for women to talk to one another, you know?"

Giving a jerky nod, Garret said, "Yeah, we guys don't have a way with words, that's for damned sure." He felt the raw guilt eating at him as if acid had been poured into his heart. He'd known those men for five years. Kira had known them for three. He should have done what she did.

"It's okay, Garret. I came away from that experience actually feeling better, not worse. It was healing for me. For them . . ."

He couldn't understand that at all. If that grief came boiling up out of him, Garret knew it would rip him apart in such a way he'd never be the same again. The PTSD had taken enough chunks out of him. He was damned if he was going to allow grief to take the rest of him. And yet, as he studied Kira's pale face, there was peace in her eyes. He was unable to understand how. Garret had never felt a moment's peace since that ambush. Not one second. Yet Kira looked calm, as if the experience hadn't ripped her apart. Maybe it was because she had internal strength that he didn't have? Maybe that was the difference? He didn't know.

Shaking his head, he muttered, "I don't understand how you could feel better after telling those families about the ambush. I really don't. It would be" — he groped — "torture to tell them. To talk about what happened over and over again." Searching her eyes, he grated, "I couldn't do what you did. You're something else, Kira. You have my respect, my admiration, for your courage under fire."

"Oh," Kira murmured, "I had to do it, Garret. If I didn't, I would feel like the grief was going to eat me up alive. If I couldn't get it out of me, it was going to kill my soul, and I knew it. Repeating it actually made it less intense for me. Sort of like opening an infected wound and letting it drain. I felt relief."

"Jesus, Kira, men and women are a helluva lot different then, because I felt just the opposite of that after my memories returned six months later. I wanted to get the hell away from those feelings, that grief, as fast as I could."

"Maybe we are hardwired differently," she gently agreed. "If I couldn't cry, talk it out, or write it in my journal, I would feel so terrible inside myself that I couldn't focus on anything. The PTSD has pretty much been a major distraction for me, but if I had to live with that grief untended, not allow it to drain, I don't think I could have survived."

Grumpily, he stood, slugged down the tepid tea and growled, "We are very different. Listen, you need to get some sleep and so do I. Why don't you come to bed?" He held his hand out in her direction. In his dreams, he wanted Kira to stand up and take his hand, and they'd walk to his bedroom. There, he would undress her, take her to his bed, fold her around his body, kiss her, taste her skin, hear her sigh with satisfaction and then love her until they were both drowning in pleasure. But that wasn't going to happen. He saw her nod and slowly unwind and place her cup on the coffee table. She was so damned graceful. Garret felt the ache intensify in his lower body. Good thing he had on jeans; she wouldn't realize how turned on he was. Garret didn't want to embarrass Kira.

"You're right," she said, gathering her journal and picking up the box of colored pencils. "Tomorrow is coming soon. I have to be over at Mr. Crawford's place at 6:30 in the morning."

Grimacing, Garret said nothing and forced himself to move. If he didn't, he was going to walk up to her, haul her into his arms and hold her fiercely. Forever. His hands itched to touch her. His body was beginning to throb. His conscience was at war within him. He wanted to gain Kira's trust so she would level with him about Crawford and his games. But to do it, Garret realized he was going to have to become starkly vulnerable. It was something he'd never done because if he had, that wall of black grief would have raced up through him and torn him apart, and he'd have lost total control. That couldn't happen. It just couldn't.

CHAPTER SEVEN

Kira tried to keep things light between her and Garret the next morning. He looked like hell warmed over. His hazel eyes were a muddy green brown, his mouth a slash, and he wasn't his normal, chipper self.

Last night she'd gone back to bed, hit the pillow and slept deeply until her alarm went off at five a.m. Garret was already up and moving about, which surprised her. Hadn't he slept at all? What was bothering him?

As she ate the pancakes smothered with bananas, strawberries and blueberries he'd made for her, she'd desperately wanted to talk with him. But there was no time. Glancing at her watch, she saw she had only twenty minutes before she had to get over to Ray's house. Last night Garret had looked terribly vulnerable after she'd admitted she had drawn all the men of the team in her journal. It was as if, out of the blue, something had zapped him. There was desperation in his eyes. And as she'd sat there, Kira felt so many different emotions — like waves of energy — hitting her. She wasn't sure how he'd taken her admission about the drawings. Maybe, looking back on it, she shouldn't have said anything. Because it had upset Garret a lot.

She forced herself to eat even though her stomach was in a knot. Having to go into battle again with Ray was the last thing Kira wanted to do. Her anxiety was already high and she could feel the howling monster that lived inside her awaken and start to snarl. The anxiety felt like a knife being rasped against her flesh, tearing her open, feeling the pain, making her bleed. Kira wished with all her heart it would go away. But it never did. The monster just slumbered and would suddenly awaken like a primal animal, defensive and ready to fight because it felt threatened. Ray Crawford threatened the hell out of her. The only solace was that Shay had been very kind to her the night before, Garret had found a fix for the situation and no one had mentioned firing her. *Not yet.*

"Thanks for the great breakfast," she told him, reaching out, grazing his forearm. Rising, she took her plate and flatware to the sink. Kira found herself wanting so badly to wrap her arms around Garret. He looked devastated. It had to be due to their talk last night. She knew how upsetting it was to think back on the ambush. But it was something she did every week, and there was no escaping the grief or memories that would suddenly bubble up. When it did, she'd burst into tears. And there was no way she could control or stop them. Nor would she try. The rolling, overwhelming sense of loss consumed her and all she could do was sob until it worked its way out. Then, always, she would feel better.

Hurrying to the wall where her parka hung, she shrugged it over her shoulders. Grabbing her red knit cap and pulling it on, she dug for her mittens in her pockets. "I'll see you at 1300," she said, struggling to pull them onto her hands.

She glanced toward the table where Garret sat. He looked pasty to her, lifeless, his eyes dull. Her heart opened to him and she wished she could stay, talk with him, find out what was going on inside him. But she couldn't.

"Don't take any shit off Crawford today," Garret growled, lifting his head, pinning her with a hard stare. "If it happens, you walk out, come and get me and we'll go see Shay and Reese. I don't want him being abusive to you, Kira."

She forced a smile she didn't feel, her hand wrapping around the doorknob. "He's just upset and trying to get used to a new way of living, Garret. It'll be all right," and she lifted her hand, pulling the door open and hurrying out. Garret's expression told Kira he didn't believe her for a second.

Adrenaline leaked into her and she felt the jittery quality sizzling through her like a wild animal on the loose. It took so much energy to control and contain those rampant feelings of threat, as if she were about to die in battle. Hurrying down the sidewalk, she realized Garret had already shoveled the snow from the night before off earlier. He really mustn't have slept at all.

Worried over their conversation, her mind starting to become distracted, Kira compressed her lips, hurrying into a trot. There was a bare hint of a pinkish dawn in the east across the wide valley, the Salt River Range ten miles away. Her breath was white vapor as she hurried along, seeing the lights were on in Ray, Noah and Harper's homes. Everyone started early on a ranch. Dawn to dusk. That was how it was.

Kira knocked on Ray's kitchen door, then let herself in. She saw him dressed, sitting at the table, a cup of coffee between his hands. "Good morning," she said, breath-less. Shutting the door, she quickly shed her parka, hanging it on a nearby wall hook. At least Crawford couldn't say she was late today. It was 6:20 a.m. As Kira turned, all she received was a dark stare. Crawford's mouth was a thin line. It reminded her of a snake's mouth, which had no lips. His brown eyes were hard and she tried to steel herself against anything he might say.

Rubbing her hands briskly, she tried to keep her voice light. "Did you sleep well last night, Mr. Crawford?"

"Bad night."

She gave him a kind look. "I'm sorry. How's the coffee this morning?"

"Better," he snapped.

What a bear. Was he like this with Shay? Washing her hands at the sink, she twisted a look toward him. "That's great to hear. What would you like for breakfast?" She saw him glare at her, look down at his half-empty cup, his brow furrowing. Kira noticed the crutch leaning nearby against the wall. He was supposed to use both crutches but refused.

"I want waffles."

Kira didn't even know if there was a waffle iron in the house. "Okay," she said, starting to look for the appliance. She opened several cupboards, not finding one.

"Do you happen to know where the waffle iron is, Mr. Crawford?"

"How the hell would I know?"

Wincing, Kira bent down, continuing to look through the rest of the cupboards. When she didn't find it, she started at one end and went through each one. No waffle iron. Pushing her damp hands against her jeans, she turned to him. "I can't find one, Mr. Crawford. Let me run to Shay's house. I'm sure she has a waffle iron we can borrow until she buys one for your house."

"What is it with women? You're stupid! And so is my daughter! She shoulda thought about this before I moved in. What the hell's the matter with her?"

Gulping, Kira straightened. She didn't dare reply. She knew a person like Crawford would more than likely explode at her, cursing and God knows what else. She walked over to the wall hook and pulled on her parka. Turning, she held his angry gaze. "I'll be back just as soon as I can, Mr. Crawford. We'll get those waffles made for you . . ."

Kira felt nothing but relief as she hurried to Garret's house for lunch. The day had turned out sunny, bright and cold. She loved the snow as it was blown by a breeze off the roof, glittering in the sunlight like sparkling diamonds as it fell to the white-covered ground. How was Garret? She hadn't seen him since that morning. Worried, she went into the house. He was in the kitchen and whatever he was cooking smelled wonderful.

"Hey," she called, hanging up her parka, turning to where he stood at the stove, "that smells great. What are you making for us?" Kira was relieved he looked a little better. But not much. Something was still eating at Garret. It took everything inside her to keep from asking about it. She knew from experience that most men dumped their feelings into a rabbit hole, never wanting to uncover them again. She'd had time this morning, after translating some letters into English from Arabic, to think through their conversation late last night.

"Hey yourself," Garret greeted, looking in her direction. "I'm making some sausage and potato-cheddar cheese soup. Cold out there this morning."

She walked over to the large steel pot he was stirring, leaned over and inhaled. "Mmm, this is wonderful." She grinned and straightened. "Let me get the table set."

"Go ahead."

Happiness threaded through Kira. It was

so easy to fall into teamwork with Garret. She retrieved two red-and-blue ceramic soup bowls, along with soupspoons.

"I've got some garlic bread warming up in the oven," he told her.

"My mouth is watering," Kira teased, smiling at him as he briskly stirred the thick soup on the stove. Kira found a red plastic basket and placed paper towels in the bottom of it, setting it nearby so he could pull the toasting garlic bread out whenever he was ready. It was endearing to her to see such a big man with a pink-and-white-checked apron wrapped around his waist, working at a stove. The image made Kira love Garret even more. He could care less about what others thought of him wearing a woman's apron. His masculinity certainly wasn't in question. She opened a drawer and pulled out two bright-red linen napkins.

"How did it go with Crawford this morning?" he demanded, giving her a concerned look.

"Oh," she laughed softly, "we had the great century waffle disaster," and she explained what had happened. "Shay had one and I used it. She's going to get that timer coffeepot today and will pick up a waffle iron for her father as well."

"He didn't start bad-mouthing you, did he?"

Kira felt the grate in his low voice. She hated lying to Garret. "He was just his usual grumpy self. He was happy with the coffee, though, so that's one hurdle completed."

"Knowing him," Garret said, taking the bowl Kira handed him and ladling soup into it from the pot, "the bastard isn't ever going to admit you did something right. Shay used to tell me that her father would only point out what she did wrong. He never praised her for anything well done." He looked pointedly at Kira as she handed him the second bowl to fill. "Is that how he is with you?"

Shrugging, Kira said lightly, "Mostly. But hey, I'm used to it. In the Army they barked at you when you screwed up, Garret. They never praised us for what we did right. Same thing here." She was hoping he'd buy her explanation but saw his hazel eyes darken with worry — for her. Carrying the bowls over to the table, she said, "Things went smoother this morning. It's just going to take time." Kira hoped Garret never heard Ray riding her verbally. She was afraid of what he might do to the invalid. Garret was so protective of her, more so than she'd ever seen before. What did it mean?

Garret brought out the toasted garlic bread and placed it in the basket. Kira already had glasses of water on the table. He sat down at her elbow, inhaling her scent. His body stirred. Kira wore a light blue sweater that lovingly caressed her curves. Her black hair was tousled, but on her it looked good. Natural. He noticed her hands trembled a little. *Crawford.* He knew it, but dammit, until he could win Kira's full trust, she wouldn't level with him about how that bastard was really treating her. It raked up his anger and he stuffed it, wanting to enjoy the time with her. He watched her take a sip of the thick, hearty soup.

"Oh, this is good, Garret," Kira purred and closed her eyes, swallowing and savoring the herbs and spice flavors in it.

He felt himself puff up beneath her praise. That was the difference, Garret decided, between them. Even in Afghanistan, Kira had been positive. She always had praise and kind words for the team members, the children, the Afghan mothers she worked with daily. Everyone felt better when Kira was around. She just naturally lifted people, made them feel good about themselves.

Hell, she made him feel something he hadn't since waking up after the ambush in the hospital: hope. Real hope. Hope for a future with her. Like the greedy beggar he was, Garret silently absorbed her upbeat smile, the sparkle in her eyes, the way that luscious mouth of hers curved. "Like the soup?"

"Like it? I love it! I remember in the village you'd do incredible things with our MREs. You'd gather them up and then concoct this unnamed food that really tasted good. Everyone loved it when you cooked for our team, Garret."

That was true and he grinned a little. "MREs are horrible tasting."

"Yes, well, you took them to an art-form level, believe me."

"Spices and herbs are the secret," he told her. Garret saw all the tension Kira was unconsciously carrying in her shoulders dissolve. Even her face softened. He knew something good existed between them. *Still.* It hadn't been destroyed, and that tugged hard at his heart. How to tell her he liked her? He knew he didn't dare admit he loved her. That would explode like an IED into Kira's life. Garret understood he had to take this slow. He had to be patient. Thank God they were living together under the same roof. It gave him an opportunity to be with her off and on throughout the day.

"Well, I know all the guys were salivating when it came to your turn to cook. We all knew we'd get something that tasted really good." Kira grinned.

"One of our team's happier memories," he agreed, trying not to sound grumpy about it. Because every time that subject was brought up, his gut clenched. Garret felt like he was sitting on a barrel of C4 explosives that was going to detonate unexpectedly some day and destroy him.

"And you did wonders with goat meat. I'd never eaten goat until I went to Afghanistan."

"It's a meat like all meats," he murmured, satisfied with how the soup tasted.

"I didn't think I'd like it, but I developed a taste for it because of the way you prepared it."

"Yeah, but Afghan food is really good. A family that's better off than most will have small tins of spices and the wife knows how to use them."

She sighed. "A fond memory." She held his dark green-and-gold eyes. Reaching out, she touched his arm. "You really made our lives better over there, Garret. I know you think anyone can cook, but that's not true.

You're really good at it."

His skin tightened as her fingers grazed his arm. He wished his flannel blue-and-green-plaid cowboy shirt wasn't a barrier between her fingertips and his flesh. Last night he'd tossed and turned with his heart and mind kicked into overdrive. It was pure, utter hell to sit there and watch the tears roll down Kira's cheeks and know he could do nothing — not a damn thing — about it. She'd needed to be held. Garret knew he could do that for her. He kept visualizing walking over to her, hauling her into his arms, tucking her into his embrace, her head nestled beneath his jaw as he held her warm and safe. Those potent images had kept him awake the rest of the night. He'd finally said to hell with it and gotten up at 5 a.m. It took everything he had to bypass her room and go to the kitchen instead. Only after shoveling the walk had he finally chilled out, literally and figuratively.

"I like to cook."

"Did you get that from your mom?" Kira wondered.

"Yeah, for sure. I can remember as a kid, my head not even reaching the kitchen counter, and I'd be there, watching her sift, measure, weigh and mix. She was always giving me tastes from a big spoon. She'd

154

cup my chin with one hand and tell me to open up, then she slipped the spoon into my mouth to taste whatever she was making."

"You were young."

"Probably six." And then Garret grudgingly admitted, "It's some of the best memories I have of my mom. We had a lot of fun in that kitchen, a lot of laughter." His heart still clenched at times when those memories rose, sweet and strong within him.

"I'm so sorry you lost her at such a young age," Kira whispered, giving him a sad glance. "She'd be really proud of you now, Garret."

"She said I should become a chef," he said. "Boys growing up at that time were considered weaklings if they were cooks. I didn't want to be a sissy."

Grinning, Kira shook her head. "You guys . . ." and she chuckled. "There's nothing sissylike about being a great chef. It's part art and part creating a recipe. Look how you made our MREs taste. That was pure art. You always thought outside the box, Garret."

He preened beneath her sincere praise and saw longing in her eyes. It was right there and so easy to read. The way she licked her lips sent fire bolting down into his lower body. Groaning inwardly, Garret could feel himself becoming aroused. Kira had no idea how much she turned him on. She turned him inside out with wanting to bury himself in her warm, liquid depths. It was a good thing she couldn't read minds or he'd be in such hot water. He didn't want this lunch to end, though it had to.

"I'm going into town to pick up some parts for the backhoe. Is there anything you need?"

"No . . . not that I can think of."

"Well, I'll see about that," and he gave her a playful look. Instantly, Kira smiled and brightened. She was so easily teased in the best ways.

"What do you have up your sleeve, Fleming?"

Garret gave her a lazy look. "Something." She pouted. Her lower lip was full, and he longed to know what it would feel like to slide his mouth across hers. Somehow, Garret knew she would be like warm honey; sweet, delicious, hot and eager. Because the need in her eyes, if he read her accurately, was proof that Kira wanted him. She was interested in him as a man this time, not as a friend and the Special Forces operator she had worked with.

She playfully hit his upper arm. "Come

on! Tell me!"

Kira was such a child upon occasion. Garret had seen it in Afghanistan so many times. Kira would walk through the village, the children tagging along, holding her hand, tugging on her blouse or dancing around her. She had asked a friend stateside to send her a soccer ball early on in her first deployment. The children loved playing with her. They'd carefully sweep their homemade soccer field out behind the village for planted IEDs. Finding none, Kira would have the boys and girls play and kick the ball back and forth to one another. Garret remembered the many times he would take time out, watch her, listen to her laughter, see the shining happiness in her eyes as she played with them. And always, Kira made sure the children won the game. She wanted to build their confidence in themselves. And she always had candy as a reward for all of them afterward. There was so much to love about her . . .

"Garret? Where did you go?"

He felt heat rush into his cheeks. "Caught me," he admitted, flashing her a grin. "I have a surprise in store for you is all. And I'm not telling you what it is. You'll find out tonight."

She considered his words and gripped his

upper arm, giving it a small shake. "You were always teasing me like that in Afghanistan."

"That's true," he admitted, enjoying her smile. "Yeah, you took the bait because you trusted me," Garret chuckled. He saw her smile widen and that same, utter happiness come to her gray, shining eyes. In that moment Garret was transported back to that village, back to one of the many happy times with Kira. She had no idea how she fed his heart and soul. Just the sound of her laughter was a healing balm for him.

"I love good surprises," she murmured. Standing, she pushed back the chair, then gathering up the empty bowls. "And it had better be a good one, Fleming."

"Oh," he murmured, giving her a sly look, "it's something you really, really like."

She snorted as she moved to the kitchen sink. "I don't know, Fleming. I remember the time you said you and the guys had a special surprise for me. You all made a big deal out of it. Every one of you were ragging on me, telling me how wonderful the surprise was going to be." She gave him a dirty look. "And you blindfolded me, surrounded me, had the camera to see my face when I opened up my surprise."

Garret's smile grew. "Oh . . . that time . . .

yeah . . . how could I forget?" and he started laughing about it all over again.

Kira laughed with him as she dried her hands on a nearby towel. "You set me up royally. That was in the first year of my deployment, when I didn't know you guys that well. There I was, sitting on a stool in the middle of a house with my hand held out for my surprise. I felt a bag placed in my hand and then you guys were telling me to take off my blindfold and look at what was in it." Her mouth went flat, but a grin leaked out of one corner. "Goat turds in a paper bag."

Garret couldn't help himself; he laughed deeply, nodding, remembering that event. "You had the most priceless look on your face, Kira." He wiped his eyes, still chuckling. "Ryan took a photo. That was one for the ages."

Kira came over to the table, giggling. "It *was* funny. All of you knew I was gullible. You took advantage of my good nature," and she gripped his broad shoulder, giving it a shake.

Feeling her hand coming to rest on him, Garret finally stopped laughing. His stomach hurt, he'd laughed so much. "Well, if it makes you feel any better, any new man or woman to the team always got a hazing.

That was our way of welcoming you on board. Aaron was smart: He watched you for about two months, learning a lot about you, your personality. He was the one who strategized the surprise."

Without thinking, Kira moved her hand across his powerful, well-muscled shoulder. She felt his skin tighten beneath her grazing touch. "I fell for it. All of it."

"Oh," Garret said, twisting a look up at her as she stood at his shoulder. "Over time you got even with all of us. I found goat turds in my pillow sack one night. Aaron found them in the tin of KitKats he hoarded. Yeah, you got even with all of us. Is it any wonder we called you Trouble after that?"

She playfully shoved at his shoulder. "Like all of you didn't have it coming? And Brady was forever threatening me with putting that photo of me holding the goat turds online."

"He was just razzing you," Garret murmured, becoming more serious, holding her warm gray gaze. "He'd never do anything to embarrass you out in public, Kira. You knew that."

"At the time I didn't know that," she confided, her voice turning fond with memory. "That was my first two months with you animals. I didn't really know you that well. And after you played that mean trick on me, you bet I believed Brady that he'd share it all over Facebook."

Feeling her light, gliding hand moving back and forth across his shoulder, Garret soaked it in like the starving animal he was. Kira didn't know how primal he really was, or how much he needed her. Her unexpected touch sent waves of heat radiating into his lower body. From the look on her face, her voice, Kira was lost in the past, not really aware of what she was doing. It didn't matter to Garret. What did matter was that Kira was touching him. In the past two days her touches had been sparing, but sometimes she would reach out, and Garret savored those precious moments of connection. Trying to relax as her hand moved back and forth across his shoulder, he wanted to soak her into his body, his heart, and keep her within his soul forever.

There was a terrible challenge directly in front of him. His heart was dying for a relationship with Kira. To get there, he had to bridge his fear and allow grief to rise up through him. Did he have the courage? Could his love conquer his fear? Garret didn't know. And even if he did, he had no idea how to go about doing it. Kira was working through her grief, that was obvious. But he couldn't go around crying. Men just didn't cry. They stuffed. When she lifted her hand away, he wanted to groan and plead with her to remain in contact with him.

"I've got to get to work," Kira told him, waving to him as she walked down the hall toward the office.

Garret watched the sway of her hips, the way her shoulders were always pulled back with pride. She'd gone through so much and carried the weight of PTSD. Marveling at her inner strength, he turned and scowled, unhappy with himself. To gain Kira's trust, he had to be honest with her. And so much of their conversation focused on a subject he wanted to avoid at all costs: Afghanistan. It was their tie, their connection. It was her healing and his demise.

Rubbing his face wearily, feeling exhaustion stealing over him, Garret wanted to crawl into her bed, into her arms, hold her close, sleep with her, love her. Nothing seemed so daunting and so out of reach right now. In order to get her, he had to surrender his backlog of grief.

CHAPTER EIGHT

Kira kept her voice light and unruffled as Ray Crawford, who sat at the table with his coffee, glared at her as she entered the kitchen.

"How are you this morning, Mr. Crawford?" Kira tried to steel herself against his black negativity as she walked to the kitchen sink and washed her hands.

"Not good."

"Oh?" Kira turned. He was wearing a red-and-black-checked flannel shirt and jeans. If he wasn't always nasty, she could almost feel sorry for him. What would she feel like if she had a stroke? That once she'd ridden a horse, run a ranch and then had it all, suddenly, yanked away from her?

"Didn't sleep well."

"I'm sorry," she said, meaning it. Taking the apron from a nearby drawer, she put it on. "What would you like to eat this morning?"

"Just some eggs, ham and toast."

He never added a please. Everything was an order. "Coming right up," she said, going to get the black iron skillet. Kira often thought of Shay, growing up with someone like him. Despite it, his daughter was a kind person. Like Shay, Kira had to work at not allowing Ray's dark, angry mood to infect her. His bad attitude was like getting caught in sticky slime, with no way out. "You have a ten a.m. appointment with your physical therapist today," she reminded him.

"I know."

As she picked up the heavy skillet from the drawer beneath the stove, she dropped it. The skillet clanged sharply on the oak floor.

"You stupid girl!" Ray shouted, jerking at the sudden, unexpected noise.

Heart banging away in her throat, Kira switched hands. Her two fingers on her right hand had been at fault. There had been some nerve damage from the bullet wound in her right upper arm. Why hadn't she thought before reaching for the skillet? Any heavy item could slip because her fingers lacked the strength to hold on to it. "Sorry," she said, quickly picking it up.

"You can't do anything right! What if there was food in it? You'd have splattered it all over the floor. Made a damn mess! You're useless!"

Cringing inwardly, Kira said nothing. She hurried to the sink and rinsed the skillet, then patted it dry. Ray continued to growl and snarl curses beneath his breath. She could feel his glare drilling two holes into her back, like bullets shattering her un-shielded body. Adrenaline had shot into her system and she was combating that, trying to focus and control her anxiety.

"One day you're gonna drop my plate of food. I know you will."

Her mouth tightened as she hurried to the stove. Grabbing the carton of eggs and ham from the fridge, she tried to ignore his abuse. It was the same all the time.

"You're just like that damned daughter of mine. She can't do anything right either."

Ignore him. Don't respond. Kira had learned quickly not to try to defend herself. It only made Crawford angrier and more verbally abusive toward her.

"Shaylene has no right running my ranch! I can do a helluva better job than she is! And then she picks losers like all of you vets, like you're something special. She feels sorry for you. None of you could make it out in the world on your own." He snorted and growled, "You're all pathetic and weak.

Losers."

Anger nipped at her. Kira almost turned around to set the record straight with Crawford. He had no idea how each of the men and women who worked there were heroes in their own right. Brave people who had sacrificed so much for their country. And yet she knew there was a part of the US populace that saw anyone in the military uniform as a warmonger, a killer. That hurt. It hurt deep. She quickly got the ham frying in the skillet and worked on setting the table.

"Are you always so damned clumsy?" he snapped.

Kira set the plate in front of him, along with the flatware. She said nothing, avoiding his glare. As she laid down the fork, he grabbed her left hand, squeezing it hard. Kira jerked it out of his strong, painful grip. Crawford was weak on the right but not the left. Her bruised wrist smarted where she'd yanked it out of his grasp.

"Don't touch me!"

Crawford studied her. "You're weak, girl."

She stood there, breathing roughly, rubbing her wrist. Her skin was aching where his fingers had dug in. "Don't touch me again, Mr. Crawford." Her voice was low, rattling and off key. Kira held his dark brown eyes and saw his nearly lipless mouth curve faintly with a smile.

"Women like you need to be beat and brought into submission. I've had horses like you. You think you're so good, so smart, but the truth of it is, you're stupid and clumsy. I'd take a two-by-four to the horse to teach him a lesson."

Instantly, her anger amped up, with her adrenaline pouring through her. She saw the enjoyment in his eyes at scaring her. It sickened Kira. "Mr. Crawford, let's get clear on this. You will *never* touch me again unless I give you permission first."

His mouth curved deeply. "You're just a weak, clumsy girl. I'll do whatever I damn well want. I don't want you taking care of me. I want you out of my hair. And if you don't like me touching you, tough."

Shaken, Kira backed away. Her throat ached with tension. Crawford was going to grab her again. Working at the stove, moving the ham to his plate, she put two eggs in next. Her hands shook. Her heart wouldn't settle down. God, he was awful. Should she tell someone what he'd just done? Or try to handle it herself? What if Shay found out? Was she used to her father physically grabbing her? Hurting her? Her wrist was throbbing nonstop. Her reaction, to jerk out of his grasp, had been instinctive. What was he planning to do if she hadn't jerked away? That bothered Kira even more.

Quickly, she placed the toast on the side of the plate and carried it over to him with both hands. Wary, she watched his hands, which were resting on the table. There was a gleam in his eyes that reminded Kira of a hunter waiting for his quarry to get just a little closer so he could make another grab for her arm. Her pulse went up as she slid the plate in front of him.

He made no move to pin her again.

Heart pounding unrelentingly in her chest, Kira turned and walked to the kitchen, relief sizzling through her. Crawford's attack had been unexpected. Shaken, she busied herself around the house, picking up the dirty clothes he'd dropped on the floor. Kira was just getting used to him, to his ways, but his actions had startled and scared her.

She started a load of wash, made his bed and straightened up the living room. He dropped magazines and newspapers on the floor. He was messy and she wanted to tell him to start cleaning up after himself. But that wouldn't be a good idea. By the time Kira was finished, Crawford had eaten. Picking up the empty plate and dirty flatware, she placed them in the dishwasher.

"I'll be back at ten a.m. for your appointment in town, Mr. Crawford."

He grunted and paid no attention to her.

Garret was glad to see Kira when she entered the house after feeding Crawford his evening meal. He'd just gotten home himself, the darkness of autumn complete. In the kitchen, preparing their dinner, he glanced to his left as Kira entered. She looked pale. Warning prickles stood up on the back of his neck. He saw Kira was upset, but he said nothing as she hung up her parka on the wall peg. "How'd your day go?" he asked. Tonight he was making a mandarin orange salad with baked perch.

"Oh, fine . . . fine . . ." she murmured, turning and smiling at him. "You?"

Shrugging, he said, "Got the parts for the backhoe and got it up and running. That's always good news." He picked up the fresh perch he'd bought in town. Placing the filets in a cornmeal-and-spice mixture, he then put them on a baking sheet. "You?"

"Fine," she answered. "I'll be back in a moment to set the table."

"No hurry," he said. Frowning, Garret watched her leave the kitchen. Something was bothering her. What was it? Instinctively, he knew it had to do with Crawford. She'd had to take him into town for his physical therapy at ten a.m. He was finding that on those days, she was stressed more than usual. Probably because she had to spend additional time around the mean bastard.

Releasing a frustrated sigh, Garret's conscience railed at him. Something wasn't right. But Kira wasn't talking. And the only way to get to her, to get her to trust him enough to let down and tell him, was to open up. *Hell.*

All day Garret had chewed relentlessly on just that. Opening up. Kira was the only person in the world he'd ever wanted to entrust himself to, but he was scared. Damned scared. Not of her but of himself. It wasn't something he'd ever done before.

Garret remembered Afghanistan, and how people had interacted with Kira. She was the only woman on the team and the women of the village had worshipped her. They trusted her, relied heavily upon her for medical help, for extra food, for clothes or shoes for their children. They always went to her instead of any man on the A team. It was partly Muslim culture in that women could never approach an unknown man. It was taboo. Still, Kira's openness and

170

warmth drew these beleaguered women like bees to a flower. And there was no question Kira was a flower in the desert of these desperate women's lives.

As Garret fixed dinner, he knew he had to open up more to Kira. Would it really be all that bad? No. But the power of the grief he'd suppressed unnerved him. It was like a dark, stalking shadow that, if unleashed, could swamp him with emotion he was afraid he couldn't control. And then he'd embarrass himself in front of Kira. Shame rolled through him. Would she stop seeing him as the stalwart warrior-knight he'd always secretly considered himself? Stop desiring him because in her eyes, a man shouldn't ever cry or lose it emotionally in front of her? That scared him even worse.

Kira entered the kitchen.

Garret turned, seeing she'd changed into a soft white angora sweater and loose-fitting, gray gym pants. She was wearing a pair of old elkskin moccasins over her stocking feet. There was a bit of pink to her cheeks and she looked less stressed. "How did it go today with the old man?" he asked, placing the fish in the oven.

"Okay," she said, pulling down plates from a cupboard near him. "So the backhoe is ready for action again?"

Garret was finding that if he got too close to something Kira wanted to hide, she automatically shifted the focus to something else. It was distraction at its finest, and he would find himself admiring her abilities had he not been personally involved with her.

"Yeah," he said, finishing up the salad. He added a half cup of orange juice to the European greens. "Reese told me another ranch in the valley is hiring us for a week-long trench dig. The ranch is building a new ditch through a pasture that will connect up to the Snake River. They want us to dig it."

"Lucky you," she said, walking to the table. "Will you be gone that whole week?"

"Yes. I won't be trying to drive fifty miles one way every night. Too much snow and ice this time of year, and besides all that, I'll be exhausted digging in half-frozen earth. October, from what Shay told me, can be as bad as December if we get a lot of hard freezes now. The soil will be a lot harder to dig."

She placed the red linen napkins next to the red ceramic plates. "I'll miss you."

He grinned and gave her a glance. "Oh, come on. The truth is you'll miss my cooking." He saw her flash him a warm smile as she placed the flatware next to the plates. A sense of peace came over him when Kira was near. It was her presence that made him feel that way, and he felt like a hoarder every time it happened.

"Well," she hedged with a soft laugh, "that's true, too, but I like your company more, Garret. I won't have anyone to talk to at night. Or sit with me when I watch a TV program."

"Hmmm; sounds like I've infected you."

Laughing, Kira said, "You're not a virus, you know." She came to the kitchen counter as he handed her the bowl of salad. Their fingers touched as he transferred it to her.

Garret saw something in Kira's gray eyes. They had been dark when she'd arrived in Wind River Valley. The way her lips curved sent heat stabbing down through him. "What? So I've spoiled you instead?" he teased her.

The bowl slipped to one side as her left hand didn't quite keep it stable.

Garret quickly slid his hands around the bowl. "Okay?" he asked, seeing how suddenly stricken she looked. She'd told him earlier that the last two fingers on her right hand were sometimes weak. He kept his large hands around hers to steady the bowl.

"Y-yes . . . thanks," Kira apologized a little breathlessly.

He saw starkness in her eyes now. Fear. Her hands were cool beneath his warmer ones. "It's okay, I've got you . . ." He saw instant relief come into her expression, the fear easing.

For a split second Garret wanted to do more, but he cautioned himself. The act of touching Kira settled her. That was a helluva realization. "Are those fingers acting up?"

She pulled away from his hands. "It seems the cold makes them less cooperative," she admitted unhappily, taking the salad to the table.

Frowning, Garret heard something in her voice. What was it? Damn, he really needed to forge a closer link with her. "What's the prognosis on them?"

"It's nerve damage. Docs said they didn't know if, over time, the nerve would repair itself and I'd get partial or full use of them again."

"It's been a year."

"Yes, but nerves grow back very slowly," Kira said, defeat in her tone. "So often I forget those two fingers don't work well at times and I pick up things and drop them. It's maddening."

"Well," Garret said, catching her worried glance, "we saved our bowl of salad, so relax. Okay?" Because she was hyper in comparison to yesterday. Something had gone on at Crawford's and damned if he could figure it out. "Come here."

She hesitated at the sink. "What?"

"I want to give you a hug. Is that okay?"

"Oh . . ." and she looked away for a moment.

"I'm not going to squeeze you to death," he teased, opening his arms. Would she come? Garret saw real consternation in her expression. "You look like you could use a hug," he finally admitted, his voice dropping gruffly. He wiggled his fingers in a gesture for her to come toward him. She did. There was a change in her eyes, moisture collecting in them, and he felt his heart wrench as he saw anguish for a moment.

Kira wrapped her slender arms around him, pressing her head against his massive chest. Garret groaned silently, his arms sliding gently around her, hugging her lightly. Nothing sensual. Nothing predatory. Just a hug. And damned if she didn't stay! He felt the soft press of her breasts against his chest, the way she burrowed her face into him, her arms tight around his waist, as if she were clinging to him like a leaf in a storm.

The sensations were hot, scalding, and without thinking, he leaned over, pressing a

175

kiss to her hair. Inhaling her scent, the way she fit against his hard body, sent him into a spiraling ache of need. He wanted to kiss her, search and explore that mouth of hers, those full lips, taste her . . .

Kira tightened and moved closer, their hips nearly touching. What if she felt his erection? Garret panicked inwardly. It was too soon for Kira to realize just how much she affected him. And right now he wanted to give to her, not take from her. She could completely misread his intentions. It could break the trust he was trying to build with her. Not wanting to, but knowing he must, Garret gave her a quick squeeze and released her.

"There," he murmured, smiling down at her. "Now, don't you feel better?" Her cheeks were flushed. There was arousal in her eyes when she lifted her lashes to look up at him. Was he honestly reading Kira right? She *wanted* him?

His brain and heart were at odds with each other. He loved her. He wanted her. All of her. Any way he could get her. How could he admit his feelings for her so she would believe him? Garret didn't know and reluctantly allowed his hands to slide off her small but so-capable shoulders.

Kira managed to give him a lopsided

smile. "I do feel better. Thanks . . ."

"Come on," Garret urged, "the perch is about ready to eat. Why don't you pour us some water?"

Kira jerkily moved her fingers through her hair. "Right . . . water . . ."

She was shaken, Garret realized. But this time he knew it was because of him. She liked his embrace. Maybe way too much; the arousal was still banked in those dove-gray eyes of hers. Kira didn't realize how much he could ferret out of her expressions sometimes. Hope flared through his chest. His erection throbbed. Good thing Levi's zippers hid most everything.

For the next five minutes silence reigned in the warmth of the kitchen. The scent of perch covered with cornmeal and Moroccan spices filled the air. It was a simple meal, Garret knew, but it would be tasty. He covertly watched Kira out of the corner of his eye as he transferred the fish from the baking dish to a platter on the counter. He liked the flush on her cheeks, the sparkle in her eyes. Just one hug. *One.* Think what could happen if she allowed him to move in to kiss her. His whole body flamed over that tempting thought.

Garret had to take solace in the fact that Kira had allowed him to embrace her. It was a huge step forward in their intimacy with each other. Another step in trusting him. He didn't know what had possessed him, urging Kira into his arms, but he sensed that was what she'd needed: a hug. To be in a safe harbor. Garret wanted to always be exactly that for Kira: a safe place where she could come. The first step had been taken. He felt delirious with joy. She had trusted him enough. *Just enough.*

As he placed the fish between them on the table, he pulled out her chair so she could sit down. "Have you forgotten about that surprise I promised you tonight?" he teased.

Kira smiled a little as she picked up the linen napkin and spread it across her lap. "No. But knowing you, Fleming, you'll spring it on me. Probably scare the bejesus out of me."

He grimaced. "Hey, when did I ever play mean tricks on you, Kira? Never."

Chuckling, Kira put one of the perch on her plate. "The pouch full of goat turds? Remember?"

"Oh . . . okay . . . well, that's fair. Yeah. One time, Kira, in our three years together I did play a dirty trick on you."

Scooping some salad onto her plate, she met his wounded expression. "That's true.

It was just one time, but I still remember it to this day. It only takes once, you know," she said dryly, holding his laughter-filled gaze.

"I did some nice things for you," Garret pointed out, filling his plate with the rest of the perch. "You liked crossword puzzles, so I went through a scrounger who could get anything and got you some magazines. Remember that?" he demanded, reaching for the salad bowl.

"Indeed I do. And that was very sweet of you."

He preened. "See? I'm not the bad guy you make me out to be."

Kira shook her head. "You're a bad guy hiding beneath that nice veneer you've got, Fleming. The jokes you played on the other guys were monumental."

He grinned. "Yeah, I was good at that."

"You were the worst of the lot."

"I'm hurt."

"No, you aren't. You loved playing pranks on the guys."

"In defense," he said, "they played them on me, too. It wasn't one-sided. I mean, we got bored, Kira. I livened things up. Kept them on their toes. They loved it."

"That you did," she agreed, eating heartily. "I'm just glad you guys left me off your radar after the goat turd joke."

He gave her a warm look. "Truth be known? We all felt kinda bad about that afterward. You were so excited and we realized afterward that we'd really hurt you. It kind of backfired on us. You aren't one of the guys. Men do that and don't take it personally."

She gave him a blunt look. "I trusted you guys. That was the problem. That was the mistake I made. I honestly thought you had some great, nice surprise for me."

He swallowed his laughter. It was funny to this day, but Garret knew it had hurt Kira's feelings. She had been new to the team and it was a hazing joke they played on all the newbies. She didn't know that, and they'd broken her trust. Garret had seen that trust rebuilt over the years, but from that point on, Kira always held away a part of herself from them. "In hindsight? I wished we'd never played it on you. You never trusted us again as you had before it happened."

Shrugging, Kira gave him a sad look. "You're probably right. After the captain explained it was a rite of passage, something pulled on every newbie in the team, I got it."

Garret saw the lingering sadness in her eyes. "How do I earn your trust, Kira?"

He'd spoken the question so softly that for a moment it didn't register on her. And when it did, he saw her eyes widen momentarily in shock over the intimacy of his question to her.

"Well . . ." she stumbled, "I guess time will take care of it. I already trust you, Garret."

He poked his fork at the salad on his plate. "Not like I want, Kira. I saw the closeness you had with the Afghan women and children. I wished from time to time that we could share that same thing between us."

Tilting her head, Kira gave him a confused look. "Really?"

"Yeah." Garret watched the shock in her expression.

"But . . ." and then her voice went low, "we had a job to perform as a team, Garret."

Shrugging, he said, "I know. But that didn't stop me from wishing that you and I could have a deeper trust between us. I wanted it." He looked into her eyes. "Did you?" He held his breath. If Kira said no, Garret knew the relationship he dreamed of with Kira would always be one-sided. It was only he who loved her. Who wanted a deeper, more intimate, trusting relationship with her. He saw her face grow concerned, and then a moment of happiness in her eyes and then it was gone, replaced by unsureness. Garret felt like his entire life was hanging on her answer.

It was.

Kira lowered her head, rummaged her fork through the salad, silent. She licked her lips and lifted her chin, meeting his narrowed, thoughtful gaze. "Yes, I did want something more, Garret." The answer had come out low and wispy. "But it wasn't possible when we were on the team."

Elation roared through him, stealing his breath for a moment. Garret forced himself to remain expressionless because if Kira knew the extent of the kind of intimacy he wanted with her, she'd run. He knew she would. And that was the last thing he wanted. "A lot wasn't possible in Afghanistan," he agreed gruffly, forcing himself to continue eating. "I always liked the nights when we were in bed in separate rooms, talking about the day with each other." How he'd wanted her in his bed.

"There was always an ease between us," Kira agreed, cutting into her fish.

Garret pushed. "I'd like to build on that now, Kira. If you're okay with it?"

"I'm okay with it," she admitted in a low tone, holding his gaze.

CHAPTER NINE

"Time for your surprise," Garret said.

Kira perked up. They had cleared the table, put the dirty dishes in the dishwasher. She was in the middle of making them coffee when Garret came over and leaned languidly against the counter, studying her. Every cell in her body reacted to that burning, casual look in his eyes, as if he were licking her like a sweet lollipop. It couldn't be her imagination.

That unexpected embrace, all triggered by him, was still making her throb with need for him. How tough it had been to just hug him and not cling to him as she really wanted. After three head-on confrontations with Ray Crawford that day, she was desperate for someone who made her feel safe. Protected. Garret provided all that to her in spades. Her skin was still tingling wherever his long arms connected with her shoulders. And when he'd pressed a kiss to her hair?

Her heart had opened powerfully and she'd held him a little tighter. Garret had responded, drawing her closer. Had he done it because he felt sorry for her? Kira knew she looked exhausted. And Garret was sensitive to her in every way. She had to stop herself from lifting her chin and finding his mouth. *So close . . . so close . . .*

Kira tried to tell herself that Garret had done this as a friend. There had been so many times in Afghanistan when he'd been caretaker to the whole team. He was just built that way; a man who could nurture, who had a strong maternal side and didn't care who knew it . . . She smiled.

"What's that smile about?"

Her lips pulled upward. "I was just thinking how much of a mother hen you really are, Garret." She saw his brows raise. "Oh, come on, you know you are."

"Well, maybe a little," he hedged sheepishly.

Snorting, Kira said, "The children called you 'Dada.' It was as close as they could come to saying *daddy* in English. And you were. The children who had lost their fathers, who had been killed by the Taliban, doted on you. And you were like a father to them. You'd sit down on a step and they'd climb into your lap, climb up on your back.

I lost count of how many times you gave the boys piggyback rides."

Garret rubbed his flushed cheek and gave her an amused look. "They were great kids. I loved them all."

One day, Kira thought, he would make a wonderful father. He'd been so attentive, gentle, always building the children's confidence. The boys, in particular, worshipped the ground he walked on.

And just a few minutes ago she'd finally . . . finally . . . found herself in his arms. She had ached for just such an event, never dreaming it could happen. But it had. Even more, he'd asked her the most important question yet: Did she want to pursue something more with him? Yes! She cautioned herself, knowing that Garret was probably wanting the same, easygoing kind of friendship they'd had in Afghanistan. Nothing more. Still, the look he gave her went straight to her heart and then, to her lower body. That wasn't a friendship look Garret had given her. It was so much more and it lifted her, lightness and joy flooding her.

"Hey, this is your night," Garret said, playfully ruffling her hair. "Go on over to the table and sit down. You have to shut your eyes until I tell you to open them. Okay?"

His touch was delicious and unexpected. She walked toward the table. "This had better be good, Fleming, or so help me, you'll pay for this. No goat turds this time around. Okay?"

He chuckled indulgently, hands on his hips, watching her sit down. "It's not a replay of Afghanistan. I promise. You'll like it."

She gave him a pout and relaxed in the chair. "Your word had better be good," she said and closed her eyes. For the next five minutes she heard the fridge open and close, heard the clink of glass and a spoon. What was he up to? His footsteps were solid and they came in her direction. Garret pulled out his chair. He set something down in front of her.

"Okay, Trouble, open your eyes . . ."

Kira opened them and stared into a bowl of ice cream. But it wasn't just any ice cream. It was her favorite: hot fudge drizzled all over it. She gave a gasp of surprise and her hands flew to her mouth.

Garret grinned broadly. "Well? Am I a man of my word or not?"

Tears burned in her eyes as Kira stared down at the bowl and then up at him. She saw the pleasure in his eyes, in the way he smiled, warmth pouring off him and embracing her. It felt so good. She looked away, swallowing several times, trying to get a handle on her emotions.

"Come on," he coaxed her gently, nudging the bowl a little closer and handing her the spoon, "eat up. You're too damned skinny, Kira. You need to put some meat on those ribs of yours. I know how much you love ice cream."

She took the spoon, tears brimming in her eyes. No matter what she did, she couldn't stop them. "Oh, Garret . . . this was so thoughtful of you . . ."

He reached out, grazing her cheek with his thumb. "Come on, eat up."

Choking back a sob, Kira gave him an apologetic look and wiped her eyes clean of the tears. "Where's your bowl?"

Garret pointed his chin toward the counter. "I'll get some later. Right now I want to enjoy watching you eat that ice cream."

Laughing a little unsurely, she scooped the rich, warm fudge along with the vanilla ice cream onto the spoon. "Oh," she whispered unsteadily, "I know what this is about. For my birthday, the first year I was with the team, you guys had five gallons of vanilla ice cream brought in by helicopter for me."

Garret sat back, a pleased look on his face. "Yeah, it was July Fourth. You were an

Independence Day baby. I talked to the captain and he managed to get the ice cream brought in with our regular, weekly shipment of supplies."

She savored the hot fudge and sweet coldness of the vanilla ice cream. "You blew me away when you guys brought in that ice cream and then sang happy birthday to me. I wasn't expecting it." Reaching over, she gripped his hands, folded on the table. "Thank you, Garret. This . . . this is so sweet of you . . . I really needed something good to happen today."

He opened his hands, swallowing one of her small ones between his. "I know it's not your birthday, but I remember that day we brought you the ice cream. It was a hundred and fifteen degrees out, hotter than hell. And the captain had ordered those five gallons to be packed in dry ice and flown out there for you."

"You guys were just the best." Kira reveled in the feeling of his roughened fingers around her hand. The calluses caused her skin to riffle with pleasure. Her lower body tightened with need. The look she saw in Garret's eyes was one of interest and desire — for her. Truly? Could she really believe he wanted her? Man to her woman? More than friendship? Hesitantly, she reluctantly pulled her hand from his to resume eating her ice cream. She needed something icy cold to tamp down the boiling heat flaring to vivid life deep within her.

"We did it three years in a row," he noted proudly.

"You guys spoiled me, no question." Her heart was pounding and it wasn't from fear. Was there regret in his eyes for a moment when she removed her hand from his? Just getting to touch Garret like this was a dessert, but Kira couldn't tell him that.

"Hey, what's that?" and he frowned, pointing to her wrist.

Her heart leaped. Kira pulled her hand away from the nearly empty bowl, set the spoon down and tugged down the sleeve, drawing it over her wrist. The bruises Ray had given her that morning had been exposed. She'd deliberately worn a long-sleeved sweater to cover up the evidence. Urgency thrummed through her as she saw Garret's eyes narrow, his mouth setting, concern in his expression. "Uh . . . it's nothing."

"Those are bruises, Kira. They weren't there yesterday."

Her heart tore. Kira didn't want to lie to Garret. Not to him. She'd never lied to him before. Pursing her lips, she whispered,

"You have to promise me something, Garret."

He scowled. "Promise you what?"

Her heart was breaking because he was clearly worried about her. "T-that you won't tell Reese or Shay." Giving him a pleading look, her hand covering the bruised inner wrist, she added, "Please?"

"Okay," he growled, "I promise. Now, what are those bruises all about?"

The gruffness in his voice was laden with protectiveness. Pushing the bowl aside, she put her forearm on the table and pulled the sweater sleeve up, revealing the three long, thin bruises around her slender wrist. "This morning," she began, her voice low and breathless, "I — uh . . . I went to Mr. Crawford's house. He was in an ugly mood. Said he hadn't slept well the night before." She closed her eyes for a moment. Opening them, Kira's voice lowered. "I took out the big iron skillet from the drawer beneath the stove and," she drew in a serrated breath. "I-I dropped it." She held up her hand. "My fingers . . . I forgot and used the wrong hand, Garret. I often drop things that have a lot of weight if I use it. I was nervous and I got distracted. Instead of picking it up with my good, left hand, I did the opposite." She saw his eyes narrow slightly, feeling the tension mounting in him. "Later, when I put the plate of ham, eggs and toast in front of him, he grabbed my left hand with his. It — startled me. I was so shocked by what he'd done that I jerked out of his grip."

"That bastard," Garret breathed savagely. "He hurt you."

Kira grabbed him as he started to get up. Her fingers sank into his cotton shirt and hard flesh. "No! Don't do anything, Garret! Please! You promised!"

He halted and reluctantly sat back down, rasping, "He's never going to lay a hand on you again, Kira. End of story." Gently, he took her hand, moving his thumb lightly across the purple bruises. Grimacing, he said, "Thank you for trusting me with this," and he searched her gaze.

Kira nodded, her throat tight. Just Garret's featherlight touch on her wrist made it feel better. "I-I wanted to tell you before, Garret."

"Why didn't you?"

"I-I was afraid. Afraid you'd go after Ray. Or tell Shay and Reese. I need this job, Garret. I've been fired from five already. It can't happen again. Don't you see?" Her voice had thinned, turned wobbly with emotion she was barely able to contain.

Wincing, Garret muttered, "All right, all

right, calm down. Reese and Shay wouldn't fire you if you told them what Crawford did to you. They already warned him about being verbally abusive." He gently held her lower arm, staring down at the bruises. They were deep; Crawford had grabbed her hard, meaning to cause her pain. "Has he done this to you before?"

"God, no!" It hurt that Garret would think she'd allow herself to be someone else's punching bag. "I-I was in shock. I wasn't sure what to do. I was afraid for my job, Garret."

"It's all right," he soothed gruffly. He reached out, caressing her cheek. "Stand down, okay? I need to get my own emotion under control."

She had never seen Garret so angry. Not in three years of working with him. Besides his gentle giant status at the village, he'd never raise his voice to child or adult. Kira had never seen him like this until right now, and God, he was absolutely terrifying. His hazel eyes were flashing fire. "I know what I should do," she said unsteadily. "I-I was going to do something tomorrow, after I slept on it. It's not right. I realize that. I've already warned Mr. Crawford he isn't to touch me ever again."

"What did he say?"

It was painful to swallow. "He said . . . he said he'd do it any time he wanted." Kira covered her eyes with her hand and whispered, "I believe him, Garret. I know he will, and that's why I was going to come clean with Shay tomorrow after I gave him breakfast." Lifting her hand away, she dug into his furious-looking gaze. "I-I just wanted something quiet, something good and safe around me tonight . . ."

"I understand more than you know, Kira. I'm not angry with you. I want to punch the bastard's lights out. I don't care if he's had a stroke, he's not allowed to do that to anyone. Especially not you." Garret looked away, his mouth set into a hard, thin line.

It hurt to have this conversation, but in a way, Kira was glad it had happened. She'd been right to trust Garret. Even more, she felt that fierce protection of his surrounding her like a warm, safe blanket. She was glad he was holding her hand gently between his. Desperate for human contact, from someone who wanted her around, who liked her a little, fed her wounded, shredded nervous system. "I'll talk to Shay tomorrow. I promise."

Nodding, he gave her a worried look. "You're exhausted, Kira. Now I understand why. Let me handle stuff here in the kitchen.

Would you like a nice, hot bath? Just a soak?"

It sounded heavenly. "Yes. That's a good idea . . ."

"Stay sitting," Garret said, releasing her arm and standing. "Let me draw it for you."

Touched, she blinked back tears. How badly she needed a little care, and Garret had sensed that. "I owe you . . . Thanks . . ." she choked out.

He ruffled her hair. "Finish your ice cream, huh?"

Garret couldn't sleep. He seethed with anger over what Crawford had done to Kira. Tossing, turning, the covers had landed on the floor on one side of his bed or the other. Glaring at the clock, he saw it was three a.m. *Dammit.* Where he wanted to be was with Kira. Wanted to hold her, protect her, kiss her, love her. He was so damned screwed. Just getting to embrace her tonight, all those little but oh-so-meaningful touches that had followed, were like food for his starving heart and soul.

Grunting, he pushed up into a sitting position, feet on the cool floor, gripping the mattress on either side of himself. Glaring at the burgundy drape-covered window, he cursed softly.

His mind rolled over Kira's promise that she was going to tell Shay about Crawford's physical abuse. Garret believed her. She had never lied to him and tonight, when it counted most, she'd remained honest with him. Kira had trusted him. His heart thudded deep in his chest to underscore the importance of her decision. He loved her so damn much, the ache in his heart was deeper than any gold or diamond mine on this earth.

Rubbing his chest, he closed his eyes, torn. Kira being harmed brought out every last damned cell of protectiveness he possessed. She'd saved his life, he'd been told later by the doctor at Bethesda. Kira had dragged his sorry ass at least twenty-five feet through a hail of Taliban bullets and gotten him to safety behind boulders. She had protected him until help arrived.

Now, as he glared around the silent room, the moonlight weak at the edges of the drapes, he so badly wanted to save her life. Oh, it wasn't the same thing, he knew, but Kira was convinced she was going to be fired if she ratted out Crawford. He knew Shay a lot better than that. Shay would be horrified. Angry. But not at Kira.

What he didn't know was how her husband, Reese, would react to the information. Garret didn't want Kira to go over to their house alone. He wanted to be at her side, to protect her whether she thought she needed it or not. He knew of her bravery, her raw courage under fire.

Garret grunted a curse, rose and pulled his T-shirt into place across his chest. He needed a drink of water. Pushing the door open, he saw a weak light on down the hall in the living room. Halting, he realized Kira was awake. What was she thinking about? He heard quiet, muffled sobs drifting down the hall.

His mouth hardened, his hand gripping the doorknob more tightly. *Son of a bitch.* This wasn't the first time he'd caught her crying. Stopping sharply, Garret fought his urges. Before, when he'd heard her crying, he'd gone back into his room to let her have the time alone. Tears gutted Garret. Oh, he understood why women cried. They needed that. But it made him feel so damned helpless.

What to do right now?

How far could he push her trust? What if he went out there? What if he asked her what the tears were all about? What if it was about the team? Garret wasn't sure he could handle that situation on top of the present one. He was too upset over her being injured by Crawford.

Standing there, a bitter taste entered his mouth. He was such a friggin' coward. Worried about the team? His grief? When Kira was hurting right now? What the hell kind of man was he? Where the hell were *his* priorities? Garret snarled a curse beneath his breath, ashamed of his actions. He shoved away from the door, heading for the kitchen, his gut taut.

Garret brought out two glasses of water. He padded into the living room, making enough noise to alert Kira that she had company. She was in her favorite place on the couch, the corner. The lower half of her body was wrapped snugly in the afghan. The surprise on her wet face, the startled look in her eyes, told him everything.

"Thought you might like some water," he said, holding it out to her. He wanted to say to hell with the water and scoop her small form into his arms, carry her to his bed and hold her. Just hold her. That was all. The desire nearly overwhelmed Garret as she sniffed, trying to quickly wipe her tears away with shaking hands.

"I woke you up," she croaked, taking the glass. "I'm so sorry."

"No. I never went to sleep," he grunted. This time, Garret sat down near her. He wasn't going to sit opposite her as he always did. Not tonight. He slugged down the cold water and set the glass on the coffee table.

She held the glass between her hands, her eyes wounded and dark. To Garret, she looked like a broken doll in that silent moment as he ruthlessly perused her. Kira was wearing a lavender, flannel, granny grown that brought out her soft gray eyes. Eyes that were now red-rimmed.

Garret found one of her feet beneath the afghan and rubbed it gently. "Tell me what your tears are about," he said and turned, looking directly into her eyes.

Kira grimaced. "That I'm a coward. That from day one, Mr. Crawford was verbally abusive to me . . . that I took it and didn't fight back." She wiped her cheek. "God, I faced so many Taliban attacks and I fought back, Garret. I didn't bite my tongue. I didn't look away from the hatred they had for us. But now? Now, everything's different . . ." She swallowed hard, hurt in her eyes. "I'm not me anymore. I-I've lost who I am. Maybe a part of me died in that firefight. I feel like a part of my soul was ripped away from me that night. As if . . . as if it were torn away forever." She gripped the glass hard. "I'm not me anymore. I would never do what I did yesterday morning when Mr. Crawford grabbed my wrist. I should have walked out the door, but instead I stayed."

Her whispered, hoarse words shredded Garret. He closed his hand around her small, delicate foot. He was sure they were perfect feet, small toes. His fingers covered the curve of her arch, letting her know he cared more than he could ever tell her. "Something was taken from us, Kira," he rumbled. He watched her chin lift, so much anguish in her eyes that it tore him apart. "And we're never going to get it back." His mouth slanted downward and he held her tearful gaze. "We're not whole anymore. War has changed us. We didn't set out to have that happen to us, it just did. I'm sorry . . . God, I'm so sorry, because if there was one person on our team who didn't deserve this pain, it was you, Kira.

"You always brought us a smile. You gave us laughter. You hugged us and you loved us when we were hurting. You were always there for us." Garret looked away, his heart feeling as if someone were cutting it in two with a dull knife. His voice grew passionate with an emotion that coursed powerfully through him. "Kira, you're strong whether you think you are or not. Maybe you're wounded, but that doesn't take away from your heart, which is still whole. Your courage hasn't changed. There's more than enough of you left for this lifetime and don't ever think there isn't." His voice dropped with hoarseness. "Because it is enough." Tears burned hot in his eyes and he cursed silently, blinking rapidly, forcing them away.

How badly Garret wanted to open his arms and ask her to crawl into them. He needed Kira with a desperation he'd never known until now. Her gray eyes were moist, filled with an emotion he couldn't name. Whatever it was, it made him feel damned good. And when she leaned over and set the glass on the lamp stand, she turned, leaning forward, her hand sliding over his hand, which was around her foot. "Has anyone ever told you you're the best coach in the world?"

His mouth twisted. "Sweetheart, I'm telling you the truth." Garret held her watery gaze, her lower lip trembling, so many raw feelings in her eyes. Her hand on his sent a river of heat up his arm, encircling his heart as he held her grateful gaze. "I'll always tell you the truth. Always."

She moved her fingers across his hand, her touch cool and light. "You've never let me down, Garret. Next time," and Kira halted, battling tears and fighting them back, "next time I start feeling hopeless, that I've lost myself . . . my way . . . I'll remember what you just said." She gripped his hand. "Thank you, Garret."

"Do you feel like going to bed, Kira? You look so damned tired." *I want to hold you. Pull you up against me, just let you rest. To sleep.*

She removed her hand and leaned back, nodding. "Yes, I'm feeling really tired."

Garret forced himself to get up. Picking up the glasses, he said, "Come on, let's get to bed." And how he wished they could be together. Understanding Kira wasn't there saddened him. Hope rose in him as he walked into the kitchen; maybe something good had come out of all her tears after all. Kira was crying for herself, Garret realized. That she hadn't stood up to Crawford like she thought she should have. Instead, she'd taken his abuse until it escalated and worsened. Garret understood Kira was scared to death of being fired, but he knew it wouldn't happen. She didn't know these good people well enough, that they wouldn't do that to her. He wondered what would happen to Crawford. Would Shay and Reese allow him to stay here or not?

By the time he placed the glasses in the sink, Kira had gone to her room, the door closed. Halting, Garret longed to hold her. He'd be fine with pulling Kira into his arms, enfolding her against his body and allowing her to feel his full protection and not make love to her. Frowning, he turned and headed into his bedroom. Closing the door, he saw the moonlight was gone, the room dark. The clock read four a.m. He settled into the cold bed and pulled up the covers.

CHAPTER TEN

"Let's eat breakfast and then I'm going over to Crawford's place at 0700 to make his breakfast."

Kira gave him a startled look. When she'd risen at 0600, Garret was already in the kitchen, making a breakfast of pancakes filled with walnuts and diced apricots.

"But," she stammered, pouring them coffee, "I'm supposed to do that." Kira saw the grim look Garret gave her. He was dressed in a black T-shirt, a dark red flannel shirt over it, his jeans and boots. His face was shaved, his sandy-colored hair still damp from a recent shower. The cutting look he gave her made Kira go cold with fear. It wasn't that she feared him. It was fear of what he might do to Ray.

"No. Not until we get this settled," he told her. "I'll tell Crawford you're under the weather today and that I'm standing in for you. He's not going to know, at least not yet, that we're going to see Reese and Shay. All right?" and Garret gave her a significant glance.

Biting on her lower lip, Kira took the cups to the table. She'd already taken out the plates and flatware. "Are you sure you can be nice to him? Because I know you, Garret. I know you're pissed he bruised my wrist. You can't go over there and rip his head off."

"Give me more credit than that, Kira." He placed two large pancakes on a plate and covered them. "Stop looking at me like I'm going to kill the bastard. I may want to, but I won't. He needs to be brought up short and told how it's going to be or get the hell off this ranch permanently." Lips thinning, Garret looked up to see how pale Kira had become as she stood uncertainly near the table. "Don't worry," he muttered. "I'm not going to do or say anything that would give him the least intel on what's about to go down. Okay?"

She chewed on her lip more. "Yeah . . . okay . . ."

"Trust me on this?"

Walking over, Kira watched him flip two more pancakes on the huge iron griddle. "I do, Garret. I guess I'm just anxious is all."

Giving her a concerned look, Garret said

quietly, "Not to mention being fully sleep-deprived this morning?" His mouth hooked upward just enough so that Kira responded and gave him a faint smile.

"I'm feeling really raw this morning, Garret. Scared," and she wrapped her arms around herself. "I never used to be like this. It's like I've gone from being confident, stable and cool-headed to this," and she jabbed her thumb at herself.

He saw the body language and knew Kira was feeling lost and had no confidence in the situation other than she knew she had to talk to Shay and Reese. "Look, you need to take some deep breaths. You're so used to fighting dragons by yourself, Kira, that you don't entertain the thought that maybe, just maybe, there are people around who care for you. That know you're a decent person. That know you would never lie about anything. They want to help you. They'll support you in this. I know they will."

"I worry about Shay and her response to what happened." Pushing her fingers through her recently combed hair, she leaned her hips against the sink, arms across her chest as Garret continued to make more pancakes. "I mean, she handled that situation with Ray for eighteen years. To what

205

extent did he abuse her, Garret? Does anyone else know? Does Reese? I'm afraid I'll open a can of worms for Shay. Maybe she's never really told Reese the extent her father might have hurt her."

Garret's eyes clouded. "Yeah, I was thinking about that last night, too. To be a survivor of abuse usually brings a lot of shame with it. And if Shay has been abused physically, I'm sure she's not going to want to be forthcoming about it in front of all of us."

"But you know she was mentally and emotionally abused?"

"Yes. She's told me as much. Over the past year, she's trusted me more and more and opened up on the subject. That's why," Garret said bitterly, "I don't trust Crawford at all. I instinctively feel he beat her mother, who's now dead. I don't know if you bringing this up to them is going to help or hurt Shay." He slid her a comforting look. "But let's keep our focus. You're the one who got injured by Crawford yesterday. And no matter how Shay takes it, I'm not allowing it to happen again."

A coldness swept through Kira. "Every time I go over there, Garret, I'm afraid. Adrenaline starts pouring through me and I get shaky and unnerved."

"I can see that. Now I understand why you were coming home after feeding him looking pale and unsure of yourself." He gave her a soft look. "I wish . . . I wish you'd trusted me enough to tell me this from the beginning. I could have helped you a lot sooner."

She closed her eyes and rubbed her face. "I was afraid, Garret. I know how protective you are of women and children who can't defend themselves." She opened her eyes and stared at him as he put the last pancakes on a plate. "I was afraid to tell you because I knew you'd do something about it."

Garret picked up the plate and slid his other hand beneath her elbow. "You're right, I would have. Come on; I need you to eat a little something. You're going to stay here until I come back. Then we'll go over to see Shay and Reese."

Ray Crawford's face turned dark and wary as Garret came into the house. "What the hell do you want?" he snapped. "Where's Kira?"

Garret shut the door and hung his jacket and Stetson on a wall peg. "I'm going to make your breakfast, Mr. Crawford. Kira's under the weather and I told her I'd take over feeding you today. Hope you don't mind?" and he unsnapped the cuffs around his wrists and rolled up the sleeves to his elbows. "What do you feel like eating?" He turned, keeping his face carefully arranged. Garret saw the rage come to Crawford's narrowing brown eyes, his hands moving into fists on the table.

"What's wrong with her?"

"A cold, I think. Nothing to worry about."

"She's useless."

Garret reined in his anger. In a quiet tone he said, "Kira isn't useless, Mr. Crawford. She's a hard worker and she cares."

Crawford cursed under his breath. "Make me some waffles! Two of 'em. And I want bacon. Lots of it."

"More coffee?" Garret asked, pointing toward the pot on the counter. He knew Kira had the new timer working. The pot was half empty.

"Yeah, gimme some."

Garret wondered, as he filled Ray's cup, if he treated Kira just like this. Or worse? Was this how he treated his daughter? He ambled to the kitchen counter, located the new waffle iron and got busy making the old man his breakfast.

"That daughter of mine is as useless as Kira."

Garret said nothing, focusing on the food. "Yesterday Kira dropped a skillet and scared the shit out of me. She's clumsy."

Gritting his teeth, Garret didn't reply. He got the bacon in one skillet and quickly whipped up the batter to make the waffles in a bowl.

"Only good thing about women is they have offspring. Hopefully good, strapping sons."

"But you had a daughter," Garret couldn't resist pointing out as he poured the batter into the waffle iron and then closed the lid. Turning, he looked at Crawford, who had a sneer on his lips.

"I wasn't happy about it. I told my wife it was her fault. I never let her forget it."

Turning before Crawford could see the expression on his face, Garret knew he'd read what was there: disgust. Pulling down a plate, he took a linen napkin from a nearby drawer. Grabbing some flatware, he placed it in front of the rancher.

"I don't see anything wrong in having a daughter," he said.

Snorting, Crawford snarled, "They're weak!"

Hardly. But Garret wasn't going there. He wanted to get through this breakfast without World War III breaking out between them.

Busying himself, he made Crawford two waffles before he was filled up. He ate nearly half a pound of bacon, so the man was tucking it away. Garret wished Kira was eating more. She'd barely eaten six forkfuls of the pancakes he'd made for her that morning. He knew she loved apricots and had found some jam in the fridge to put it into the mix, hoping that would tease her into eating more. Kira was probably stretched thin at home, anxious and worried about the coming talk with Shay and Reese. This was dirty family laundry, the skeleton in the family closet, and Garret could hardly wait to air out the whole damn situation. Anything to protect Kira from this monster father poor Shay had been forced to grow up with.

"Ready?" Garret kept his hand beneath Kira's elbow as they stood in front of Reese and Shay's home. Garret had called over earlier to let them know they'd be heading their way and now they knocked on the door. Kira was in her green nylon parka, a red muffler around her neck, the red cap in place. Errant strands of black hair peeked out along her wan cheeks. The day was cloudy and windy. It was 8 a.m. and he'd seen Noah and Harper heading down to the barn as Kira and he had walked over to the main house.

"No," Kira whispered, grimacing, "I'm not ready, but this has to be done."

"That's the spirit," he said, holding her unsure gaze. Squeezing her elbow, Garret added, "We'll get through this together, Kira. Just like old times. The team always sticks together and helps support one another as they make it through the gauntlet."

Garret couldn't say anything else before Reese opened the door. He nodded hello to them, stepping aside. Wearing a dark blue flannel shirt and jeans, Reese was leaner and two inches taller than Garret.

They wiped their boots, hung up their coats on wall pegs and followed Reese into the warm kitchen that smelled of cinnamon rolls baking. Shay was in there, just pulling them out of the oven with two heavy mitts on her hands.

"Hi, guys," she greeted, giving them quick smiles. "Take a seat at the table. You must have smelled my cinnamon rolls, Garret. That explains why you're here."

"I didn't, but I'm good for timing, Shay. Are we getting some?"

"Oh, for sure." She laughed.

Garret pulled out a chair for Kira. There was a coffee cup at the head of the table and one on the opposite side of him. Reese brought over two more mugs and poured them coffee. Garret could see concern in Reese's eyes. The man missed little. He'd been a captain in the Marine Corps and ran a company, which was a huge responsibility. Not something everyone could do successfully, but Reese had. And now he was managing this sick, broken ranch, nursing it slowly back to health. Garret respected Reese. He worried about Shay.

"How many?" Shay called from the kitchen. "Kira?"

"Just one, thanks, Shay."

"Two for me," Garret called out, grinning.

"I thought you were going to plead for three. Even four, Garret."

Reese brought down brightly colored plates.

"Well," Garret hedged, giving her a wily look, "I might ask for seconds. Would you give them to me, Shay?" He saw her face was flushed, her cheeks a deep pink, her eyes glowing. Reese made her happy. He gave her the emotional support she needed. And he was protective of her, which was a good thing in Garret's book.

"Oh, we'll see," Shay said with a laugh, taking off her apron and laying it on the counter. She fluffed her hair and came to sit down opposite Garret. Reese took the chair at the head of the table.

Reese gave Kira a searching look. "Are you okay? You don't look well."

Garret tensed inwardly but remained relaxed-looking outwardly. He saw Kira lift her chin to meet Reese's concerned gaze.

"I need to tell both of you something that happened yesterday morning," she said, including Shay in her glance. Taking a deep breath, Kira told them what Crawford had done. And as she did, she saw Shay's face go absolutely white. Reese's eyes narrowed and his mouth tucked in at the corners, as if he were withholding a lot of unexpected emotion. When she pulled back the sleeve of her yellow sweater to show them the livid blue-and-purple bruises across her inner wrist, she heard Shay gasp.

"Oh, God!" she whispered, instantly leaning forward, her hands gently enclosing Kira's extended wrist. "Oh, no . . ."

Tears flooded into Kira's eyes. She instantly knew Shay had been physically abused by her father. It was in Shay's expression, in the strained tenor of her voice. Her hands were gentle around Kira's wrist. "I'm okay, Shay. I really am. It's just that I couldn't let this go without talking to both of you." She turned to Reese, whose

213

eyes were now hard and unfathomable. "I talked to Garret about it and we both agreed I needed to come over this morning to let you know."

"Why didn't you come as soon as it happened?" Reese demanded quietly. "Why did you wait, Kira?"

Shay released Kira's wrist and looked at her husband. "Because she was afraid, probably, that we might fire her or something." She looked at Kira. "Am I right?"

"Yes," Kira admitted hollowly. Her entire body felt like it was in a war with itself. Unconsciously, she rubbed her stomach. "And to be honest? It wasn't until Garret got home last night, and he saw the bruises, that I decided to tell you everything." She gave the couple an apologetic look. "I'm really sorry this happened. I shouldn't have tried to pick up that skillet with my injured hand." She felt Garret's fingers come to rest on her shoulder, gently smoothing the yellow sweater she wore. There was such strength in his light touch, and she felt his care wrap around her. "I was going to do it eventually, but Garret assured me you two would want to know sooner rather than later."

Reese gave his wife a tender look. "We do want to know."

Shay wiped tears from her eyes. "God, I'm so sorry, Kira. This is my fault. I didn't warn you that my father might . . ." and she choked, burying her head in her hands, sobbing.

Kira felt terrible. Reese excused himself, stood up and gently pulled Shay's chair back and gathered her beneath his arm.

"We'll be back in a little while," he assured them. "Stay here. All right?"

Swallowing hard, Kira gave a jerky nod. She was so grateful for Garret's arm across her shoulders because she felt like a rubber band that was going to snap at any second. "Y-yes, we will. I'm so sorry . . ."

Reese lost his hard look, his eyes alive with moisture. "You have nothing to apologize for, Kira. Absolutely nothing. I'm glad you came to tell us."

Kira waited until they disappeared down the hall. Miserably, she looked to Garret. "Crawford hurt her so badly . . ."

Grim, he snarled in a low tone, "Yeah . . . the bastard . . ."

Her stomach shriveled into a hard, painful knot. Kira kept rubbing the area slowly and at last it started to ease her tension. "I didn't know what to expect this morning," she told him helplessly.

"I'd always had a suspicion Crawford had

beat the hell out of her mother and then, when she died, he started on Shay. Men like him need a whipping post and Shay was a convenient one when her mother wasn't there to protect her from him anymore."

Trembling inwardly, Kira heard the rage within Garret's voice. His eyes were implacable. The only time she'd seen that look was the night of the ambush, shortly before he was struck in the head with the second bullet. A shiver moved through her and she pulled her arms around herself, feeling guilty and responsible for upsetting Shay.

"Don't go there," Garret rasped, his hand stilling on her shoulder, his fingers brushing the nape of her neck. "This has nothing to do with you, Kira. From the look on Reese's face, I'd say he was blindsided, too. I don't think Shay told him what her father had done to her. She tried to downplay it. Believe me, my old man whaled the tar out of me, and I always downplayed my bruises when one of my teachers saw them. I was ashamed. I didn't want to admit to anyone I was getting the shit beat out of me by my drunk old man."

Her heart felt deep compassion for Garret. "I'm so sorry you had to go through that."

He shrugged. "It's over. It will never happen again. Shay's a woman and her father doesn't respect her. Even now, under the right circumstances, he might go after her, physically hurt her again. He has to be stopped once and for all."

"I can't blame her for her reaction," Kira said thickly, drowning in his narrowed hazel eyes. "I feel so bad for her. For Reese. I agree; I don't think he knew all of it."

"He does now. And I'm sure Shay is sorry she didn't tell you the whole truth about her father. She left you unprotected, probably hoping her old man wouldn't do to you what he'd done to her."

The finality of Garret's growling tone made her want to shrivel up and hide. Kira knew it was a combination of the PTSD symptoms and her own inadequacy that made her unable to believe she wouldn't be let go from the job.

"W-what do you think they're going to do?"

"I don't know, Kira. There are lots of options on the table." And then Garret slanted her a look. "And there's no option on the table to fire you, so relax."

She gave him a small, hesitant smile. "Yes . . . okay . . ." Reese hadn't looked angry at her. He'd looked completely upset over his wife's unexpected reaction, the tears in his eyes, shaking Kira deeply. "I don't know how Shay survived it all, Garret. I really don't." She lifted her hand. "And to come home to a broken ranch that she had to save, while having to deal with Crawford, all with the fear he'd be abusive toward her again . . . God . . ."

"She's a strong woman," Garret agreed quietly. He began to move his hand lightly, slowly back and forth across her shoulders once more. He needed the contact with her, needed to help her in some small way. Garret could see his touch soothed Kira. He saw it instantly in her expression, and now he could literally feel her muscle tension dissolving beneath his hand.

"Shay tries so hard. She cares so deeply . . ."

"You're built the same way as her."

Startled, she blinked. "Me? Oh no . . ."

"That's what I see."

Shaken, Kira shook her head. "Look at me. It's been a year and I'm still a certifiable mess."

"You're a brave person struggling to get well. That's what I see."

"I think you're prejudiced."

Garret held her gaze and gave her a slight smile. Lifting his hand, he smoothed a few strands of hair away from her cheek. Instantly, she flushed, and he saw her black pupils enlarge. Kira liked his touch. Liked this subtle form of intimacy from him. His hope rose even higher. And whether it was right or not, Garret could visualize Kira in his arms, in his bed, him loving her fully and completely.

How he wanted to give back to this woman who had fought so long and hard by herself. She'd had no one, striking out on her own like so many vets did when returning home. The raw urge to support her, help her and be there for her, was eating him alive. And yet he had to pace himself so as not to frighten Kira off or shut her down toward him. Worse, the drama with Crawford was infecting everyone like the plague, distracting all of them. A black anger moved through Garret, but he squelched it. Kira needed him, not his own damned rage aimed at Crawford.

He squeezed his hand on her shoulder, his voice lowering. "If I'm prejudiced it's because you've always been a shining light in my life, Kira. I've seen you in so many situations: dangerous ones, happy ones. You're a person who deserves respect and support. Nothing less." Garret forced himself to remove his hand, and damned if he didn't see regret come to Kira's eyes as he did. Did she want his continued touch? Garret wanted to ask her, but it was the wrong time and place.

"Thanks," she offered softly, giving him a shy look. "So often I've fallen so far from my old self, Garret, that I forget there are still parts and pieces of me intact, deep within me. I'm not sure a shrink would understand what I'm saying, but that's how I see it: I'm cobbling myself back together, one piece at a time. And sometimes I can't find the piece I'm looking for."

"Because it's gone?"

"Yes."

Garret's mouth moved into a soft line. "You'll rebirth that missing piece sooner or later, Kira. I've found that to be true for myself. And in time I think you will, too. If you were always honest in the past, you'll be honest now and in the future. If sunsets made you cry, that will come back, too."

"You're so romantic, Garret." She marveled at his sudden insight. "You have the soul of a poet. Did you know that? I've never seen this side of you before."

Growing a bit uncomfortable, he groused, "How could I expose it in Afghanistan? The team would have thought I was going nuts. I couldn't talk to them like that. But I can with you."

She brightened a little. "I like this side of you. Stop hiding it, okay? I love what it does for me," and she placed her hand over her heart. Kira saw his cheeks turn ruddy, his gaze skitter away from hers. Garret was actually embarrassed. And he was right: The man she lived with now versus the one in Afghanistan was different. But in the best of ways. She adored his gentleness and patience with her, but that had always been shared between them. Garret was like a big, patient bull. He was that way with everyone. "I really want to know what you think, how you see things," she admitted in a low tone. "I like discovering these facets of you, Garret. You're surprising me."

His mouth quirked. "Good surprises? I'm not that bag of goat turds?"

She laughed quietly and shook her head. "I always saw you and the other guys like the knights of King Arthur's round table."

"And which one was I?"

Now it was her turn to flush. "Don't laugh: Sir Galahad."

"You're quite an idealist underneath that team cover you wore."

"Well, what was I going to do? Share that with all of you? You'd have laughed me off the team. Right?"

"Probably," Garret grudgingly admitted, a

wicked grin on his face. "So, does that make you beautiful Guinevere?" He watched her cheeks grow red. Kira hadn't paid that much attention to herself feminine-wise. She didn't wear makeup, she didn't do her hair except to wash it and pull a comb through it. Yet her grace, the sway of those small, beautifully shaped hips of hers; she was all woman. She might have worn male-type clothing, but that took nothing away from who she was: a nurturing, loving person.

"I've never seen myself like that," she admitted.

"I like you just the way you are, Kira. Your hair is longer, though, and it looks good on you."

She studied him as the quiet descended between them. The clock on the wall showed that ten minutes had passed. "Thanks. I like you just the way you are too, Garret."

"No," he deadpanned, "there's nothing fancy about me," and a small grin curved one corner of his mouth. He saw the worry gathering on Kira's brow. "They've probably got a lot to talk about in there," he told her, moving his head in the direction of the hall, where Reese and Shay had gone.

"I don't think this is going to get settled fast," Kira agreed. "Do you think we should leave? They can come to get us when they're really up for a discussion."

Garret nodded. He pulled out a notebook and a pen from his pocket. "Let's leave them a note. I can get busy repairing equipment in the barn and you can go back to your translating duties. They know where to find us."

Relief flowed through Kira as she slowly stood and pushed back her chair. "Let me clean up the kitchen for Shay. It will only take a moment."

Nodding, Garret penned a quick note and left it where Reese would see it on the table. He was sure Shay was going to be emotionally totaled for hours to come, and neither Shay nor Reese needed the pressure of thinking they were sitting in the kitchen waiting for them.

Lifting his head, Garret saw Kira quickly and efficiently clean the table, wrap up the warm cinnamon rolls and place them on the counter. His heart swelled with love for her. Even though she was under a lot of pressure herself, she still thought of others. It was one of the many things he loved about this woman he wanted to someday claim as his own.

Chapter Eleven

Reese felt relief flow through him as he picked up Garret's note and read it. His gut was in utter turmoil as he put it down on the table and turned, moving to the bedroom where Shay had gone. His love for her was fierce and he wished there was some way to shield her from what her father had done to her.

Mouth tightening as he walked down the hall to their bedroom, he ached to put a stop to her suffering and pain. But how did a person divorce a parent? The emotional ties were too deep.

As he walked into their bedroom, Shay was sitting on the small sofa in the corner, wiping her damp cheeks, giving him a shamed look.

"They've left," he told her gently, coming to sit with her once more, taking her into his arms. Shay came willingly, tucking her head against his jaw, her arm going around his waist.

"I've screwed up so badly," she uttered, her voice wobbly. "I should have told Kira the truth about my father. I-I was so ashamed of it, Reese; that's why I didn't tell her."

He moved his hand gently over her mussed hair. "I understand. We'll all get through this, Shay."

"I-I should have told you, too," and she sniffed, wiping her cheek. "I'm sorry, Reese . . . so sorry . . . I was hoping when my father came back to the ranch all that would be behind him. That he wanted to be here to get better, to take back the part of his life he loved so much."

Kissing her hair, he rasped, "In my experience, an abuser doesn't get better unless he wants to, Shay."

"I should have realized that," she whispered. "I left Kira wide open to him. And . . . he hurt her. I can't ever forgive myself for that . . ." She pressed her face into his shirt, fresh tears coming.

"Kira will live," he reassured her in a thick voice, continuing to smooth his hand slowly up and down her back. "She'll forgive you. What's more important is that we do something about it. Your father won't be allowed to do this to anyone else ever again." He eased her away just enough to look down at her shattered expression. "We need to decide what to do. Whether he can continue to live here on the ranch or not. He's recovering and getting better every day."

Nodding, Shay said, "Yes, we need to do something, but what? He wanted to come back home. I couldn't blame him. I'd hate being in a nursing home, too."

Cupping her chin, Reese looked deeply into her moist eyes. "Has he been abusing you again, Shay, since you've been home?"

Swallowing hard, she whispered unsteadily, "When I came home after getting out of the military hospital, at first he was just verbally and emotionally abusive toward me. He didn't want me back here, Reese. He wanted me gone. He told me there was no place for me at the ranch, that it was running fine without me."

"Which," Reese said grimly, "it wasn't. He'd chased off all the wranglers and the ranch had fallen into a state of disrepair. All the fences needed to be replaced and he'd lost all his pasture leases, which was his main source of income. Ray had no money coming in when you arrived."

Sitting up a bit, Shay pushed her dark hair off her cheek. "Yes, it was a mess. It took me about a month to realize what had happened." She gave her husband a sad look. "One morning here, in the kitchen, I was making us breakfast. This was after his stroke. I asked him about hiring a wrangler. He flew into a rage." Her voice dropped and Shay looked away, shame in her expression. "He slapped me. I was so shocked. I don't know why, because after Mom died he used to hit me all the time when he got angry."

Reese smoothed his fingers across her cheek. "I'm so sorry I wasn't here to protect you, Shay."

"Well," she murmured, "this time I was older and more mature. I'd spent years in the military, in combat zones, and I didn't stand there taking it. I balled up my fist and hit him in the jaw as hard as I could." She shrugged. "It shocked him. His nose was bleeding."

"Did he come at you again?"

"No. He cursed me. But he never . . . ever . . . tried to hit me again."

"You took a stand," Reese said tautly, moving his hand across her shoulders. "He never expected you to hit back."

"Yes, well, it was a heck of a step forward in our relationship, but he became even more angry and screamed at me, day in and day out. And then," she sighed, looking into the quiet bedroom, "because of the stroke, he needed more help than I could give him. I drove him to the nursing home and never regretted it. I wasn't ever going to allow him to hit me again."

"The stroke got him out of your life in a sense." Reese snorted. "Maybe it was a good thing in disguise."

Shay gave him a guilty look. "I can never say this to anyone else but you, Reese. Really, I was relieved that he'd had a stroke and needed twenty-four-hour medical attention. It was my excuse to get him off the Bar C. Because I was getting ready to leave the ranch once and for all. I wasn't going to stay here and continue to get abused by Ray even though the ranch was dying. I no longer loved him. He'd beat it out of me over time. He'd killed Mom with his rages, his alcoholism. He was still drinking like a fish when I got home from the military. He had a friend buying him liquor." She rubbed her arm and frowned. "I wasn't going to take it anymore."

"And then you put him in the nursing home and you decided to stay to try to save the Bar C."

Wiping her eyes, she nodded. "Yes. The ranch is coming back to life a little at a time."

"Listen," he told her, holding her unsteady

gaze, "you've worked miracles here not only for the ranch but for all of us vets. You should be proud of what you're doing, Shay."

"The only fly in the ointment is Ray." She shuddered. "I can't even think of him as my father anymore. All he ever did was make me fearful of him. I must have spent half my childhood either in the pastures, the barns or my bedroom, hiding from him. Trying to stay out of his way."

Kissing her wrinkled brow, Reese said, "You're so brave, so brave . . ."

Shay snuggled into his arms, resting her cheek against his broad shoulder. "I don't feel brave right now. I've let Kira down. I owe her a huge apology. I should have told her and I didn't. I was too ashamed . . ."

"Look, we can fix this," Reese urged her, kissing her temple. "We need to pull ourselves together, look at this and get Garret and Kira back over here to discuss strategy."

She moved her hand across his chest. "You're right. But I don't know what to do. I don't want to go over there and cook for him. I-I just don't have anything left inside me to protect myself from his black moods, his anger."

"No one is asking you to do that," Reese rasped, giving her a hug meant to buoy her.

"And I don't want to put Kira back in the line of fire either."

"Let's talk this out with them. You're close to Garret and I want to hear what he has to say, what he recommends. Kira will have input, too. They're trustworthy people. We'll figure this out with them. All right?"

She reached up and kissed his recently shaved jaw. "Yes. But first I need to apologize to Kira. She walked into Ray's lair not realizing what he could do to her."

Reese nodded. "Garret told me the other day she was jumpy about being fired. She was worried if she didn't do a good enough job for Ray, we'd let her go."

Stricken, Shay sat up. "We wouldn't do that! She's bringing in decent money through her translation skills. Why would she ever think that?"

He gave his wife a tender look. "Because she was fired from five other jobs in a row, that's why. And that's probably why she wasn't going to report Ray's mental and emotional abuse to us. She was going to take it, just gut through it."

"That's awful," Shay muttered, rubbing her face wearily. "Kira shouldn't take anything from Ray. Not a thing."

He rose and kissed the top of her head. "Do you feel like tackling this now? I'll

230

round up Kira and Garret."

"No, but I will," Shay said grimly, standing. "It's my responsibility to fix it."

"We will," Reese promised, sliding his arm around her shoulders, drawing her against him, holding her tightly for a moment.

Kira kept her cold, damp fingers in her lap as Reese and Shay settled down on the opposite side of the trestle table in their warm, cozy kitchen. She found solace with Garret at her side. She saw the devastation in Shay's wan face and her bleak-looking blue eyes. Her heart went out to her because she was clearly shaken. Kira wished she could do something about it. Reese was the strong, quiet one, his eyes speaking eloquently of the emotions he was experiencing.

"I need to apologize to you, Kira," Shay said in a low, trembling voice. "Ray used to beat my mother before she died. When she went, he started taking his anger out on me. I-I didn't tell you that he'd been physically abusive toward me and I should have. I didn't protect you. I can't tell you how awful I feel about not doing that. It was the coward's way out."

Kira winced. "It's okay, Shay. I understand."

"No, it's not okay. I left you vulnerable to

him." Her mouth tightened and she held Kira's gaze. "This is about me, not you. You did nothing wrong. And I take full responsibility for it. I hope you can forgive me someday."

Reaching out across the table, Kira gripped Shay's tightly clasped hands. "You're already forgiven. Don't worry about it. Okay?" and she released her hands.

Shay gave her a miserable look. "I hope you'll stay with us, Kira. I don't want you to leave. You're a good, hardworking person, honest and caring. This is all my fault, not yours."

Reese added, "Kira, we want you to stay. We need your input as to what happened over there with Ray. You were there. Tell us, please?"

Girding herself, Kira gave Garret a quick glance. He nodded his head but remained silent. Relief flowed through her as she realized they weren't going to fire her. Taking a deep breath, she told them everything. Shay looked absolutely devastated by the time she finished. Reese was tense, his face growing hard. These were military people. They knew how to put their emotions aside to think through a problem. Kira felt Garret's hand come to rest on her shoulder, a silent signal that sent a wave of reassurance through her.

"I think this is bigger than you two realize," Garret said, finally breaking his silence. He slid a glance toward Kira. "Didn't Ray tell you one time that he was going to take back the Bar C when he got better?"

Shay gasped.

Reese scowled.

Kira's eyes widened. "Oh, God, I forgot all about that!" She turned to the owners. "Yes, yes, he did say that to me one time. I'm sorry, I forgot to tell you about it."

"There's a lot that happened to you over there," Shay said, "so don't beat yourself up on forgetting some of the details."

Reese pinned Kira with a dark look. "Ray said that? Those exact words?"

"Yes, he did."

Reese gave his wife a searching look. "He told you he wanted to come home because he missed the place. He lied."

"Right. He never told me he was coming back to take the ranch back," she admitted, her voice thin with disbelief.

"Could he?" Garret demanded of them.

Reese sighed. "Technically? The ranch was originally from Shay's mother's side of the family. Her mom left it to Shay with a provision that reads that Ray is in charge as long

233

as he is physically capable. If he's incapacitated, the ranch legally belongs to Shay. But if he gets well? I don't know. There's no provision in the will for that possibility. It's a legal no-man's-land."

Garret leaned forward, clasping his hands on the table. "I think Ray's a wolf in sheep's clothing, Shay. I think he's going to get better to the point where he'll hire a lawyer and then contest the will to take back the reins and ownership of the ranch. It's clear to me he wants the Bar C back and he's willing to fight for it in court and take it away from Shay."

The table went silent. Kira saw the pain in Shay's eyes at his statement. Reese looked grim, his eyes flashing with concern at the possibility.

"And I took his money, which was roughly a hundred and fifty thousand dollars, out of the ranch account and put it into a savings account for him," Reese added. "I was protecting the nest egg he'd saved so he could continue to pay for his nursing home stay in case the ranch defaulted by missing a monthly payment."

Shay reached out, her hand falling over Reese's forearm. "You couldn't know. You were protecting him in case I couldn't keep this place solvent. If Ray's money hadn't been pulled out of the bank account, he might not have been able to pay for the nursing home where he was staying. He could have been dumped out on the street."

"Yeah," Garret said, "like we vets were after the military released us from the hospital and our military service."

Kira rubbed her brow. "This is complicated."

Reese sat back, moving his shoulders. "Ray is going to physical therapy three days a week. He's getting stronger."

"But he's had a stroke," Garret pointed out. He looked at Shay. "Has the stroke affected him mentally?"

"Sure. He's a lot more emotional. Angrier, more often. He's almost out of control sometimes."

"What about his mental capacity?" Reese pushed.

Shay shrugged. "He's forgetful. He mixes things up. I don't know whether he's lying and he knows what he's saying or not. He repeats a lot of things from the past, and when he does, it's usually a different twist on what really happened."

Garret slid a glance at Reese. "It may well be that your ace in the hole is his deteriorated mental capacity. If he takes this to court thinking he can get the ranch back with the money you helped him save because he's physically able once more, it's his mind that could make a judge not allow him to become owner again."

"God, this is a nightmare," Shay whispered, disbelief in her tone.

Reese reached out, placing his arm around her shoulders for a moment. "Would Ray do this? Take us to court?"

Shay nodded miserably. "Every time I go over to see him, he regales me with stories from the past about the ranch, how much he loves it, how much he misses it. I think he would do it. God, I hope I'm wrong." She gave Reese a distressed look. "We don't have the kind of money to fight a court battle."

"I know that. But let's just take this a step at a time."

"Yes," Garret growled, unhappy. "Shay, you need to keep a log or journal of your father's daily mental status. If this goes to court you're going to need conversations and proof of his mental incapacity."

"Yes," she whispered. "This keeps building into a worse nightmare scenario. I feel like we're fighting so hard to get the ranch on its feet, but every time we go one step forward, we get knocked back down on our knees."

"It's the nature of the beast," Garret soothed. "But one thing's in our favor: We've all been in the military. We've all seen combat. We know what it takes to hold the line and fight back and fight smart."

"That's all good," Reese agreed, "but we need to deal with what's going on right now with Ray." He looked at Kira. "I don't want to put you back over there under the circumstances."

Kira shook her head. "Listen, if he's really gunning to take the ranch away from you, I think I'm in the perfect position with him. Don't you? He talks and raves all the time when I come over to make his meals. I can start recording what he's saying, keeping a daily log of it. And if it does come to a lawsuit, I'll be a witness." She gave Garret a hopeful look, but he was scowling. So was Reese.

"Look," Reese said, "it's clear that I need to go over there and tell Ray he can no longer behave as he has toward you, Kira. Whether you go back there to care for him or not is another thing we have to determine."

Kira leaned forward. "I think it's fine that you talk to him. Give him boundaries, things he can't do to me or Shay or anyone here at the ranch. But he does chatter a lot

237

when I go over to make him meals. If he's really plotting to take back the ranch, I'm the perfect foil. I have a very good memory. I'm a translator, and I don't forget very much of what's said to me. When I leave his house, I can go over to ours and write down the conversations. I can type them up and give them to you to keep, just in case."

"Reese, I'm going over with you," Garret growled. "I think Ray needs to understand we're not going to allow him to abuse anyone. At any time. And I think you need to tell him if he does, you and Shay will remove him from the ranch. He can go back to the nursing home or wherever else he wants to go."

Shay's eyes widened and she looked from Garret to Reese. "He's liable to explode over that."

"So what?" Garret bit out. "What's he going to do? Have another stroke that finishes him off?" Giving Shay an apologetic look, he added, "Sorry, Shay, but I'm really protective of Kira. She shouldn't be going over there at all. He's a mean, miserable bastard who has always taken out his rage on others. That has to stop. Now. Forever. And if we don't give Ray really strong, restrictive boundaries, he'll push through them, as usual. He's got to know that whatever Reese tells him is the law, and he'll act on it. Immediately."

Crestfallen, Shay nodded. "You're right, Garret. I wish . . . I wish he weren't my father. I have no love for him, but I'm his daughter. There are days when I feel so torn that I don't know what to do."

"Let me continue to make his meals," Kira pleaded. "So long as he stops his abuse, I can handle the situation. I can be your eyes and ears should it ever come to a court battle." She gave Reese a pleading look. "Please let me continue over there?" She saw the hesitation in his eyes.

"Are you sure, Kira?" Garret gave her a worried look.

"I'm positive. If you guys go over there and tell Ray he has to change, I can handle the rest." She saw Garret's green-and-gold eyes go dark with concern. "You don't have a choice in this. Ray is going to get a little stronger every week. I truly think he's going to get to the point where he can ride a horse and do some of the work around here. He's only forty-nine years old."

"Could it be that we're wrong?" Shay asked softly. "Maybe he's not trying to take the ranch back."

Reese gave his wife a gentle look. "You

know him better than us. What do you think?"

Garret spoke up. "Shay, I've been around your old man for over a year now. Given what you've shared with me as a friend about him, I think he's serious. He's on a mission to jerk this ranch out from under your feet. Don't try and idealize him; it will only set you up for a fall, in my opinion."

Kira felt her heart thud with pain for Shay. She looked devastated and utterly exhausted. "It's okay, Shay. If I'm over there as a spy of sorts, recording the conversations we have, it's intel we could use should you ever need it."

"Garret, you're right about Ray." Shay shook her head and gave them an apologetic look. "He's always been a wolf in sheep's clothing. And he might have had a stroke, but it didn't change that side of him. He's always been protective of this ranch. Always bragged how it's a family treasure and he's done such a good job of keeping it going." Her mouth twisted. "Which we know is a lie because he's an alcoholic and he let the ranch slide into the position it's in now."

"He's still drinking, Shay," Garret added gently. "I can't prove it yet, but I know he's drinking. I know you don't want to hear it, but you've got to take off your rose-colored glasses about your father. My old man, Cal, is an alcoholic. I grew up with the bastard. And Ray was made from the same mold. I'd bet my right arm that he's getting alcohol from someone."

"Then," Reese said, "we need to prove it. It's just that much more ammunition for our side if this goes to court." He gave his wife a warm look. "I'm sorry, Shay, but your father has a lifelong history of drinking. We need everything we can discover about him."

"I know," she whispered brokenly. "Garret's right. We need to find out for sure."

"I'll do that," Kira told them quietly. "Once we get Ray to agree to stop the abuse, I can do the footwork on this. I go in and make his bed, clean up his room and do the washing. He wouldn't think anything of me opening and closing dresser drawers or his clothes closet. If he's drinking, he's hiding it. But I can start actively looking for the bottles."

"And when you find them," Garret said, "take cell phone photos of them. Make sure the photos are date-stamped, too. You can start watching how much he's drinking because the bottle is going to show it. You take photos and leave the bottles where you find them. It's that simple."

"That's a good idea," Reese agreed. "You okay with doing all this black ops stuff, Kira?"

She smiled a little. "Just like old times, isn't it? Only it's not Afghanistan, it's here."

Garret gently moved his hand across her bunched shoulders. "You were a good operator over there. You know how to conduct a search. Ray doesn't respect women anyway, and he's sure as hell not going to suspect you're looking for his stash. He'll think you're too stupid to find it. Let him think that. It works in our favor."

Distressed, Shay said, "He told me he stopped drinking after he had the stroke."

Garret gave her a sad nod. "Take it from me, Shay: If an alcoholic or, for that matter, anyone hooked on any kind of drug, doesn't want to stop, he won't. My old man is still drinking like a loon."

She opened her hands. "But his doctors all have said that if he keeps drinking, he's going to shorten his life by twenty years."

"It doesn't impact them that way," Garret told her grimly. "Ray is going to continue to drink. There's nothing you can do about it. No one can. I'm sorry, Shay. I know how much this hurts you. I know you wanted the best for him. But he controls and makes his own decisions about his life."

Reese sighed. "Yeah. For sure. Okay," he said, looking at his watch, "Garret, you and I need to have that talk with Ray. I don't want Kira going back over there to make his lunch without him knowing we aren't putting up with his abusiveness anymore."

Garret rose. "Let's go. I'm more than ready to confront him."

Kira started to rise, but Garret placed a hand on her shoulder. "Why don't you hang with Shay for a while? Make us a fresh pot of coffee. Maybe get those cinnamon rolls out. We'll come back here as soon as we've had that talk and fill both of you in. And later, I'll get to Noah and Harper to let them know what's going down."

"Yes," Kira said, seeing Shay nod in agreement over the idea, "we'll wait here."

Reese said, "Good planning. Ready, Garret?"

Grimly, Garret said, "More than ready. Let's go."

CHAPTER TWELVE

It was nearly eleven a.m. when Reese and Garret returned to the main house. Kira sat stiffly, anxiety running through her, hands tightening around her coffee mug, as the two cowboys entered the kitchen. Both were looking grim.

Garret poured them coffee and they sat down at the table. Then he grabbed one of the cinnamon rolls.

Reese sat down, giving his attention to Shay. "Your father is pissed off as hell, but he got that we were serious about how he was treating you and Kira."

Garret said, "Kira, he knows he has to treat you with respect. He got that message in spades."

Nervously, her fingers moved around the warm cup. "You think he really did?"

Garret smiled a little. A wolfish smile. "Reese put the screws to Ray. Told him that if you complain about his behavior to you, he's out of here permanently."

"Oh, I bet that went over well," Shay muttered, worried.

"He started with a bunch of gibberish about still owning the ranch," Reese told her. "I cut him off, told him that he had no legal legs to stand on, and that because you and I are the owners, we set the rules. And if he doesn't follow our wishes, he'll go back to the nursing home or wherever else he chooses to go."

"What did he say to that?" Shay asked.

"He was shocked we came over and confronted him. I don't think anyone has ever done that before," Reese said. "He's a bully, Shay. And a bully, when confronted, melts away. He didn't say anything. He just sat and listened."

"He agreed to be *nice* to everyone," Garret told them. "I'll believe that when I see it, but for now, we have to trust Ray to do what he said he would." He held Kira's searching gaze. "He'll never touch you again," he said gruffly. "Ray knows that if it ever happens, he's dealing directly with me."

"And that he's off the ranch permanently," Reese added. "He's not getting any second chances."

Kira said, "I hope this works. I really do."

"Lunch is in an hour," Garret said, "so

let's see how Ray reacts to you."

She nodded and sipped her coffee. Garret had eaten two cinnamon rolls already. Her stomach was rolling with nausea and she had no desire to eat anything. Kira wasn't going to tell any of them how this was affecting her, but the glint in Garret's eyes alerted her that he knew she was feeling anxiety. For her, it was like entering a war zone when it came to dealing with Ray Crawford. And he wasn't someone who could be relied on for logical actions or reactions. It made her feel nervous and flighty, but she wanted to put herself in the line of fire for Shay and Reese. These two people loved the Bar C for all the right reasons. If Ray ever got the ranch back, he'd destroy it, given time.

"In a way," Shay offered, "I feel like we're on a battlefield and Ray is our mutual enemy. And he's a powerful one. I know his stubbornness. When he sets his mind to something, he never veers from his goal."

Kira reached across the table and touched her hand. "It is a war, but it's one worth fighting. I'm happy to support your and Reese's vision for this ranch."

"Thank you," Shay said, gripping her hand and squeezing it. "You're the person

who's really under fire with Ray. I worry
—"

"Don't," Kira said strongly. "I've survived
things I shouldn't have already. I'll make
this work." She saw some hope come to
Shay's blue eyes. The woman had been
totaled by what had happened and she felt
badly for her. Kira was so glad she had a
father who loved her, who was a good man
and nothing like Ray. They had both lost
their mothers, but even then, Kira felt lucky.
Her mother, while having deep depression,
still had been a constant in her life, or at
least tried to be. Shay's mother had been an
abuse victim, so Shay had no one to protect
or support her growing up. Kira now understood why, even when she was beaten down,
she still had confidence in herself. Shay
didn't, and that was where Reese's love and
support had become vital as she rebuilt and
strengthened her weakened foundation.

"I'll still worry," Shay admitted.

"I'll be there for her," Garret promised.

Kira felt her heart open wide with a fierce
love for this man who'd made it clear he
would protect her. She gave Garret a soft
smile. Reaching over, she briefly touched
his arm. "You always were."

"Always will be," he growled, pinning her
with a burning look.

■ ■ ■ ■

Kira saw a remarkable difference in Ray's demeanor when she entered his house to make his lunch. He was sitting at the table with a book of crossword puzzles, pencil in hand.

"What would you like for lunch, Mr. Crawford?" she asked, trying to sound light and relaxed, though she felt anything but. She went to the kitchen counter and tied on the red-and-white-checked apron.

"Not too hungry. How about just a tuna sandwich? Some sweet pickles?"

The tone of his voice was shockingly different. Still, Kira saw anger banked in his eyes, although he refused to meet her gaze.

"Of course." Kira felt so tense that she might snap, but she kept taking deep, slow breaths to minimize her anxiety. She forced herself to focus and not use her weak hand to pick up anything heavy. In no time she had his food prepared and brought over to the table. She didn't expect a *please* or *thank you* from Ray. That would be asking too much.

"I'll go tidy up your bedroom," she said, taking off her apron. It was something she did either after breakfast or lunch.

"Whatever."

Well, okay, she could live with his minimal replies. At least they weren't laden with frustration and impatience as before. Kira hurried through the living room, picking up the strewn parts of a newspaper from the floor. In the bedroom, she partially closed the door. Hurrying to the dresser, she quietly opened every drawer. In a middle drawer, beneath a stack of T-shirts, she found a bottle of whiskey. Taking her iPhone, she snapped a picture of it, then sat it up on the dresser to see where the level was. The bottle was half empty. She took another photo.

She felt some triumph as she placed the bottle back into the drawer. Kira knew the proof would further devastate Shay, who hoped her father was on the wagon. The pain she was going through was awful and unending. Kira felt for her. In no time, she had the bed made, the bathroom cleaned and picked up. Taking the dirty clothes to the washer on the porch, Kira's duties were complete.

As she put on her parka to leave, she asked, "What would you like for dinner tonight, Mr. Crawford?"

"A roast with potatoes, carrots and celery. I want gravy, too."

"Okay, sounds good. I'll be back later to get it started." She left, and as she hurried through the cloudy day, snowflakes lazily twirling around her, Kira saw Garret talking with Noah and Harper in the barn aisle. She was sure he was filling them in on what was going on.

Once in the house, she wrote down everything and made a file for the pictures. Her translation duties were next and she hurried to her office. In about fifteen minutes Garret would be coming over for lunch.

Garret entered the kitchen. "Kira?" he called down the hall. "You around?" He'd just got finished talking with Noah and Harper. It was 1300 and he was hungry.

"I'm in here," she called from her office. "Just a moment . . ."

"Okay," he said, going to the kitchen. He'd started a navy bean soup early that morning with a ham hock, and now he lifted the lid, inhaling the scent, satisfied it was ready. He heard Kira's quick footfalls coming down the hall as he whipped up some corn bread batter. Twisting a look over his shoulder, he said, "How'd it go with Crawford?"

"So far, so good," she said. "Need help?"

"Yes. Could you get out the paper cups?

I'm going to make us some corn bread muffins to go with our soup."

She nodded and turned, opening a cupboard. "Ray was very subdued."

"Was he nasty to you?"

"No." She pulled out an aluminum pan and put the paper cups in them. "He hardly looked at me. It went okay. I found a bottle of whiskey in his dresser drawer."

Garret halted for a moment, bowls in hand. "You did?"

"Yes. I took photos." She frowned. "We have to tell Shay and Reese."

Grunting, he said, "We'll do it after lunch. You have those photos saved on your laptop?"

"Yep, I'm ahead of you." She sighed. "I feel so bad for Shay. She's hurting."

"I know," he said, slipping her a concerned look. "How are you holding up?"

"Okay. I mean, it was nerve-racking for me, but I just kept it light and breezy. He was really, really subdued. Amazing."

"He'd better stay that way."

Hearing the checked anger in his tone, Kira slid the pan toward him so he could pour the batter into the cups. "How are Noah and Harper taking all this?"

"Harper, being the wry wit he is, said this sounded like a soap opera in the making.

Of course he was teasing."

"He's a very sensitive guy. He was a combat corpsman. I can't say I disagree with his analysis. Just wish it wasn't happening to us. We're the last people you want in that kind of scenario. We have our own PTSD drama going on inside us, 24/7/365. We don't need another one on top of everything else. It's super stressful."

Sliding the muffins into the oven, Garret straightened. "Shay's a mess, and she's going through a lot, with the physical abuse being uncovered. But she has Reese and he'll help her. And we'll be there to support her, too."

Sobering, Kira said, "We all need someone." It came out sounding wistful, and she saw Garret's eyes suddenly narrow on her. It wasn't upsetting. It was . . . well . . . comforting. She saw so much in his hazel eyes for a split second and then it was gone. How she wished he would really open up to her.

"We need one another," Garret agreed thickly, "no question. I wish I could do more for Shay, but we all know the internal battleground where she was wounded. It comes down to each of us doing the hard inner work to heal it. Reese can be there to listen to her, and I know how important it is for a woman to be able to talk." He gave her a teasing grin.

"Phooey, like men don't need to talk, too? Give me a break, Fleming."

His lips curved. "I like you feisty. You always were over in Afghanistan."

She sighed. "Yeah, I lost a lot of myself back there. I know that." Brightening, she held his smile, feeling warmth and something wonderful but unnamed flow powerfully through her. "But around you, it seems to all come back."

He came over and cupped her face, angling her chin just a little upward so he could hold her soft gray gaze. "See? You think you've lost parts of yourself, but you know what? I think it's still there. Just under some rocks and dirt is all." He released her and stepped back. "Let's have some coffee while we wait for the muffins to bake."

Shaken by his unexpected intimacy, her flesh dancing with delight where he'd placed his roughened palms against her, Kira could barely breathe for a moment. The look in Garret's eyes made her run hot with longing. It took her by surprise. The man was sex on a stick as far as Kira was concerned. There was nothing about Garret that was a turnoff. He was everything she wanted. "Yes . . . coffee," she agreed, a little breathless. Anything to get this hunger within her tamped down. Every cell in her body knew Garret would be a tender lover. Her skin tightened just imagining him kissing her, running his hands over her body. Kira was amazed, as always, at how Garret could incite her body to a riot of keen longing.

Garret placed the mugs on the table and sat down. "Tell me about the whiskey."

She pulled her cell phone from her pocket, brought up the photos and handed it to Garret. Sitting down, she took a sip of the hot, black coffee, hoping it would calm her down. Mystified because, as intimate as Garret had suddenly become, he seemed far removed from that now. In part, she knew a black ops person had a single-focus ability like no other. But in the moment he'd devoted all his attention to her, she'd felt like she was the sun in his world. Garret always made her feel special, fully desired and wanted. She saw his mouth purse as he studied the photos she'd taken.

"Okay, good work," he praised, handing the phone back to her. "Check tomorrow after lunch. We need to understand how much he's consuming daily."

"What about the person he's getting to buy it for him?"

Garret sipped his coffee. "First, let's see

how much he's drinking. That would be key testimony in a court case should this thing go to trial. Then, we'll find the guy whose doing it for the money."

"I didn't smell any alcohol on his breath. I made a point of getting close enough when I put down his food in front of him."

"He might not be drinking every day."

"I hope this doesn't escalate, Garret. Shay and Reese can't afford a hundred-thousand-dollar court case if things go in that direction."

"I know."

"That kind of money isn't just laying around."

"Noah has a horse he's been working with since he's been here. It had been abused by its previous owner."

"Broken by it?"

"As in a broken spirit, yes. Noah has been trying to put him back together again. The sheriff's department is interested in buying some trail-trained horses for finding lost children and hikers in the Salt River Range. That's a twenty-thousand-dollar horse once he gets it fully trained. Did you realize that?"

"No. I knew it took a year or more to make a trained trail horse, but I had no idea."

"Noah says the horse is coming along well."

"What do you mean?"

"Talk to Noah sometime in depth, but he'll tell you there's a fast and a slow way to train a horse to a high level of performance. The fast way uses negative training methods. The slow way uses positive reinforcement. The horse was trained by a man who used what I consider torture to get the animal to do what he wanted. Noah has been working to gain his trust and uses positive reinforcement instead. The horse is responding well, and Noah thinks in another three months he'll be ready to be put up for sale. He's going to stipulate that a woman officer or deputy work with the horse because the horse's trust in men is pretty well shot. Maybe it could be Sarah Carter's horse."

"Except that he trusts Noah."

"Everybody trusts that dude," Garret said wryly. "Even me, and I'm not good at trusting many people."

She tilted her head, thinking over his statement. "You always trusted me from the moment we met. How do you explain that?"

Garret managed a one-cornered smile. "It was easy, Kira. Anyone with two eyes in their head would trust you the moment you stepped into their life."

She felt a powerful flare of hope in her heart as he gave her an intimate look that couldn't be construed any other way. "I never knew you felt that way about me."

"Couldn't say a thing in Afghanistan. We were a team and there wasn't any room left over for any kind of relationship other than the professional one we maintained."

"Yes," Kira said, remembering the hundreds of times she'd wanted to reach out and touch his arm, his hand. Just small gestures to let him know she appreciated him, but Kira knew that such errant contact would cause problems in the team. It was okay to be a friend — at a distance. Nothing close. Nothing . . . well . . . intimate or suggestive.

"I wanted something more with you, Kira, but at the time it wasn't going to fly."

Kira's heart bounded once, hard, in her chest as Garret's roughened voice fell across her. At first she thought she was making it up because there was nothing she wanted more than continued intimacy with him. She took a sip of coffee. Her heart warring with her head, considering his statement, she folded her hands in front of her. "We were always good at working with each other," she began, feeling a throb in her throat. Kira longed to have the diplomatic words she needed, but she was far from being a diplomat. Her parents had taught her to be honest at every juncture. And sometimes true honesty and diplomacy clashed. She pushed some strands of hair from her cheek, tucking them behind her ear.

"We grew to be best of friends," Garret said.

"Yes . . . yes, we did." Kira felt his gaze burrowing into her, as if he could see right through her and read her mind. Sometimes she thought Garret could do that. He seemed to sense or somehow read her emotions.

Feeling as if she were on a balance beam, Kira knew she couldn't blurt out how she really felt about him. At least not yet. He was offering her something, though, even if she didn't know where it might lead. Maybe just a deeper friendship? She wanted so much more than that. Compressing her lips, she stole a look at his serious expression. "My mom and dad always taught me that friendship was the best basis for a deeper relationship of any kind."

"Were your parents friends first?" he wondered.

"Yes, they were. They met and became friends because they worked at the timber company together. Mom was an office assistant at the time. My father was an axman, out in the woods cutting down trees. She was a budding wildlife photographer, and on weekends he'd drive her around on the back roads in the area, showing her where there were deer and other animals to photograph."

"As I recall, you always had a camera in your hands in the sandbox."

"Yes." She smiled fondly over calling Afghanistan the sandbox. It was. "I guess I picked up my mom's love of photography."

"You were always taking photos of the children, mothers and anything else who would stand still two seconds."

Laughing, she said, "That's true." And then she became somber. "I lost all my photos, and my camera, after that ambush."

"What do you mean?"

She traced a pattern in the wood of the table. "Well . . . I woke up at Bagram hospital and things were hectic. I tried to find out about the rest of the team . . . about you . . . but no one knew anything. I passed out and woke up a day later in Landstuhl. I asked a nurse what happened, and he told me only you and I had survived. I was devastated. It was only after I was transferred to Bethesda that I thought to ask where my duffel bag was. Everything I owned was in that bag. We all had them at the Afghan village. My camera and the cards that held all the photos were in the duffel bag. When it finally reached me, half the contents were missing, including my camera and the cards. They're all gone. I wished I'd had those photos so I could give them to their wives, parents or girlfriends, but they were lost."

"Damn," Garret muttered. "I'm sorry, Kira. I know how much pleasure photography gave you."

"It was a way to escape the bone-crushing poverty those poor Afghans lived with every day. I could take a photo of a mother with her baby and then show it to her on the screen of my Canon D7. I just loved the way she would look so surprised. Usually they'd burst into tears because they'd never seen anything like it before. I was planning, once I got stateside, to make copies I could send back to them, but that never happened."

"Do you have a camera now?"

Shaking her head, she said, "No." She held up her left hand. "My last two fingers don't work well. I have to hold the camera still to get the photo. My dad, bless him, wanted to buy me another Canon when I came home.

He wanted to give me Mom's old 35-millimeter camera, but I didn't take it. I had trouble holding it in this hand." Pain worked through her chest. "It was just one more thing I'd done before but now couldn't."

"And it devastated you?"

She gave him a searching look. "Yes. Because photography has always been an escape for me. I can see the radiance in a child's face, the beauty in a woman's face or a colorful landscape. I can lose myself in them. Even the Afghan desert had its beautiful moments, the way the sun slid across the land, creating depth, shadows and textures."

"I think," Garret said, "you see beauty no matter where you are, Kira. It's one of the many things I've always admired and liked about you."

She felt his thick voice move through her like a lover's caress. Oh, if only it was so! The tightening of her lower body, that primal animal that resided within her, wanted Garret to touch her, explore her, but she forced herself to stop thinking in those terms. "Thanks."

"Maybe someday you'll get another camera."

"Well, not right now. The Canon I want

costs over a thousand dollars and I don't have that kind of money. And I won't ask my dad either. I have to get back on my feet and earn it."

"Working here, you can save for it."

"That's what I'm hoping. Fingers crossed."

Garret pushed away from the table. "Okay, time to take those muffins out of the oven," and he gave her a tender look. "You just sit there. My turn to wait on you."

A frisson of warmth wound through Kira. "You're spoiling me, Garret."

He chuckled as he pulled on a mitt and opened the oven door. He pulled out the corn bread muffins. "You deserve a little care and attention."

What to say to that? She sat there, watching him fill two bowls with the fragrant navy bean soup sprinkled with carrots, onions and celery. So many memories of Afghanistan, of working with him and the team, flowed through her. It was partially pain mixed with happiness. Every day it seemed to her Garret was becoming more open toward her. She loved the way he touched her, even unexpectedly.

Kira said nothing, watching him work at the counter. Garret turned and approached, placing a bowl of soup in front of her. He sat down at her elbow. "Okay," he said gruffly, "dig in. Eat all of it. I need to get that weight back on you."

Kira felt a blush flowing up into her face as she drowned in his green-and-gold eyes. Her heart wrenched in her chest, wanting closer contact with Garret. Wanting to kiss him and knowing she couldn't, Kira reached out and touched his upper arm. "This is a wonderful meal. Thank you."

Garret lay awake, naked, on his bed, his hands behind his head. On the dresser opposite the bed, the clock read two a.m. He'd awakened out of nowhere, but that was so usual that he thought nothing of it anymore. The room was quiet. He heard the hoot of an owl somewhere outside. It wasn't that close, giving the sound a haunting quality. Moonlight leaked silently around the drapes.

Garret wondered if Kira was sleeping. He hoped so. Closing his eyes, he smiled to himself, always wanting to remember the priceless expression on her face as he'd cupped her face with his hands. The way she reacted had moved him deeply. Kira liked his touch. That much he knew from his bold action. For the past twenty-four hours, since she'd been hurt by Crawford, he'd wanted to hold her. It was out of the question, but he was driven to do something. The look in her flawless gray eyes after the shock of his gesture was pure, melting beauty.

Garret had an answer to an important question that had always hung silently between them. Kira had enjoyed his touch. He'd seen it register in her eyes and something else, too. Arousal? Could that be right? Could she really desire him? Only time and patience would tell. It felt damn good to do something nice for Kira. Garret wanted to do so much more for her.

Worry dissolved around him and he dragged in a sigh of relief because Kira had agreed to allow their relationship to flourish. Jesus, if she only knew how much he wanted it to grow, that he wanted a long, exploratory, intimate relationship with her. He knew she wasn't ready for that kind of admission from him yet. Still, just stealing a touch here and there, he felt like a greedy, sneaky thief, but he didn't care. He was driven to connect with Kira. Had to feel her firm, warm skin beneath his fingertips. Just getting to cradle her face in his hands those few stolen times had fed his heart and soul.

His brows fell. He wondered if Crawford was going to continue to be *nice* to Kira.

Every protective hackle rose in him toward her. He was damned if the man was ever going to hurt her again.

CHAPTER THIRTEEN

Kira showed Reese and Shay the evidence of Ray's continued drinking through mid-November. Garret sat at her elbow, quiet as usual. For the past three weeks they'd had weekly meetings, going through the information Kira was compiling for them. That and the iPhone photos of the bottle of whiskey Ray preferred and consumed regularly.

She pushed the hard copies of the photos for the last week toward the couple, showing how much Ray was drinking. It hurt her to see Shay wince visibly, her eyes dark with pain. Did an alcoholic ever realize the anguish he or she was putting the rest of the family through? Kira didn't think so. She felt Garret slide his arm around her shoulders lightly, as if reading her mind and reassuring her, even though she'd said nothing. How she looked forward to those times when he embraced her. It was never often and always unexpected, but she lapped up the contact like a starving dog.

"This week," Kira said gently, holding Shay's gaze, "your father has been drinking a cup of whiskey a day."

"Then," Reese said, looking at the photos and scowling, "he's drinking more, not less."

"Yes," Kira confirmed sadly.

"But he's still being nice to you?" Shay asked.

"The same as the first day after Reese and Garret talked to him. He won't meet my eyes. He pays attention to the crossword puzzle magazine in his hands."

"He doesn't seem to be opening up and chatting with you like before," Reese observed.

"No, he's really closed down toward me." Shrugging, Kira added, "Probably because he's worried about getting thrown off the ranch."

"For now he's meek," Garret warned them. He picked up his coffee and took a drink. Setting it down on the table, he added, "I've seen my old man go through periods like that. It always happened after I confronted him. But at some point he turned back to his old, wonderful self and became angry and abusive toward me again." He slid a glance toward Kira. "I'm just waiting for him to make that change." Gesturing to the photos between them, he added, "And this week Ray has been drinking more than ever before, so something is eating at him."

"He hasn't said anything to you at all, Kira?"

Kira shook her head. "Nothing. The minimum of words to answer whatever questions I might ask him."

"You're taking him to his primary care doctor tomorrow," Shay said, grimacing. "I'm wondering what those tests will show. I'm worried his liver function is going to show up being worse."

"It has to," Garret said. "He's been drinking roughly a bottle of whiskey a week."

Reese gave his wife a look. "Can you call his doctor to ask Ray to be screened for alcohol in his blood? Elevated levels?"

"Yes, of course. I was going to call him today anyway, to let him know what we've discovered."

"Whatever you do," Garret warned her, "don't let the doctor tell Ray we know he's drinking again. We're still trying to find out who's supplying him; we need that for evidence in case you ever wind up in court. Besides, even if the doctor let him know he's aware he's hitting the bottle, Ray would just keep on drinking."

"No worries," Shay promised. "He's a good doctor and will understand."

Reese studied the photos. "We need to talk about Thanksgiving."

Shay sighed and looked at Garret and Kira. "We want to invite everyone here for Thanksgiving. Last year Garret made all the fixings though I helped him a little. This year," her voice lowered with worry, "my father will be here with us. I can't not invite him to the dinner, but at the same time I don't know what kind of mood he'll be in. I wanted the day to be special, happy, like last year."

"He'll stand down and behave himself," Garret told her. "And I'd like to make the dinner again if you don't mind."

Shay brightened. "Oh, I'd love that, Garret."

He grinned a little and turned to Kira. "You weren't here, but it was a very good meal I fixed for all of us."

"The gravy," Shay sighed, "was divine. Garret's so good at cooking. We call him the Gravy King."

"I'd love to help you," Kira said, "if you don't mind me underfoot?"

"Sure, we work well over at our house. No reason we can't do it over here, too."

Kira smiled. "Then that's settled, Shay. Garret and I will do the honors. All you, Noah, Harper, Reese and Ray have to do is show up."

"I worry Ray will spoil it," Shay admitted hesitantly.

Reese shook his head. "I think Ray knows where he stands with us. I don't believe he'll pull anything," he told his wife.

"I don't either," Garret chimed in.

"But it won't be the same," Shay stressed softly. "Last year was so much fun. We had so much laughter, so many jokes and good times. I know Ray will drag it down. He's always so pessimistic."

"You know," Kira said, looking at all of them, "maybe we can use a different strategy. How about, because Ray is so used to me, that I ask him to help us with the dinner? Get him involved? It will just be me, Garret and him in the kitchen. That might loosen him up. Maybe make him feel important? Like he's part of the team?"

"That's a good idea," Garret murmured, giving her a proud look. "I can handle it if you can, Kira."

"Sure. I deal with him daily; maybe this is what he needs. Maybe it will show him that we're a big, sloppy, happy family of sorts?"

Shay looked dumbfounded. Kira felt happiness thread through her. "I really think he's lonely over there. He's at a point where he could use his walker if he wanted to go outside. We keep the sidewalk clear and free of ice and snow, but every time I ask him if he'd like some fresh air, he just grunts like an old grizzly bear and shakes his head."

"He loves the outdoors," Shay said. "He's always hated being indoors."

"Maybe he's depressed," Kira wondered out loud. "My mother had terrible depression, and he has all the signs and symptoms of it. Like he's given up and has no connection with the joy in life, the beauty of it."

"He's an alcoholic," Garret reminded her grimly. "Liquor steals a person's soul, just as recreational drugs do. It takes them out of reality."

"This time of year," Reese said, "the Salt River Range is beautiful. You can see it from our back door."

Kira gave Garret a beseeching look. "What if I could cajole him into coming with me to the barn? You're always working out there on all the equipment. Maybe Ray would find some interest in that. He's a guy. He knows mechanical stuff like you do."

"I don't care," Garret said. "With the amount of alcohol he's drinking daily he's high all the time. I don't know that anything like what you're suggesting would be of interest to him, Kira." He gave her a look of regret.

"I think it's worth a try," Kira said stubbornly, waiting for Shay and Reese to approve her idea.

"My father was always tinkering on the equipment," Shay said. "Midday it's the warmest it will be and might be a good time to drive him over to the barn, Kira."

"Sure."

Garret studied Kira beneath his lashes as she worked at the kitchen sink, preparing grilled cheese sandwiches for lunch. She was slender and small, her movements graceful as she turned the sandwiches in the skillet. Her black hair was resting on her neck and looked winsome. Garret was glad she was allowing it to grow longer; it brought out her natural femininity, which had been hidden in Afghanistan. The hair was now below her nape and soon, in another month or so, would begin to touch her shoulders. He smiled, liking the way blue highlights danced through her hair because of the bright, sunny light filtering through the window over the sink.

The sky was finally free and clear of storm clouds, the sun shining strongly on the two feet of snow that had fallen in the valley over the last couple of days. It took the snowplows a lot of time to clear some of the back roads and the road to the Bar C was no exception. It wouldn't last long, this sunny weather, but Garret wanted to get out in it instead of being inside the barn.

"Did you know Shay has a small Canon camera?" he asked.

Kira looked up. "No."

"Yeah. I asked her yesterday if she would lend it to you and she was fine with it." He saw Kira's eyes light up with interest as she transferred the toasted cheese sandwiches to a plate.

"Really? She's okay sharing it with me?"

"I told Shay you were a photographer and that you lost your good Canon and all your photos. She brought the PowerShot SX50 out and it's in the foyer of their mudroom. There's a card in it and the battery is charged."

Kira handed Garret his plate and sat down. "Wow, that sounds wonderful." And then she laughed a little, putting a paper napkin across her lap. "Not that I have a whole lot of time to spend on anything but work."

Picking up the sandwich, he gave her a slight grin. "I'm going into town after lunch.

Want to come with me? There's always deer or elk along the highway just before we get into Wind River. If we stopped it should give you some good shots of whatever we see. Would you like to do that?" Garret wanted quality time alone with Kira. She needed it for a lot of reasons, especially working with Crawford, but he was being completely selfish in wanting her all to himself. He had a plan and he was going to damn well implement it.

"Sure, I'd love to!" And then she frowned. "Are you sure Shay doesn't mind me using her Canon?"

"Positive. She told me she's a fair-weather photographer and has no interest in using it during the winter months."

"Gosh, that's eight or nine months out of the year," Kira remarked.

Garret saw a flush come to her cheeks, her gray eyes suddenly taking on a sparkle of excitement. In that moment she looked like a child who had just been told she was going to Disneyland. His heart swelled. He'd do anything to make this woman happy. And with her love of photography, that was an avenue he wanted to help her pursue. "Maybe you can show me how to take good photos?" he teased.

She smiled. "Sure. I never saw you with a

camera in Afghanistan, though."

"Always hope for the hopeless," He chuckled. Kira was right: He wasn't a photographer. Never really had interest in it until just now. It was just another way to get her to trust him, to share something they both enjoyed.

"Well, sure. You really want to learn how to use one?"

"Why not? I've always appreciated other people's photos. And you're a natural teacher, so what is there not to like about this situation?" It took everything he had not to reach out and graze her reddening cheek. Garret was finding all these subtle, but oh-so-important, body language signals from Kira telling him she was happy. And that she wanted his company. It was a slow but a very promising way to get to know her better without the stress of danger and war surrounding them.

"Okay, sure. It's just that I've never used a PowerShot. I know it's not a pro's camera, but it's just one tier down from my beloved D7. I'm sure it will have the same dials, controls and such. It will be easy to introduce you to using a Canon to photograph with." She smiled. "And then you'll take some shots. Later, we can go over them here at the house and I can show you the strengths and weaknesses you have as a budding photographer."

"Emphasis on budding," Garret assured her. Frankly, he didn't care how good or bad he was. He just wanted Kira's closeness, her attention. It would give him a chance to maybe, if he got lucky, briefly touch her shoulder. Maybe her cheek. Garret cautioned himself; he knew to move too fast would upset the delicate balance they'd so far achieved.

Now he sat with her on the couch some late nights when neither could sleep. Kira would be bundled up in the pink afghan around her lower body and he could sit a foot or so away from her. It was a wonderful time, he felt, for both of them. There was a comfortableness beginning to blossom between them, as if Kira wanted his continued nearness. She never pulled away from him. Never left the couch because he was too close to her. Never dodged his hand if he lifted it to touch her shoulder. Garret felt his hope deepening.

If someone had told him at eighteen, when he'd joined the Army, that he would wait over four years for the woman he loved, he'd have laughed his ass off. At eighteen he was in a hurry for everything. Instant gratification was his mantra. Now, at thirty, Garret could look back on that time and shake his head, wondering what the hell was the matter with him. Yes, time and maturity had changed him, and so had the ambush that only he and Kira had survived.

Most of all, because he had survived it, the last year of his life made Garret seriously ask *why.* Why had he lived and the others died? He wasn't married. He had no children. Why was he alive when he felt there were others in his A team who were far more important, more valuable to the human race and to the world, than him? As they shared meals, he watched Kira from time to time, noticing her appetite returning. She was slowly starting to regain some of her lost weight. Her cheeks were beginning to fill out, not looking as hollow as before. Garret could see why Kira had been allowed to survive. She was literally a sunbeam in everyone's life. She automatically lifted people up when she was around them. He had no idea what the hell he contributed to this world except that he breathed. And, okay, he was good at driving heavy equipment. Big deal.

"Were you planning to leave for town right after we eat?"

"Yep. We'll get the Canon and take off." He saw the sudden jolt of joy in her expression and so badly wanted to lean over, cup her chin, bring her mouth to his and take her long and deeply. How many nights had he lain awake, fantasizing what her lips might feel like beneath his? He'd lost count over the years. There was something satisfying about waiting for Kira. Garret couldn't put it into words. He often wondered if he had turned into a Victorian-era character, wooing the woman he desired for years before even approaching her about getting married. Maybe the Victorians had it right: There was something magical, something new and exciting, slowly unfolding between himself and Kira. And they were becoming friends. He remembered her saying her parents had been friends long before they'd gotten married. It must be in her genes.

"I need to be back by three p.m.," she said. "Mr. Crawford wants pork loin roast for dinner and that needs to bake for two hours to be done in time for his dinner at five."

Garret wiped off his mouth with a paper napkin, wadded it up and dropped it on his emptied plate. "Not a problem. Takes fifteen minutes to get into town. We'll have nearly an hour to spend photographing, if you want."

"I'd love it! I'm so excited, Garret."

∎ ∎ ∎ ∎

The sky was such a brilliant blue that even with his Stetson pulled low over his eyes, Garret wished for his dark glasses. He stood with Kira on the plowed berm. Down the snowy slope was a small, narrow meadow near a stream. There was a small herd of elk who had come out of the mountains to dig for grass beneath the snow. As Kira started to take photos, Garret watched the animals and knew they would have died without that grass.

His gaze moved from the elk herd to Kira. She stood snapping photos. He shielded her from the cold breeze, standing behind her and a little to her left. The wind was brisk. Kira was wearing her red knit cap, red muffler and green nylon parka. It was only fifteen degrees out and that didn't include the windchill factor, which dropped the temperature even lower. He was bundled up in his well-worn sheepskin coat, a black knit muffler around his collar and neck. His gloved hands were stuffed into his pockets. Garret noticed a number of people had also pulled off the roadway to watch the elk below.

He felt happiness winding through his

chest just watching Kira at work. She clearly loved photography, was fully and completely involved in the movement of the elk. Some of the bulls were playing with one another, their racks impressive. Garret knew the bulls would lose their antlers in April or May of next year, just in time to grow a new one for the breeding season in the coming fall. The female elk often stayed with one another. Yearling elk babies still remained at their mothers' sides. Garret could literally feel Kira vibrating with joy. Her cheeks were a bright red, her lips parted in a half smile that made him burn for her.

Kira was awkward in how she held the camera. From time to time it would slip because of the lack of strength in the last two fingers of her hand. Garret wondered if there was a way to help her keep the camera steady. Frowning, he decided that when he got time, he'd go on the Internet to see if something was available to help her do just that. It hurt him to see what the bullet wound to her arm had done to change her life.

Kira wasn't one of those people who let something like that stop her. What she did instead was to rest the camera on a nearby fence post to support it. That allowed her to shoot without a problem. He was proud of her pluck, her ability to make the most of what she had. Garret knew there were people who would allow such an issue to stop them cold in their tracks. But not Kira. He was so damned glad he'd asked Shay if she had a camera. The radiance in Kira's face made him soar as never before.

"Oh!" Kira cried. "Look at that! They're fighting!"

Garret saw two big, thousand-pound bulls with six-point racks on their heads, getting serious with each other, the clashing sounds of their antlers echoing even up the hill where they stood. "They're probably bored," he said, smiling.

"Great shots!" she cried, clicking away. "Oh! Wonderful! Wonderful!"

She was like an excited child. Garret wanted to turn her around, sweep her into his arms and hold the joy that was palpable around her, absorb it into himself. Would she ever approach him with that look in her eyes? That kind of eager excitement? He didn't know, but the ache of his erection told him he wished she would. Still, just being with Kira, discovering this side of her, made Garret determined to find other ways to draw her out. If photography was a path they could share, he'd willingly throw himself into learning about it, lock, stock and barrel. Because he loved her and he wanted her happy. He absorbed her sighs, her oohs and aahs as she clicked away. Garret didn't want to be anywhere else on earth except right there, where he was at that moment.

Kira finished shooting and turned to him. "Thank you!" and she threw her arms around his shoulders, giving him a hard, quick hug.

Surprised, Garret barely had time to react. And then it was too late. Kira released him, standing back, giving him such a radiant smile that it nearly brought him to his knees. He'd never seen such unparalleled happiness sparkling in her eyes. Was it because of the camera? It had to be. Maybe more? Garret hoped so, but he was on very mushy ground with that question and possible answer. He smiled and tucked some strands of hair behind her ear. "Hey, I like seeing you like this. I've never seen you happier."

She grinned and handed him the camera. "This is the first time we've done something fun since I last saw you, over a year ago. For me, it's a celebration, Garret. The best kind. Come on; I'll show you how to use the camera."

He pulled off his gloves and stuffed them

into his pockets. The camera was small in his huge hands. It was just the right size for Kira's delicate ones, however. He fumbled with it for a moment. "This is a little thing," he muttered.

Laughing softly, Kira slipped her hand around his arm, pulling him toward the fence. "You can learn to use it, big guy. Come on, stand here," and she tugged him forward.

Garret enjoyed her closeness. He leaned down to hear her softly spoken instructions, her lips so close to his ear. The warm moisture of her breath flowed across his jaw as she leaned up on tiptoes, pointing to the right side of the camera, giving him more instructions. He shouldn't have been so damned slow to learn, but it was an advantage now. Garret wasn't a camera aficionado, but Kira's enthusiasm infected him in the best way. She was leaning into him because he was so much taller than she was and she had to arch her hand across his broad shoulder to point to certain functions on the Canon. Finally he was set and she eased away. Garret missed her closeness.

For the next few minutes he chose certain elk and pressed the button down. The camera clicked away and he actually found it very easy to use. The best part was that when he'd take some photos, Kira would urge him to stop. Then she'd take the camera from him, dial backward and they would look at his pictures, their heads nearly touching each other. Her enthusiasm was contagious as she pointed and talked in breathless exclamations over some of his photos. One time she lifted her chin, their mouths inches from each other. Instantly, Garret felt his lower body clench. Her lips were full, parted, and the shining look in her eyes totaled him. How badly he wanted to dip his head and take that sweet, sweet smiling mouth with his own.

Garret barely resisted, struggling to pay close attention to everything Kira was saying because he did want to learn from her. If a camera was a way to her heart, he'd damn well learn how to use one, no questions. Besides, he enjoyed the photos he'd taken and learned a lot about the framing of the elk and which were better shots than others. Later, he handed the Canon back to her. This was Kira's day, not his.

Reluctantly, he looked at his watch. It was time to go. Garret watched Kira with the camera. She was fast, and there was no question she had an eye for her subjects.

Lightly touching her shoulder, he told her they had to leave. He saw how crestfallen she looked for an instant, and then she rallied and smiled. That was the old Kira he knew from Afghanistan. She might be disappointed, but in the next second she rallied and became her usual bouncy, positive self.

She tucked her hand around his arm and they walked down the slight slope to the truck parked on the berm. For him, it couldn't be a more beautiful day in every respect.

In the cab, Kira sat in the passenger seat, the camera held lovingly in her lap, both hands over it protectively as he drove them to the ranch. "What will you do with the photos on that card?" Garret wondered.

"Well," she said, frowning, "do you know if Shay has a card reader? Or the cable that goes with the camera?"

"No. How about you scoot over there and ask her when we get back? I'll drop you off at her house and you can walk home."

"Great idea. Thanks."

"I like seeing you this way," Garret said, meaning it, giving her a quick glance. Kira's face was flushed, her hair tousled because she'd taken off her cap. Her eyes were like shining diamonds and Garret could feel her unbridled joy. He soaked it up like a sponge.

"What way is that?"

He saw her fine brows draw down a little,

curiosity in her expression.

"I remember times almost like this in Afghanistan. Usually you were with babies or younger children, playing with them, holding them, loving them."

She sobered and sat back, her smile disappearing. "Yes, I remember those times." Rallying, she added, "I miss so many of those villagers to this day, Garret. I wonder how they are. I worry that they no longer have the medical attention we were able to provide them. If they're getting enough to eat . . ."

"Hey," he growled, gripping her hand for a moment, squeezing it, "don't go there. We did what we could while we were there. We can't save the world. You know that, Kira." Reluctantly, Garret released her fingers.

"I know . . . but it was three years of my life, Garret. I can't just forget about it. Those villagers were a part of me," and she pressed her hand against her parka, over her heart. "Our guys . . . God, the guys . . . all ten of them, will be a part of me forever."

His mouth thinned. Garret didn't want to go there. Talking about it had extinguished the glowing happiness that had been in Kira's eyes. It was always a downer to speak about that ambush. He wished Kira could stuff it like he did, but he knew she wasn't built that way. It was the one thing that scared him the most, talking about the loss of their friends.

"Well, why don't you focus on those photos? I'll bet Shay has something you can offload them with and onto your laptop so you can see how good they are." He saw Kira instantly perk up. She was so easily moved. So responsive. Garret knew she'd be equally responsive and sensitive as a bed partner, and he wanted to be the man not only to appreciate everything she brought to both of them but to love her like no man had ever loved her before.

CHAPTER FOURTEEN

Kira could hardly contain her excitement after dinner that night. Shay had a card reader. Being able to download the photos onto her laptop was wonderful. She called Garret into their office and he pulled a chair up next to hers.

"Come see your photos," she said. She'd felt her entire body go on alert when he'd sauntered into the small office. The warmth in his hazel eyes always made her feel good, lifted her.

"Sure," he said. "But why don't you show me yours first? How am I going to learn from the master if I don't see her shots first to compare against my own?"

"You're right," she said, "but your photos are really good for a beginner, Garret."

He placed his arm across the back of her chair and leaned forward to look at her MacBook Pro, which had a large screen. "Okay, show me yours."

"Well," she said, "I took at least three hundred shots and I've reduced it down to twenty-five."

"What did you do with the rest of them?"

She liked his nearness. He was a mountain of a man, and instinctively, Kira inhaled his scent, which always made her feel desire for him. "Usually I just trash them, but I kept them this time because I want to use them to show you why they shouldn't be kept."

He frowned. "You'd throw them away?"

"Sure." Kira gave him a patient look. "Not every photo is a good one, Garret. I'm ruthless about getting rid of all but the best." She saw him grimace. "It's not like getting rid of one of your children." She laughed. Just having his arm resting across her chair, not even touching her, made her feel shielded. It was the way Garret was: protective of her. He always had been.

"I don't know," he teased, giving her a crooked smile, "you sure act like each of these photos is a kid of yours."

Meeting his grin, she flashed up the twenty-five photos from her laptop. "You'll see over time that I'm not throwing the baby out with the bathwater." She enlarged each photo so only one was on the screen at a time. "Here are what I consider the best of the twenty-five I saved."

Garret leaned in and studied it. The picture was of the two bull elks, both down on their front knees, antlers locked. She'd captured the front half of each elk, the focus on their heads and expressions. "That's a powerful photo," he praised her, giving her a quick look. He saw a flush come to Kira's cheeks.

"Thanks. Let me show you what's good about it," and she pointed her finger, quickly explaining to him composition in general, the light, the camera speed and so much more. When she was finished, she turned, meeting his eyes. There was only six inches between them. She could see the beard on his face, smell his scent, see the burning quality in his green, brown and gold eyes as he studied her. The desire to kiss Garret was powerful. Kira swallowed convulsively and quickly broke contact with his interested gaze. Feeling inwardly shaky, she brought up a second photo. On each of the twenty-five, there was something she wanted to teach him.

"So, let's go to your photos," she said after viewing hers, giving him a quick smile, "now that you know what to look for." Garret had been Special Forces. Those men were alert, intelligent and didn't miss much. Ever. As she brought up his best twenty photos and arranged them, she asked him for feedback on each of them.

There were no surprises as Garret began to honestly evaluate each of his photos, pointing here and there at them. The pleasure of sharing something she loved so much with him made her feel things she'd never felt before. There was no question she loved Garret, but now it was as if the photography was giving them a focus they could openly share. Kira couldn't name a time when she'd felt this happy. This content.

When he was done, she asked, "Okay, Garret, so which one of your photos is your best?"

"This one," he said. It was a headshot of a female elk with white vapor shooting out of her flared nostrils.

"You're right," she murmured, giving him a pleased look. "It's a keeper."

"You're going to destroy the other nineteen?"

She heard the pang in his voice. "Not if you don't want me to. These are your photos, Garret. I can burn a DVD or put them on a thumb drive and you can keep them."

"Is that what you do?"

"Well," Kira hedged, "in Afghanistan I

didn't have a card reader and the laptops we used were Army-only stuff. I didn't have a photo program like Photoshop or Lightroom to dump them on if I did. I just kept them on my cards. I deleted all except the best ones."

"Yes, could you transfer them to a thumb drive?" He gave her a wry look. "As time goes on, I can go back to my beginnings and see I really should have deleted them."

Laughing, she shook her head. "No, that's fine. Photos are like children to most people who photograph things. I do understand."

"What about these really good photos?" Garret asked, pointing to the three she'd kept of her own photos.

"Oh, I'll burn a CD and keep them."

"Is there some way to sell them?" he wondered.

"There are any number of what's known as stock photo websites where you can upload your photos, put a price on them and hope you can make some money."

He stared at her. "That's an income stream for you, Kira."

She hesitated and sat back. "You're right. Why didn't I think of that?"

"Why don't you go to one of those stock photo websites and upload the one of the bull elks fighting?"

"I think I will." She shrugged. "Now, you have to realize those photos could sit there for a year or more and make no money. It depends upon what a person coming to the website needs for a project."

"Still," Garret persisted, "you're a damn good photographer, Kira. Someone will like your photos."

"You have to understand that stock photos are used in a hundred different ways. It could be for someone's blog, a newsletter, maybe for a website. It's not about people wanting to buy my photo to frame and hang it on their living room wall."

His brows rose. "This is a whole new world you're introducing me to. Who determines the price if they want to use your photo?"

"Well, there are lots of i's to dot and t's to cross on that," Kira said. "When you put up your photos on a stock site, you determine how much it's worth. Some go for as little as a dollar. Others for hundreds, even thousands of dollars." She clicked the mouse and went to a stock site on the Internet. "I would set the prices on my photos differently. There would be a price if it's used on a blog versus used in a video or TV program, for example. There'd be a different price if it's used in a commercial advertisement. Plus, you make it a one-time-only use and retain copyright on your shots at all times."

He gave her a look of praise. "You're an astute businesswoman. You know that?"

Heat swept up across her face and Kira drowned in the admiration she saw in his eyes. "Thanks. My dad said the same thing. I told you, when I first got home after the hospital he tried to buy me a camera to replace the one I lost. He urged me to make a livelihood out of photography."

"I think he was on to something," Garret agreed.

"At the time," she admitted hollowly, "I was a mess. I was so grief-stricken, so overwhelmed with PTSD, I couldn't think straight, much less take good photos. I was lost, Garret. Really lost."

He brought his hand down and smoothed it across her tense shoulders. "Well, a year's passed and you're climbing out of that hole now, Kira. But I think your dad knew what he was talking about. Would you like to become a professional photographer selling your photos online? A second career to being a translator?"

"Oh," Kira sighed, smiling, "I'd love that! But it takes a while to build your portfolio, to get enough photos out there and start making a name for yourself in the photography community."

He gave her a lazy shrug. "So? Why not? Shay's fine with you using her camera. Why don't we take time out at least a couple of times a week, an hour here or there, and go look for areas where you'd like to shoot?"

Kira felt such a sharp stab of hope. "If I could earn money doing translations *and* selling my photos, that would be perfect." She searched his face, seeing how serious he was about the idea. "But the PowerShot isn't a pro's camera, Garret. I'd have to save money to get a professional one."

"Why not let your dad get it for you?"

Shaking her head, she said, "No. That's something I have to do for myself. He's already given me enough over this past year to survive. All I want to do is be able to call him weekly, keep in close touch with him and not take any more of his hard-earned money. He's not rich. He's a hardworking man who owns a small lumber company. I do not want to spend his retirement savings. He'll need that someday."

"Okay," he said, "that's a good plan. Your translation duties are increasing. That means more money you can save to buy the camera."

She glowed beneath his look, which sent

her heart tumbling with joy. When he removed his arm from around her shoulders, she missed that sense of care he always bestowed upon her. "It's a solid plan," she agreed.

Rising, Garret said, "It's supposed to snow the next two days. Maybe on the third day, if we can manage it, I could take you up to the Grand Teton National Park entrance area. There are a couple of moose that always hang around the bridge area, eating the willows along the banks of the Snake River. You might get some good shots of moose if you want them."

"Oh, I'd love that!" She drowned in his smile, feeling as if Garret were embracing her invisibly. "My strong point as a photographer is wildlife and landscapes. This is a perfect time to capture a portfolio of winter landscapes."

"Good," he murmured, halting at the open door. "Let's plan on it."

Thanksgiving was hectic for Kira. With Garret's help, they got Ray into the truck and drove him up to the main house. There, Shay and Reese greeted him at the door. They guided Ray to the head of the trestle table in the warm kitchen so he could watch Kira and Garret work. He was as short with his sentences and always grumpy with Shay. Kira had smelled alcohol on this breath earlier that morning and knew Shay did, too, by the anguished look in her eyes.

Shay said nothing to her father. Ray was able to get along with a cane now and pushed everyone's offer of help aside with a sharp gesture of his hand. She had smiled a hello to him and brought him a cup of coffee after he sat down. Shay and Reese left Kira and Garret alone with him; they had ranch duties to attend to. Ray made it tough on everyone, especially his daughter.

"Are you any good at peeling potatoes?" Kira asked Ray, wrapping the apron around her waist.

"Dunno. Never tried it before. That's women's work."

She kept her smile in place. "Well, Garret and I want to make mashed potatoes for the family this evening and we need potatoes peeled. It would help us if you could do it." Kira knew he was working hard to get his weakened right hand to work again. And using a peeler would be good physical exercise for him. She saw his brown eyes remain flat and hard. His mouth was always a straight line, almost lipless.

"Yeah, I'll give it a try."

"Good," Kira said. "And if it doesn't work

out, no worries, okay?"

"Yeah."

Kira hurried to get a large wooden cutting board to place in front of Ray. She gave him the peeler and ten recently washed, large baker-sized potatoes to peel. Showing him how to do it, she asked, "Think you got the hang of it, Mr. Crawford?"

"A numbskull could do it."

Right. Kira said lightly, "Well, let me know if you need any help."

Ray said nothing, holding the first potato over the board and trying to peel it with his right hand, which didn't always work well.

Kira turned away, knowing Ray didn't need the extra pressure of her watching him. Joining Garret at the sink, she saw him give her a concerned look. She smiled a little, silently letting him know everything was all right.

To say he was protective of her right now was an understatement. The energy practically flowed off him toward her. Garret was more tense than usual and she understood why. Her heart went out to Shay and Reese. Both were equally strained this morning. The feeling in the ranch house was that Ray would ruin the happiness of the holiday for all of them sooner or later. Kira was going to try her best to distract Ray and hopefully get through the day without a major flap.

Noah ambled into the kitchen, his hands in his jeans pockets. "You need any extra hands in here?" he asked Garret, nodding a hello in Kira's direction.

"Naw, we're okay," Garret said.

Noah's face broke into a grin and he leaned casually against the counter. "If you let me mash those potatoes, I'd probably screw it up. I'm no cook."

Kira laughed outright, peeling the carrots on the other side of Garret. "Oh, come on, guys. Mashing potatoes isn't that hard to do."

Kira smiled and focused on the mound of carrots in front of her. Harper ambled into the kitchen. She loved the ragging the men did on one another. Originally from Appalachia, he was six feet tall, with short, dark brown hair and dancing blue eyes. He'd been a Navy corpsman attached to a SEAL unit near the Pakistan-Afghanistan border for four tours of duty. Normally, he was very quiet, almost shy around people. He wasn't outgoing and she was glad to see him taking part in the rivalry between the three of them.

Harper was lean and, like herself, not as heavy as he should be. Often, he spent time alone and liked it that way. Garret called him a loner, but Kira understood why. Sometimes, she would take a break from her translating duties and go visit him. Harper was a good mechanic, plumber and electrician. There wasn't much he couldn't do when it came to those areas of expertise. Right now, he was replacing all the old wiring in the barn with newer, up-to-code electric cables. It was a long, intricate job, but he was a hard, consistent worker.

"Hey, Harper, is it true?" she asked, looking up at him. "Shay said you had a job to replace electric cables at another barn in the valley?"

He grimaced. "Yeah. I'm taking off after tomorrow and heading south to do it. Two-story barn."

"Not a lot of fun in this cold weather," Kira said, giving him a concerned look. She saw him shrug his broad shoulders.

"It's something I enjoy. No one is going to be looking over my shoulder while I do it."

"Yeah," Garret said, "you'll be alone and like it."

Kira saw a flash of pain in Harper's large, intelligent blue eyes, but he said nothing. She knew he'd been married but, after his last tour, come home with severe PTSD. His relationship with his wife, Olivia, had disintegrated, and Harper had signed the divorce papers and left. He'd become homeless because he couldn't stand being around people for very long. Kira loved the gentle, soft-spoken man fiercely because in his off time he volunteered his healing skills to Taylor Douglas's clinic in town.

"Aren't you working on becoming a paramedic?" she demanded.

"Sure," he murmured, resting against the counter, his arms crossed over the chest of his blue flannel shirt. "About halfway through the course right now."

"How are you doing?" Garret asked.

"Okay. Carrying a B average."

"Good," Kira said. Harper hadn't finished high school. He'd had trouble reading. She knew he wanted to graduate as a paramedic and then try to join the Wind River Fire Department. They had a separate medical unit from the firefighting component. Harper loved being a medic and was good at what he did. Until then, Kira knew his other skills would contribute to the Bar C, as well as save money for his future.

As a vet, he could use government money to get through college. He was so shy, but he'd been that way ever since she'd met him. Sometimes he'd be down at the horse training area, helping Noah with the training. Kira felt sorry he'd lost his wife; Garret had told her how much he loved her. Harper saw himself as broken, as all the other vets did, unable to bridge the gap and be normal again where it counted.

Kira wiped her hand off on her apron and touched Harper's shoulder. "You're a wonderful medic. I know the people you help will be so much better off because you were there for them." She saw his cheeks go ruddy and his gaze dart past hers. It looked as if he didn't believe her. PTSD had taken so much from all of them. She wanted to cry at that moment and swallowed, battling back her emotional reaction to Harper's quandary.

"You want me to do something to help?" he asked. "Maybe set the table?"

"Sure," Kira choked, her eyes still moist. "That would be great. Thanks, Harper."

Never let it be said that vets weren't part of a team; they knew how to pitch in and help. Kira returned to her carrots.

"You got any other horses in the pipeline that can make us some good money?" Garret asked Noah, who was now chewing on a stick of celery.

"Yes. I'm going up to an auction in Idaho Falls in four weeks. I've been working with that six-year-old black quarter horse gelding, Poncho. He's a kicker, but I'm trying to break him of it."

Kira frowned. "That's a dangerous habit."

"Tell me about it." Noah held up his hand and showed the swelling on it. "Got this from Poncho this morning."

Frowning, Garret said, "Damn. You okay?"

Grinning, Noah said, "Yeah. I had our resident corpsman, Harper, look at it early this morning. He said I'd be fine, cleaned up the scrape and off I went."

Shaking his head, Garret muttered, "Whoever made Poncho a kicker ought to be shot."

"Oh," Noah said mildly, pushing away from the counter, "don't get me started on that topic. Love is the way to train up these horses. They're superintelligent. My way of training just takes more time, which is why some other horse trainers are using pain and punishment instead. It gets them through the pipeline faster, but the horse becomes a risk to the rider and everyone else around them."

"No, pain is never a good way to train a man or an animal," Garret agreed, pulling over the twenty-pound turkey to stuff it. "Have you talked to Shay and Reese about it? Getting another horse trainer to help you?"

"Yeah, Shay's going through the Veterans Administration to try to locate someone who would come out here to work with me." He shrugged. "I'm not very hopeful. Not a lot of vets were horse trainers before they joined the military."

Kira handed Noah a peeled carrot. "Here, keep eating. You really need to put on more weight."

He smiled and took the carrot. "Thanks. And are you the pot calling the kettle black, Ms. Duval?" He wriggled his eyebrows.

Laughing, Kira said, "Guilty as charged."

"Hey," Harper called, "why don't you help me set the table, Noah, instead of eating everything in sight? Save some for the rest of us, okay?"

Kira giggled and returned to the carrots, placing them in a large pan to steam. Later she would drizzle them with warm honey and melted butter. "You two are like brothers, I swear."

Noah reached over her, grabbing a bunch of plates. "Just ignore him."

Harper walked over, taking the plates Noah handed him. "Me? No, Bro, it's you. You know how I know?"

"No. How, genius?"

Harper pointed at his right hand, swollen from Poncho's kick. "I don't know of any idiot who would willingly work with a broken horse like Poncho. This is the second time he's kicked you inside of a week."

Grumping, Noah said, "It's not the horse's fault. It's the human who trained him. He's confused."

"Yeah," Harper muttered, "right. You couldn't get me to be a horse trainer for nothing."

"It's just a matter of patience and time," Noah told him smugly.

Kira said nothing, thinking that was exactly what was needed between her and Garret: patience and time.

CHAPTER FIFTEEN

Garret covertly watched Kira deal with Ray Crawford throughout the day. She knew he liked crossword puzzles and had thoughtfully brought one of his magazines along so he would have something to do. After peeling the potatoes, he got up with the aid of his cane and went into the living room. There, Shay remained with him for a while, relieving Kira of her duties with the grumpy bastard. He didn't like Crawford and knew he had an agenda. The older man wasn't saying much to anyone, but then, he wasn't nasty either.

Near five p.m. everyone sat down for the sumptuous dinner, the fragrance of the baked turkey and the sage-and-chestnut dressing filling the air. Shay had placed Ray at one end of the trestle table, Reese at the other and her on the right of her husband. Garret was glad to sit with Kira, with Noah and Harper opposite them. Garret gave the two vets credit; they kept up a friendly patter, although they never directed anything toward Ray. He ate in silence, which put a pall over the entire table.

Most of all, Garret felt for Shay. She was stressed out to the max with her father among them, knowing he disliked vets. He gave her credit for her always including him in the talk around the table, although he barely acknowledged her. Garret saw the anger banked in Reese's eyes for his struggling wife, who was trying to smooth things out. He understood better than most, with an alcoholic in the family, that the disease strained and darkened every event. It destroyed all happiness, too, between the other members of a family.

Toward the end of the dinner, when Garret and Kira were serving up warm pumpkin pie with whipped cream, he decided to help Shay a little. She looked devastated and was unable to hide it. With PTSD, it was nearly impossible to hide how one felt. As Garret served Reese and Shay, he said, "What do you think of the odds of getting a military vet with horse training experience out here? Have you heard anything from the VA yet?"

Kira looked up a little as she served Ray his dessert. Then she went back to the kitchen to retrieve Harper and Noah's pie.

Shay gave Garret a relieved look of silent thanks. "No, not yet. Reese called and they said they were looking but for us not to hold our breath."

"That's all?" Garret asked dryly. He walked to the kitchen to get Kira and his pie.

"Yes," Shay said. She picked nervously at the pie with her fork. "We told them it was urgent, that we needed someone right away."

Garret sat down, giving Kira a warm look. She sat at Ray's left elbow. To his relief, she seemed to be feeling steady compared to poor Shay. Returning his attention to the couple, he asked, "Are you wanting a specific type of horse trainer?"

Noah said, "We'll take anyone they can give us." Giving Shay a smile, he said, "They've called since we put in the request. We all know the VA is like a fat, bloated worm that doesn't react fast to anything."

"Is there some other way to get a trainer?" Garret pressed Noah.

"Not that I know of."

"Hate working with the VA," Garret muttered, digging into his pie. He slid a glance to his right. Kira was eating heartily despite the tension at the table and he was glad. Every day she seemed to have more purchase and confidence with Ray. That was good, and he relaxed a little inwardly. Soon this dinner would be over, and so far, no one had stepped on a land mine with Ray. He noted the rancher was cleaning his plate as well.

Harper spoke up in his soft, Appalachian drawl that was neither fully Southern nor fully Northern. "Y'all ever thought that maybe you'll end up with a woman horse trainer?"

Noah shrugged. "I'm not gender-prejudiced. If she can do the job, has the chops for it, I'm all in. I just need someone who is really, really good with horses that need to be broke and trained."

"But how many women vets have that kind of experience?" Shay wondered.

"Not many," Noah said.

"Yeah," Garret said, "but look at Kira. She was a woman put into a male combat environment. There could be other women out there who have worked with horses before going into the military."

Kira nodded. "That's true. The top-secret program I took part in could very well have someone like that in their ranks."

Noah smiled a little. "Well, that would be a good place to go to find out, because a woman's energy is way different from a man's. Horses respond very well to a woman trainer versus a male one if the animal has been hurt by a male."

Kira brightened. "Noah, that gives me an idea. Let me make a call tomorrow and I'll see what I can find out."

"Sure," he murmured, giving her a grateful look, "anything to get Poncho's attention on someone other than on me." He chuckled. "Maybe he likes women."

"Things went well tonight," Kira said to Garret later as they went back home after dinner. Garret hung up his Stetson and shrugged out of his coat.

"Yeah, better than I expected. Crawford was good. Well, as good as he can be. He's still a snarly bear at best." Turning, he saw Kira go into the kitchen. They had a lot of leftovers they'd parceled out to the other vets. "You really handled yourself well with him."

"I'm getting used to his new normal," she said, turning, giving him a slight smile. Opening the fridge, she put the leftovers inside. "And I think Ray was really trying today."

"He was trying all right," Garret said. The clock on the wall read 6 p.m. The next storm had arrived over the valley and snowflakes were falling fast and thick outside. "But he seems to respond more positively to you than to Shay right now."

Shutting the fridge, Kira said, "Poor Shay. My heart just bleeds for her. Ray is angry at her and Reese. It's obvious."

"Well, he's pissed at me, too. I was there when Reese laid down the law to him."

"His focus is on them," Kira said. "Are we going to try to find out who's supplying Ray with his whiskey?"

Moving toward the living room, Garret nodded. "You're taking Ray in for his PT two days from now at one p.m. I'm going to do a little black ops work at that time. I'll follow you into town and be your eyes and ears."

"You have the camera," she reminded him, sitting down in the corner of the couch and pulling off her boots. Picking up the pink afghan, she tucked it around her lower body and snugged it around her waist. "If you can get photos, that would be good."

"I'll have it with me." He sat down nearby, leaving about twelve inches between them. There was soft, instrumental music, all Christmassy, playing in the background on the radio. "If I get photos, I'll go to the guy who's buying Ray his whiskey. Let him know it's not appropriate and tell him to stop doing it."

Sighing, Kira said, "I wish we didn't have to do this."

"I wish Ray would consider what he's doing to his family, to all of us, but it isn't going to happen." His mouth turned into a slash.

She leaned forward, her hand brushing the fabric along his arm. "I never knew how alcoholism could infect a family . . . everyone. I'm so sorry it happened to you, Garret."

He shrugged and sat back, relaxing. "It taught me one thing: never to touch alcohol. I've seen firsthand what it does to a family. It destroys it."

Leaning into the corner, Kira studied his harsh profile. Garret wasn't movie-star good-looking, but his face was strong. "I noticed you never took beer when we managed to get some in from time to time when we were at Bagram."

"No, I don't touch the stuff." He smiled faintly, holding her soft gaze. "Coffee is my bad habit."

She smiled a little. "Do you think your father will ever stop drinking?"

His voice hardened. "Not until he dies from it, like Crawford is presently heading straight to his own demise."

"I like a glass of wine sometimes. For

special occasions. I guess, being in the military, coffee is the norm."

"There are worse things than coffee."

Kira wanted to ease out of her corner and slide next to Garret, place her arms around his shoulders, but she stopped herself. He looked bereft in that moment, the sadness and probably grief about his father apparent. Instead, she gently nudged him with her toe. "Hey, could we take a drive tomorrow so I can get some shots down by Moose Lake in the park? It should be a beautiful time with fresh snow having fallen."

"Sure, but let's see if this storm passes quick enough. They're saying we'll get six inches tonight. If the plows get out and salt the highway, we should be able to make it into that area, no problem."

"Good," she murmured. "I think we deserve some time out. And I can teach you a little more about framing a bright snow landscape shot."

"I'd like that."

A warmth settled in her heart. What would it be like to love Garret? Kira wanted him so bad. She saw the way he looked at her. Felt him wanting her. No longer did she deny it, but there was another question: Was Garret seeking a long-term relationship with her or not? What really lay between them?

Kira had never been built for one-night stands. Everything told her Garret wasn't that kind of man either. Even at Bagram, when some of the team was allowed a break from their village duties and flew to the huge Army base, Garret never caroused. And, to be honest, the other members of the A team were either married or engaged, so they didn't either. None of them had gone after women that she could remember. It said something about their love, their loyalty, to the women in their lives. Her heart squeezed with pain. Now that was all lost. Gone. Forever.

Moose Lake was oval, frozen-over and covered with snow. On one side of it were tall Douglas fir, decked out in heavy winter overcoats of the white stuff. The sky was cloudy with a few riffs of blue sky every now and again. Everything was quiet, that special, muted silence Kira loved so much.

They moved from the parking lot to the lake. They had a few hours and Kira eagerly trod through the knee-high snow, Garret cupping her elbow to keep her upright. In her gloved hands was the small Canon PowerShot.

Garret looked around. The grizzly and black bears were well asleep now, hibernating. The Snake River wolf pack was now the alpha predator of the area. He knew the wolf pack wasn't known to frequent the park at all. Still, it would have been an incredible shot if the large pack of fifteen wolves had shown up here. He knew Kira would be thrilled. He grinned just thinking about it.

She wore her red knit cap, the red muffler around her neck and shoulders. The snow was deep for her and Garret patiently cut his stride so she could walk without stumbling or falling.

Their breaths were white jets coming from their noses and mouths. "Look," Garret said, halting and pointing to the right. "Tracks."

"What are they? Do you know?"

He craned his neck. "Maybe fox or bobcat?"

"What I'd give to see a wolf!" She looked up at him, grinning.

Garret wanted to absorb her sparkling gray gaze that tugged so powerfully at his heart. Her cheeks were flushed and he was seeing the old Kira again, realizing how much of a damper Crawford put on her. He was glad he'd suggested this little outing, thanking Canon and the photographic gods and goddesses for the opportunity. "Probably won't," he cautioned.

"Do you see any other tracks?" she asked, pushing forward, heading to the west side of the small lake because the sun's position would be behind her and excellent for good photographs.

"Yeah, lots," he said, looking here and there as they trudged through the snow. "Where do you want to set up to shoot?"

Pointing, Kira said, "Over there. You always shoot with the sun behind your back."

"Why?"

"You'll get a black shadow instead of all the colors and details you wanted if you shoot directly into the sun. The sun is in the eye of the lens. Not good."

"Okay, then," Garret murmured, giving her a smile, "let's get over there."

Once in position, Garret stamped out an area with his boots where Kira could move around a little without slogging through a bank of snow. It was a small circle but large enough for both of them. The shadows were long and the tree trunks thin, dark lines across the snow. He watched as Kira put the camera on manual and then adjusted a lot of things he still wasn't familiar with.

"Now," she said, "the camera is ready. I've guesstimated the F-stop, the ISO and other functions. All I need to do now is take a test photo to see if my settings are correct for the light and conditions."

Garret enjoyed her enthusiasm. "Okay, go for it." He watched her adjust her bulky gloves, which had sheep's fleece inside them to keep her fingers warm. It hurt him to see the camera nearly fall twice because the weakened fingers on her left hand wouldn't hold it correctly. Each time, she caught the camera and patiently readjusted it until she was satisfied.

He watched her place her elbows against her body to keep the camera as still as possible and then click. Once she had the test shot, she lowered it and turned to him. Their heads were nearly touching as she told him about the shot and the light.

"It's good," she said.

He heard the pleasure in her voice. "Then shoot away. I'll stand watch for bears." He grinned, drowning in her shining gray gaze.

"They're hibernating. You're going to take some shots, too."

"I will, but you go ahead," he urged. The stillness enfolded them. After the swift-moving front had come through last night, the cutting, icy wind had left with it. Now there was a stillness that fed Garret's soul. It always had. This was what he loved about the winter. It had an incredible, healing

317

quiet that silently embraced him. The only thing he heard were the clicks from the camera.

Then he caught movement near the lake and narrowed his eyes.

"Kira!" he rasped in a low tone, "wolves at eleven o'clock!"

She gasped, turning her camera in that direction. "Oh," she whispered excitedly.

Disbelieving, Garret watched a black alpha male, the leader of the pack, come silently out of the tree line, leading confidently through the chest-deep snow toward the back of the lake. A white wolf wasn't far behind him, more than likely the alpha female. They skirted the edge of the lake, where the snow was only ankle deep, heading toward the deeper, denser forest on their side of it. Garret saw eight more gray wolves following them. His heart pounded with excitement at their unexpected arrival. He heard Kira making happy sounds in her throat, pure pleasure, as she snapped away, following the swiftly moving pack. In less than ten seconds, the wolf pack disappeared into the other tree line, disappearing into the darkness.

"Oh my God!" Kira squealed, turning, jumping up and down, the camera in her right hand. "Oh my God, Garret! It was a wolf pack! I got them! I got them!" and she stopped jumping and turned on the camera to look at the shots.

Garret watched her hunch over the camera, her eyes riveted to the screen. He heard her gasp and she moved over to him, body against his, holding the screen up toward him.

"Look! Look, I got him! Oh, God, this is *such* a great shot!"

He'd seen Kira like this in Afghanistan, but never here, as he steadied the camera, looking intently at the screen. She'd expertly caught the head and neck of the black wolf and it was a stunning shot against the white snow. Garret lifted his head, smiling. "Wow. This is a great photo." He handed the camera back to her. "Look at all of them," he coaxed, happiness soaring through him.

She made more purring sounds in her throat as she quickly dialed through the rest of the shots. Garret looked over her shoulder and honestly, he couldn't see a bad photo in the bunch. She'd clicked on automatic and had at least twenty shots, both close-ups of individuals and of the entire pack strung out along the edge of the lake. He wasn't prepared for Kira turning around and throwing her arms around his neck, her lips crushing his.

Garret's world exploded, anchored to a screeching halt as Kira's warm, soft mouth pressed against his. Her breath was swift, punctuated with excitement. Her arms were damn strong. Stronger than he'd given her credit for being as she hugged him fiercely with all her woman's strength. Only in reaction did his arms sweep around her body, nearly lifting her off her feet, crushing her as close as their heavy clothing would allow.

Her mouth . . . oh sweet Jesus, her mouth tasted like delicious cotton candy, heat combined with eagerness as she kissed him hungrily. There was such enthusiasm, boundless joy and need all wrapped up in her lips sliding against his as he opened his mouth to allow her to explore him more deeply. All sounds, the coldness, everything . . . disappeared around Garret. All he felt was her moist, ragged breath against his face, her fierce kiss that took no prisoners and her arms holding him as tight as she could. There was no space between them. He couldn't get enough of Kira as she melted into him, her body languid, trusting, fused to his. Her mouth was like the petals of a rose slowly opening beneath his exploration and onslaught. His entire body became galvanized, heat roaring through him as she cherished his mouth with an eagerness that caught him completely off guard.

Without thinking, because she trusted his arms, his body surrounding hers in that magical moment, Garret groaned deeply. Kira's taste was like a perfume awakening his body from a deep, dormant sleep. She was bold and he absorbed her lips, feeling them give and take beneath his. And then she gave the signal she wanted to be let down, to be on her feet once more.

Garret placed her solidly on the packed snow, unwilling to leave her mouth, which was sending his lower body into a spasm of agony, but he didn't care. He'd crawl through hell just to feel her mouth gliding, sipping and hungrily relishing his.

Reluctantly, Garret felt her mouth leave his. He barely opened his eyes, staring into her cloudy, aroused-looking gray ones. She gripped his arms, clinging to him as if she were unsteady. Their breaths were sharp and punctuated, thick vapor rising between them, their gazes locked together. Slowly, she eased her fingers from digging into his biceps. He opened his arms, allowing her space between their once-fused bodies. Kira's lips glistened, were pouty and swollen from the fierce kiss they'd shared. His heart was thudding in his chest and a quiver roared through him as he kept his hands on her shoulders, staring down at her, disbelief and shock still funneling through him. Kira had kissed him. Him! His throat closed and he felt a lump form that he tried to swallow away. His mind was mush. Garret was always good with a verbal comeback, but this time he had none, absolutely none.

Kira gave him a confused look, touching her lower lip with her gloved hand. Her cheeks were flushed as she stared wonderingly up at Garret.

"Why did you kiss me?" Garret growled unsteadily, refusing to let her go. She felt wobbly and he suddenly realized the power his kiss had on her. The thrill of knowing her reaction was heady, racing through him like an unleashed animal, howling through him. Seeing arousal in her shining eyes, the joy in those huge black pupils staring up at him in wonder, made Garret dizzy for a moment. Fighting the euphoria, the shock still singing through his veins that Kira had kissed him, he didn't know what to say.

With his gloved hand, he caressed her cheek. Garret felt as if his whole life hung on her reaction to their kiss. He saw her close her lips, compress them, then look away for a moment. Did he see fear in her eyes? *Impossible.* But why? Why would she suddenly look fearful and unsure of herself? Garret didn't understand, and he so desperately wanted to. So many words, an avalanche of them, wanted to tear out of him. His mind spun with questions. Had Kira kissed him in the heat of the moment? Was that what this was about? Just joy being expressed with him as a friend? Nothing more? Nothing deeper? More meaningful? He wanted that one, branding, forever kiss still tingling on his mouth to mean Kira loved him. She'd kissed him like she damn well meant it. She wasn't innocent. She'd had relationships before they'd met. If only . . . and a gutting pain went through his heart. If only Kira meant that kiss with him for the right reasons.

Too soon, his brain screamed at him. *Too soon. Can't go there. Don't dare . . .* Wrestling with his wild, fluctuating emotions while his mind called for logic and calm, Garret had never felt like he did right then with Kira. When she turned and lifted her chin to hold his gaze, he saw as many emotions in her eyes; it was impossible to know what she was really feeling. Why had she kissed him? He had to know. His fingers caressed her shoulders lightly, a lover's touch, silently urging her to speak to him.

Giving him a flustered look, Kira whispered unsteadily, "I don't know what happened to me, Garret. I was so happy . . . I wanted to celebrate it with you was all . . ."

He tried to swallow his hurt and disappointment. Kira had kissed him in the heat of the moment. Nothing more. Searching her eyes, he still saw arousal banked in them. Or was it only that he wanted to see that reaction?

Managing a sour smile, he released her shoulders. "Seeing a wolf pack, getting it on film is worth celebrating." Garret wasn't going to take out his disappointment on Kira. He instantly saw relief in her expression. How could she have kissed him so passionately and then said what she had? Garret had had enough relationships in his life to know the kinds of kisses a woman could give a man. Was there celebration and joy in her mouth clinging to his? Absolutely. But there was more. And he desperately wanted Kira to be honest, completely honest, with him.

Warning himself that he was expecting far too much too soon, Garret forced himself to slow down, take a long, deep breath and stop pushing Kira. He'd seen fear in her eyes and he didn't know what that was about. Fear of him? Fear of something from the past?

He gave her a genuine smile laced with real warmth. Sliding his hand beneath her elbow, he said, "Come on, it's time we started back."

"Yes," she agreed, looking at the watch on her wrist. "Oh, darn it. My watch died. What time is it, Garret?"

He pulled his wrist out enough from beneath the sleeve of his coat to look at his Rolex. "Three thirty p.m., or 1530 to us military types."

"You're right, we need to get back. I have to get started on Ray's dinner soon."

Watching her shift gears, the sudden mask of responsibility meshed with concern fell over her expression. Garret eased her forward, taking the same steps back in the deep snow in order to reach the truck. He wished mightily he could release Kira from having to take care of Crawford. More and more, he saw how much it dampened her spirit. Just now, he'd seen the old Kira from Afghanistan. There, she'd been a wild child, spontaneous, affectionate with all the village kids and animals, always with a smile for everyone. She truly had been the team's secret weapon in winning the hearts and minds of that village and its elders. Everyone had loved Kira, without exception. And so did he.

CHAPTER SIXTEEN

Kira had no time to analyze her actions with Garret. As soon as she got home, she put the camera in the office and then took off for Ray's. It was four p.m. and she was running a little late. Her heart sang with joy as she replayed kissing Garret. In the crazy heat of the moment, she couldn't help herself and had turned and kissed him.

Touching her brow as she entered the house, she wondered what had happened to her. Why then? Groaning, Kira had to tuck that beautiful, unscripted moment away. Her lips still remembered the imprint of Garret's mouth on hers, the power of his kiss. He'd stolen her breath away and sent her spinning and melting into his arms. She had fully trusted herself with him.

Ray was at the table when she entered the kitchen. He barely looked up at her, a crossword magazine in his hands.

"You're late."

Kira smiled a little and tied on the apron. "Not really. All you're having tonight are turkey leftovers. It's easy enough to heat them in the oven for your five p.m. dinner."

He grunted and returned to his magazine.

Okay, then. This was such a typical response from him that Kira blew off his scowl and took all the leftovers from the fridge, placing them on the counter.

"I got PT tomorrow at three p.m., you know."

"Yes. I'll be driving you in. The roads have been cleared from last night's snow."

"Is that why you were late? You went somewhere with Fleming?"

Surprised, she turned in his direction. "Yes, we went and took some photographs up at Moose Lake."

"Get anything?"

Kira returned to her work. This was the first time Ray had shown any interest in anything she did. She told him about seeing the wolf pack.

"That's not the Snake River pack," he told her. "Their alpha male is gray."

"Garret was saying that there's a second pack that's formed in the valley. The black wolf was once part of the Snake River pack but got chased off by the alpha male. Later, he hooked up with a female white wolf and started a second pack."

"Women have no business in a man's world."

Suddenly he was being chatty. Kira remained silent, put the food on a plate, wrapped it in foil and slid it into the oven.

"You need to give a set to Wyoming Fish and Game, too. They're the ones who'll be real interested in those pictures you took."

"I will, for sure," she agreed.

Ray penciled in some letters into the crossword puzzle. Turning, Kira went to the sink, wishing she could run away from this man. All of a sudden Ray was being conversational. What had spurred him on? The liquor? Kira didn't know and was unsettled by the shift in his tactics and demeanor. How she wished the food in the oven would get hot enough to serve to him sooner, not later. When she served him the meal, though, she had her answer. She could smell the liquor on his breath.

Kira felt relief as she stepped into the house. Garret was getting their supper ready, which was warmed-up turkey leftovers for them, too.

"How'd it go?" he asked, lifting his chin, staring at her as she hung up her parka.

Grimacing, Kira told him what had happened. She walked into the kitchen to get plates down from the cupboard. Garret's mouth quirked and she could tell he was affected by her story.

"Ray's probably drunk," he said flatly. He cut up some French bread, then slathered it with melted butter and diced garlic, brushing it between each slice.

"Is that why he's suddenly chatty?" she asked, setting the table.

"Could be. You said the odor around him was strong. Could be he drank more than usual. Who knows?" He placed aluminum foil around the bread and slid it into the oven to heat. "You look upset."

Kira turned and shrugged. "Yes. He started saying all vets were weaklings."

Garret wiped his hands on the towel and hung it up. He poured them fresh coffee and gestured toward the table. "Come on, let's go sit down. It's going to take the food about fifteen minutes to heat."

Kira felt his powerful sense of protection surround her as they sat down at each other's elbows at the table. The tightness in her stomach dissolved. Did Garret know how much she loved the sense of safety he always bestowed upon her? Kira wanted to tell him but didn't feel it was the right time. There was a new warmth she saw in his hazel eyes, too. Was it because of her spontaneous kiss earlier that day?

Everything was shifting between them, and Kira realized she had a lot to do with it. She hadn't been completely forthcoming about their kiss, about what it meant to her. What to say? How much to reveal about her love for him? Garret had kissed her like a man who wanted to love his woman. It was no light kiss. Not a kiss between friends. That molten moment had turned into a kiss between two lovers and she knew it. There was so much to think about. To sort out.

Kira tossed and turned. The clock on her bedstand read two a.m. Her mind and her heart would not turn off about her kissing Garret at Moose Lake. All she had to do was close her eyes and allow their kiss to embrace her once more. She could still taste Garret on her lips and never wanted it to go away.

She hadn't thought about what might happen when they kissed, but her whole body was still vibrating with need for him since then. It hadn't been a gentle kiss on her part either. Kira realized she'd kissed him with all the pent-up longing she'd held for years for Garret. And there was nothing platonic about it. It was the kiss of a hungry, sex-starved woman wanting her man and letting him know it.

What had startled the hell out of Kira was the ferocity of her kiss, her mouth curving and taking Garret's mouth without any hesitation. She sighed, lay on her back, pulling her arm across her eyes. She'd kissed Garret like a female alpha wolf telling the male she wanted to mate with him. It had been a raw, primal kiss and still, the sensations, the memories of it, were floating like liquid lava throughout her entire lower body.

Moaning, she turned over, burying her head in the pillow, gripping it, unsure of what to reveal to Garret. Should she come clean about what she hadn't said to him? That yes, it had been a totally crazy, spontaneous kiss at first. But when he'd gotten over his initial shock, he'd kissed her back. And the man had kissed her like his life depended upon it. She knew he had, and that was what startled her so much. Kira hadn't kissed him with any intention but to share her unparalleled joy over unexpectedly seeing the wolves. And it had turned hot and hungry between them. As if . . . as if Garret wanted to kiss her as much as she'd wanted to kiss him.

Her mind rocked with the what ifs. What if Garret did care about her beyond friendship? What if it went deeper than that? How deep did it go? Kira was afraid because she was unsure of Garret's endgame with that kiss. Had he deepened the kiss between them because he wanted sex? Only sex? He was a man after all. Was this only about raw sexuality that needed to be fulfilled? Was that all it meant to him?

She couldn't go in that direction. No matter how sex hungry she was, Kira wasn't able to make love to a man who didn't mean something serious and ongoing to her. She just wasn't built any other way and she couldn't go against what she knew was right for her.

Kira had had two powerful relationships in her life. When she was nineteen, Neal, an Army sergeant, had pursued her until he'd gotten her in his bed. And she'd fallen in love with him. But nine months later she'd found out he was married and had two children. Mortified, Kira had broken it off, vowing to never trust another man.

But she had, at twenty-one, when she'd fallen hopelessly in love with Alex Edwards, a Special Forces A team weapons sergeant. It had been the best year of her life. She'd discovered what love was really all about. They'd shared bodies, hearts and souls with each other. A year later he was killed a month after deploying to Afghanistan, and her whole world had crumbled around her.

Sitting up, Kira pushed her fingers through her hair, her heart roiling. It had been a year later, after being put into the undercover operation, that Kira had met Garret. Almost instantly she'd fallen in love with him. And for three years she could do or say nothing about it. The ache for Garret was always there, a part of her daily work world in the village because he often accompanied her on her duties. They had an easy friendship, a lot of jokes, laughter and fun shared between them.

But never a kiss. Because it had been off-limits. Taboo. But the kiss he'd given her today, that raw, male, primal kiss, had told her he wanted her in every way possible. She'd never realized just how much Garret had wanted her until that afternoon. Her world had shifted drastically as a result.

But what to do about it? How to approach Garret? Or should she? What if Garret was interested only in sex with her while they lived in the house together? Nothing more? Just sex. Kira knew it would be world-class sex because Garret was sensitive to her and her moods. The way he'd gentled that initial powerful kiss, rocked her lips open further, moved his tongue teasingly against hers, had sent her body into wild longing. He would be a wonderful lover; there was no doubt about that.

But Kira wanted a lot more than a sexual relationship with Garret and wouldn't settle for anything less. When she loved a man, she loved him with all her being. There had to be deep emotional ties with the man, nothing frivolous, nothing inconsequential.

How to talk to him about this? Kira knew, judging from the look in Garret's eyes at the kitchen table that night, that he wanted her. It was clear to her because she saw a starving desire in them. He was't trying to hide it. Kira felt fear and longing all at the same time. Fear that Garret wanted something far less meaningful than she did. He didn't realize she was unable to love fully, with all her heart, unless there was something serious and long-lasting going on between them. How to tell him that? And Kira was concerned that they lived in the same house. What if their relationship didn't work out? What then? Could she lose her job? These were daunting questions with no answers.

Tomorrow she had to take Ray to his doctor in Wind River. She was planning on seeing Brook Russell, a friend of Shay's whom she'd met in town and befriended. They had gotten along wonderfully, and Kira cherished their friendship. She was planning on dropping over for a quick visit to see her and her daughter, Lily, while Ray waited to be seen by his doctor.

Three-year-old Lily looked wonderingly up at Kira as she leaned over and smiled down at the child in Brook's arms. She was dressed in a pair of light yellow coveralls, a pink, long-sleeved sweater beneath it, complementing her ginger-colored hair. Brook sat down and placed her daughter in her lap, taking off her knee-high boots, which were wet with snow. Lily's large, blue eyes never left Kira as she knelt down beside her, placing her hand on the little girl.

"She's precious," Kira said to Brook. "So beautiful."

Brook had long, blond hair she had tied into a thick, single braid that lay down the back of her pale green cowl-necked sweater. Her eyes were sky blue, just like her daughter's.

"Precious for sure," Brook said with a grin, handing Kira first one wet boot and then the other. She pulled up Lily's socks over her small feet. "She's just like her daddy, always on the go. A real type A." Brook set her daughter down and Lily immediately took off through the living room toward the hall to her bedroom.

"Someday," Kira said wistfully, boots in her hand, "I want one just like her. You're so lucky."

Brook was one of Shay's best friends, both having been born in the valley. Shay and Brook had attended school together. She pushed her hands against her jeans and rose. "Come on; join me out in the kitchen while you wait for Crawford. Would you like some coffee?"

"Love some. Where do I put Lily's boots?"

"Oh." Brook pointed to the mud porch. "Out there. Thanks."

Brook had married Brian Russell when she was eighteen. He'd gone into the Marine Corps and she'd gone to college to get a degree as an RN. At twenty-five, Brian had been killed in Afghanistan. Brook had found out she was pregnant with Lily and come home to Wind River. Still grief-stricken, Brook had needed a job, and Taylor Douglas, the physician assistant, had hired her to help run her clinic.

Brook, at twenty-eight, was only now coming out of her grief, from what Kira could tell. She'd once told Kira that she would never marry another military man. And Kira could understand why she felt that way.

Looking around, Kira admired the cedar log cabin Brook and Lily lived in. The kitchen was an extension of the living room, open concept. Kira sat at the table while Brook busied herself in the kitchen making their coffee. "This house feels so warm and nurturing."

Brook tilted her head, nodding. "It is now. I was a mess when I came home after Brian was killed, though."

"The house has been a calming influence for you?"

"The very best kind," Brook murmured, her voice laced with emotion. "Just being near my parents has helped me and Lily so much. They love being grandparents. Family is so important."

"Shay has said she was so happy you came home after your husband was killed."

Brook brought two mugs to the table. "I was glad, too. My folks are here and that was the most important reason to come back to Wind River. When I arrived here, it was my parents who helped me find this cabin. I was such an emotional mess at the time, Kira. Shay helped me get a job with Taylor's medical clinic."

"And look at you now," Kira said, her voice filled with admiration. "You look beautiful, so happy," and she found herself

337

admiring Brook's strength to survive the loss of the man she loved so much.

"It's been a long road back," Brook assured her. She gave Kira a smile. "Garret and I are buddies. We've been close ever since he came here a year ago. He's sort of like a big brother to me. I don't know if you knew that."

"No," Kira said. "But he's an easygoing guy who makes friends wherever he goes."

Brook brought over a plate of Oreo cookies. "He's really focused on you."

"What do you mean?"

Sitting down, Brook nudged the plate in Kira's direction. "He likes you. A lot."

"Well," Kira stumbled, "we worked together for three years in Afghanistan. Did he tell you that?"

Brook smiled and relaxed against the hard-backed chair. "Oh, yes." She gave Kira a searching look. "You mean the world to him, Kira."

Blinking once to underscore her shock, she said, "What do you mean, Brook?"

"Anytime I run into him in town, the conversation is always about you. He's got nothing but praise and respect for you. He once told me how you'd rescued him and you'd both survived that ambush when no one else did. He didn't say anything beyond that because it was top secret, but I could read between the lines, having been a military wife."

Somber, Kira picked up an Oreo. "Yes," she whispered, "we were the only two survivors . . ."

Reaching out, Brook's hand fell over hers. "He cares so deeply for you, Kira." She gave her a searching look. "I don't know if you realize that."

Shaken, Kira shook her head. "We've always been friends." Did she dare confide their kiss from the day before? Brook Russell was a very gentle soul, quiet and incredibly caring and sincere. She made Kira want to confide in her. Garret had been right; she and Brook had become fast, close friends. Every time she had to take Ray for an appointment or to the gym, she dropped over to see Brook and her daughter.

Removing her hand, Brook nodded. "Friendship is the best basis on which to build a relationship. The first thing Brian offered me was his friendship when we were freshmen in high school."

"Garret really makes me feel calm when he's around me," Kira admitted.

"Does he make you feel safe? Because Brian always gave me that."

"He does," Kira acknowledged. "Sometimes I call him a big, gruff teddy bear, which he hates," and she laughed a little.

"Is it something you feel coming around you, like invisible arms holding you?" Brook asked.

"Very much like that." Kira frowned and gazed into Brook's amused-looking blue eyes. "Why? How do you know that?"

"Because," she said quietly, holding Kira's confused eyes, "I didn't realize it at the time, but Brian told me about it later. He said he fell in love with me right from the start. He couldn't help himself. And of course he hid that little nugget of information from me for a long time. He proposed to me after we graduated from high school. I married him when I was eighteen. It was an amazing thing to me. He didn't even have to touch me. Just be nearby. I was so grateful to him for giving me that." Her eyes sparkled. "It wasn't until far into our relationship that I realized what had happened and why."

Kira swallowed hard and stared at Brook. "That's exactly how Garret makes me feel. He doesn't have to touch me, but just being in his presence helps me so much . . ."

"Maybe there's something more going on between you and Garret?" Brook wondered.

Shock flowed through Kira. Brook understood exactly how she felt. Then she shook her head. "Did Garret put you up to this? To talk to me, Brook?"

Her mouth curved ruefully. "No. He hasn't said a word. It's just what I'm picking up around the two of you, the way you look at each other. There's something special between the two of you."

CHAPTER SEVENTEEN

December 20

Kira sat out in the living room with her journal across her lap at three a.m. The house was quiet, the drapes drawn, and she was curled up beneath her warm afghan. A nightmare had awakened her. Would they ever stop?

Outside, it was snowing. The weather forecaster had predicted another ten inches from the latest storm coming over the valley. With it being only four days until Christmas, Kira knew it would affect traffic in the valley and last-minute shoppers. But her heart and mind weren't on the holiday. They were squarely focused on the A team. Wiping tears drifting down her cheeks, she stared down at her journal.

She heard a door open and close down the hall. It had to be Garret. Had he heard her screams earlier? She'd awakened herself with them. Twisting a look over her shoulder, she saw him emerge from the darkened hall, his eyes half open, his short hair mussed. Even in a dark blue T-shirt and blue flannel pajamas hugging his legs, he stirred her lower body to life.

"I woke you up, didn't I?" she asked, giving him an apologetic look.

"No, I woke up on my own," he mumbled, wiping his face. "Want some tea?"

"Sure," she whispered, turning her attention to the journal. So much of her anxiety diminished because of his presence. Brook's observation weeks before had impacted Kira strongly. And since then, they'd become even closer friends, talking on the phone when they could and going out to lunch together, which wasn't often, but Kira enjoyed the company of another woman who understood the military. Brook was so easy to talk to . . .

"Where did you go?" Garret teased as he set a mug of tea down on the coffee table in front of her.

She smiled faintly and looked up at him. He had such an intense, rugged look. "I was just thinking was all," she whispered. Watching him move around the table and come to sit close to her made her feel that delicious sense of protection. The couch dipped beneath his weight although he sat a good twelve inches from where her feet were tucked beneath the afghan.

"Did you have a nightmare?" he asked, studying her as he leaned his elbows on his thighs, the mug between his hands.

"Yes. I get so tired of them, Garret. I just wish they'd go away."

He grunted, his mouth pursed. "Libby Hilbert brought up a good point last week at our meeting," he said in a low tone. "That these nightmares are a way of working out the shock and trauma of it. Each time the dream is a little less potent, a little less intense than the one before."

"Yes," Kira sighed, "I know she's right because I've seen it in myself. I see less intensity in my dreams than before I came here." She moved her hand lightly across the open journal. "But it's still so painful."

"We've got a lot to work out from Afghanistan," he soothed, giving her a concerned look. "Is that a drawing of Aaron Michelson?"

She looked down at her pen-and-ink drawing of the CO of the A team. "Yes. I made a number of drawings of all the guys." She shrugged. "When I lost my photos I wanted to do something to remember certain days or times with them."

"Can I see?"

Kira had never handed Garret her journal. She hesitated fractionally and then nodded. He put the tea on the coffee table and took the large journal from her, settling it across his knees.

"You're really a fine artist, Kira. Another talent of yours."

Warmth flowed through her. Above all, she didn't want Garret to see the section she'd devoted to him. There were at least six drawings of him she'd made at various times, and she'd written thoughts that, if he read them, would give away that she loved him. "Thanks."

Garret's mouth pulled into a slight smile. "I remember this incident. The chief of the village got in a flock of geese. He was trying something new, wanted eggs in the diet of his people. Special Forces had worked with him on it." He tapped the drawing, which showed the captain with the chief surrounded by about forty white, honking geese. Kira had drawn the many children who had made a circle around the geese, keeping them penned in with their small, skinny bodies. "That was such a hilarious day," he said, a chuckle rumbling through his chest. Looking up, he said, "You captured it perfectly, Kira."

Her heart opened to the boyish, sleepy-eyed look Garret gave her. She cherished these times because he was vulnerable and open to her. Being half asleep, she was sure, was partly why.

Several strands of hair dipped down over his broad brow as he read the writing that went with the illustration. She saw his expression soften as he read. His large hands, those long, strong fingers, curved over the journal, as if to caress and care for it. She ached to have those hands trail over her body. There was no way Kira was going to tell Garret that since their kiss, her dreams had changed, become sexually charged and explicit regarding him. That one kiss had broken a dam of emotion, sexual need and love for him wide open within her.

"I like that you wrote about that incident," he said, giving her an admiring look. He gently touched the nearly hundred pages of the journal, the paper thick and cream-colored, able to handle drawings like this. His fingers lingered over the other pages in the journal.

"It has the date, the names of the people I drew and what happened."

"And you did this because even though you were taking photographs, this was another way to record it?"

346

"Yes." A little fear moved through her and she hoped Garret wouldn't start riffling through the rest of the journal. If he ever saw the portion on him . . . Her mouth went a little dry. Opening her hands, she stretched them toward him, wanting her journal back.

Garret handed it to her. He picked up his tea. "When you saw the families of the guys, did you show them these drawings?" he wondered.

"Yes . . . yes, I did. I was afraid to at first, but Aaron's wife, Denise, was so grateful that I'd sketched him that I went to a place that had a copier and made archival-quality copies of every one of them for her. She treated them like they were a Christmas gift, saying she was going to keep them for their children in a special scrapbook."

"She'll probably show them the drawings when the kids are at an age where they can understand and appreciate them."

Kira nodded, sipping her tea, feeling the invisible cloak of his care powerfully surround her. His hazel eyes were no longer cloudy with sleep. Instead, she saw the desire in the green-and-gold depths of them — for her — she was sure.

It had been nearly a month since they'd kissed. Kira hadn't decided if that was a good thing or not. Garret had made no further attempt to kiss her again. But then, she hadn't either. She was convinced she was an emotional invalid of sorts when it came to love. Brook had laughed outright at that definition of herself, telling her nothing could be further from the truth. But she felt fear about broaching the topic with Garret. Afraid of what he might say. Kira knew she wasn't emotionally strong enough to take his rejection at this point.

"Every wife and girlfriend of the guys wanted my sketches. It made me feel good that I could do something so positive for them. I was heartbroken that my camera and cards had been stolen. I couldn't give them the photos I'd taken. Sometimes I still cry for their loss because those photos would have given them so much more."

Garret sat back, resting the mug on one thick thigh. He reached out, squeezing her foot beneath the afghan. "No, you gave them something of equal value, Kira. It's good that you know how to draw, that you put down the date when you drew each of the guys. Those are going to be forever keepsakes for their families. You did such a good thing for them."

She felt his care and something else. Her heart said it was love for her, but her mind questioned it. "I was glad I could do it."

"By going through your journal? By looking at each of the guys and remembering incidents around the village? This helps you get through all that grief?"

"Very much so." She closed the journal, smoothing her hand across the dark leather that had so many scratches and such wear on its surface. "I find that when I have the nightmare about the ambush, I can look through my journal and cry. But it's a release, Garret. I remember our good times, the laughter and the jokes we played on one another. I can cry and feel relief and better afterward."

"Do you find that working through your grief in that way makes it easier over time? Like our nightmares lose some of their intensity with each dream?"

Her mouth curved faintly and she gently moved her hands across the journal. "Yes . . . exactly. I've always been glad I've sketched all the guys. It's been a very healing journey for me in one way. In another, it's opened me up and I can't escape my grief; I have to move through it." She gave the journal a fond look. "All the pages have tearstains on them."

His mouth thinned and he nodded, looked away for a moment.

Kira saw the pain in Garret's eyes and

knew now that he hadn't even begun the journey to work through his own grief. It had come up a couple of times at their weekly therapy sessions, and it was then she'd realized the terrible load he still silently carried inside himself. She'd talked to Brook about it, and they'd both agreed that women were far more willing to work through their feelings than any man was. A man had to be dragged kicking and screaming to do the same thing. Garret was no different and her heart twinged with anguish for him, understanding the heaviness he must be carrying within him.

"We need to put up a Christmas tree," Garret said, wanting to get to a safer topic.

"I'd like that."

"How about today? We can go out and find one. I'll chop it down and we'll bring it back here and decorate it."

"I don't have any decorations. Do you, Garret?"

Shrugging, he said, "No, but we can make do with what we have. There are cranberries in the fridge. We can make popcorn and string it." He gave her an amused look. "You could draw some decorations with your colored pencils and we could hang them. What do you say?"

She smiled and thought about it, seeing

the life come back to his hazel eyes. "Sure. Because I don't want to spend my hard-earned money on holiday decorations right now."

He grunted, finished off his tea and stood. "Sounds good to me. Why don't we hit the rack? Get some sleep? After you feed Crawford his breakfast and we eat, we'll go find a nice little tree."

"I'd love that," Kira said softly, suddenly emotional.

Kira tripped and fell in a snowbank as she helped Garret drag the five-foot blue spruce through the knee-deep snow. There was a cloudy, gunmetal-gray sky above them, a few snowflakes still twirling around them. Garret had found a hill not far from the main ranch that was covered with evergreens of all widths and heights.

Last week Reese and Shay had gone out to find their own tree. They'd invited everyone in to decorate and had a wonderful evening doing it. Maybe Kira shouldn't be glad, but Ray hadn't wanted to take part in the decorating, even though he'd been invited. He hated Christmas, he'd told her. Didn't like it at all. That had been fine with all of them, and Kira had loved the evening spent trimming the huge, seven-foot-tall

Scotch pine Shay had chosen.

The snow flew up around her and she closed her eyes, flakes on her lashes, as she turned over on her back. Opening her eyes, she saw Garret leaning over, extending his gloved hand toward her, concerned. She laughed. "I'm okay. I tripped over my own feet!" and she gripped his hand. He pulled her gently to her feet.

"You look like a snow woman," he chuckled, releasing her hand, moving his fingers through her hair, brushing the snow from the black strands.

His touch was galvanizing and Kira absorbed his closeness, secretly taking in his strength, his height, his masculinity. His fingertips grazed her cheek and she looked up into his eyes. And she was lost. His hand stilled against her cheek, their breath white vapor as they stood so close to each other. He was going to kiss her.

It was as if the cry of the nearby chickadees in the trees was turned down in volume. The stillness of the snow on the tree-clad hill embracing them. The look in Garret's eyes, the narrowing of them upon her making her heart suddenly race. Her hand had a mind of its own as she hesitantly placed it against his massive chest. Garret wore his Stetson and he leaned down, cupping her jaw, holding her gently in place as he lowered his mouth near hers.

Her breath hitched as she felt the warm moisture of his breath against her face, holding the burning, intense look in his eyes, feeling her body begin to tremble with such need that it made her want to cry out for Garret. Her fingers dug into his Sherpa jacket and she fractionally leaned up, her mouth barely grazing his.

It was enough. Just enough. Her eyes shuttered as she felt him respond, felt his mouth curve tentatively against her own. This time the kiss wasn't primal or wild. It was, instead, asking her for permission. Asking to allow him to kiss her more deeply. Oh yes!

Kira leaned into him, sealed her lips more strongly against his, letting Garret know she wanted this kiss, too. It wasn't one-sided at all. She heard a growl of pleasure rumble deep in his chest as she felt his arm come around her shoulders, drawing her slowly against him, allowing her time to decide whether or not she wanted this kind of closeness with him. Kira took that half step toward Garret, his arms opening to her. She wanted nothing else but to have this man kiss her once more. She'd loved dreaming about this ever since his first kiss. Now . . .

a second kiss, and a liquid pool of heat began to ache in her lower body.

Garret eased from her lips, whispering her name against them, one hand cupping her cheek, holding her at just the right angle so he could caress her wet lips and savor them. She raised her hand and rested it against his chest, becoming lost in the melting movement of his exploring mouth against hers.

This kiss was so different: tentative, searching, silently asking how far she wanted to go with him. Hot tears stung her closed eyes as she, in some small, functioning part of her brain, realized Garret was testing her, seeing just what exactly she wanted to share with him. She could feel him anchor himself, hold himself in check as her mouth opened further, like a flower blooming beneath his. There was such tenderness in his kiss this time that she couldn't control the tears that slid silently down her cheeks. She felt their warmth meld where their mouths were fused together. She felt Garret's love so powerfully just in the way he kissed her. It was a kiss of hello, of searching and finding a like heart within her.

Slowly, so slowly, Garret eased from her wet lips. He barely opened his eyes, feeling his entire lower body burning with unquenched need for Kira. Her thick lashes lifted, revealing drowsy eyes awash with arousal, and it made him want her even more.

Gently, he wiped the tears from her cheeks with his thumbs. He didn't know why she was crying, but it affected him deeply, tearing him up because their kiss had been so fragile and beautiful. And when he grazed her red knit cap with his gloved hand, she managed a small smile, drowning in his gaze. He reveled in her hands against his chest, and even though there were so many layers of clothing between them, his skin smarted and wanted more of her touch.

"I like what we have," he told her gruffly, holding her in his arms. "I like where we're going with each other, Kira," and he wondered if she felt the same. Dark strands of her hair, dampened by the snow, curved around his hand. He saw her eyes widen slightly, heard a small gasp escape her. Was that a good sign or not? He didn't know. Garret waited because he couldn't do anything else. He felt as if the world had gone away, that they were the only two people on the earth right then. And Kira was in his embrace, her slender body resting fully against his. He wondered if she could feel his erection; he'd never wanted to bury himself in a woman as much as he did her. Kira had to know, now, that he wanted her. She wasn't innocent. She knew about relationships.

"Garret," she began, her voice barely a whisper, "I-I don't know where this is going," and she gave him a helpless look filled with confusion.

His mouth curved a little. "I don't either, Kira, but I like it. I like you. I want to continue to explore what we have." Again, he saw the fear in her eyes. It was real. And it was there. "We'll take it slow," he promised her thickly, taking those wet strands and pushing them behind her ears. "At the pace you want. No pressure, Kira. Okay?" Because he had to say something; it was time. Garret felt as if he were standing on the end of a plank that might give way beneath him. There was surprise in her expression, but also a hunger that was easy to read. At no point had Kira drawn away from him or asked to be released by him.

"Y-yes, I need to know that, Garret. I need time . . ."

He gave her a warm look, caressing her cheeks with the thumbs of his gloves. "Tell me what your tears were all about."

His deep voice moved through her, she closed her eyes and a huge well of old feelings bubbled through her. Garret deserved her courage, not her cowardice. Opening them, she held his green-and-gold gaze, his expression so serious. "Your kiss was so beautiful . . . so . . . caring. It made me cry." She saw all the worry dissolve on his rugged face, saw it replaced with something that made her swiftly beating heart sing. His beautiful mouth, so male and strong, lifted at the corners.

"That's good, then?"

"Yes."

There was no mistaking his male pride that she'd given him her honest, full answer. Heat cascaded through Kira and she moved her palm against his chest. "I wish . . . I wish I knew where this was going, Garret."

"Trust me, Kira," He looked deeply into her upturned face, seeing the fear alongside her arousal. "I won't rush you. We'll talk. We'll go at the pace you want."

She licked her lower lip and gave a jerky nod. "Yes . . . thank you . . . I just need time."

So did he, but Garret didn't go in that direction. To do so would be to open himself up, to own the fact that he'd loved her for nearly four years. He was sure Kira would be totally stunned, maybe shocked, to hear that. Instead, he leaned down, placed a light kiss on her wrinkled brow and then opened his arms to release her. Garret didn't want to, but under the circumstances, it was the wisest thing to do. If she would guide him, let him know how far or fast to go, it was more than he had hoped for. Clearly she wanted him. Garret didn't know who wanted the other more; there was such a savage, intense hunger thrumming through his taut, aching body.

"Come on," he urged her gently, cupping her elbow. "Let's get this tree to the truck. We've got some serious decorating ahead of us this afternoon."

She smiled tentatively and took huge steps through the deep snow back to the tree on the bank. "Could we go into town on the way back to the ranch? I'd like to stop at the stationery store to buy some construction paper. It won't cost much and it will make the tree look so pretty."

"Anything you want," Garret promised. He released her elbow and leaned down, picking up the tree trunk between his hands. "You follow behind me." Because he knew her left hand was weaker than her right and he didn't want her falling again trying to haul the tree by herself.

"Okay," she agreed.

Garret could hardly contain himself, wanting to roar to the world that Kira was willing to explore what they had together. As he dragged the tree through the deep snow, he was grinning. He couldn't help it; hope soaring through him, lifting him, making him nearly dizzy with the possibility that finally — God, finally — there was a door open between them. That he had a chance to woo her, show her that he loved her, that his kisses weren't about just sex, but about something so deep and vulnerable, that his heart and whole life were focused upon it.

There were so many obstacles in the way, and as Garret hauled the tree down the slight slope to the truck, he didn't try to kid himself. Kira had PTSD like he did. Was it possible for a relationship between them to develop with all their symptoms playing hell on them every hour of every day? He knew as he hefted the tree into the truck bed, shaking out the snow from the thick branches, that he needed to communicate with Kira as never before. But one look into her eyes, dancing with such happiness, and Garret was a goner. She'd liked that kiss as much as he had. There *was* something solid between them . . .

As he opened the door for Kira and helped her in, Garret melted at the smile she gave him. All of a sudden his anxiety turned molten and joy flowed powerfully through him. He closed the door, walking around the front of the truck, not even feeling his boots hit the icy road. The day might be snowy and gray, but inside his heart the sun was shining bright and bold. Climbing in, he started the truck and drove carefully down the long road that led back to the ranch. He'd drop the tree off at the house and then they'd go into town and Kira could get her construction paper.

Garret felt as if his whole world had magically shifted as he drove to the ranch. If this was what love released felt like, he wanted it, wanted to absorb it like the starving beggar he was. Wanted to reach out and grip Kira's gloved hand, though Garret stopped himself. He could see her profile, saw her thinking. He'd promised not to press her and he had to hold to his word. She had kissed him in return and the taste of her on his mouth made him want her so damn bad he could hardly think straight.

Christmas this year was going to be better than last, he thought. Shay had gone to great lengths to make him, Noah and Harper feel welcome at her ranch. And now this Christmas had brought him a gift from the past: It had brought Kira back into his life when he thought he'd lost her forever. Garret didn't know what kind of providence was at work, but he was damned grateful it was happening to him.

His mind moved to her journal, a journey of sketches and information about her three years with the A team. He wondered what she had written about him. He didn't have the courage to ask such a thing, knowing her journal was a private, intimate part of herself. Maybe someday she would share it with him. He'd seen what she'd written about their captain. Her feelings. And Garret wondered what feelings she'd had toward him those years they'd spent together in Afghanistan. For now, as Garret slowly drove the truck toward the group of houses, he was more than satisfied. Their kiss this time had been fragile, exploratory and tender; it was as if they were reintroducing themselves to each other. It took everything Garret had to sit still, focus on driving, not give out a loud, triumphant whoop of joy.

CHAPTER EIGHTEEN

Kira tried to gird herself for what was going to happen up at Reese and Shay's home. It was December 23 and the morning was sunny, a blindingly bright blue sky outside the kitchen window. She heard Garret walk in and turned. His face was grim-looking.

"You don't think this is going to work, do you?" He was dressed in a bright red flannel shirt, jeans and boots. They'd just eaten their breakfast and she was cleaning up in the kitchen.

"What? An intervention with Crawford? Hell no," Garret muttered, coming over to the sink and pouring himself another cup of coffee. "Want some more?" he asked, holding up the pot in her direction.

"No, thanks. My stomach's tied in knots. I've never attended an alcoholic intervention before."

Garret snorted and sipped the coffee as he stood near Kira. "It only works if the alcoholic wants to make changes in his life. Crawford doesn't."

She frowned, drying her hands on a towel. "You'd think that after you found the guy selling him the whiskey and his stash was cut off he'd get it."

"Yeah, well, since he's been cut off, Crawford has been anything but co-operative." He gave her a significant look. "I know you keep telling me he's still nice to you, but I have a hard time believing it, Kira."

She knew he was worried. "Ray hasn't changed. He's still short on words, always grumpy, but he's never tried to touch me again or curse me out."

"That's because he's getting stronger every day and he thinks he's going to eventually get his ranch back. He's playing a waiting game with all of us."

"Shay thinks the intervention will work. With all of us at her house with Ray, confronting him about it, she hopes it will help him stop drinking."

Shaking his head, Garret said, "Ray might be cut off for now from his liquor, but that doesn't mean he won't go out and buy it himself once he's ambulatory again. That day is coming, Kira. I promise you that. He has no intention of stopping his drinking.

He's a carbon copy of my old man."

She took in a deep breath. Two days ago, trimming their small tree and putting it in the corner of the living room, had seemed like a miracle compared to the seriousness of today. "I wish . . . I wish this was better timed. It's Christmas."

"Reese is pushing hard for this intervention. He sees what it's doing to Shay and he wants to put an end to it one way or another. He's tired of seeing his wife hurt daily by Ray."

"I know."

"Reese loves Shay and he's protective of her. I don't blame him. I'd be doing the same thing if I were in his shoes."

"But what does Reese hope to accomplish with a family intervention if he doesn't think Ray will try to quit?"

"That Ray will get the hell off the property. He wants him gone and, again, Kira, I don't blame Reese. Legally, he can't force him off the ranch. But he can make it so damned miserable for Crawford to remain that he leaves on his own accord. Reese isn't doing this for himself; he's doing it to help protect Shay. I've seen her going down little by little ever since Ray has been living on the ranch."

"Yes," she admitted softly, turning, arms

across her chest as she leaned against the counter. "I try to be a good friend to her, Garret. She's so twisted up inside because he's her father and yet, at the same time, he's slowly killing her." She opened her hands. "Well, maybe not killing her in a physical sense, but she's depressed. I can see it more and more every day."

"So does Reese. He's going to defend Shay and this is his way of doing it. Shay wasn't sure about the intervention, but he's made it happen."

"Do you think Shay realizes her father is a lost cause?"

"I think she does," Garret said, scowling. "When you're the kid of an alcoholic, the connections between parent and child get screwed up. And with Crawford having a stroke, that's convoluted Shay's world tenfold. She's in denial because of guilt."

"You can't divorce your parents."

He shook his head. "I sure as hell divorced myself from Cal. I knew he was toxic and I didn't want him poisoning my life in any way, shape or form after I turned eighteen."

She slid him a gentle look. "But Shay's predicament is different. She's trying to save the ranch in spite of Ray. Yet she's connected to him emotionally and legally. It's messy, Garret."

"Yeah, it is. I was talking to Reese about it yesterday. He knows it can backfire on them. If Ray decides to stay anyway, it just makes things worse for Shay because after the intervention, he'll know his ability to get whiskey is going to be gone forever. He'll know we're on to him and that as long as he can't drive himself into Wind River, he can't buy liquor. Ray knows we're all actively trying to make him stop. And I'm sure it's pissing the hell out of him." Garret gave her a worried look. "And when we go to that intervention, you let me handle him if he comes at you. Okay?"

"Thanks. I'm feeling really vulnerable about this whole thing, if you want the truth. Ray knows I'm the one who found the bottle. He doesn't know the extent of what I've done yet, and when he does, I'm sure he's going to focus his anger on me. From his viewpoint, it will be my fault that this has happened."

"For sure he's going to try to make you his whipping post, but I won't let him."

Kira felt Garret's dogged shielding of her far more strongly than ever before. She saw it in his narrowed eyes and heard it in his tight, low voice. There were a lot of emotions in his expression. She released her arms and turned, walking over to him. It was the first time she'd touched him since their kiss getting the Christmas tree on that snowy slope. Reaching up, sliding her hand up his jaw, feeling the sandpapery quality of his flesh beneath her fingertips, she whispered, "You have no idea how glad I am you're here at my side." She saw the look in his dark eyes change as she made contact with him. Giving him a small smile of appreciation, Kira backed away. She wanted to kiss him, but his cup of coffee was between them, and besides, the intervention was going to take place in half an hour. "Thank you, Garret, for all you do to help me."

"I have your back, Kira. You've always known that."

Her skin riffled at his thick, low comment. She felt his care, that protective sense wrapping around her even though he'd made no move to physically embrace her. "Yes." She gave him a look and said, "I'm afraid. I hate this kind of angry, tense confrontation. I always have. With my PTSD, my anxiety is already climbing." She shrugged. "I feel like I'm going into a firefight, pure and simple."

He eased away from the counter and set down the mug on it. "Come here," he growled, stepping toward her, opening his arms.

Kira came. She desperately wanted to feel safe in a highly unsafe time for her. Blindly, she turned, moving into Garret's arms, sliding hers around his waist, resting her cheek against his chest. Closing her eyes, she sighed as his arms wrapped comfortingly around her. She stood with him, her body against his. She was half his size, and he felt like a mountain of warm male flesh protecting her when she really needed it. Kira felt him kiss the top of her head and she nuzzled into his soft, flannel shirt, hearing the slow thud of his heart beneath her ear. All her razor-sharp anxiety began to dissolve. And when Garret moved his large hand gently across her tight shoulders, she quivered with need. Kira was so hungry for his next touch, his next embrace. She'd had to hold herself in check since the kiss on the hill.

"It's going to be all right," Garret said against her ear. "We'll get through this combat together, Kira, like we have everything else."

His words were barely above a rumble and the sound of his deep voice flowed sweetly through her, erasing all the tension and anxiety inside her. Kira tightened her arms around him, feeling his hand move slowly up and down her back. Garret's touch felt so good and she absorbed it hungrily, needing him more than ever, afraid of the coming meeting.

"I worry," she muffled against his chest, her eyes tightly closed.

"About what?"

"That — that I might get fired. Ray could turn this around, Garret. He could accuse me of being the reason for this intervention."

"He can try," Garret soothed, kissing her hair again, moving his hand down her back, "but it won't work. Reese will see through it in a heartbeat."

"But Shay might not. I know she's tied in knots and so confused about her father and her own identity. I don't think she'd willingly believe him that it's my fault, but I worry . . ."

Garret squeezed her gently and said, "It's not going to happen. Yes, Shay has a lot of trouble disconnecting herself from her father, but she's smart enough not to blame you for it." He smiled a little, resting his cheek against her hair. "You're such a worrywart, Ms. Duval. Who knew?"

Laughing a little, Kira clung to him, never wanting this moment to end. Garret's arms were strong but not crushing. She loved his cheek against her hair, loved the intimacy that just naturally sprang up between them.

"I guess I am a worrywart," she admitted, a hesitant smile pulling at her mouth. "It feels so good to be held, Garret. Thank you."

"Any time you want to be held, you come to me," he rasped, moving his hand in a slow circle across her back. "Anytime . . ."

Ray Crawford sat in a chair in the middle of the trestle table. At one end was Reese and at the other was Shay. Garret sat opposite of Ray, with Kira at his side. Noah and Harper sat on either side of Ray. Beneath the table, Kira reached out and gripped Garret's hand. It told him so much about her blossoming trust in him and he gently curved his fingers around her small hand, giving her what he hoped was enough strength to get through this confrontation.

The tension in the kitchen was palpable. Shay was pale, her eyes dark and worried. Reese, on the other hand, looked like hard stone, implacable resolve in his eyes. Garret had no problem holding Crawford's angry gaze as he looked at his daughter and then at Reese.

"What the hell is this all about?" he demanded.

Garret felt Kira tense at the man's angry voice. He kept his hand firm around hers.

"This is an intervention," Shay began in a

low tone. She placed her palms flat on the table. "You told all of us when you came to the Bar C that you'd stopped drinking. We know you've been paying a young man to buy you whiskey on a weekly basis."

"What?" he snarled, glaring at her. "That's pure bullshit!"

"No," Reese said in a low, controlled voice, "it's not, Ray."

Ray glared at him. "You have no proof!"

Shay brought out several photos from the file beneath her hand. "Look at these, Father. You tell me if we're making this up." She slid them toward Ray.

Garret felt pleasure as Crawford's eyes widened for a moment as he saw the photos of the whiskey bottle he hid in his dresser drawer.

"What the hell!" he exploded, standing up. "That house is mine! It's private! Who's been snooping around without my permission?" And then his lip lifted as his gaze swung to Kira. "It was *you*!"

Garret felt Kira go into battle mode. Every muscle in her body tensed. His hand tightened. "Stand down, Crawford," he snarled. "And sit the hell down. You yell at Kira one more time and you'll deal with me. Now sit," Garret ordered, holding the man's black glare.

Reese pushed the photos closer to Crawford. "This isn't about Kira. The fact is that you've lied to all of us. You're drinking; the smell is all around you. Your breath, Ray, is what tipped us off. Kira washes and folds your clothes and puts them away for you. She couldn't help but run into that whiskey bottle you had hidden in your dresser drawer. You didn't think she would find it?"

Ray sat down, wiping his mouth, looking at the photos Reese pushed at him.

Garret sat tensely, feeling Kira shaking. It wasn't obvious, but she'd leaned just a little against him and he could feel it. Dammit! He wanted to get her out of this confrontation. It took everything in him to control himself, not to curve his hand into a fist and nail Crawford in the face for yelling at her. He slid her a look, seeing she was as pale as Shay. He wished neither woman had to undergo this kind of battle.

Reese went on. "This is an intervention, Ray. That means that the whole family, everyone on the Bar C, knows you have an alcohol issue. Your doctors have already told you that you'll get cirrhosis of the liver. If you keep drinking, you're going to cut off your life by twenty years. Your daughter loves you and the rest of us want the best for you, which means you have to stop drinking. We care enough about you to talk openly to you about it. We want to find ways to support you and help you stop drinking."

Garret gave Reese a helluva lot of credit: The man was genuinely sincere, holding Crawford's gaze, his voice low and filled with emotion.

Garret didn't care about the bastard. He'd had eighteen years of an alcoholic shoved down his throat, watched it kill his mother, so he had no compassion for Crawford at all. Garret felt like a wild dog wanting to rip a man's throat out and kill him because he was killing his family with his decisions. Just as Cal had killed him and his mother.

Ray glared at all of them. "How could you?" he snapped at Shay.

Shay reacted as if shot. She straightened, opened her mouth, then closed it. Her eyes went wide with shock.

Garret started to speak just as Reese stepped in. "Ray, if you can't be kind to your daughter, if all you can do is yell at her, then you yell at me. I won't allow you to continue to hurt her. She's your daughter."

Crawford glared at Shay. "This is all your fault. You did this!" and he jammed his finger down on the table.

"No," Reese said, "I did. This was my

idea, Ray. Look at me."

Garret had to give Reese a lot of credit under the circumstances. He could feel his gut tie into a painful knot. He felt Kira quivering like a frightened deer next to him. He saw Shay look as if she'd been gutted. Noah and Harper's faces were hard, anger in their eyes, but they remained silent.

Only Reese, his steely reserve and patient-sounding voice, broke through the anger at the table. Garret's protective mechanism was working overtime. He wanted to shield both women from this out-of-control bastard.

Ray jerked his gaze to Reese. "You? Who the hell do you think you are?" He jabbed his finger at Reese. "You're nothing but a broken-down military vet. You couldn't take care of yourself. You had to come crawling to Shay for help. You're just like all the rest of them!" and he jabbed his finger toward Garret, Kira, Noah and Harper. "I don't have to do a damn thing here. I *own this ranch*!" he roared. Ray shoved to his feet, breathing hard, glaring at them, his hands flat on the table. "You all listen to me. You are *not* the owners of this ranch. You never will be! I'm the owner, by God!" and he slammed his fist down on the table.

Garret started to release Kira's hand,

springing out of his chair.

Reese instantly grabbed at Garret's left arm, forcing him to sit back down. He slowly unwound and rose to his full height. "Ray, you're out of control. And we're the legal owners of the Bar C. Nothing is going to change that. Now you have a choice here: You can stop drinking, start acting respectfully toward everyone on this ranch or you can leave. It's your call."

Garret was controlling himself, feeling every cell in his body going into fight mode. Kira sat there, frozen, her face etched with anguish. He saw Shay had tears rolling down her cheeks, her hands gripped in front of her on the table. He heard Crawford's loud, raspy breath. Saw the man's face turn a bright red color, hatred for all of them in his small, brown eyes.

"None of you," Crawford grated, "deserves my respect!" He shoved the chair violently back and it went flying across the floor with a bang. Turning, he grabbed his cane, heading for the hallway. Every line of his body was stiff and jerky as he moved. His mouth was set, his jaw jutted forward.

Garret sat there watching Crawford disappear down the hall. They heard the door open and then slam shut. He turned, seeing the man limping down the cleaned sidewalk, heading back toward the other houses down the slope.

He heard Kira sniff and turned, frowning. He saw such devastation in her wounded eyes and automatically slid his arm around her, hauling her against him. He saw Reese move toward his wife, opening his arms to her. Shay sobbed and got up, flying into his waiting embrace.

Sitting there, smoldering with rage, wanting to hurt Crawford as much as he'd just hurt these two women made Garret grind his teeth. Shay's sobs filled the air and he winced inwardly. Kira had buried her head against his shoulder, her hand on his chest, curled into him, her whole body tense.

"Garret?" Reese said in a low voice, "Take Kira home. This intervention is over."

He nodded and gently unwound Kira from his embrace. "Come on," he urged her quietly. "Let's go home." Noah and Harper nodded toward him, their faces stony and grim.

Nodding jerkily, Kira gave Reese and Shay a worried look.

"We'll be okay," Reese assured her quietly. "Go home and take care of yourself, Kira. Let Garret help you."

Garret rose and took Kira's hand and pulled the chair out for her. When she stood, he drew her beneath his arm, giving her a sense of protection. He wished he could do so much more for her. He held Reese's eyes, alive with unspoken anger as he held his weeping wife.

"What are your plans?"

Reese gave him a flat, hard look. "Crawford's gone. And he's going to know it very shortly. I'll take him off the ranch myself."

"Let me help you."

"Need more help?" Harper asked.

"No, thanks, we have it," Reese told him and Noah.

Reese nodded. "I'll drop over and get you later, Garret." He kissed Shay's hair, soothing her with soft words.

"Come on," Garret coaxed Kira gently, leading her toward the hall.

Kira couldn't stop the tears as she sat down on the couch with Garret at their house.

He got her beloved pink afghan and wrapped it around her shoulders. She didn't want that; she wanted Garret. Giving him a pleading look, she whispered, "Will you be my blanket instead?" She saw his hardened face melt with so many feelings that it choked her up. In a heartbeat, Garret sat down on the couch, opened his arms and pulled her against him, holding her tightly.

It was exactly what Kira needed. His strength. His mountainlike stability in a world that was in chaos outside as well as inside her.

She buried her face against his neck and jaw, her eyes shut tight, one arm winding around his waist. Just the way he kissed her hair, her temple and her wet cheek, sent a powerful longing through her. Garret could be so tender with her, as he was right now. Each stroke of his fingers through her hair, across her shoulder and down her back took a little more of her rampant anxiety away from her.

"T-that was an awful meeting," she muffled against his chest. "Ray's a horrible person. But he's still Shay's father . . ."

"Don't feel sorry for the bastard," Garret breathed savagely, grazing her arm. "He brought this on himself through his own choices. No one did this to him. He took it on himself, Kira. All I care about right now is you. Just you. Forget him. He's not worth your time or care."

Quivering, she felt as if her entire insides were made of jelly and she couldn't stop it from happening. It was all part of her PTSD; when severely stressed, that unsettling symptom appeared. Garret held her, cosseted her, made her feel safe in a world that wasn't. "What do you think Ray is going to do?"

Garret pressed a kiss to her temple, gently wiping the tears from her cheek. "Reese and I will go over to talk to him. I think he'll tell Crawford he's not welcome here any longer."

Kira sniffed and raised her head enough to meet Garret's gaze. "What does that mean? Legally? Can Reese do that?"

"He and Shay are the owners of the Bar C, Kira. It's his right to throw anyone off this ranch he wants to." Grimly, he added, "I think Reese has had it. He's a man of a lot more patience than I am. He kept giving Crawford a long rope to hang himself on and he finally has."

"I-I felt so sorry for Shay. My God," she sniffed, wiping her eyes. "That hurt her so much, Garret. I'm crying for her, too. How awful she must feel."

"I know, I know, sweetheart, but right now, you're my focus. I want to take care of you, help you through this. I know how hard it was for you to sit there and take Crawford's shit." His mouth flattened. "It's not going to happen again. Not ever," and Garret leaned down, caressing her lips in a butterfly-light kiss.

A soft moan caught in Kira's throat as

Garret's mouth glided across her lips. She tasted him: the coffee he drank, the salt of her spent tears flowing between where their mouths clung to each other. And as he cupped her jaw, bringing her more surely against his lips, her skin tingled wildly. She clung to Garret for solace, out of love for him and because she needed the safe harbor he offered her. She felt the moisture of his breath against her cheek as she opened her lips, telling him she wanted so much more from him. Her body ached for him as his mouth rocked hers open and took her more deeply. She pressed herself more surely against his chest, wanting more of his mouth on hers, wanting even more contact with him.

Slowly, Garret disengaged from Kira. He looked into her half-opened eyes. "Kira, if we keep going . . ."

She nodded, easing away from him, touching her mouth. She had his taste on her lips. Seeing the burning look in his eyes, the arousal, she understood what she was saying. "Yes . . . you're right. I'm sorry —"

Garret reached out, cupping her chin. "Don't ever be sorry for kissing me, sweetheart. It's just that you turn me on, turn me inside out, and I don't want to stop at just kissing you." He held her gaze.

Kira felt her lower body melting with need for Garret. She saw he wanted to make love to her. It was right there. Right in front of her. Clear. No guesswork. Sitting there, legs tucked beneath her, she felt her whole world tilt and change. Whether she wanted to or not, Kira whispered, "I understand . . ."

"Maybe," Garret grimaced, "another time. But not right now. I know Reese isn't going to wait long before confronting Crawford. Once he gets Shay taken care of and settled down, he'll be coming over here to pick me up."

Feeling tortured by so many emotions — her feelings toward Ray, her hurt for Shay and Reese — she nodded. "Of course. You're right. God, what a mess this turned out to be."

"No one said interventions were fun," he growled. Garret eased her away from him and stood up. "I'm sure Reese is going to remove him today. I don't know to where, but from the look in his eyes, he's no longer willing to subject Shay to her father. Not when he's like this."

"Right," she whispered. Rubbing her face, she placed her feet on the floor. "I should go over to be with her, once you two get Ray off the ranch."

"That would be a good idea. She needs

someone."

There was a knock at the back door.

Garret turned. "It's probably Reese." He looked down at her. "You'll be okay?"

"I'm fine," she said, lying. Right now Shay was far more hurt than she was. And Kira wanted to be there for her. And she didn't want to concern Garret, who had worry in his eyes. "Go. I'll be with Shay until you guys get back."

CHAPTER NINETEEN

Kira fixed Shay some lunch even though she said she wasn't hungry. Just the act of puttering around the kitchen helped calm her anxiety. An hour earlier, Reese and Garret had left with Ray in the truck. There were three suitcases in the rear. Hearing the door open and close, she looked up to see Noah and Harper sauntering in.

"Thought we'd drop by to see if we can be of help," Noah said, taking off his coat and hat and hanging both on a peg.

Harper was next, nodding hello to Shay and taking off his coat and hat. "You've had a stressful morning. Can we do anything for Shay or you?"

Kira felt warmth and gratitude toward the two vet wranglers. She motioned to the table. "I'm doing okay, thanks. You guys have a seat. Shay is lying down, so let's keep our voices low. I'm making tuna sandwiches for lunch. Would you both like some?"

Noah wandered over, peering over her shoulder at the bowl of tuna. "Let me help you." He rolled up his sleeves and washed his hands at the sink.

Kira smiled a little, thinking Noah was like a wolf in a pack. He was a team player. "Sure."

"Can I make coffee for everyone?" Harper volunteered, coming up and standing on the other side of Kira.

"Perfect," she murmured. Giving him a quick smile, Kira saw the concern in both men's eyes.

Cutting up the sandwiches, Kira placed them on a large platter that she handed to Harper. Noah grabbed a sack of potato chips off the top of the fridge. Kira brought the pot of coffee over to the table. As she poured each of them a mug, Harper distributed the sandwiches and Noah dropped a handful of potato chips on each plate. It wasn't much of a lunch, but it would do.

Kira sat down, Noah sat beside her and Harper sat opposite her. "Had Reese filled you in about the upcoming intervention?" she asked them.

"Yes," Noah said. "I didn't think it would go well, if you want the truth."

"Me neither," Harper agreed. He studied Kira. "You look pretty peaked to me. How are you holdin' up, gal?"

She loved Harper's soft Appalachian drawl. "Stressed out, but nothing like the way Shay is feeling right now. She got hit broadside by her father's attack. I feel so bad for her."

"It's gonna take her time," Harper said between bites. "She's a strong woman; got more grit than she realizes. She'll pull through this rough patch okay."

"Reese did the right thing for Shay," Noah muttered, anger in his tone. "Crawford's a mean dog. Even dogs don't do that to one another. Crawford treats her like hell. It's not right."

Harper chuckled a little. "Yeah, Crawford could learn a thing or two from your horses, couldn't he?"

Kira felt surrounded by their warmth. No one was more gentle than these two men. Noah, because he worked with horses, and Harper, because he'd been a combat medic. Each had sensitivity and she could feel them circling the wagons around her and Shay. She didn't want to look in a mirror, knowing she probably looked pale and drawn.

"Where're they taking the old man?" Noah wondered.

"I don't know. We'll find out a lot more when they get back." She wished Garret would call her, but that was being selfish.

"Reese had a plan," Harper told them, giving them a quick glance.

"Oh?" Kira asked, curious.

"Yeah," Harper said quietly, reaching for a chip. "Reese asked me and Noah a couple of weeks ago what we'd do if we were in his shoes."

"Really?" Kira raised her brows.

"Hey," Noah said. "He was a company commander, taking care of a hundred-plus Marines, Kira. And judging from what we see, he was a damn fine CO. He's treating us like his company now, and that's not a bad thing."

"He wanted our ideas and opinions," Harper confided. "How Crawford being here was impacting us and our jobs. The man cares, that's obvious."

"Yeah," Noah said, "even about us."

"I wonder if he talked to Garret. Reese never spoke to me about it," Kira said.

"You're close with Shay. Reese probably knew from her how you were feeling," Noah pointed out. "Plus, you were in the bullseye, Kira. You had to see Crawford three times a day, seven days a week. I'm sure Reese probably had a pretty good handle on how you felt about things. Garret would certainly give him observations and feedback on how it was affecting you on a daily basis."

Harper reached out and patted her hand. "Kira, you wear how you feel on your face. You know that, don't you?"

It was her turn to grimace. "I know." She sighed.

Noah finished off his sandwich in quick order, ate all the potato chips and dumped more onto his empty plate. "I think Reese looks at all of us as Marines under his care. As the CO, it's his job to take our temperature, ferret out how we feel and to get ideas from us. He's done that before and he'll do it now and in the future."

"So," Kira said, "Reese probably knows exactly where he's going to take Ray."

Harper grinned. "Bingo. Now you're catchin' on, gal."

She smiled a little. "That makes me feel better, actually. I had horrors of them dumping Ray back at the nursing home back in Jackson Hole or something."

"Naw," Harper said, giving her a wink. "My bet is he's already got a condo or apartment rented for Crawford. I think he's seen this coming for a while. As a CO, you do long-range planning where and when you can. You know your people and you create strategies accordingly. Plan B, C and

D. Crawford just got handed Plan B, whether he knew it or not. Reese is a good tactician and strategist."

"I think after he talked to us weeks ago," Noah chimed in, "Reese decided to get Crawford out of here as soon as he could because of how it's continued to take Shay down."

It made sense to Kira and she actually relaxed a lot more, realizing how strategic Reese had been. He was protecting Shay because he loved her. He wasn't going to keep putting her into the line of fire with her father, who refused to be decent to everyone. "Well," she uttered in a hushed tone, looking toward the hallway to make sure Shay wasn't nearby, "I'm personally glad he's gone."

"I'd be, too, if I were in your shoes," Harper said, giving her a sympathetic look. "Now you can focus on doing translations."

"And photos," Noah reminded him. "How's that going for you, Kira?"

"Much better than I ever hoped," she admitted. "I'm not making a huge amount of money, but every little bit helps. I think as I expand my portfolio over the next year, I can bring in a nice, tidy sum every month for the ranch and for myself."

"That helps all of us," Harper agreed.

"Hey," Noah said, stretching his neck and looking out the front window, "the guys are back."

Instantly, Kira's heart beat faster to underscore her relief. "Is Ray with them?" She was sitting at the wrong angle to see the truck pull into the driveway.

"Nope," Harper said. "He's not with them."

Kira bit back a sigh. She heard a sound and turned. Shay was coming down the hall, rubbing her face, looking drowsy. She got up and went to her.

"Reese and Garret just got back," she told her, quietly guiding her to her chair at the table. "Would like something to eat, Shay?"

She shook her head. "No, thank you. Maybe some coffee?"

"Coming up." Kira headed to the kitchen. She heard the front door open and close. Reese and Garret's voices were low, but carried down the hall. Pouring three cups, she met the two men as they walked into the warm kitchen. Her gaze went immediately to Garret, who nodded slightly at her. She saw anger and darkness in his eyes as he shrugged out of his jacket and Stetson. Reese's face was unreadable and Kira wasn't sure what that meant.

Reese sat down after kissing Shay's cheek.

He thanked Kira for the coffee.

"Have you guys eaten?" Kira asked. "We have tuna sandwiches." She stood near where Garret sat down and instinctively placed her hand gently on his shoulder. He looked tense. She could feel the tautness in his muscles. There was tightness at the corners of his eyes as well. He turned a little, giving her a slight smile of thanks.

"No, we haven't, and I could eat," Reese said. He held out his hand to Shay and she took it. "Come here," he coaxed, "and sit down with us?"

"Garret? You hungry?" Kira asked.

"Starving. Could you make me two sandwiches, please?"

"Sure."

"Two for me, too," Reese said, giving her a look of thanks.

Noah got up. "I'll help you out, Kira."

In minutes they had the sandwiches ready. Harper passed the men the chips, and pretty soon they were eating hungrily, without much talk going on at the table. Kira refilled their coffee cups and then sat down next to Garret, her hand resting on his thick thigh. He closed his hand over hers. She could feel the tension in the kitchen, but it was nothing like before. She saw the hollow look in Shay's face and knew she needed to hear about her father.

Reese didn't take long. He left the second sandwich on the plate, wiping his mouth with a paper napkin. Wadding it up, he looked at all of them. "Ray is now at the White Water Condo complex. He's got a nice two-bedroom condo on the first floor and it's completely furnished. Garret went and got him groceries, so he's well stocked. He's at a point where he's quite able to make his own meals and take care of himself." He took Shay's hand and squeezed it gently. "Your father is fine. He's not happy, but I think in time he'll cool down and adjust."

"I was so afraid he was going to have another stroke," Shay admitted hoarsely, rubbing her eyes.

"Right now," Reese said gently to his wife, "we need to climb down off this cliff we've all been living on since Ray came back to the ranch. It's no one's fault, but an alcoholic can turn a family inside out, creating nothing but continued drama and ongoing stress and chaos." He smiled a little, looking at everyone, his voice low with emotion. "Tomorrow is Christmas Eve. I'd like to invite all of you over for dinner. Garret has agreed to fix it for us."

Harper rubbed his hands together, grinning widely. "That's great! I always look forward to your vittles, Garret."

"We're going to have ham wrapped in bacon and pineapple, red-eye gravy and mashed potatoes. I'm going to make two pecan pies for dessert. I know that's a big favorite of yours, Harper."

The medic's grin widened even more. "That's a Christmas gift to me," he said, a sudden catch in his voice, gratefulness in his tone.

Kira's heart melted. She'd heard Harper's folks, Bailey and Irene Sutton, who lived in Ontario, Oregon, desperately wanted him to come home. But Harper couldn't handle home, like so many returning vets. Both his parents were originally from Virginia and were hill people. She felt such love and pride for Garret; the meal he was cooking was purely Southern and truly would be a gift for Harper, who had a gleam of gratitude in his gray eyes.

"Oh, and some homemade biscuits," Garret added, giving Noah a wicked grin.

"Good," Noah said, "I was hoping you'd make them. I've never tasted anything as good as the ones you make, Garret. My ma would kill me if she heard me say that."

Kira saw Shay respond to the happy, positive banter around the table, a little color tingeing her cheeks. A fierce love for Garret rose in her chest. She wished they were alone. Wished she could throw her arms around him, hug him, kiss him and thank him for his big, generous heart. Not much got past Garret, and she knew he realized everyone was hurting from this morning's battle with Crawford. The stress he generated had been ongoing for all of them.

"Long-term, Reese? How's my father going to make his appointments?" Shay asked in a soft voice.

"Either Garret or I will drive Ray to any appointments he has." Reese gave both women a serious look. "Neither of you will ever do anything for that man again. We want you out of his sight. Neither of you deserves to be around him." He sighed and gave Shay a tender look. "I know he's your father and I'm not saying you can't visit him. But for right now, I think it's wise you steer clear of him. He's not in a good place and frankly, I think he's going to continue to drink. There's nothing any of us can do about that."

Shay closed her eyes, dragging in a ragged breath, her hands tightly clasped on top of the table. "What you're saying is true. I just have a tough time with it is all."

"Well," Reese soothed, "maybe you'll have

the time now to put yourself back together instead of always being torn apart by him. Give yourself some time to sort everything out."

Garret held Shay's sad gaze. "Listen, Reese and I have this. We're your guard dogs. Ray knows he has to call one of us on our cell phones. He's not allowed to call here to the main house. Right now, you need time and space to heal. You don't need ongoing daily upsets." And then his lips hooked upward a little. "Besides, I want you hungry and looking forward to my Christmas Eve meal."

Shay rallied and gave Garret a watery smile. "You're right. And I am going to start taking better care of myself. I promise."

Garret pointed his chin toward Reese. "He's just the guy to get you back on your feet, so let him help you, okay?"

The table had turned into a low-key therapy session, but Kira wasn't surprised. Dr. Hilbert had given them tools to deal with stressors and other issues. She was so proud of Garret. Everyone looked to him because he'd been here the longest of all the vets who'd come to the Bar C.

Kira's respect for Reese was also growing, now that she'd seen the man in action. He had a strategy to protect the woman he loved and he'd pulled the trigger on it to ensure Shay would get exactly that. Kira knew Garret was very much like Reese. He, too, was a long-distance planner, and she'd often seen him do that in Afghanistan.

"Look," Reese told them, "it's one o'clock. Let's all get back to work. Routine helps de-stress all of us. Garret, we'll see you here at about ten a.m. tomorrow. Can you have dinner ready for us at five p.m.?"

"Sounds good," Garret murmured, draining the rest of his cup and standing, "I'll be here." He offered Kira his hand. "Ready to go home?"

"How are you holding up?" Garret asked her, taking Kira into his arms, holding her, allowing her to decide how much space should remain between them. All morning he'd ached to hold her. Every protective hackle he had was up and in place for her. He'd seen the devastation, the shock on her face, when Ray had rounded on her during the intervention. It had taken everything Garret had not to cock his fist and deck the man with one swing. He didn't care if Ray had had a stroke; his savage rage aimed at Kira outdistanced any concerns Garret had for the older rancher's health.

She smiled tiredly and walked into his

embrace, sliding her arms around his waist and resting her head against his chest. "I'm fine now," she murmured, closing her eyes as his arms came around her.

"Do you feel like doing some translating? You look pretty stressed," he said, kissing her hair as it tickled his chin and jaw. Garret wanted to love her. Right now. But it was bad timing. He didn't want her so stressed out that she couldn't be a fully focused partner. She deserved so much more than that. Just having her lean against him, her breasts pressed against him, their hips lightly grazing each other, was more than he'd ever expected. Savoring her against him, the scent of her, the citrus fragrance of the shampoo she used, conspired to make him thicken.

"No, not really. I just feel like a mess inside, Garret. I think I'll go draw in my journal, make some entries . . . something that doesn't require much of me. Just a way to come down from this and relax."

He squeezed and then released her. Because if he didn't, Garret was going to do the unthinkable: lift Kira into his arms, carry her down the hall to his bedroom and make slow, passionate love to her.

Someday . . . someday Garret wished more than anything else he could tell Kira he loved her.

"Why don't you go do that? I need to help Harper down at the indoor arena. A lot of the renters are coming in to ride their horses before Christmas."

She eased out of his arms. "I know. That indoor arena was a great business decision on Shay's part. We're full up with thirty renters and their horses. It's bringing in some good money for the ranch."

Garret drowned in her exhausted-looking gray eyes. He nudged some strands of hair off her cheek. "Hey, forget about the business, sweetheart. Go play. Put some good stuff in your journal. Grab that pink afghan, sit out on the couch and relax, okay? You don't have to make Crawford any more meals. I want you to rest this afternoon. I'll make us dinner tonight."

She reached up, grazing his hard, implacable jaw. "Thanks for the nudge. I think I might take a nap later, on the couch. I'm drained, Garret. It's been a marathon with Ray and I'm totally exhausted."

"I know you are," he rasped, dropping a kiss on her brow. He turned her around and said, "I'll see you about dinnertime."

Garret entered the kitchen quietly at four thirty. The last of the indoor arena horse people were leaving as night started to fall. For the next two days the arena would be closed for the holiday. It would give all the wranglers some needed downtime and relaxation. Closing the door, he heard soft instrumental music coming from the radio in the living room. He hung up his coat, hat and gloves and walked quietly across the tiled floor to the living room in his wet cowboy boots.

Garret saw Kira sleeping on the couch, all curled up beneath her afghan. His heart wrenched with love for her. He saw there was color back in her cheeks, and that was a good thing. Moving quietly — he had been black ops trained after all — he approached the coffee table in front of the couch where Kira slept. Her huge, rectangular journal was open across it. He frowned, honing in on it. Her pen was in the center, but what he also saw drew his immediate attention. On the open pages facing the chair opposite the sofa was a sketch of himself.

Quietly sitting down, he wondered what Kira had written about him beneath the drawing, as well as on the next page.

He examined the head-and-shoulders sketch of him in his floppy hat, a three-quarter rendering. He was bearded, smiling, dressed in his cammies. Kira's ability to capture his likeness startled him. Garret leaned forward, amazed at her talent.

His throat tightened as he read her lazy scrawl.

Today, Garret's smile went straight through my heart. I love his laughter. It booms out of him and touches everyone around him. I wonder if he realizes how happy he makes me feel when he laughs. There was a goat kid trapped in a nearby ditch, next to one of the fields, and the little boy, Ahmad, was struggling wildly to get the kid loose. Garret came along with me and saw the problem. Ahmad is eight, and he was crying with frustration and fear because he couldn't get the kid free. I watched Garret soothe the child and then gently get the kid's wedged hoof and leg out of that pile of rocks. His hands are so huge, like a giant's hands, but I watched how gently he handled the shaken, frantic kid, who was baahing at the top of its lungs. The kid's mother was nearby, bleating frantically for her baby. Once Garret made sure the kid was okay, he released it and it went running back to its mother. They both ran down the road, happy.

What touches me most about Garret is

how he relates to the Afghan children. He drew Ahmad to him where he was crouched, pulled the boy between his legs and helped brush his tears off his face with those big hands of his. I watched Ahmad stop crying, crowding deeper into Garret's arms, wanting to be held by him. I had to turn away. I had tears in my eyes because he was so loving toward Ahmad. The child has a nasty father who beats him with a strap nearly every day. And I know none of us want to see it happen to Ahmad. The captain is trying to get the chief of the village to make the father stop beating Ahmad. The child is only eight. My God. It's so heartbreaking.

I think Garret knows the little boy needs a good father. And he always goes out of his way to hug him, give him special treats, praise him and try to rebuild his broken confidence. It's so easy to love Garret. I wish I could tell him just that, but it would never fly. Not here. I can't break the unity of our team. It's so hard sometimes not to want to become intimate with Garret. I know he doesn't know how I really feel about him and he never will. I'm just glad he treats me like a good friend. It's more than enough to be able to live in the same house with him, listen to him laugh, listen to how he thinks and watch him focus on the village and his care of these poor, struggling Afghans. I just wish, in my heart of hearts, I could throw my arms around him and tell him how proud of him I was today when he helped Ahmad. If that kid had broken its leg, his father would have beaten the poor child mercilessly, blaming him for it. Goats are a sign of wealth, and every goat is worth a lot of money and prestige. Ahmad would have suffered terribly if the kid had to be killed due to a broken leg. Garret came and saved the day. But that's who he is: so protective of those who need protection. I love him fiercely for that.

Garret slowly stood up, not wanting Kira to suddenly awaken and find him reading her journal. His heart thrashed in his chest and he swallowed hard, a hundred emotions roiling around his chest. He moved quietly back to the kitchen, his mind in shock over what he'd just read.

He stood at the sink, looking at the night fall over the valley. Placing his hands on either side of the cool stainless steel, he closed his eyes, hanging his head, Kira's scrawled words branding every inch of his heart. She loved him? The date on that page was nine months into their first year of deployment to that Afghan village. Stunned, he shook his head, opening his eyes, wondering how blind he'd been. Kira loved him? Had she never not loved him? For damn sure she'd never said a word about it to him.

Garret understood her need to hide her feelings from him. Hell, he'd hid that he loved her, hadn't he? Both of them were mature enough, smart enough, to know that to allow their love to be known to each other, would have torn the team apart in insidious and dangerous ways. Both had kept that secret locked in their hearts, silent.

He stood, rubbing his chest where his heart lay. Garret began to think about the ambush and the time after he was wounded. If Kira honestly loved him as her words seemed to indicate, she must have gone through such painful grief over not being able to find him after the ambush. Worse, he'd had amnesia for six months, not even knowing his own damned name, much less knowing he loved Kira.

All that had changed when his memory returned. And that was when Garret had turned over heaven and hell trying to locate Kira. To hear her father, Les, who was in tears on the phone with him, telling him that she'd left his home and he didn't know where she'd gone had gutted Garret. Kira had been gone from both their lives and it had hurt like hell.

"Dammit," he muttered darkly, turning, staring through the quiet kitchen. His heart roiled with anguish, need and love for Kira. He wondered if later entries in her journal still talked about her love for him. Had she fallen out of love for him because she couldn't initiate a relationship with him in Afghanistan? Her father had never mentioned anything like that to him. Wouldn't it stand to reason that Kira would tell her father if she still loved him? And wouldn't Les have told him? Garret rubbed his jaw, feeling the bristles of his five o'clock shadow beneath his fingers. Scowling, he stood there trying to figure it all out.

All he had to go on was one journal entry by Kira, written early in their deployment. Things could have changed, and yet he was sure she wasn't in any long-distance romantic relationship during those three years. He had lived with her and knew she sent e-mails regularly to her father, but there had been no hint that there was a man in the States waiting for her.

Garret didn't know whether to shout to the heavens for joy or to stop and get logical about that entry in Kira's journal. *One entry.* Were there others? *Maybe.* Kira's journal was private. It wasn't like she'd showed it to him. She'd probably been exhausted and accidentally left it open on that page when she left it on the coffee table. Oh, she'd shown him sketches of some of the team members, but she'd never handed the journal over to him to look at her sketches of him. No, it was like a diary to her, and now Garret felt guilty about looking at it more closely and reading it. He should have walked away. He should have . . . Hell. He loved her. He'd been curious. It didn't make what he'd done right and Garret knew that, but it was human nature.

Had Kira continued to love him throughout the years or not? If she had, the ambush, the PTSD afterward, had changed her markedly. The love she held for him had probably been destroyed in the wake of that one life-changing event. Or was it possible that she had continued to love him through those years, regardless? Garret found it impossible to believe that Kira had held a torch for him that long. Especially when he'd disappeared off her radar after the ambush. What had she thought when she hadn't heard from him again? That was enough to kill anyone's love.

He stood there, feeling ripped up over his unexpected discovery. Now he was sorry he'd allowed his curiosity to push him to take a peek at her journal. He didn't know what to think. Or what to do. One thing was for sure: he felt a mountain of grief overwhelming him because at one time she'd silently and secretly loved him. And he hadn't picked up on it. Not at all . . .

CHAPTER TWENTY

Kira was awakened by the sound of pots and pans being moved around. She yawned and stretched, the living room mostly dark except for the light coming from the kitchen. Garret was home. It felt so good to think that. *Home. With her.*

She slowly pushed the afghan aside and sat up. Drowsy, she realized she hadn't closed her journal before she fell asleep. Her mind wasn't working well; she leaned forward, closing it and pulling it over to her. The love she felt for Garret was so strong that she needed to go back to the pages in it to read every entry and sketch she'd made of him through the years. It gave her solace now, as it always had. It was as if her words, along with the sketches, fed her starving soul and spooned her hope of a future with him. They were now, slowly, becoming intimate with each other. It thrilled Kira as nothing else ever had.

Slowly, she pulled on her boots and stood up, rubbing her face. Tucking the journal beneath her arm, she walked into the kitchen. Garret was at the counter, putting together their meal. He turned his head slightly in her direction.

"Hey, sleepyhead," he teased. "Did you just wake up?"

"Yeah," she murmured, giving him a soft smile. "What time is it?"

"Eighteen hundred." And then he corrected himself. "Civilian time is six p.m. Do you feel better?"

"Much," she murmured, going over to the oven. "What are you making? Smells delicious."

"Baked chicken with rice and veggies. Should be done in about twenty minutes."

She turned, seeing the table was already set. Giving him a teasing look, she said, "You're such a house frau, Fleming." She watched his serious features melt and that smile she loved so much appear, lifting her, squeezing her heart with longing.

"And aren't you glad, Trouble?"

Laughing, Kira nodded. "Better believe it. I like the idea of a man in my kitchen."

"Not just a cook either," he reminded her archly. "Chef quality."

She groaned and nodded, hesitating at the

entrance to the hallway. "A five-star chef for sure. I'm already thinking about that red-eye gravy you're going to make from the ham drippings for tomorrow's dinner." She saw pride come to his hazel eyes. It felt good to praise Garret. "Give me ten? I'll be back," she promised.

"Gosh, I'm stuffed!" Kira said, placing her hand over her stomach, giving Garret a look of thanks. He was a master at using spices and the chicken was savory, making her eat a lot more than she'd intended. Satisfaction gleamed in Garret's eyes as he picked up their plates, taking them to the sink.

"You have to have some room left, Kira. I made ginger cake with lemon sauce."

She groaned. "I'm going to gain too much weight, Garret," and she tugged at her waistband.

"You're at least twenty pounds underweight," he reminded her, sliding the plate in front of her. Handing her a fork, he added, "And from now on, you're in my hands. You need that extra weight back, Kira. You'll never endure the winter cold without a small layer of fat on your body." He lightly pinched her forearm. "Look at that; you're a skinny chicken right now compared to the woman you were in Afghanistan."

She grinned and saw the amusement dancing in his eyes as he sat down. There was a piece of ginger cake at least twice the size of hers on his plate. But to be fair about it, Garret was doing a lot of hard, physical work every day out in cold, freezing weather. He worked mostly in the indoor arena, helping Harper clean out the thirty horse stalls. That was demanding, backbreaking work. And when they got done with that chore, they had to clean leather, bridles and saddles. The place was nearly spotless. They were vets; they knew what clean meant and were willing to work to achieve that goal.

More than anything, another part of what she loved about Garret was that no job was beneath him. He was a man who did his best no matter what he was asked to do. She felt so proud of him. Garret had never been a slacker and he didn't know what the word *lazy* meant. All she had to do was feel the roughened quality of his hands on her and it told the story of his hard work.

"You know," Garret murmured between bites, "Christmas is here. When did you and your parents open gifts?"

"Why, Christmas morning of course." And then she smiled a little. "Wait . . . I remember once you said you used to open them on Christmas Eve."

Shrugging, Garret said, "Yeah, when my mom was alive, we did. She was like a kid: loved Christmas and couldn't wait to open her gifts." He frowned. "Not that Cal ever bought her a damned thing. When I was young, I didn't understand that he was a drunk. When I was nine, I went out and bought my mom a small gift. She loved dragonflies, and when I was walking home from school, I passed a shop that had a small dragonfly pin for sale. It wasn't much, just costume jewelry, but I bought it for her."

Kira sighed. "That was so sweet of you. Did she like it?"

Garret nodded. "Yeah, she cried, it meant so much to her. My father always drank heavy on Christmas Day, so she had chosen Christmas Eve for me to open the gifts she'd gotten me." His voice grew emotional. "I'd never seen her cry until the time I gave her that piece of jewelry. And she kept hugging me so much I felt like she was going to suffocate me."

Touched, Kira reached over, grazing his hand. "That's such a beautiful memory to have of her." She saw the pain, the memories, in his lowered eyes, feeling his loss deeply. "She sounds like she was a wonderful mom to you, Garret. I really wish I'd known her."

He dragged in a ragged sigh and shook his head. "Cal killed everything he touched. The only reason I didn't die under the bastard's watch is because I left the moment I turned eighteen."

"And you love children so much," she murmured sympathetically, holding his dark eyes. "You're a natural father. I saw it in Afghanistan, how you became like a second father to all the boys in the village. They loved you so much and you gave so much to them in return."

"Yeah, I liked the little rug rats," he muttered.

Kira felt sadness cloaking him. "The holidays always bring out the best and worst in all of us," she agreed quietly.

"Did you see? Santa Claus left you something under our tree." He hitched a thumb toward the living room.

Brows raised, Kira said, "Why, no," and then she prodded his lower arm. "What did you do?" She saw him smile a little. "Garret? Did you buy me a gift?"

"Sure. Why wouldn't I?"

"Darn it," Kira muttered darkly. "I got you something, too, but it was supposed to be a surprise. I was going to sneak it out before Christmas morning and put it under the tree for you."

"And I ruined your surprise."

"Yes."

He reached out, ruffling her hair. It was something he'd always done to her because it got such a reaction out of her. She squeaked and dodged his hand this time, too, laughing with delight.

"You're the troublemaker, Fleming, not me," she challenged, smiling into his eyes.

"Naw, not me. You got that reputation all on your own, Ms. Duval. Now, do you want to open your gift on Christmas Eve or Christmas Day? I'm fine with either." And then Garret gave her a wicked look. "But as I recall in Afghanistan, every Christmas when you'd get a package from your dad, you'd tear it open on the spot. Forget about Christmas Eve or Day, you didn't care. Right?"

She felt heat moving into her cheeks. "Well, yes, but that was over there. It wasn't really very Christmassy in Afghanistan. Oh, I know we decorated some spindly tree one of the guys found, but it wasn't like being home." Her voice grew merry. "Besides, when I'd get my gift, you were always poking at me to find out what was in it, not to wait until Christmas. Really, Garret, you're nothing but a big kid under that man's body of yours. You were just as curious and eager to see what was in my dad's package as I was."

Chuckling, he lifted his hands. "Guilty as charged. So? When would you like to open your gift?"

She held his warm gaze. "It makes no difference to me. It's kind of nice to be celebrating a real Christmas with you and really? You're my gift, Garret. It doesn't get any better than that for me." She saw his eyes narrow slightly, felt that powerful, invisible embrace go around her, flow through her. Was it love? Was that what she was feeling? Because it felt like it even though Garret had never used the word. Never spoken about his feelings for her directly.

"Okay," he rumbled, "then let's open them Christmas morning."

"This I have to see," she teased. "You're worse than a kid about Christmas, and I've seen it."

"It'll give you time to wrap my gift, then."

She gave him a dirty look. "I suppose you know what it is?"

"No. There hasn't been much time to do anything but deal with Crawford's tempests in a teapot."

She grimaced. "You're right about that. I

haven't wrapped your gift yet." She waved her finger in his face. "And don't you dare go snooping and look for it!"

He gave her a look of mock horror. "Me? I wouldn't do that to you, Kira."

"You did it in Afghanistan. You were well known by every guy on the team; if they got a Christmas gift, you'd sneak into their house, carefully unwrap it and look to see what was in it. And then you'd rewrap it and make it look like no one had seen what was inside. Good thing the captain caught you doing it the third year." She laughed, shaking her head. "I'm black ops, too. I'll make *sure* you don't find your gift beforehand."

His mouth curved ruefully. "I'm not going to try to find it. I promise."

"Sure. You're the fox in the henhouse, Fleming. I've got your number. Don't even try it."

The joy Kira felt at Reese and Shay's home the next evening was night-and-day different from two days earlier. Christmas music played on the radio, wafting quietly in the background. The tall Scotch pine had been fully decorated and stood colorful and bright in the corner. Beneath the spreading branches was a red quilt that had been in

414

Shay's family for a hundred years. She had told everyone her great-great-grandmother had made the quilt and it had always been spread beneath the tree, the gifts on top of it. Kira liked that kind of family tradition.

She'd just arrived and was standing, admiring the tree, when she saw Garret walk into the living room. He had a green apron around his waist and a large oven mitten on his left hand. For the celebration he wore a dark green country shirt with pearl buttons, the color bringing out the green in his eyes. "Everything smells wonderful," she said.

"You sure look pretty," he said, coming up to where she was standing.

Shyly, Kira touched the long blue denim skirt that brushed the tops of her boots. She'd dug into her duffel and found a bright red sweater with a mock turtleneck and decided to dress up for the occasion. "Thanks."

"How'd the call go to your father?"

She sighed. "Always good. He was glad to hear I'm doing better. He was worried."

"I know."

"He said he got my Christmas gift yesterday, so he'll have something from me."

"What did you get him?"

"One of the fall photos I took of the

Tetons. My dad loves nature, especially mountains. He's never been in this area of the country and I know he'll love it."

"He can hang it somewhere he can see it," Garret said. "I'm sure every time he does, he'll think of you."

Her heart warmed. "I miss him so much. He asked if maybe I could come home next Christmas. If I felt well enough to come home for at least a visit." She gave Garret a pained glance. "I'm hurting him and I feel awful about it."

He touched her shoulder. "You're doing the best you can, Kira, and I believe he knows that."

"That's true," she whispered, sad. "He never begs me to come home. He knows I'm struggling. I love him so much. I really do miss him: his counsel, his holding me when he knows I need a hug."

"Maybe by next year you can go home," Garret said. "Not everyone has parents who love them like Les loves you."

Kira lifted her chin, seeing the loss in his eyes. She slid her arm around his waist, giving him a hug. "I know. I shouldn't take it for granted." She released him and stepped back. "I value my father so much. I love talking to him once a week. He's always been there for me, even after I ran away."

He slanted her a warm look. "I have a feeling you'll be home for Christmas next year."

"I hope so," she murmured. "I just need to keep getting stronger, less anxious. More focused."

Noah ambled into the living room, his hands shoved in the pockets of his jeans. "Hey, you two lovebirds, did you see? There's a gift for each of us under that good-looking tree."

"I've put my gift under it," Kira said, pointing toward a red-foil-wrapped gift. She liked Noah calling them lovebirds. Her heart had sped up.

Noah came over and nodded, looking at all the brightly colored presents beneath the tree. "This is my first Christmas with Shay and Reese. I didn't know they'd be getting us each a gift. I didn't have one to give." And then he brightened. "Maybe a ride on Poncho, who isn't kicking humans anymore."

Laughing, Kira walked over and threw her arm around Noah's broad shoulders for a moment. "Don't worry about it, okay? Gifts are exactly that: you give what you can, and if the gift is yourself, that's more than enough."

Noah hugged her back and released her. "Ever the optimist, Kira. You do my guilty soul good." He moved closer to the tree. "What's this? A second gift for me?" He picked up a large green-foil-wrapped present in both hands.

Kira grinned. "That's from me to you. And it's nothing special, Noah. Just a small gift is all."

He made a face and gently put the present down beneath the tree. "I didn't get you anything either, Kira. Want a ride on Poncho?"

She laughed. "No worries, Noah. You're my gift. You let me come down and help you train some of your nicer horses. I love doing that."

Garret said, "I'm off to the kitchen. Noah, if you have a moment? Table has to be set."

"Roger that," Noah said, leaving with him.

Kira stood by the tree, feeling incredibly happy. She had done a pen-and-ink drawing of Shay and Reese, a portrait to their shoulders, standing next to each other. She felt some anxiety, hoping they would like the framed, signed sketch from her.

For Noah's gift, she'd drawn him next to two of the horses he had trained. She thought he would like it. And Harper's gift was a drawing of him on horseback, moving down the fence line with that wrangler slouch of his. He was on his favorite quarter horse, Jeb, and she thought it had come out looking nice.

Her heart swelled as she thought of Garret's portrait, hoping he would like it but not sure. She had withheld his from the tree here and instead put it beneath their own. There was a silver-wrapped gift for her already beneath the boughs there and she'd seen on the tag that it was from Garret. When he'd left the house, she'd gone in and lifted the box. It had some heft to it and she shook it a little, hoping to hear something. But she didn't. Curious, she had gently set it down next to her gift for him, curiosity burning through her.

She looked out the window. Night had fallen long ago, but the porch light out front exposed the heavy snow falling silently around the house. It was a perfect Christmas for Kira. She was with people she loved. There was peace in this house now, not upset as before. Shay had dressed up in a golden sweater and black wool slacks and wore a pair of small pearl earrings. Everyone had dressed up and it had felt good to Kira to get out of her own wrangler clothes for a little bit. Even Reese was dressed in a pair of gray slacks and a black sweater, looking every bit like the Marine Corps captain he'd once been. It was so nice to see him and Shay together, love clearly in their expressions for each other. It made Kira's heart lift with joy. She heard Harper and Garret jawing and joking with each other in the kitchen, bringing another smile to her face.

"It's a very different energy tonight," Shay said to her, coming over and sliding her arm around Kira's waist and giving her a hug.

"Isn't it, though?" Kira looked at her, seeing dark circles she'd covered with base makeup. "How are you doing, Shay?"

"Better." Folding her hands in front of her, looking up at the tree, she whispered, "I keep thinking of my father. He's alone at that condo. He has no one."

"He made his choices," Kira said gently, smoothing her hand across Shay's shoulder. "It's not easy on you or him, but he put himself into this predicament. You didn't."

"I know." Shay rallied and gave her a weak smile. "I should be thinking of how happy everyone else is. The difference in the guys between when Ray was here and gone is shocking."

Keeping her expression neutral, Kira said, "Garret lived with an alcoholic for eighteen years, Shay. He knows what it does, how it affects everyone like a deadly infection. In time your father will adjust. He's got a roof over his head, food and medical care. He's strong enough to do so much more than he could right after the stroke."

"Nothing stays still forever." Shay gave her a wry look.

Kira shrugged. "Love is eternal."

"Love, yes. It's . . . well, beautiful. Reese is so wonderful to me, so patient. I don't know what I'd have done without him. He's such a wise people manager."

"That's because he ran a company of Marines," Kira said with a grin. "The guy has hands-on experience with a tough group of men and women. I thought he was amazing in the crisis with Ray."

Shay said, "He told me he was going to get Ray out of here. He saw what it was doing to you. Garret came to him a number of times, worried and with legitimate gripes on your behalf. Reese listened."

"I knew nothing about that."

Shay smiled a little. "No. You were under enough stress. Reese had to figure it out and then ran it by Garret first. Later, he consulted with Noah and Harper. We all wanted you out of the line of fire. I especially knew what you were going through every day and I didn't have the will or the courage to step in and take over for you."

Kira squeezed Shay's cool, damp fingers.

"Listen, you lived with Ray for eighteen years. He wore you down and wore out his love and welcome with you. I know you see that."

"I do. It's an ongoing process for me to separate out our father-daughter relationship and the fact that he never loved me. That's the hardest part to accept, that a parent doesn't love his own child. I just don't get it, Kira. I mean," she touched her heart with her hand, "if Reese and I have children someday, I'm going to love each and every one of them."

Kira saw the agony in Shay's eyes, the questions unanswered between her and Ray. "I'm sure," she said thickly, "any child you and Reese have will be the most-loved kid in the world. Hands down."

"You can count on it."

"Sometimes," Kira said wistfully, "parents teach children by their example what not to be or do. In your case, as well as Garret's, you learned what not to do. You took a positive, healthy road and made good choices for yourselves instead. You need to be proud of yourself for that, Shay. A lot of kids get run under an alcoholic parent and never come up for air. It ruins them forever. At least you two had the internal strength to overcome it and go in the right direction."

"Mmm, you're right." Shay hugged her. "You're wonderful for me, Kira. You remind me of all the good things I've done, the positive choices I've made. Thank you."

Later Kira sat beside Garret at the long trestle table, the air thick with laughter, talk and smiles. Everyone ate as if they were starved. The scent of freshly baked biscuits slathered with butter and honey made Kira down two of them instead of just one. Everyone was relaxed and in a good mood. Even Shay rallied, and there was a lot of trading of military stories among the group. She felt the camaraderie, the love among all of them . . .

At one point Reese told a story about one of his Marines falling into a ditch used by the village as a latrine. It had been during a night patrol and an IED had been fired. The Marine had lunged into what he thought was simply a farm ditch. Wrong. Kira laughed until tears rolled down her cheeks. So did everyone else.

Afterward, Kira sat on the U-shaped brown leather couch in the living room with everyone else as Shay and Reese distributed the gifts beneath the tree. She was surprised to see a very long pole wrapped in red foil handed to her. Frowning, she looked at the tag. It was from Garret. She turned, giving him a questioning look.

"It's a gift," he said smugly. "You're just going to have to open it to see what it is. I'm not telling."

Grinning at him, she playfully jabbed him in the ribs with her elbow. "Come on. Can't you give me a hint?"

"Sure," he said, his smile increasing, "it will help you."

Snorting, Kira muttered, "That's not a hint, Fleming. Feels like a crutch to me."

"Well, in two seconds we'll all get to open our gifts and you'll see."

Kira could hardly wait to see the look on everyone's face when they opened the framed sketches she'd drawn for them. Why had she been afraid they wouldn't like them?

Shay burst into tears when she saw their portrait, her hands over her lips, looking with such love at Reese as he held it out for her to see. And she saw moisture in Noah's eyes as he looked at himself standing next to his horses. He gave her a watery smile of thanks, holding that framed drawing as if it was life itself. Harper hooted and held up his sketch in its dark green wooden frame.

"Look! It's me and Jeb! Doing what I hate the most: fence mending!"

Everyone howled.

Most of all, Kira wanted to know what

Garret's reaction would be, but she'd have to wait until they got home to see that.

"Hey," Garret coaxed, "open up my gift. It's time now."

She smiled and put the long pole out in front of her, opening up one end of it. "What is this? A pole to hit you with, Fleming?"

He chuckled. "God, I hope not."

Everyone laughed heartily.

Her smile slipped as she peeled the paper off and realized it was a monopod. Most camera buffs had a tripod or a three-legged affair on which they'd affix their camera to take a stable shot. A monopod was one-legged and allowed the photographer to put the camera on top of it. Kira gasped as she looked it up and down. It was a good one, made of graphite, lightweight but sturdy.

"Like it?" Garret asked, holding her gaze.

"It's perfect!" she said, suddenly emotional, running her fingers down the sleek black surface.

"This way," he said, his smile slipping, becoming serious, "you'll be able to balance the camera with the three fingers of your left hand. No more camera almost slipping out of your hands."

She sniffed and wiped her eyes, self-conscious. "I knew this is what I needed, but the Canon PowerShot won't fit on this."

"I know. It's for a Canon D7," he said.

"Well," she said, giving him a grateful look, "I'll put this in my bedroom in the corner, where I can see it every morning. And it will inspire me to keep saving money for another D7." She saw Garret's eyes twinkle, but he only nodded, saying nothing more.

"It's a step in the right direction for you, Kira."

She wanted to lean over and kiss him, but she wasn't ready for everyone to know how she felt about him. "Thank you," she whispered, gripping his hand and squeezing it hard. "You're helping me to make a dream come true . . ."

CHAPTER TWENTY-ONE

Kira could hardly sit still while Garret slowly and carefully unwrapped her gift to him. They had walked back in the snowstorm to their home after everyone broke up after dessert, Garret's ginger cake with lemon sauce.

She sat on the edge of their couch, their knees touching, watching him and wanting him to hurry opening it. Would he like it or not? She held her breath for a moment as the paper came off and he turned it over, frowning. And then she saw his face grow soft, emotion in his eyes as he studied it for a long time. Silence cloaked them and then he lifted his chin, holding her gaze.

"This," he rasped, "is incredible, Kira. Thank you," and he stared down at it.

"Do you like it? I was afraid . . . well, afraid that it would bring back too many bad memories for you, Garret." She had painstakingly rendered the entire Special

Forces A team standing together with them in the sketch as well. They were all smiling, their arms around one another in a semicircle, staring outward at the viewer. They were dressed in their normal Afghan cammos and floppy hats, the weapons they wore every day, a pistol on their hip or in a drop holster on their thigh. Some of the men carried knives on them as well, plus a cartridge web belt.

"Damn," he whispered, choking up, "you are good, Kira. Every one of the guys look like they really did." He moved his hand across the glass, as if to reach out and touch each one of them again, his frown deepening.

Her throat tightened. "I'd taken a photo of us that third year. I don't know if you remember. I'd shown Ahmad how to hold the camera and snap it. I tried to resurrect the photo from memory."

She saw so many feelings, raw and alive, come to his eyes as he stared silently down at it, his hand moving almost in a caress across the large drawing. It was two feet wide and two feet long. She'd taken some of her translation savings and gone into town to a good frame shop and bought one for each of her sketches for the vets' Christmas gifts. The frame she'd chosen for this one was dark green, a reminder that they'd been in the Army.

"This," Garret rumbled, his hand stilling over the sketch, "is priceless, Kira. Thank you."

She felt tears burn in her eyes and hastily brushed them away. "You really like it, then? It's not a painful reminder that we lost them? I was so hoping you'd see it as a celebration of our lives together . . . something we all experienced, that we had such great times together, too. Laughter . . . jokes . . . you know . . ."

Garret's mouth softened. "Yeah," he said roughly, sliding his fingers across the thin wooden frame, "we had a lot of good times, too. And this reminds me of that, our better days. Happy times . . ."

Pressing her hand to her heart, Kira closed her eyes and whispered, "Thank God. I was so hoping you'd take it in the spirit I sketched it." Opening her eyes, Kira saw the sadness in his gaze, knowing this sketch would bring back everything to him. But maybe, just maybe, it would also remind Garret of the joy they'd shared together as a group of people who wanted only to help the struggling Afghan people.

Maybe the good times could gently assuage the grief she knew Garret still had locked inside himself. Help to bleed it off a little at a time instead of him being afraid it would overwhelm him if he allowed any of those feelings out of that box he kept buried deep within himself. Kira knew it was taking a risk, but she also knew Garret couldn't keep on living without dealing with those emotions sooner or later either. She hoped the sketch would be a relief valve, a slow way of healing him as he looked at it from time to time.

Garret set the picture on the coffee table and brought her into his arms. "Sometimes," he said, his voice low and thick against her hair, "I think you're more magic than real, Kira."

She snuggled into his arms, feeling happiness thread through her as her cheek rested against his shoulder, her arm went around his torso. "Oh no," she laughed softly, "I'm very real and wounded. You know that. I'm just glad you like the drawing, Garret. I didn't do it to depress you."

He closed his eyes, resting his jaw against her hair. "You must have spent a lot of time making it. That's a hell of a lot of work and you put so much detail into it."

"It was," she admitted, rubbing her cheek against him. "I had to use the other sketches from my journal to get each guy's face exactly right. I didn't want to get it wrong. I want to always remember them, Garret. They're a part of us forever."

He pressed a kiss to her cheek, sliding his fingers through her loose hair, nudging the strands across her shoulder. "It's a very healing gift for me. You knew that, though."

"Guilty," she whispered, lifting away from him, meeting his dark, burning gaze. "I know you haven't grieved yet, Garret. I was hoping the picture would open up that process a little, in small amounts, over time. I wanted the guys all smiling. Because we loved them and they loved us. They deserve not only our missing them but also to remember the good things about all of them, the laughter; the fun times, too." She reached up, cupping his recently shaven cheek, a finger resting against his flesh. "You have to let that grief out and start working through it all. We both know that. And I felt this was an easier way of opening up that dark place within you. Maybe a gentler way of starting the process?"

Garret took her hand, placing a kiss on the back of it, his eyes never leaving hers. "Like I said, I see you as magic in my life, Kira. I always did. That's never changed." He held her hand and looked at the sketch on the coffee table. "I'd like to hang that in the hall, where I can see it all the time. Do you mind if I put it there?"

Hope rose in her chest. "No, I think that's a wonderful place. Then I can see it, too. When I was drawing it, I remembered so many things about the guys; their wives, girlfriends . . . their children . . . and it made me feel happy because they were smiling. It made me feel good, not sad. Maybe, over time, it will do the same for you, too."

He sighed and nodded. "It's not going to be easy," he warned her. "I'm scared of letting any of it loose within me."

She pulled her hand from his, running her fingers down his arm. "Garret, I'm here. I want to be a support for you. Let me?" She searched his agonized gaze. The words *I love you* nearly tore from her lips as she silently willed him to say yes to her offer. There was such a war going on inside Garret that she could almost feel it. For a moment she saw his eyes grow moist, and then that disappeared. His grief was on the surface; she had known that since meeting him here at the ranch. Giving him a playful shake, she smiled and said, "We can do this — together. Like we've done everything else. Okay?" She patted his shoulder. "I might be small, but I'm mighty, Garret. On hours or days when the grief brings you to your knees, you can cry on my shoulder if you want. I'll just hold you. I won't let you go."

He shook his head, the corners of his mouth flexing inward with pain. "You're so damned fearless when it comes to anything having to do with emotions, Kira." He caressed her cheek. "You always were. It scares the hell out of me. But you throw yourself into them, work through them and come out on the other side okay."

She leaned up, placing a swift kiss on his mouth. "Trust me, Fleming, you can do this. God gave you a heart, too. He gave you a rich palette of emotions and bright, beautiful feelings. If I can do it, so can you. Society taught men they shouldn't cry or feel, but they should. I'm here. I'll walk you through it. You can talk to me about anything. I won't let you down. I have your back." She saw a glitter in his eyes, knowing it was tears threatening to fall. How Kira wished he would cry. It would help get the process started, but these darned A team guys pretended they were impervious to the normal slings and arrows life threw at them. It wasn't so, and Kira knew it. She eased out of his arms, not wanting to allow the happiness of the night to completely dissolve.

"Can I open my gift now?" she asked,

pointing toward it. Instantly, she felt a shift in Garret, a rakish grin coming onto his lips. There would be other times, she knew, when she would go the distance emotionally with Garret's grief. The next two days, however, she wanted only good things to happen between them: laughter and smiles.

She would gently steer him in a direction of lightness, not darkness. They'd seen enough darkness already. She craved the happiness she knew they could have with each other.

Unwinding, Garret said, "Stay put. I'll get it for you."

She laughed. "What? You don't trust me with it?"

He smiled a little and leaned down, picking it up. "I trust you with my life," he said and he gave her a meaningful look that quickly made her smile disappear. Damn, he didn't want her to go in that direction. Kira had saved his life already. And in so many ways, Garret silently acknowledged, since she'd stepped back into his life, he was better off for it. As he had been in Afghanistan. Every day with Kira under his roof in that village had been a secret pleasure known only to him. He'd savored their quiet hours with each other as he was doing right now. Handing her the gift, he made sure it was safe in her outstretched hands.

Sitting next to her, he leaned back, watching the delight on her face as she tore, like a child, into the paper. Garret could hardly wait until she saw what it was. How would she react?

Kira gasped and snapped a look up at him. "No! This isn't what it says, is it, Garret?" and her eyes were huge with shock.

"Open it," he said quietly, gesturing toward the box.

"Oh my God," she whispered unsteadily. "Is it really? Is it, Garret?" and she ran her trembling hands over the box. A picture and the printed name of the Canon D7 camera was on the top and bottom of it.

Garret couldn't help but smile. "Find out, huh? Open it. It's not going to bite you, Kira." She looked stricken as she opened it and took off the top of the snug wrapping. Kira gave a little cry, her hand flying to her lips, her eyes wide with joy. Garret wanted to crush her in his arms in that instant, but he stopped himself. The look on her face was priceless and he burned it into his heart forever.

With a sob, Kira gently pried the D7 out of the box, holding it as if it were very fragile and might suddenly disappear.

"Oh, Garret. How? How did you do this?"

and she turned, lifting the camera in his direction. "This costs sixteen hundred dollars. You don't have that kind of money. None of us do."

He gave a lazy shrug. "Is it what you wanted?" He swallowed against the lump forming as tears streamed down her face. Kira gave a jerky nod, her fingers caressing the camera, touching it here and there, as if making sure it was real, not a figment of her imagination. "Dreams do come true," he told her huskily, holding her watery gaze. "Merry Christmas, sweetheart."

Sniffing, she shakily wiped the tears from one cheek, gripping the camera with her good hand. "Garret . . . oh, you shouldn't have done this. It's so expensive."

"You're worth it, Kira. You have no idea how good it makes me feel to see that look in your eyes right now." Because she was incredibly happy, her gray eyes were like soft, glinting diamonds. Her lower lip trembled as she stared down at the D7 in her lap, her hands gently stroking it, as if the camera were a much-loved child. For a split second Garret thought hotly of Kira pregnant. With his baby. She would make one hell of a loving mother and he knew it. If only . . .

Sniffing, Kira managed a choked laugh

and carefully set the camera on the coffee table. Scooting over to him, she threw her arms around his shoulders, holding him tightly, burying her face against him. "T-thank you, Garret . . . but it's too expensive." She released him and sat there, staring at him. "How did you do this? How?"

"It doesn't matter," he told her, reaching out, brushing the tears off one cheek with his fingers. "What matters is you're worth it and this camera is going to help you get better, Kira. That's all I care about. Okay?" He saw her trying to figure it out. She was damned smart and Garret hoped she wouldn't put it together.

"No!" she breathed suddenly, gripping his wrist. "Oh, Garret, you didn't! Tell me you didn't sell your Rolex to get the money for this camera."

Busted. He eased her fingers from around his thick wrist, pulling it to his lips, kissing the back of it. "It's just a watch, Kira." He saw fresh tears roll down her face and she sat there, shaking her head, her eyes filled with pain.

"No . . . no, that's not true. You loved that watch, Garret! You bought it when you graduated from Special Forces school. I know how much it meant to you." She made an unhappy sound, shaking her head. "You shouldn't have done this!"

"I wanted to," he said patiently, holding her hand, moving his fingers slowly up and down her arm. "And it's okay, Kira. It's just a watch. Nothing more."

"No!" she cried, pulling her hand out of his. "That Rolex meant the world to you. It was something you treasured."

His heart squeezed in his chest as he saw upset in her eyes. "Listen to me," he said quietly. Framing her face with his hands, he held her tearful gaze. "You are a treasure to me, Kira. Do you understand that? Money can't buy you. What you give me is worth far more than any money or any watch. I wanted to make you happy. I didn't realize just how much photography meant to you until just recently. I've seen it lift you up, help you. Don't you think I want only the best for you? If I had to sell a measly watch for that camera, I'd do it again in a heartbeat. You're my world, Kira. Not that watch. It's nothing compared to you. I want you to take that camera and start using it. Please?" He saw anguish in her eyes, her face glistening with tears. It hurt him to see her cry.

And then, Garret thought *to hell with it* and leaned down, gently curving his mouth across her lips, tasting their wetness, the salt of her tears. A moan rose in Kira as he deepened the kiss, wanting her to share in the joy of the moment, not remember him selling his Rolex. Her mouth was incredibly soft, opening, blossoming beneath his and his entire body went wildly hot and hungry. He cautioned himself because right now Kira had been overwhelmed emotionally by receiving something she'd thought she'd never have again: her camera.

Gentling his mouth against her lips, he sipped from her, tasting her, kissing each corner of her mouth and then reluctantly easing away. Garret opened his eyes, drowning in the glinting silver deep in her gray gaze, telling him she enjoyed this kiss as much as he did. "You," he whispered roughly, "are a treasure. My gift, Kira. You always have been. You always will be." He couldn't keep his secret any longer and it felt so damn good to release it, to let her know. No matter how she took his raw confession, Garret was glad he'd finally spoken the words. He wanted to tell her he loved her, but that would have probably shocked her even more than she already was.

He watched her thick, black lashes drop against her flushed cheeks, a fine tremble moving through her. She opened her eyes and gripped his upper arms, staring up into his eyes.

"H-how long?" she whispered brokenly. "How long, Garret?"

Confused, he frowned. "How long?" He saw her eyes grow as confused as he felt. Garret didn't know what she was talking about. Kira licked her lower lip and he saw her struggling to think beyond the hazy lust created by their kiss. He wasn't thinking too clearly either. Concerned, he rasped, "I don't understand your question, Kira."

She managed a small shake of her head, her eyes wide and vulnerable-looking. "How long have I been your treasure?"

Her words were feathery, sounding far away and strained. It slammed into Garret what Kira was really asking him. God, did he dare tell her the truth? All of the truth? She was clinging to his gaze, searching his eyes with a desperation he could feel within himself. If nothing else, Kira deserved his courage and his truth. She'd risked her life to save his. He could do no less for her now.

"I've loved you ever since you came onto the A team, Kira."

Garret saw shock roll through her expression. Tears filled her eyes. What had he done? Had he hurt her? Disappointed her? Worse? He didn't know, but he could no longer sit on the truth of loving her. She

440

made a small, strangled sound in the back of her throat and he frowned, using his thumbs to push the tears off her cheeks. "Talk to me," he demanded hoarsely. "Why are you crying?"

Kira managed a choked sound and pressed her cheek into his palm, closing her eyes. "I've loved you forever, Garret."

Now it was his turn to feel shock punch through him as he registered her barely whispered words. He felt her tears collecting in his palm, felt the firm warmth of her skin against his cupped hand. It took long moments for the dots to connect, to realize that they had both fallen in love from the get-go. His whole foundation rocked and he couldn't speak.

Kira lifted her head, pulling out of his arms, trying to stem her tears. Garret sat there, staring at her, wondering if he'd heard right. Maybe he'd made up her response? Hadn't heard her correctly? He was almost afraid to say anything, to break the precious feeling that made him feel utterly bound to Kira. Everything was so fragile between them right now. So . . . possible . . .

Kira sniffed and looked up at him. "You've loved me from the start? When I first came into the A team?"

His brow scrunched; her words were halting, afraid. He saw the fear of rejection in Kira's wide, flawless gray eyes that overflowed with joy and terror. Clearing his tight throat, he rasped, "Yes. From the start. It just happened, Kira. I didn't expect to fall in love with you." And then his mouth quirked. "But I did." Reaching out for her hand clenched in her lap, Garret laid his over hers. "Know this: I never stopped loving you for one second. Not even after the ambush. My memory was gone for six months, but when everything suddenly downloaded and I realized I loved you, I immediately called Les. He didn't know where you were, Kira." His fingers tightened over her damp, cool hand. "When you'd call your father, you never told him where you were."

"I remember you telling me that," Kira whispered, her hands pressed against her face. "I'm so sorry, Garret. I-I didn't know." Her hands fell to one side and her voice was raw. "I thought — -I thought you didn't want to reconnect with me. I thought my love for you was one-sided. My side. I loved you, but you didn't love me." Her face crinkled and fresh tears fell. This time Kira didn't try to wipe them away as she hung her head, looking haunted, an apology in her expression.

"Come here," he coaxed, his voice low with feeling as he eased her into his arms. Garret sat back and settled Kira against him. To his relief, she didn't resist. It felt so damn good to have her cheek resting against his shoulder, her arm around his middle. He smoothed the sweater down across her back, his hand coming to rest against her hip. "I love you, Kira. I've never, for one second, ever stopped loving you." He felt her move her head, tipping it back so she could look up at him. Her eyes were stormy and he slid his fingers through her hair, some of the strands damp from her tears. "I've sat on telling you so ever since you walked back into my life here at the Bar C. I wanted to tell you, but Jesus, I was afraid to, sweetheart. I was afraid it was one-sided. I didn't know you'd fallen in love with me, too."

She swallowed hard. "I love you, Garret. I never stopped . . . never . . . not even when I couldn't find you after the ambush. No one would tell me anything."

"Because we were black ops, Kira. The Army circled the wagons around us. We disappeared off the radar. I'm sorry . . . so sorry this happened." He saw the agony in her eyes. "And it must have been a special hell for you, thinking I didn't care about you. That I'd just walked away from you afterward." He drew her against him, holding her tightly, feeling her quiver once, her fingers digging into the fabric spanning his chest. Taking a deep, ragged breath, Garret released it, feeling so much relief. Kira loved him. Had always loved him. It had been mutual. His head spun with shock, elation and grief . . .

Kira whispered, "Don't be sorry, Garret. You didn't do anything. You were injured." She moved her hand across his powerful chest, feeling his flesh tighten beneath his clothing. "It must have been a shock when I showed up at the Bar C." She lifted her head, meeting his somber gaze.

"Helluva shock," he admitted. "But the best damn shock I'd ever gotten. I couldn't believe you were there at the table with Shay. At first I thought I was seeing things." He smiled a little, grazing her cheek. "It was the happiest day of my life."

"When I saw you, I about came unglued. I didn't know you were here. I thought I was seeing a ghost. I didn't know what to do . . . what to say."

"You seemed pretty unflappable from where I was standing," he said wryly, leaning down, kissing her brow. "I was pretty close to fainting from the shock of it all."

Kira nodded. "That made two of us, believe me." Kira searched his eyes. "What now, Garret?"

He shrugged, holding her and never wanting to let her go again. "Move forward? We know what we have has already stood the test of time." His mouth curved faintly. "Four years we've loved each other even though we couldn't speak about it or act on it. Kinda reminds me of the Victorian era." He saw the corners of her luscious mouth tip upward, some of the darkness leave her eyes. Each time her hand moved across his chest, he wanted to groan with pleasure. How long had he waited to have her in his arms like this? To be able to freely speak of how he felt about her? And the biggest bombshell of all was that she loved him as much as he loved her.

"We couldn't act on it while we were on the team and we both knew it," Kira said quietly. "We knew better."

"Yeah, it wouldn't have worked. It would've broken the team's back." He slanted her a tender look. "But I've got to 'fess up, Kira, I damn well was glad you were living in that small house with me. You have no idea how much I enjoyed our private talks, getting to know you. I've got all those memories back and they kept me company even after we were wounded and separated."

She looked at the coffee table, her voice warm. "I had my journal." And when she looked back up at Garret she saw guilt in his expression. "What?"

"I have another confession to make." He gestured to the journal. "I came in here last night to see how you were and you were asleep on the couch. When I got closer to you, I glanced at the coffee table and saw a sketch of me in your journal." He gave her an apologetic look. "Curiosity got the better of me. I should have controlled myself, but I wanted to see it."

"Oh no," she muttered.

"Yeah," he said, "I read what you wrote. About the kid getting its leg stuck in that rock pile?" He saw Kira press a hand over her eyes.

"You read that I loved you," she whispered.

"Yes."

Kira sighed and pulled her hand away from her eyes. "Then . . . you knew . . ."

"After getting over the shock, I tried to think my way through it all," he admitted, frowning. "That entry was dated nine months into your first deployment with us.

I didn't know if you still loved me in year two, three or after the ambush."

Kira pulled out of his arms and said, "I'll be right back. Don't move."

Garret watched her slide off the couch with that feminine grace of hers, his body burning with need for her. She walked quickly across the living room and down the hall. He knew she was retrieving her journal. When she returned, he saw the happiness in her eyes. She sat down next to him, opening the huge journal so it lay across his lap as well as hers. Fingers moving through the thick, creamy pages, she stopped at one.

"I have ten sketches of you in here," she admitted shyly. "Twice as many as any of the other guys. This is the first entry, three months into my first deployment with you and the team."

Garret looked at the pencil sketch. She had drawn him as he slept on his sleeping bag on the floor of the mud-and-rock hut they'd lived in in the village. He was in his tan T-shirt, mouth partly open, sleeping deeply, his hands around the pillow. Kira was incredibly talented; he saw all the tiny details in the large drawing. His gaze drifted to her scrawl beneath it.

I wish I could lay beside Garret. He always makes me feel safe even though we're always in an unsafe environment. Even when he snores at night and wakes me up, it makes me feel protected. I turn over, smile and go back to sleep. It's as if he's always on guard. I'm falling in love with this guy. I don't know how it happened or why. He's so kind to others, always a smile and a hug for the boys of the village. I find myself selfishly wishing he would throw those strong arms of his around me. But I know it can't be. But God, I wish it could happen.

CHAPTER TWENTY-TWO

Kira felt her heart swelling with euphoria as Garret sat quietly with her. She turned the pages until she found the second drawing of him. "This was sketched three months later." She gave him a rueful look. "By that time I knew I was in love with you. I fought it at first, but by the end of the first six months, I knew you were the man I wanted in my life forever." She saw his eyes narrow on hers with an intensity that made her body clench with need. She pulled her gaze from his, moving her hand lightly across that sketch and the next page, where she'd poured her heart out.

Garret studied the sketch. She had drawn him with several little Afghan boys around him as he crouched down near one of the fruit tree orchards. There was a skinny mongrel of a dog with them as well. She'd drawn it looking toward him, the boys with their hands on his massive shoulders, a third child kneeling down in front of him. They were all smiling. "I remember this," he said quietly. "That's Ahmad on the right side of me."

She nodded. "Yes. I was walking toward you, going to help you with the ditch digging to improve the village's irrigation system when I saw this happen. You knew your size and height scared the kids and you were always either kneeling on one knee or crouching down to make yourself look less threatening to them. Ahmad had just been beaten by his father and you'd seen him crying and trying to hide it. You put your arm around him and tried to make him feel better. The other boys came over later." Kira gave him a soft smile. "I mentally photographed that moment, and that was when I knew, for certain, that I had fallen in love with you." She reached out, touching his hand. "You're a gentle giant. For those three years, those boys got so much love from you. Ahmad adored you. I can't even begin to know how he felt when we were ambushed. I'm sure he doesn't know if you survived or not."

Shaking his head, Garret rasped, "I loved that kid. His father never stopped beating him. It tore me up. I wanted to kill the bastard. He was abusive, like my old man."

"You did what you could while you were there, Garret." She searched his pained expression. "That's one of the many reasons I fell in love with you. Despite your size, you were incredibly gentle with the kids, with me . . . everyone."

Sitting back, he said thickly, "Cal's a big man. I knew what it was like as a thin, skinny kid, how threatening he looked to me. I knew from that experience how the kids saw me. I didn't want them to be afraid of me like I was afraid of Cal."

Her heart tore a little and she saw the memories in his eyes. She gently closed the book, knowing that for him to see the other eight sketches would simply be too much to digest. Over time she would show them to him. They could be a catalyst to help him unload the grief he held. "You've had a rough life," she said quietly. "I realize how lucky I was to have my mom and dad. I had a happy childhood in comparison."

Garret nodded and placed the closed journal on the coffee table. He looked into her eyes. "This Christmas has turned into nothing but one shock after another." A corner of his mouth hooked upward. "But good shocks, Kira. We need to talk now that we know the truth about how we feel about each other."

She studied him in the silence. "This is the best Christmas ever."

"Yeah," he teased, "you got your D7 back."

"No," she said, "I got you." Kira reached out, sliding her hand into his, seeing it swallowed up. Fearlessly, she held his gaze, rife with emotion. "The best gift of all will be if you'll let me come to bed with you, Garret. I want to be with you, lay with you, love you, if you'll have me. You have no idea how much I wanted you when we were in Afghanistan. Look but don't touch. Never, ever speak of how I felt about you. I could do nothing, and it about killed me." And then she rolled her eyes. "Well, you know what I mean." She saw his hazel eyes, the gold in their depths, intensify as he studied her. There was a delicious warmth embracing her and she now knew it was his love surrounding her.

"I want the same thing, Kira. Are you sure? Do you want more time?"

"I'm very sure. Maybe you need the time? To think this through?" She saw him give her a wry look, his fingers closing firmly around hers.

"I've never been more sure of anything in my life, Kira." He stood up and pulled her gently to her feet.

Kira felt as if the world and all its troubles, pressures and demands, melted away beneath the hungry look in Garret's narrowed eyes as he drew her to him. She nodded and slipped her arm around his waist and they walked through the living room and toward the hall. To his bedroom. His bed. For so long she'd visualized this moment, dreamed about it, and now . . . it was real.

He pushed open the door to his bedroom and she saw he'd made the bed. How like a military man to ensure his room was clean and picked up. She remembered sleeping on the hard-packed dirt floors with their sleeping bags and blankets. In summer, there was no air-conditioning and in winter it was always cold.

He shut the door and turned to her. She lifted her chin, drowning in his dark, intense gaze, his fingers sifting through her hair, gentle, making her scalp race with tiny shivers of delight. "We may need to stop before we start," he told her wryly. "I don't have any condoms on me, Kira. Never thought I'd need them. I'm clean; no diseases."

She heard the amusement in his lowered tone and rested her hands against his chest. "We're in luck, then. I just finished my period three days ago. I'm clean, too." Garret's expression lightened and she saw naked hunger in his eyes, sending a deep wave of longing through her. He'd settled his hands on her shoulders and she rested lightly against the front of his body, more than a little aware of his erection. It amped up the starvation she felt for Garret. "I'm okay with it if you are."

"Sounds good to me."

"Me too," she whispered, easing away from him, pulling the sweater over her head. She wore no bra, just a white silk camisole. Kira felt no shyness about being naked in front of Garret. She'd waited too long and wasn't going to be detoured. There was appreciation in the look he gave her.

"You always were a wild child," he murmured with a grin, beginning to undress himself.

She smiled and removed the camisole. Instantly, Garret's eyes warmed, his gaze lingering on her small, upturned breasts. It made her feel desired.

Kira walked over to the bed, shimmying out of her denim skirt and hanging it over the back of a nearby chair. "I'm close to nature. I don't see myself as a wild child." She watched him undress far more quickly than she had. There was a night-light on the wall near the door. It shed just enough luminescence in the room to show the outline of his powerful body.

The cooler air caressed her breasts, puckering the nipples. Heat thrummed through her lower body as she removed her panties and set them aside. Garret stood unmoving, watching her, but it was his eyes that told Kira everything. If it were possible, he looked more like that huge, shadowy wolf, primal, raw, his hard body powerful, calling to her. And he wanted her. There was no denying that.

"Come here," she whispered, holding out her hand to him. As he started to walk toward her, she added in a low voice, "I haven't had sex in years, Garret."

He took her hand and guided her onto the bed. "That makes two of us." He lay her down on the bed, coming to her side. "We'll take it slow and easy," he promised.

She had dreamed of this moment for so long. His weight depressed the mattress as she lay stretched out on her side, the pillow beneath her head. She watched the economy of his body, the muscles tight and honed. He was beautiful. Utterly, mouth-wateringly beautiful. As Garret stretched out beside her, less than a foot between them, she felt the heat rolling off his body and inhaled his male scent like an aphrodisiac.

"You look worried," he rasped, moving his

hand lightly down her arm, across her hip, then stopping.

"A little," she admitted, somewhat breathless, her heart pounding in her chest. She saw the glint in his eyes soften and felt his callused pads move in a soothing motion across her hips.

"We'll go slow, Kira. Just talk to me, all right? I'm not a mind reader. I need to know how you're feeling, what you want."

"I will. I'm just a little . . . well . . . nervous. It's one thing to dream about making love with you, another when the dream becomes reality. You're here beside me. Really here," and she gave him a slight smile, reaching out, allowing her fingers to drift across the fine, dark hair sprinkled across his chest.

"From where I am, I see the most beautiful woman in the world. You're perfect, Kira. You're more beautiful than I'd ever imagined."

Her smile deepened as she held his burning gaze, feeling incredibly desired. She felt her breasts tighten as his gaze swept across them, felt as if Garret had caressed them physically. The heat and gnawing in her body was almost too much to bear because she wanted him so much. To feel him moving into her, take her, make them one.

"That makes me less nervous."

His brows moved down and he sat up, his hand gliding gently over the puckered scar where the bullet had gone through her slender calf. "I've never seen this scar," he murmured, worry in his tone. "Is it still painful for you?" and he hitched a look in her direction.

Just the way he skimmed her wound made her want to cry, but she quickly forced the reaction aside. His fingers were rough from outside work, and her flesh sang beneath his touch. "It gets cranky in cold weather, I'm discovering. No big deal. Really."

He studied it in the semidarkness and then lay down, propped up on one elbow, moving his hand to her upper right arm where she'd received the second bullet. "It hurts me to know you were wounded," he told her quietly, fingers moving across the depression and scar.

Kira felt her heart open even more if that was possible. "We both got hit in similar places that night." She could see the thin, fine scar along his temple where the bullet had grazed his flesh, leaving him with amnesia for six months.

"Yeah," he rumbled, shaking his head, his hand grazing her torso, outlining her hip, "we're a pair, aren't we? You're still beautiful to me, sweetheart. You always were and you always will be."

All the years of waiting, of carrying a deep loneliness for Garret, unable to kiss him, to savor him, to love him, conspired like a storm within her heart and body. Kira slid against him, her belly pressing into his erection as she cupped his jaw and slid her mouth over his. Maybe she was a wild child after all, bold enough to take what she wanted to share with Garret.

All of those thoughts dissolved the moment he groaned, slowly lay on his back, took her with him. He repositioned her body over his, her legs between his as he took her mouth, ravenous to taste her, his hands roaming firmly down her back, cupping her cheeks and lifting his hips against hers.

Fire erupted deep within Kira and she gasped as she felt the power of his erection, dampness swiftly following between her thighs. A low moan of pleasure followed as his hands curved around her breasts pressing into his chest. Sparks of heat leaped through them and she couldn't remain still against him, his body too beautiful as it swayed against hers, teasing her in the best of ways. The past met the present for Kira as she melted into his exploring hands, feeling the sexual tension rise between them, the ache in her lower body almost painful with wanting more from Garret.

Lost within his mouth, his tongue stroking hers, inciting her, he rolled her onto her back, his gaze locked with hers. She felt like a wild animal finally released, and as he nudged open her thighs, his hand trailing languidly down across her belly, caressing her, his fingers meeting the warm fluids collecting at her entrance, he smiled. It was a very male smile of being pleased with her body's response coupled with intense need for her.

Eyes closed, Kira moaned as he moved a finger slowly into her, testing her, teasing her. Gripping his thick biceps, Kira thrust her hips against his hand, wanting so much more, wanting him. Her body hummed and burned as he eased his finger from within her, settling over her, his large frame covering her like a warm blanket. As he nudged her entrance, her world started shredding apart. And as he captured one of her nipples, suckling her, she cried out, her body naturally arching upward, pulling him to just within her entrance.

She knew she was small and she felt her body shift and open to his slow thrust into her. Fire flowed from each nipple as he lavished each one, in no hurry, tasting her as if she were some delicious dessert to be utterly savored, one sip at a time. Kira wanted this, wanted him, opening to him even more, feeling the momentary burn as he stopped, allowing her body to accommodate him. The burn soon dissolved and she made a low sound in her throat, lifting her hips, inviting him deeper into her. Just the feeling of his maleness, his muscles taut and powerful, felt as if he were holding himself under tight control, and Kira knew he must be doing all of that. He hadn't loved anyone in years either, and she could hear a swift intake of breath between his clenched teeth as he eased into her waiting body for the first time.

Her universe shifted, boiled, and a small cry tore from her as she met and matched his slow, deep thrusts, absorbing him, his need for her. And each time he suckled her, another sob rose in her and she bucked against his hips, hungry for more. She felt pressure and gnawing build rapidly with each of his languid thrusts. She understood he was being cautious, but her starving body didn't want it at that pace. She opened her eyes, meeting his, her hands gripping his hips as she let him know she wanted more. Much more. Kira saw a gleam in Garret's eyes, the same hunger she felt, and when he pushed hard and deep into her, she gasped, arching into him.

Closing her eyes, she met and matched him, feeling her entire body tighten. Barely aware of anything except the sweat between them, the movement of their bodies in primal union, she felt Garret's large, callused hand move down her flank, capturing her hip, anchoring her.

And then her world exploded and she screamed, her body frozen in the white-hot grip of an orgasm that shattered through her. At first it was painful because it was so powerful and then, a second later, it turned into a throbbing, rippling pleasure that kept coming through her, never ending until she felt faint from the release. The scent of Garret's male body, the taste of his sweat on his shoulder as she kissed his flesh and the pumping of his thrusts triggered even more pleasure within her. She floated, barely aware of anything except Garret. Kira suddenly felt him tense. He gripped her hard, stiffening, a groan ripped out of him. As weak as she felt, she pushed against him, wanting to prolong his release, to give him the same lavish pleasure he'd just gifted her with.

The rumbling growl from deep within his

chest vibrated through her. His fingers tangled into her hair, gripping the strands, straining against her. His breath was hot and moist, punctuated against her cheek and temple as he froze and then suddenly collapsed on her. A soft smile of fulfillment pulled at her lips as she curved her arms around his back, moving her fingers in soft motions up and down along his spine. Never had she felt happier than at this moment. They were coupled, and the love she felt for Garret soared into a heady place. Kira closed her eyes, joyous.

Garret groaned as he pushed upward, not wanting his massive weight to squash Kira beneath him. He felt shaky with release, weakened in the best way possible. Worried, he eased out of her, knowing she was so small and tight. The look on her face was bliss, her lips slightly parted, eyes closed, a flush sweeping across her upper body. Her black hair was tangled, lending to that image he'd always carried of her being a wild woman in disguise. Her hands were small and dainty and she looked fragile against his bulk. But he knew from experience that no one had a braver or a more courageous heart than this woman of his. He propped himself up on his elbow and eased to Kira's side, bringing her up against him, her cheek resting on his upper arm, her smile lingering on her wet lips.

"Are you feeling okay?" he asked, caressing her cheek, watching her lashes flutter. The joy sparkling in her eyes was there for him. If Garret had thought he'd hurt her in some way, he knew now that he hadn't. The flecks of silver deep in her gray eyes told him how satisfied she was. And so was he. It felt good to pleasure Kira, to give back to her when, over the years, she'd given so much to him.

"Mmm, wonderful," she whispered, lifting her hand, skimming his cheek. "Couldn't be better. You?"

He grunted and said, "Good." He slid some precocious strands off her clear brow, drowning in her large, half-open eyes. "I like that smile in your eyes and on your mouth."

"You should," she murmured lazily, sighing. "You put them there."

"Really? Are you all right, Kira?" Because he wasn't your average-size man in any respect. And she was small in comparison.

"I'm going to be sore," she admitted, "but so what?" and she gave him a satisfied smile. "It's been a long time for both of us."

"Yeah," he groused. "Too damned long."

Kira slid her hand up his thick upper arm. "But now, you know what?"

"What?" He leaned over, skimming her smiling mouth. "Tell me," he whispered against her lips.

"We can make love anytime we want. The waiting is over."

A rumble of laughter rolled out of him. Kira gave him a wicked look, her smile deepening, the pleasure still shining in her luminous eyes. The love he felt for her was so powerful it rendered him mute for a moment as a wave of happiness tunneled through him. He lifted his head away a bare inch, holding her amused gaze. "I like that idea."

"Mmm, so do I." She laughed in a wispy way and slid her fingers through his hair. "If you only knew how many times I was so horny I wanted to jump your bones, Fleming, you'd probably die of shock because you would have lost count."

He laughed with her. "Oh," he growled, kissing her temple, trailing small nips to her earlobe and then her slender neck, "I don't know about that. I went around with a perpetual hard-on. Damn good thing those cammos we wore were so bulky. Otherwise the guys would have outed me from the get-go." He absorbed her rich laughter, liking the amused look in her eyes.

"I never saw it either."

"Black ops," he intoned, grinning.

Kira snorted and laughed. "You're so full of it, Fleming."

"No, I'm full of you," and he slanted a long, hot, hungry kiss across that smiling mouth of hers. It was like kissing hot, living sunlight as she returned a molten kiss with equal hunger and love. And it was love; Garret was sure of it. Gradually, he ended the kiss, caressing her lips, tasting her, soaking up that careless, satisfied smile of hers. She was wanton and wild, just as he'd thought she would be, and it made him feel good. As a lover, she was willful and bold, and she let him know without any words exactly what she wanted from him. It didn't get any better than this. There was a natural trust between them that had been building for years. Just the way she'd opened herself to him, willingly, pulverized Garret with gratitude.

"Maybe," she said, "but you still have your moments."

"Guilty." His chest felt filled with so much joy he thought he might explode. Kira's returning smile tore at his senses.

"I still love you," she whispered, her smile dissolving, seriousness in its place. "I just can't believe we're here, Garret. Together. We loved each other all that time. We both carried the same secret."

Garret knew what she was saying and brought her flush against him, taking her mouth, his hand drifting down to her hip, caressing her long, curved thigh. She was like dessert drizzled with rich chocolate, soft, alive, willing and supersensitive to his every touch, every kiss he gave her. There was love in every movement of her hips against his, her mouth lush and exploring against his.

They had had four years of unrequited love for each other. Neither able to say anything. It was a torture Garret never wanted to live through again. Looking back on it now, he couldn't believe he'd managed it. But he had. And so had Kira. She was an incredibly strong woman.

He heard a sweet sound vibrate in her throat as he caressed her breast, feathering the nipple with his thumb, feeling her respond sensually, her leg coming over his, pinning it so that her hips could coax his erection back to life. Garret was shocked at how hard and thick he was already becoming. That had to set a new record.

It was Kira, he realized, taking her lips, moving his tongue across her lower one, listening to her hum in that sweet way, her hands ranging down between them, fingers curving around his awakening erection. Garret swore she could bring a dead man back to life with the way she moved her fingers languidly around him. He groaned, thrusting into her hand, wanting more, wanting her.

This time everything came at a slower pace, one where each of them could acquaint the other with their bodies, their scent, their texture. This time there was no urgency.

Garret lay Kira out on the bed, sliding his fingers through her hair, feeling the strong silk of the strands, watching her eyes grow cloudy with arousal, knowing that massaging her scalp was pleasuring her in another way. He had nothing against sex, but he also liked to taste, smell and feel all parts of his woman, to worship her in quiet, subtle ways, all designed to build another orgasm.

Her body was like a recipe, providing food for his body, for his heart and soul. Kira fed him with the way she looked at him through half-closed eyes, those sweet sounds that made him feel good and that he was giving back to her. And when her body moved as he caressed her here and there, that combination of languid movement on her part, the sounds whispering from between her lips, the way her expression grew hungry and engaged, all were one hell of a turn-on for him as well.

This time Garret kissed, nibbled, licked, lightly nipped his way from the nape of her neck all the way down to her small, dainty feet and perfectly formed toes. He left no part of her untouched. He wanted to love her in a different way, letting her know he would lavish every inch of her, without exception. He paid particular attention to the two depressions and scarred areas where she had been wounded. At one point he looked up and saw tears in her eyes, as if she realized by kissing and licking them, by soothing them with his mouth, he was trying to take away the pain and bad memories . . .

When he arrived at the juncture between her thighs, he heard her sigh with anticipation as he stroked her entrance with his fingers, feeling the fire burning brightly within her once again.

Garret couldn't resist the urge, ever so slowly, to enter her once more, watching and delighting in her expression, those erotic sounds coming from the back of her throat, that hardened him even more if that were possible. And this time he kept the pace languid, like a deep, slow-moving river so that when he brought Kira to orgasm, he'd triggered a powerful avalanche of pleasure that brought her to ecstasy.

And only then did he allow himself to partake of her, releasing hotly into her loving, damp body.

Her nurturing arms surrounded him afterward as he lay half on top of her. His mind had shorted out, and as he curled his body around her, his heart opened fully and Garret allowed himself to feel the full depth of his love for the woman in his arms.

CHAPTER TWENTY-THREE

There was a knock at their back door on Christmas morning. Garret rose from the table. He and Kira were enjoying a cup of coffee after breakfast. "Stay there. I'll see who it is," he told her.

Kira nodded. Her body was warm and satiated. She'd awakened at dawn with Garret and they'd made love a third time. The hunger she felt for him, to sleep in his arms and then to wake up and love him again, was like a dream come true. The soreness in her lower body testified that it wasn't a dream, but a hot bath later would take care of that. She heard voices and realized it was Noah and Harper. She smiled as they entered the kitchen and lifted her hand to them.

"Hey, guys. Merry Christmas."

Noah grinned and handed Garret a wrapped gift to hold. "Merry Christmas, Kira. Harper and I are here to deliver your gift." He hung up his jacket and hat, taking the wrapped box from Garret.

Harper smiled shyly and said, "Merry Christmas, Kira. You look happy." He hung up his gear, following Noah to the table, where they both sat down.

Garret went to retrieve two more mugs and brought over the coffeepot. He poured the coffee and replaced the pot on the counter. Turning, he walked over and sat down at the head of the table, Kira at his left elbow. "You two are up early considering this is a day off."

Harper grimaced. "Sort of a day off. Noah and I just got done feeding all the horses."

Kira smiled at them. "It's cold out there. Your noses look like Rudolph the Red-Nosed Reindeer."

Harper touched his and said, "It's going to be ten above this afternoon. Warm for this time of year."

Noah pushed the large gift toward Kira. "Here," he said, "this is from Harper and me."

Kira moved her cup aside and gave him a quizzical look. "What is it?"

Crowing, Harper said, "Like we're going to tell you?"

Noah snickered. He picked up his cup and drank some of his coffee. "You need this,

Kira. Open it."

She felt a thrill go through her as she tore into the wrapping. She could never understand people who very carefully opened a gift, ensuring no tears in the paper or anything else. As the paper fell away, she gasped.

"Oh!" she cried. And then she broke into a huge smile, her hands moving over the Lowepro camera bag. "You guys," she whispered tearfully, giving them a grateful look. "You shouldn't have done this! These bags don't come cheap."

Harper reached across the table and squeezed the hand resting on the black ballistic nylon bag. "Actually, it was Garret's idea. He told us he was getting you a camera and that you needed a bag to carry it in."

"Yes," Noah said, "and between us, we could afford it, so wipe that stricken look off your face, okay? We didn't sell our children into slavery to buy that for you."

Garret chuckled.

Kira shook her head, giving Garret a dirty look. "You set them up."

"Well," he hedged, amused, "sort of."

"Phooey, you did."

"Do you like it?" Noah pressed.

"I love it. Professional photographers prefer a Lowepro camera bag," she said as she unzipped the top and opened it up. There was plenty of padded space for the camera, the lens and anything else she wanted to protect while in transit. "It's wonderful. Thank you . . . both of you," and she stood up, walked around the table and gave each vet a kiss on the cheek and a huge hug.

Noah, embarrassed by her emotional outpouring, rubbed his warm cheek and chuckled uneasily. "Now, since the old man is out of here, you can devote your spare time to going out with this dude," he hooked his thumb in Garret's direction, "and start shooting landscapes and wildlife and making more money."

Kira touched their shoulders, squeezed them and walked back to her chair, which Garret pulled out for her. "You guys are real coyotes. I had no idea what Garret was up to."

"Do you like the camera, Kira?" Harper asked.

"I love it. It's exactly like the one I had in Afghanistan."

"Can we see it?" Noah asked.

"Sure."

"I'll get it for you," Garret said, "stay sitting."

Kira gave him a look of thanks. She ran

her hand lightly over the dark blue bag, her heart swelling with love for these two men. When Garret was gone, she asked, "Did he threaten to break both your arms if you didn't get me this bag?"

Chortling, Harper said, "No, not at all. He just got us in the tack room about four weeks ago and told us what he was going to do for your Christmas gift. So we ordered it online and it was delivered." Harper looked over at Noah. "He did the wrapping."

"This will be a gift that will keep on giving for years to come. It's a well-built bag. Thanks so much." Kira choked up as both men's faces filled with pride. She knew how hard both of them worked. Money never came easy.

"Hey," Noah said, "I've got some news. Reese and Shay got a call from the Pentagon this morning. Remember, Kira? You said you'd make a call there?"

"Yes, to General Ward. She runs the black op I worked for. Did she call?"

"Reese said it was an enlisted woman," Noah said. He brightened considerably. "She said she had been a Marine sergeant who was a horse trainer before she entered the military. She was a WMD handler in Afghanistan at one time." He frowned a little. "Said she was wounded in an IED explosion, her dog killed. She lost part of her lower left leg. She's just now getting out of the hospital after being there for over a year. She's being given an honorable medical discharge and the general assistant thought we might be interested in hiring her."

"Wow," Kira murmured, "that's wonderful."

"Do you know who she is?" he asked.

"I can't say much, Noah, but yes, there were three women WMDs in our group who went into this black ops mission. It could be any of them. Did the general give her name?"

"Yes." He dug into the pocket of his dark blue flannel shirt, producing a scribbled note. Unfolding it, he said, "Dair Wilson." He looked up at her. "Do you know her?"

Kira smiled. "Oh, yes. Dair is a one-of-a-kind woman, Noah. She's about your age, single and she's part Comanche. She comes from a family near Laramie. Her grandmother, a full-blooded Comanche, was a horse trainer of some repute."

"When she was in the Marines, what kind of dog was she working with?" he asked, excitement in his tone.

"Combat dogs."

Rubbing his hands together, he then put

them in a prayerlike position. "Let her come here, then. I've got two horses and I need help working with them. I was so hoping we could find someone with that exact kind of background."

Kira smiled. "It would be so great if Reese and Shay are able to hire her."

"What's she like?" Noah asked, leaning forward.

"She's a warrior, very focused, with a very dry sense of humor. Of the three dog handlers in our group, she was the quietest. I think it was because of her Indian genes. Her mother runs a kindergarten off the reservation. Her father is white, but Dair never liked to talk about him. She listens a lot and says very little."

"A good horse trainer is all of those things." Relief was in Noah's voice. "Reese said Dair would be traveling here to our ranch in a couple of days." He gestured toward the window. "That is if we get a break from all this snow."

"Supposed to clear up for about five days," Garret told him. "Why don't you two go enjoy your day off?"

Noah and Harper got the hint and finished their coffee and left. The kitchen grew quiet. Garret leaned his elbows on the table, studying Kira. "Okay, what's the scoop on this woman? I saw you pulling your punches with Noah. What didn't you tell him?"

Kira zipped up the Lowepro and set it in the wooden seat next to her. "When we went through the one-year training course with Special Forces, there was a lot of trouble at her mom's home. Her mother divorced her father when Dair was ten." Her mouth tightened. "Her father abused both of them, Garret."

"Not good."

"Yeah. It was pretty bad. Her father went after Dair out in the garden. He broke one of two bones in her lower right arm. Her mother flew into a rage, kicked her husband out of the house and filed charges against him. She put him in prison and divorced him. Pretty awful, if you ask me."

Rubbing his face savagely, Garret snarled, "Men like that should be castrated as far as I'm concerned. They have no place on this earth."

"Dair's mother was an abused wife. But she finally fought back when he broke Dair's arm." Taking a deep breath, Kira said sadly, "Dair turned to animals for solace. Those she could trust. But she doesn't trust men at all. I wasn't sure she'd make it on the mission, but she was fine working with the guys because she had a dog between her and them."

"The dog kind of a safety net for her?" Garret mused.

"I think so." She frowned. "Gosh, I don't know if Dair will want to work with Noah or not. He's a man."

"Maybe she's changed since you last saw her. Matured a little more."

Shrugging, she said, "I don't know. Last time I saw her was four years ago. She was still the same then. We were sent to different black ops groups and lost touch with each other, for the most part."

He reached over, smoothing his hand down her arm. "Look at it this way: Noah's the type of man who's good at handling trouble of any kind. If he can make Poncho stop kicking people, he's got the tools and awareness Dair might need."

"Oh, I don't know," Kira murmured worriedly. "Dair's distrust of men is pretty strong. But maybe you're right; maybe she's changed."

"And she was wounded," Garret reminded her. He gave her a sad look. "We both know how a major experience in combat has affected us. It changes everyone, maybe even her. She's an amputee now, and I'm sure that has also altered her worldview plenty."

"Yes," she murmured. "If she hasn't come

to terms with her distrust of men, I don't think Dair will agree to work with Noah."

"Time will tell," he said. "Hey," Garret called softly, standing, "do you feel like taking a drive with your new camera? Maybe try it out on some nice late-morning landscape shots?"

She perked up and smiled. "I'd *love* to do that!" She quickly stood and grabbed her Lowepro.

Garret felt wave after wave of fierce love for Kira as they stood at a low wooden fence on Moose Road, outside of Jackson Hole. The sun was still in the east and she'd found some moose ambling across the road. Being able to use the D7 on the monopod had been the perfect fix for the weak fingers.

She was making happy sounds only he could hear as he stood nearby, watching the two bull moose with wide sets of antlers graze alongside the asphalt road where the snow had little accumulation. The animals were eating willow branches. Their huge, funny-looking heads, dark brown eyes and floppy ears made them look like clowns to him. To Kira, they were absolutely beautiful, each with that ten-foot spread of antlers. Never mind they were seven feet tall at the shoulder and weighed twenty-five hundred pounds.

After a few shots, she would stop, press another button and look at what she'd photographed. And then she'd excitedly show Garret. He would never get over her bubbling joy, the shining look in her eyes. Her red knit cap was slightly askew, her black hair escaping around her, giving her the look more of a child at play than the serious, hardworking adult he knew her to be.

As he continued to look around — his black ops training would always be with him — the pasture on the other side of the fence was pristine white, covered with three feet of snow. The sunlight glanced off it, the flakes, tossed into the air by an inconsistent breeze, shining like thousands of scattering diamonds. Kira's cheeks were flushed a deep pink and he leaned over, brushing a kiss on one of them. He saw her eyes widen with nothing but love for him. It made him feel so damned good.

As he stood there enjoying the brisk morning, watching Kira give her camera a good workout and listening to the low, excited comments she made as she shot, he smiled. How far they'd come. And, in a fluke he'd never expected, Kira had walked back into his life. What were the odds? Garret knew she still chaffed and worried about their mutual PTSD symptoms, but they had Taylor and Libby helping them cope. And they had each other. Love might not cure PTSD, but it sure as hell set it in the corner and made it behave. His mouth drew into a grin, thinking about it. There was nothing like good sex and orgasms to relieve the constant anxiety of PTSD. Endorphins, those happy hormones that made people feel good, were released during sex and helped diminish stress. More sex was a good solution in his book. And judging by Kira's eager appetite, she was not only sensual as hell but sexual as well, enjoying their time in each other's arms as much as he did. Life didn't get any better than it did right now.

"Okay," Kira said, turning, the monopod in her gloved hand, "I'm done."

"Think you got some good shots?" he asked, taking the camera from her and carrying it to the truck.

She stuffed her hands into the pockets of her parka. "Yes. I'm so excited, Garret!"

He slid his arm around her shoulders, drawing her close to him, giving her a squeeze. "I'm excited for you. I know those photos will be great. And I'm sure when you post them to that stock photo website, people will buy them."

She gave him a warm look. "You're such a cheerleader, Fleming."

He chuckled and opened the door to the truck for her. "That's my nature, Ms. Duval. Hop in. I'm taking you to town. We'll celebrate with lunch and a cup of hot chocolate at Kassie's Café."

"Oh, that sounds great!"

"Garret? What do you think Ray Crawford is going to do?" Kira asked, her hands around a large pink mug of hot chocolate. They sat in a booth near the window of Kassie's Café, watching the main square. At this time of year only tourists who wanted to ski came to Jackson Hole. Most drove through Wind River Valley, stopping for gas and maybe something to eat and were off again, with fifty miles to go to the major tourist city. There weren't many people out and about on a sunny, cold day.

He frowned and sipped the rich chocolate. Wiping the whipped cream off his upper lip, he said, "Right now Ray is adjusting. He's got his first PT tomorrow and I'm taking him to it. I'll find out more about his mood then, but I'm sure he's angry about being tossed off the ranch."

Kira picked up the juicy hamburger she'd ordered earlier. The café was busy because it was one of the favorite places for locals. "Your father is an alcoholic. What do you think Ray will do?"

Shrugging, he picked up a French fry from his plate, which also had a huge hamburger on it. "He made it clear the day of the intervention that he wanted the Bar C back. I'm sure he's going to work damned hard to get his body into shape from that stroke. He's only forty-nine, and before the stroke, I heard he was a lean, tough hombre, physically fit and capable of doing all the ranch work himself."

"But with his drinking? And the stroke has affected his memory. Do you think he'll achieve all that again?"

"I don't know. It was clear to me he was going to try to take the ranch away from Reese and Shay, legally speaking. He's got a lot of money stashed away and can hire a good lawyer and hit them with a lawsuit."

She scowled. "That isn't right."

"Depends upon who's looking at the situation, sweetheart. From Ray's perspective, he lost his ranch due to a stroke. If he can come back and show the court he's mentally capable of once more running his ranch, that will be the crux of the legal case. Ray has to find a lawyer who can show the court and a jury that he's mentally and physically fit once more."

"But that will is a contract of sorts," Kira objected.

"Yes," he said patiently, "it is. But what if Ray introduces Shay's PTSD and the fact that she's got anxiety? That could be seen as a mental incapacity, too. To a jury, and with the right lawyer, she could be painted as unstable and unable to run a ranch because she can't take the stress of the demands placed on her."

Groaning, Kira gave him a panicked look. "I never thought about that."

Grimacing, he growled, "Think like a lawyer and you will, Kira. It's a dicey situation and I have no idea what will happen next. Ray is a loose cannon in their lives."

"And in ours, too."

"Yes. Because if the law allows him back on the ranch, I won't stay. I won't work under that bastard."

Wrinkling her nose, she said, "I wouldn't either."

"If such a thing did happen," he said, reaching out and squeezing her hand, "it would take years. Things are backed up in courts for one, two or three years into the future. Reese is very aware of the situation, Kira. He's a guard dog for Shay and he's already making business decisions that show

484

she's competently running the ranch. They're still in the red, but give them another year with that indoor arena in place and they'll be in the black. Plus, Noah's training business is starting to bring in some serious money. Harper is going to college presently, taking paramedic courses. And he's planning on going to the fire department or the local hospital to get a job after he graduates. It's all future money that will help the ranch stabilize. Things aren't lost, so stop looking like they are." He smiled a little.

"Okay," she muttered. "That means I really have to amp up my translation business, plus get more photos sold on that stock website."

"You will," he said. "And for now? Let all that go. You concentrate on you. And me. And us."

Garret saw Kira in the living room, taking the ornaments off their Christmas tree. It was December 31, New Year's Eve, and they had decided it was time to take the tree down. Outside the picture window, once more snowflakes were lazily falling out of the low, gray clouds across the valley. Kira was in a pair of black wool slacks, wearing a pink, long-sleeved blouse with a bright red sweater vest over it. With her black hair and the flush to her cheeks, she looked beautiful to him. He'd just finished making them lunch and their afternoon job was to remove all the decorations.

Kira looked up from placing the construction paper ornaments she'd made in a special cardboard box she'd set on the coffee table. "Who just called?" she asked.

"Oh, that was Shay. She's calling everyone to let us know that Dair Wilson is going to be arriving by pickup truck on January 2."

Straightening, Kira said, "That's wonderful. I can hardly wait to see her again. I wonder if she knows I'm here."

"Probably she does would be my guess." He came and stood next to her, looking at the tree. "You're making fast progress here."

"I hate taking it down," she admitted. "I love Christmas, the lights, the colors. It's all so beautiful." Slipping her arm around his waist, she leaned into him as he curved his arm around her shoulders.

"That's because you're an artist," he said, kissing the top of her head. "You see beauty in everything, Kira." Garret eased her back just enough to catch her gaze. "And that's one of the many, many things I love about you. You see the good in life, not the bad."

"And I photograph the good so it will lift

people's spirits when they see one of my photos."

"Hmmm," he said, tilting his head, looking critically at the tree. "Did you miss something under the tree?"

Frowning, she looked. "There aren't any more gifts under the tree, Garret."

"Sure?"

Kira gave him a quizzical look. "What are you up to?"

A corner of his mouth lifted slightly. He pointed beneath the branches. "I think you missed one present, sweetheart. Take a look. Behind the trunk, maybe?" He saw amusement in her expression as she pulled out of his embrace.

"What have you done now, Fleming?" she muttered, walking over to the tree. She crouched down.

"Nothing," he said innocently, going to the couch and sitting down, watching her get on her hands and knees to look toward the rear of the tree. Satisfaction moved through him.

"This had better be good," she grumbled, sliding in beneath the lowest boughs of the tree, straining to reach a small package in the corner.

"Oh," Garret said, "I think it will be. Once you get it, come here and sit down beside me to open it."

Kira grabbed the silver-wrapped present. It was no larger than a cup in size, a square with a big, bright red ribbon on top of it. Kneeling there, she looked at the tag. It said: *To the woman I love.* Turning, she gave him a tender look. "This is lovely, Garret."

"You're lovely." He gestured for her to get up and come sit beside him. Her eyes were wide with excitement. Garret enjoyed her excitement, her sensual mouth curving into a careless grin as she walked over to the couch and flopped down beside him.

"You can't afford to keep giving me gifts, Garret. You really can't."

He placed his arm around her shoulders, giving her a wicked look. "You should be given a gift every day of your life, Kira. Open it."

She tore into it, the paper flying in all directions. When she opened the box, she found it stuffed with more paper. His heart stopped for a moment as he watched her dig into it, her fingers finding the box. As she drew it out, realization dawned on her face, her gaze flying to his as she held up the red velvet box.

"Garret! You didn't!" and she gasped as she opened it. Stunned, she looked at the platinum wedding ring set and then up at him. "Oh, Garret!"

He patiently removed the box from her hand and eased the engagement ring out of the surrounding velvet. "Do you like them?" he asked, his voice deep with feeling. He took her left hand, knowing those two last fingers didn't work, and eased the ring on one of them.

"T-they're beautiful!" she choked, tears gathering in her eyes.

He held her shocked look, the tears making her gray eyes soft diamonds. "This makes it official," he told her in a low voice, holding her eyes. "I love you, Kira. I want to marry you whenever you want to marry me."

Pressing a hand to her lips, she stared down at the one-carat solitaire diamond on her hand. "Oh," she whispered brokenly. "I never expected this, Garret. I really didn't."

He smiled and kissed her lightly on the lips. "Why not? How long have we been in love with each other, sweetheart?"

"Well," she blubbered, unable to take her gaze off the engagement ring, flashing like fire on her hand, "it just never came up. I'm happy with the way things are with us right now, Garret." She lifted her eyes. "I love you. I never stopped loving you."

"Then," he growled, "let's make it official.

There's no one else I want to share my life with than you, Kira. I'm in no hurry, but I think you need to know that I want you forever."

Tears trickled down her cheeks and she pulled her hand out of his, self-consciously wiping her cheeks with her trembling fingers. "This cost so much money . . . how?"

He gave her a wry look. "My Rolex. I was able to get your camera and the rings. Okay?" She was such a worrywart when it came to money. "I've already told you, you're more important than the watch, Kira. Don't keep giving me that look like we're going to the poorhouse. We're not." He pulled her hand from her lips and urged her into his arms, embracing her, feeling her willingly melt against him, her brow resting against his jaw. "Will you marry me, you stubborn woman?"

She laughed a little, tilting her head across his shoulder, meeting his gaze. "You know I will! I love you so much, Garret. So much . . ."

That was all he needed to hear. He could see the raw love for him shining in her eyes. "We've had a rough, long journey," he told her in a tone, his lips grazing her cheek. "All I want now is for you to be my wife, my best friend, my lover. Everything else in our lives will sort itself out over time. What do you say?" He gave her a look filled with love for her alone.

"Yes," she whispered, leaning up and skimming her lips against his strong mouth. "Yes, a thousand times over. I love you so much!"

ABOUT THE AUTHOR

New York Times and *USA Today* bestselling author **Lindsay McKenna** is the pseudonym of award-winning author Eileen Nauman. With more than 135 titles to her credit approximately 23 million books sold in 33 countries worldwide, Lindsay is one of the most distinguished authors in the women's fiction genre. She is the recipient of many awards, including six *RT Book Reviews* awards (including best military romance author) and an *RT Book Reviews* Career Achievement Award. In 1999, foreseeing the emergence of ebooks, she became the first bestselling women's fiction author to exclusively release a new title digitally. In recognition of her status as one of the originators of the military adventure/romance genre, Lindsay is affectionately known as "The Top Gun of Women's Military Fiction." Lindsay comes by her military knowledge and interest honestly — by continuing a family tradition of serving in the U.S. Navy. Her father, who served on a destroyer in the Pacific theater during World War II, instilled a strong sense of patriotism and duty in his daughter. Visit Lindsay at www.lindsay mckenna.com.